André Carl van der Merwe was born in Harrismith in the Free State. He studied fine art in Cape Town, and has worked in the fashion, art and architetual fields. *Moffie* is his first novel to be published in America.

MOFFIE

André Carl van der Merwe

MOFFIE

Europa
editions

Europa Editions
1 Penn Plaza, Suite 6282
New York, N.Y. 10019
www.europaeditions.com
info@europaeditions.com

Library of Congress Cataloging in Publication Data is available
ISBN 978-1-60945-050-2

van der Merwe, André Carl
Moffie

Book design by Emanuele Ragnisco
www.mekkanografici.com

Prepress by Grafica Punto Print – Rome

To all the people who suffered prejudice in the army
and the tortures of Ward 22. To those who are still suffering today
—in schools, at home and at work.
I dedicate this book to you. May we all one day live
in a world of compassion rather than self-seeking superiority.

CONTENTS

So in everything, do to others what you would have them do to you, for this sums up the Law and the Prophets.
—MATTHEW 7:12

ZAMBIA

LUSAKA •

ANGOLA

• ONDANGWA

Livingstone •
HARARE •

ZIMBABWE

NAMIBIA

BOTSWANA

WINDHOEK •

GABORONE •

PRETORIA
(1 MIL.)

MIDDELBURG •

JOHANNESBURG ■ MBABANE •

SWAZILAND

HARRISMITH •

LESOTHO
MASERU •

Durban •

SOUTH AFRICA

500 km

STELLENBOSCH
(BANHOEK) OUDTSHOORN •

CAPE TOWN •

Port Elizabeth •

BACKGROUND

The invasion and conquest of the German colony, South West Africa, in 1915 by South African forces laid the foundation of South African control over the territory later known as Namibia.

'Apartheid' (literally meaning separateness, and implying segregation of races), as a policy of the South African Government from 1948 to 1994, set white South Africa on a path of confrontation with its disenfranchised indigenous nations and the rest of the world.

Military service for white male South Africans was introduced, first by a drafting system in 1952, and from 1967 as a compulsory 12 months military training period, later extended to 24 months. In addition these trained soldiers were called up for further annual 'camps,' as more manpower was required for the government's military campaigns.

Most government schools had a cadet system where male students were taught to march and shoot a rifle. These militarising actions ensured that the South African Defence Force of the nineteen seventies, eighties and nineties was the most powerful in Sub-Saharan Africa.

Military service could only be avoided on the grounds of ill health, mental incapacity, by emigration or four years in jail for conscientious objectors.

South Africa's military involvement in Namibia started in 1966 and ended with the independence of Namibia in 1989. During this time the same policies of segregation led to conflict with SWAPO (the South West African Peoples' Organisation). The armed wing of this organisation, PLAN (the Peoples' Liberation Army of Namibia), started a campaign of armed incursions into South West Africa in 1965. In 1966 the first shots were fired in the 'Border War,' in a skirmish between the South African Police and Air Forces and a PLAN unit in the north of Namibia.

The collapse of the Portuguese colonies of Mozambique and Angola in 1975, and independence of Rhodesia escalated the guerrilla incursions into South Africa and Namibia dramatically and even greater demands of manpower and resources were made on the country and its economy. An internationally imposed arms embargo against the country forced South Africa to become militarily self-sufficient. Young recruits would have to do two or more stints of Border Duty during the course of their National Service.

International pressure intensified and within South Africa the realisation of the evil of Apartheid and the attrition of the war led to a groundswell of resistance against the National Service system and political change slowly started taking place. In 1989 the imminent independence of Namibia led to the withdrawal of the South African forces from the area.

In South Africa, the broadening of democracy has led to a diminished role for the South African National Defence Force (SANDF), with national service being abolished in 1994.

Additional reading:
http://en.wikipedia.org/wiki/Koevoet
http://en.wikipedia.org/wiki/Umkhonto_we_Sizwe

MOFFIE

PART ONE

As we pull away from the kraal, a woman staggers from her hut through an opening in the primitive fence. Her wailing, the painful suck-gasping when her cry is spent, rasps through me. At this moment, I know that I am witnessing anguish so deep, so all-encompassing that nothing in my nineteen years could have prepared me for it.

It is hot, but I am shivering. Everything about this scene is harsh: the sounds, the smell of exhaust fumes, the metal of the Buffel. It hammers me like a tenderiser. The noise when the driver changes gears, which would normally pass unnoticed, hits the soft places deep inside me. Nothing gentle can survive here.

I see the devastated woman's ragged run. It is as if she is trying to rip the pain from her chest. Her tattered clothes flutter like streamers bursting from inside her.

We round the kraal, and the fence draws a curtain between us. She is looking up when the bullet enters her body. Then she falls, face down, crumbling as if her frame has been whipped out of her. There is a small puff where she falls, the response of the dead dust to this stolen life. Above her broken body hangs her husband—or what is left of him.

I have been thrown into hell; herded into the Defence Force, into the abattoir of its border war like an animal to slaughter, with no say over my own destiny. Forced to kill people I don't know, for a cause I don't believe in.

My best friend Malcolm is sitting next to me. We are the only national servicemen on the back of the vehicle. We are the only ones who haven't killed before, and we are the only ones who didn't volunteer for this life of war. The other soldiers have chosen this existence. Killing has settled in them, and they are different for it.

I want to look at Malcolm but I can't. I want to talk to him. I want to tell him how I feel, but sharing my fear could prove too much, could make me lose control, and all I have left is this thin line of restraint. Nothing else is within my power.

I should be watching out for terrorists, but the radio has told us that we are still a few clicks away from where the other soldiers are waiting—at the last point of contact—where we will resume the chase. But now, before even processing the possibility of a contact, I have to fight my inner battle.

I put my head down, double up in the moulded seat of the landmine-protected vehicle and pull my rifle in to prevent it from snagging on the bushes. For a second I imagine a bullet travelling along this tube, a bullet aimed and triggered by me. I picture the first round waiting in the chamber, right here under my face, and instinctively I check the safety catch.

Then I place my hands on either side of my head, like blinkers on a carthorse hauling scrap in Maitland. 'You must pull yourself together,' I say to myself. 'You have to stay calm. Focus on good things, positive things.'

There have been positive things in this, the most significant year of my life. Large enough to balance the outrage that is the Defence Force. I have experienced three remarkable relationships in this unmitigated hell.

Malcolm, whose friendship I have been waiting for all my life; Ethan, my love; and Dylan, whose image now induces a pain that outstrips the fear. Dylan, dark around those sad eyes that saw so much.

*

The shriek of the radio tears me away from him. It hisses and talks in pockets of squelch, in short sharp bursts. I look up at the untainted nature around me: cicadas, insects, plants with fragile new growth, small bird's nests. Through all of this we thrash like blunt scissors through silk. My skin crawls when I think of the delicate beauty we are disturbing in our baneful quest.

The sun bites at my already burnt arms and neck. Heat enters the fibres of my brown shirt, changing its smell. The goose bumps on my skin rub against the fabric, and drops of sweat trickle down from my armpits.

To the side of our crude progress, slightly higher than the Buffel, I watch the smooth flight of a yellow-billed hornbill. I study its flight, like Da Vinci would have. But I study it to escape. I think of my childhood, searching for the safe places before the great divide of these past months.

Uncontaminated fragments from years ago rise up in me: my grandmother scraping burn off the breakfast toast so as not to waste; the names my mother had for our favourite food: rolypoly-pudding-and-pie, apple-crackle-daisy-tart; games I played in our back yard. So soft are these memories that I shiver for their protection.

If I die, so will they.

But time has caked grey survival and greasy denial into my memory like layers of grime in an old kitchen. Looking back on such an ordeal, it always seems less terrifying than at the time. So, to be true to my story, I trust the notes I made during that time.

At night I escape and uncoil the binding threads of memory. I implode into a hypnotic state, where I float over fields in the Northeastern Free State and live the recurring dream of my youth: I am weightless, floating, but held securely, and I know that divinity flows through me. I know I am connected, but free.

PART TWO

1

At the age of three, woven into me are the love of my elder brother, the love of the rolling hills that surround our small town, and the love of the Zulu woman who cares for me during my mother's long illness. Within this trinity I am totally secure. Frankie and I are one; the physics of this synthesis is not questioned. We move as a unit—only sometimes he moves separately. When I lie on the large softness of Sophie's breasts, I have no connection with fear. This security stays with me for the rest of my life—people around a fire, their huts, the land, and I, swaddled in different kinds of warmth. My parents, our house, food and shelter simply form the lining behind the true fabric.

Frank and I, little-people march, break away from Sophie and run ahead. She calls us back and takes our hands. Then, when the path levels out again, she lets go and we run ahead. Frank will be going to school next year, but the implications don't concern me. I have never been exposed to the ripples of such events.

Like an abundant woman's body, the hills are gentle and soft. Ahead of us, drawing us, are three huts and a fire. Above them the setting sun splits the indigo sky. Smoke swirls in pockets around the people in the yellow light of the fire.

I smell the early night scent of the soil that the valley releases only at this time of day. It is fertile, like sex, an exhalation of virility, and seeping and drifting through it is the fragrance of burning wood. These smells are in me, an unseverable link to

that part of my life. It is often the most delicate that remains
resistant to the erosion of time.

Sophie, Frank and I are drawn into a universe of concentric
circles: the fire, then the people, then the thatch-roofed clay
huts lit by the flames and final light in this ether. I can't see
inside the huts, but they invite me. They want to receive me
and hold me. A large blanket is wrapped around me and I
snuggle into it, pushing away a frayed edge to open my face.

On my lap is a yellow enamel plate. The chipped black line
around the edge hugs the contents of putu porridge, milk and
sugar. The smell of the blankets, the people, the fire and the
happiness wrap around me; a softness so deep that no evil
exists here.

Black faces shine as the light of the fire licks the smooth con-
tours of their features. Gleaming white teeth break through
large-lipped laughter. Sparks climb up above the fire like glit-
tering nebulae and spiral beyond the oval window of my blan-
kethouse.

The deep, hollow voices of the men, like old trees, contrast
with the high-pitched yell-singing of the women. Babies in
blankets tied above full hips sink in and out of this hypnosis.

A glimpse of paradise.

I know that this is how we are meant to feel. But this right,
taken for granted, will be stripped by the immense contrast
waiting on the periphery. Waiting, perhaps, for me to feel the
loss in order to completely grasp what happiness is.

At this time my parents are the roof and walls of my existence; my backup. My true home is made up of Frankie and
Sophie's devotion. My sister, Bronwyn, is only a mild chafing,
mostly disregarded by the two of us.

Although Frankie is two years older than I am, we are like
twins, like two parts of the same being. I live one half of what
we see, feel and think, and he the other half, making each experience whole.

*

The year of the Cat ends and the year of the Dragon begins; my last year at the foot of the Drakensberg *(Dragon mountain)*, in the warmth of its fire. Three years earlier, in 1961, when I was born, South Africa gained its independence from England and became a republic—an event that would impact on my life more than any other world event. The new government is run by a small minority of whites, mostly Afrikaners, my father's people, who set us on a tragic course—all in the name of God.

2

This is it. The time has come . . . Waiting for my mother to call me, I am aware of a depression that has settled in the sad morning light of the curtained room. My knees are pulled up into the hollow under my chest. I am lying still, hardly making an imprint on the mattress. So terrified am I that I have not moved from this position all night.

The light reflects off the wood-panelled walls onto my blue tog bag. In it is the kit we've been instructed to take. A narrow shaft of light through a slit in the curtain becomes distorted over the objects in the room. It is like a door opening into the room; instead of me passing through it, it passes over me. If I close my left eye I can make the light jump forward, then back again when I open it and close my right eye. I am too afraid to look at my watch.

Outside the sounds that find their way into the room are as familiar as ever: the almost human murder-screams of the pigs being fed, the birds chattering before immersing their wings in the first morning light, the murmur of the farm labourers on their way to work.

When there is such drastic change, surely everything else should also adjust to the altered state? When one steps into misery, all else should follow suit, for it could mean the destruction of a soul.

The familiar sound of my mother's footsteps on the wooden staircase, the first three steps of wood on brick, and then the hollow sound of suspended wood as she turns the corner. On the wall above this corner is a drawing of a blue beach buggy with impossibly wide tires, the wheels turned in boyish expectation. In the right-hand bottom corner my name is signed.

People have a rhythm, born from an internal tempo; or perhaps it is the ratio of their skeletons to their weight. It is as unique as the markings on a finger. I know my mother's sound like a calf knows the blazes on its mother. With her comes the scratching sound of my dog's nails as she jumps from tread to tread. My mother will say, 'Rise and shine!' and then Dot will jump on the bed and my mother will say, 'No-no, off-off!'

Two years. Two years! Today the knock on the door is different, my voice is different, unwilling, but the door opens with the same ride on its hinges. The Defence Force hasn't got to my dog yet. That will only happen tomorrow when she rushes up the stairs and doesn't find me in this bed.

Where will I be tomorrow when she comes looking for me? Where will the train be when she starts whimpering for my mother to open the door? In the bent reflection of my chrome lampshade my mother stands.

'It's time, my boy.'

'I know.'

As I am pulled into myself, I swing my legs over the side of the bed, bring my body up and sit on the edge, bent over.

While I'm getting dressed I look through the window at the valley. Above the house the strong mountains hug my separation. On the one side the morning light layers colours across the cliffs. On the other side the mountains are dark, heavy against the bright blue sky. Smoke from the labourer's cottages has drifted over the narrow road and lies amongst the peach trees like a phantom horizon below which the other world can still be seen. Outside my room is the large molehill-pimpled lawn that I've so hated mowing on Saturdays.

I walk down the wooden stairs to the smell of egg and a noise from the portable radio that no one seems to be listening to.

Bronwyn is not-having-to-go smug, and my father is happy that I am going to be taught some lessons—lessons he could never teach me, lessons I refused to learn: his doctrine, blast-frozen in Calvinistic self-convincing, a safety belt of dogma and fear.

What is certain is that I will suffer, mainly because of my views, my unwillingness, my desires. Only my mother feels sympathy. Her love is larger than politics and the threat of communism taught by my school and my father. Now she only sees her son being sent to war, and nothing is more important.

'You must eat, Nicholas. It will make you feel better and you don't know when you will get food again. How long is the train journey to Middelburg?'

'I think three days.'

'Nonsense, two days at the most,' says my father, who always repudiates whatever I say.

'The train stops at every station to pick up conscripts.'

'Still, it won't take three days.'

I don't argue.

'Come, eat just a little. Can I get you something else?'

'No, he will eat what you've given him or nothing. Too bloody spoilt, that's his problem.'

'No thanks, Mom, I'm really not hungry.'

'Leave him, Suzie, if he doesn't eat he'll faint, like the sissy he is.'

At this my sister giggles and she and my father grin at each other. Yellow egg yolk drips from his bottom lip and runs down his chin.

'I'm just glad it's not my job to get you into shape. I feel sorry for those instructors.' He chuckles, looking at my sister for support.

'For heaven's sake, Peet, Nicholas is leaving today! Why make it unpleasant?'

'The sooner they whip some discipline into him the better.'

The egg has coagulated on his chin, settling in his goatee, stopping its movement just below his smirk.

'You are going to see how the real world works, my boy,' he says to me, and then to all of us, 'It's going to be good for him. Best thing to get boys away from their mothers' apron strings. Little babies. At your age I was a man.'

How dare he talk like this? What does he know? He never went to the army. It is his government, it is what he stands for, that I have to go and defend. I am going to fight for him! The thought churns my empty, knotted stomach.

'I don't believe in what I'm being forced to do.'

'Please, let's not get into that now.' But our anger is larger than my mother's pleading.

'It's your bloody government that you voted for that I now have to fight to protect!' My sister, two years my junior but in her third-parent capacity, says, 'Don't say bloody.' She knows this will irritate me.

Again my mother tries to keep the peace while my father with the egg on his face lectures me on politics in between insults. So I retaliate. Then he calls me a moffie and I say, 'If I am one, I am what you have made me.'

When he lashes out, it is a split-second lapse of restraint rather than a calculated attack. It is a strike-and-grab blow, the corner of the table preventing his full weight from following his fist and allowing just enough time for my mother's pleas to stop the attack. But the blow is strong enough to knock me off my chair.

I sit on the mottled, dusty carpet supporting myself with

one arm, the other hand stopping the blood dripping from my nose. There is a measure of freedom in my anger, for it is stronger than my fear. In the kitchen doorway my dog cowers, ears flat and eyes darting between my father and me. I get up and go to the bathroom.

Behind me my mother is crying. This is what brings regret; she hardly ever cries. They are arguing—I hear her anger through her tears. They are arguing about him hitting me just before my leaving for the army. What if I don't come back? How will he feel then? The part I hate to hear is, 'And how can you call your own son that? You should be ashamed of yourself!'

'What?'

'You know what I mean, Peet.'

'You mean a moffie?'

'Yes, it's the most despicable thing you can call anybody, never mind your own son!'

'You know what I meant.'

'What did you mean?'

'I meant he is a sissy, not a homo.'

'Well, you should know better. I never want to hear that word in this house again. Sissy is bad enough.'

'Well, he is one, and I hope they flog it out of him in the army. I sure as hell have had no luck with him.'

Between my arms supporting me on the edge of the basin, blood drips into the running water. A dark red drop sucks from my nose. As it hits the water, it expands into a stringy, paler red and then spirals down into the drain. In it I detect frail, slimy mucus.

I see myself framed in the mirror. A red streak flows from my right nostril. Some blood makes its way over my lip and I suck it into my mouth, tasting the metal and salt. Behind the rage in the mirror is my mother.

'When the bleeding stops we must go.' She keeps quiet for a while. Between a sigh and a sob she says she thinks it's a good thing that my father and I will be separated for a while. I know she hopes that time will bring change.

But we have crossed an invisible line, like a layer between two temperatures. So complete is the destruction of this forced kinship, that it cannot be undone.

I feel hate—shocking, driven hate—and I use it as the fuel to face this day. I wish Frank could be here to see me off; I miss him with raw self-pity.

They insist on coming to see me off. I question my father and Bronwyn's motives but say nothing.

He leaves the house dressed in his usual fastidious way; no trace of the lack of control that drove his fist into my face. His clothes are drab and outdated. So are his rules, which are to be accepted without question. Beating or mentally abusing your child is condoned, particularly if the child doesn't conform.

We walk to the pale green, spotlessly clean Chevrolet and put my bag in the trunk. It looks small and insignificant. Like my life, I think. The painstaking cleanness reflects this man who is my father, and I see him personified by the car. 'If you don't keep it clean, you don't respect it.'

I look back at the house through the rear window and try to catch a last glimpse of my dog. She looks forlornly at the car and turns to the spot she has chosen to wait for my return. Near her hangs the box that was the home of two squirrels I had saved and reintroduced to freedom.

As I get out to close the first gate behind us, I see moisture dripping from the exhaust. The smoke and vapour of the cold engine seem to muffle the sound of the idling car. Suddenly everything I see is crucially important, chastising me for my previous indifference, mocking me: And now you are going and we are staying.

To the right of the kitchen door is the table where I stitched my mother's hand after one of the pigs had bitten her. To the left of the gate is the spot where Bennett beat the woman with a piece of pipe and she fell and hit her head on the lawn mower still smelling of freshly cut grass and pulverised dog shit. All my observations are vividly laid out in front of me, waiting to be acknowledged.

We drive past the side of the house in which I have experienced so much sorrow, but now don't want to leave. The structure suddenly looks sad, droopy and empty. But the largest void is Frank-shaped. Touching my tender, swollen lip, I move my finger up into my nose and pick at the caked blood. Then we are through the second gate.

Once we've crossed the last bridge, the gravel road ends, the rattling stops and we accelerate on the asphalt bordered by the greenery that shelters this winding road out of the valley.

On the left is the old tree trunk where we used to wait for the school bus. We round the slow bend past Van Breda's packing shed and I turn around to look back, not caring about Bronwyn's malicious pleasure.

Through the back window I stare back at Banhoek, stainless in the morning light and slightly warped by the curve of the glass.

Every inch of the road out of the valley is layered with tiny adventures: the popping sound of jacaranda blossoms as I cycle over them, pockets of air with different temperatures and smells of the rich valley life, the late afternoon sun on closed eyelids. Yes, I love this valley; it's what happened to me here that scarred. Strange that it never tainted the place—but then, it is so incredibly beautiful.

And through it all runs the cord of sexual discovery. How mortified he would be if he knew about the sex, his son's exploration of the unmentionable, the other races. Yes, to him that would be the ultimate evil.

'The heart is dirty.' This is what the black woman said about my parents, right there, at that very spot, when I caught up with her as she was leaving the valley after being fired, ostensibly for stealing. Is this how she felt when she spoke to the little snot-nosed child clinging to her with a fistful of her skirt? She, too, didn't know what was waiting for her outside the valley.

I have learnt so much here: a new kind of love, the first hate. A hate that had started way back but had broken soil here—all part of my initiation between these mountains. Acne, alcohol, sex, religion, loss, revolution, assault, no rights, failure and fantasy, all of it learnt here. But the torture, that's what I will never forget, the soul-scarring realisation that I am what I have feared and prayed I wouldn't be.

We pass the shop with its dry wooden floors and high shelves, old glass display counters with cheap jewellery and sweets. I recall the sounds of the trading mingled with the smell of soap and paraffin in the dimly lit room.

The owner was murdered here when the revolution reached the valley. At that time death seemed so distant, only for the old and tired. Death was for others, but now it seems so close. For two years I will be on the vehicle of its pursuit.

There is little conversation in the car. In front of Bronwyn our father sits neatly. Far to the opposite side our mother looks small and withdrawn.

Over and over in my head I feel-hear the words, 'This must stop, this must stop!' Then it becomes a plea. 'Please, please, dearest Lord, I beg of you, let something happen, anything, for this to stop.'

When we turn down into Helshoogte, the valley of my youth becomes obscured and I catch sight of Table Mountain in the distance; where I will board the train . . . today.

A pool of parents, family and friends has formed on the plat-form. We enter the station in rough formation after having enrolled at the Castle, and we walk towards our families. They probably still see us as the same people, but on the threshold of our departure we have already been altered—spirits now, walking amongst them, touching them in conversation, but they don't own us any longer.

Soot and dirt of trains and many partings lie beneath our feet. Above us the light-blocks through the canopies of the different platforms illuminate the rusty colour of oxidised decomposition, coating stone and concrete. Everything has a metallic dirtiness and the smell of coal, metal and travel.

I secure a compartment with Gerrie, the only boy from my group of friends to be called up to the same camp. Under his skin are the swollen signs of worry; a brighter red where he has picked at the numb pain. As I put my bag on my bunk, I briefly remember the day we were chosen for student council. Did that really happen to me? Was I really chosen by the people who two years prior didn't even know my name? From zero to hero . . . and now back to zero . . .

When I left the hall that day, I was in a state of shock; like hearing about a death, similar in intensity, yet so completely on an opposing clef. I walked from that hall, and for the first time I experienced a feeling of triumph, feeling the sun and the throng of people as they came rushing out, congratulating me, and for once I felt confident. Even during initiation by the previous year's prefects (when we were dumped in a truck with pig shit and covered with a canvas, punched, beaten and dropped off to walk home in the middle of the night, covered in shit) I didn't care, because I was one of the chosen. Chosen despite the fact that I didn't play rugby, just chosen for who I was, or for the part I had allowed them to see. Chosen, for who they thought I was.

My father becomes agitated. Bronwyn is standing next to him,

unnoticed. The atmosphere on the platform gives no indica-
tion that I'm about to start a journey to hell.

The whistle is like a chain of sound running up and down
the carriages. Sound with length. Everybody starts talking faster
and louder. The whistle has issued a declaration. It cuts like an
ice-cold chainsaw through my spine. My mother catches my
expression and says, 'Nicky, you'll be fine.' She looks at me
intently, and nothing else exists. I can feel my face drain of
colour, and the African sun slicing through the dirty roofing has
no effect on the shiver running through my body.

The large hooks join like iron hands between the cars, lock
and take up the slack to carry us away, griping with loud metal
clunks between the links of this shackle. The screeching of releasing brakes and dragging metal on metal—discordant, jarring sounds—gives the impression that the machine is aware
of the long trek and bemoans it . . . or the unwilling ones it is
carrying.

I hear the nearest wheels go over the first joint in the tracks:
Dik . . . dik. I hold my mother's stare. The invisible cord of tenderness starts stretching.

We juggle for position, filling every window. I fight only to
see my mother's face, and she stands there knowing my need.
I focus so intently that all else smudges into pixels, with her
face in the centre.

Dik-dik . . . dik-dik, the sounds shorten in step. Eventually
I only see the spot that is her face. Then a pylon sweeps past as
we enter a long bend. As the train obediently follows the tracks,
the pylons arrive faster. Where is she? I search until I can no
longer see the platform.

The sound changes as I pull my head back in.

'We're fucked,' someone says.

3

The journey is in no way as I imagined it to be.

For the first part of the day, with tension unravelling, massaged by increased familiarity and the rhythm of the steel wheels, there seems to be a jostling for position. By the time we snake through the Hottentots Holland Mountains all restraint has evaporated.

Bizarrely my life has now swung even further around, fixing a course directly opposed to what I yearn for, dragging me over uncharted territory.

We travel through the semi-desert of the Karoo that I learnt to love as a child. For hours on end I block out my reality, escaping to the wild outdoors. The contrast tortures me—I see where I want to be, but I'm so far removed from it, like a caged bird hanging at a window to a forest.

There are three realities: the outside, the trepidation inside me, and then the chaos behind me bristling against my neck like the cold breath of the devil, who knows what awaits me.

I take a wire-bound notebook from my top pocket—the first of many such books I will use to diarise what happens to me over the two years. I write:

The light of the train runs like a scanner over a strip of ribbon, lighting the Karoo desert. From where I cup out the light, with my face close to the glass, I see a transient betrayal of the nocturnal mystery. Untouched-ness is richest in feeling. Our lack of exposure to it has numbed us to the subtle gifts that nature gives, like the emotion locked into a soft desert wind and the scent in its wash when you stumble upon its mystery while opening a gate on a gravel road and you realise for the first time its size and power.

At De Aar, in the heat of day two, the train is delayed for thirteen hours outside the town. The toilets are a mess and the passages filthy. The railway staff have been hiding in the guard coach since yesterday. In a matter of twenty-four hours the train degenerates to a septic, sick serpent moving towards some disgusting hole.

Fights break out, people vomit and defecate in the passages. One guy gains instant fame by managing to puke at will—his nickname is Skomgat.

Drunken men from different social standing, language and culture, made equal by a mutual fate, open our compartment door and demand alcohol. The five travelling with me are part of the decay that is setting in. Gerrie hovers in-between, on a fence of fear, leaving me alone to defend my Kiwi shoe polish and Robin starch, products I didn't even know existed until a week ago.

By the afternoon of the second day of my two years I start longing for the discipline of the organisation awaiting me at the end of this journey. It is, after all, run by adults—the government elected by people like my father, people who are staunchly religious and regulated. Not people I relate to, but people who stand for discipline and order. And anything must be better than this anarchy.

Deep into the day we stop again, this time at a station called Potfontein. Through my window I notice an elderly black man dressed in an ill-fitting but clean suit, its life extended by need and poverty. He carries the signs of this harsh climate, but there is gentleness and calm in his weathered face.

Window down, my arms resting on the frame, I analyse the scene as if composing it for a painting. There is fortitude in the man's posture, a humble tolerance of life and circumstance. He seems to have moved beyond struggling, to have arrived at acceptance.

I draw a small sketch of him. Next to it I write:

I've met such a man; in an intolerable corridor—neither of us wanted to be there—me trapped by youth and he by colour. We became friends . . . No, he took me between the scars to his trust where I had a glimpse of a different wisdom. A man like this has cried and sung for my loss. He doesn't know the alignment of the planets, but he knows their touch on a cold, crisp Karoo night, away from the lights that react obediently to the white man's control.

From another coach someone starts swearing at him. He looks up and then down. For some reason, what happens next stays with me as my real introduction to the Defence Force. The old man suddenly appears to embody everything that is simple and tender in the world of which I am no longer a part. I wish the train would start moving.

With a dull thud a beer bottle hits the platform next to the bench where he is sitting. A white triangle of glass and froth explodes and he gets up, but then decides to stay when he hears the conductor's whistle and the train starts moving.

I hear cheering as someone running beside the train hurls a full plastic bag at the elderly man and it bursts against the side of his head. A cold fury lodges in my stomach. The perpetrator jumps onto the step between two coaches, as if onto a podium, holding on to the handles on either side. Why do the rivets and screws retain their hold? Why don't they drop him under the wheels?

As the vomit-smeared man bends to pick up his stained hat, I see the sign on the back of the bench: Non-Whites Only.

The sun is low over the vast space and the colours are deepening, the light softening. The sounds around me become rounder, less sharp than in the middle of the day. I change seats to feel the air on my face. When I feel the panic clamp around me, I will search for this balm, try to capture it, to remember what 'can be,' I write:

What do the bridges consist of that I'm traversing from my old world to this one; bridges built by others? I'm looking for bridges that go back—no . . . no, ladders that move higher. That's what's calling me . . . to an entirely different plane.

Poupan, Kraankuil, Witput, Modderrivier. Later that night more conscripts board the train at Kimberley. I feel their frightened energy . . . and then I try to sleep.

Bloemhof, Orkney, and early in the morning at Potchefstroom more people board the filthy train—they don't have the luxury of experiencing the process of decline.

Slowly we crawl through the outskirts of Johannesburg. The pollution over the graffiti-scarred homes, factories and grime demoralises me even more. Old caravans are dying in backyards; mangy animals, filth, futility and crumbling structures line our route.

I will the engine driver to go faster, but he seems to slow down even more, savouring the hangover of the humanity outside. The dirt of being close to a railroad lies on all the surfaces, but even cruder are the marks people make in despair.

We leave Johannesburg station, our last stop, and the people of this train become more subdued. The nervous laughter turns to giggling, and by late afternoon it is quiet. We sit staring blankly ahead, consumed by what we have heard is waiting for us. It settles on us like a damp bandage.

As the quiet train moves into rural stretches between towns, massive thunderclouds start building up and casting shadows on the dark land. There are small settlements in the shallow valleys, small white dots in partial shade. The marks of man seem frail on the plains beneath the billowing vapour.

Gerrie is sitting opposite me. Behind him the backrest of the seat that becomes a bunk bed at night forms a blue background to his anxiety. He cradles his guitar and strums softly;

stops and starts until a song emerges. When we round a corner, the sun comes out and lights up his face.

He repeats certain chords over and over until they are linked together and become recognisable. In the previous days, when he sang, volume was important. Now I only hear emotions lying gently in the chords—deep emotions. He looks at the floor but sees the clouds. He plays a very deliberate, unhurried interpretation of Joni Mitchell's *Both Sides Now*.

> *Rows and flows of angel hair.*
> *And ice cream castles in the air.*
> *And feather canyons ev'rywhere,*
> *I've looked at clouds that way.*
> *And . . .*
> *If you care, don't let them know,*
> *Don't give yourself away . . .*
> *It's life's illusions I recall*
> *I really don't know life at all.*

Someone who knows the area, or has memorised the stops, says quietly,

'One more station then we're there.'

Every moment becomes a large door slamming irrevocably shut behind me. In carefully selected steps, down, down from where already there is no return, the closer we get, the more solid they become, the more heavily they shut, the more thoroughly they seal.

It is almost dark. We sit in concentrated twilight in the unlit compartment. As the train creeps into Middelburg station, we see them on the platform: the instructors. Their stance is menacing, army-aged; a worn-turned-hardened army threat.

Metal screeching, painful-sounding; then a jerk, heavy with friction. Shouting. The men burst onto the train, hitting and kicking the sides of the passages and compartments, flinging doors open and swearing. The words are mostly fuck, *poes* or cunt . . . and move, move, move!

Shit you will shit! You are going to vomit blood, troops! You are going to vomit blood for a long, long time.

We are given a 'rofie-ride' to the camp in the back of Bedford trucks, under dark canvas, on raw, splinter-emitting benches. We can only see out the back, unable to brace ourselves against the turns and sudden stops. So we fall about, which is the dri-ver's intention. Everything is immediately childish, spiteful and senseless—I have no wavelength of logic to tune into.

At the camp there is some comfort in the darkness, the chaos and the fact that we all face the same fate. We are allocated tents in groups of six. Nobody knows what to expect; some say we will be woken up in the night, beaten and drilled and exer-cised until we pass out. Others say the instructors are going to attack us with *balsakke* (tog bags) filled with rocks and iron. I think of ways to protect myself and go to sleep curled up with my arm over my face.

4

The shapes in the house have started to change. Furniture has been moved to one side and there are large boxes everywhere. When the carpets are rolled up, Frank and I skate on the woodblock floors that Sophie has polished. The rooms sound hollow and our voices louder than usual.

We are excited, but Sophie has a private sorrow about her. She holds me close and there is a tautness in her body. I look up and see tears on her round cheeks, which she wipes away with the back of her hand, but they stay shiny. To me it feels as if she is overflowing with tears, so I avoid her and play in the maze of boxes with Frank.

Whenever I have supper with Sophie in the kitchen, I eat by candlelight. My father says it's not allowed, because I'm not black, but I only want to eat when it's dark and peaceful. What I really crave for is the dark night and a fire with people huddled in blankets in front of their round homes called huts—the first English word I learn.

A big truck with a compartment above the driver's cabin comes to take away all our furniture and the boxes. Frankie and I sleep on the floor, on a blanket-bed. We don't feel the hardness, only the adventure.

I look up from the floor. My parents are moving about as people do when they've been awake for some time. It is light and our mother tells us to get up.

'Frankie, see that Nicky gets up now. Come on, boys, we don't have time. Be a big boy, Frankie, and help your brother brush his teeth.'

I'm sleepy-slow and Frank is urging me to go to the toilet and get out of my pyjamas. Milk and rusks that Sophie baked, no putu porridge this morning, no breakfast, just sluggish drinking and eating and our hurried parents around us.

'Come now, boys, let's not make your father angry, come-come. Say goodbye to Sophie you two, quickly, and get to the car, quickquick!' I hug Sophie and say goodbye. Her embrace is rigid.

My mother looks at Sophie. 'Don't upset the little *baas* (master) . . .'

I walk to the car. Before I get there, I hear a wail and words I don't understand because they are drowned by sobs. Sophie bursts past my mother and runs to me. She calls out her name for me, 'Isipho!'—my gift! She moves towards me, charged with momentum. She has lost her composure and the quiet peace that dwells in her. I have never seen her like this, and it unsettles me.

Bent over and weeping, she picks me up. A sound like shouting comes from deep in her throat, 'Ngizokubona . . . Ngizokubona, Isipho, Isipho, Isipho.' She is sobbing and crying and saying over and over, 'I see you, I will see, I will see you always, my gift, my gift,' and then we are both crying.

I hear my father's angry voice, but my mother says, 'Wait, Peet, he's like a child to her, just let her be.'

'I don't care. What will the neighbours think?'

'Forget about the neighbours . . .'

Then my mother speaks to Sophie, and her grip relaxes. She sits down on the garden wall, her body round and hunched up. She doesn't move, and when my mother tells her to help with the bags, she ignores her for the first time in her life.

Suddenly I feel a loneliness, as if something has been taken out of me. It's confusing and overshadows the excitement of the journey ahead. Thus, at the age of four, I leave the rolling foothills of the Drakensberg. I leave forever where the dragon pushes its feet into the earth to steady its mass that towers above in the blue Lesotho distance. I leave a life of happiness.

Later that morning we have tea, which extends into lunch, with my father's family in neat, suburban Bloemfontein. In the bathroom there is a machine with big straps that, my mother explains quietly to Frank and me, is to shake one's fat so that one can become thinner. I wonder for how long the woman has had the machine, because her fat looks hard, solid.

Her husband is shipshape, like his house.

We are not allowed to play in the house. We sit down and have 'Hertzog-cookies' with our red Kool-Aid. Only one of each, and for the rest we have to sit still and keep quiet. The lounge suite is beige-brown with armrests in the shape of wagon wheels. Everything is carefully covered with crocheted squares to protect the gleaming surfaces. There is a lot to look at: ornaments, mostly bright and shiny, like different synthetic species herded together in polished packs; collections of all sizes of shiny dogs, frogs, chickens. The dog assortment is so large that it almost takes up a corner of the room. Small tables bear arrangements made out of feathers or shells, or plastic flowers in clay pots surrounded by glazed figurines, boats made out of matches, and little carts made from pegs hold bottles of something wrapped in silver wire. The pictures on the walls are of old cars or 'arrangements' of beads or sand on fabric, jigsaw puzzles glued and framed, and backlit silhouettes on glass.

The woman looks angry and speaks almost exclusively to my mother. When she walks, there is a chafing sound that I trace to the top of her legs where, under the stiff dress, I imagine her stockinged legs rubbing against each other.

She has a sour-sweet smell. Her head looks flat from the back and runs straight up from her neck to her tightly curled and lacquered hair. On either side of her mouth deep grooves bracket her down-turned mouth, which seems to be made of something other than flesh. She and her house are both cluttered with precise behaviour.

Her husband asks us if we play rugby. I say, 'My mother says it's a stupid sport because people get hurt.' This seems to shock him, and he replies that if we don't play rugby we'll grow up to be sissies. The only time he talks to us after that is to say goodbye. He squeezes my hand with a swollen grip. I pull away, which embarrasses my father. We snigger in the car when Frank calls him Banana Fingers. My mother also laughs, giving us the freedom to ride the joke all the way out of the Free State.

By late afternoon, about 400 kilometres south of Bloemfontein, we turn off the N1 to my father's family farm, situated between Richmond and Britstown. We will stay there for five days before going on to Cape Town.

Frank and I stand behind the front seat, riding the potholes in the gravel road. We are thrilled by the sound of the stones hitting the undercarriage of the car, the wide expanse and the feeling of adventure. Off the tarred road we become part of the landscape, the textures, sounds and smells.

The sky is bigger here, with clouds on different levels catching the late sun, reflecting colours of different weight. Unique aromas of the wild Karoo float through the car.

There are farm gates that Frank and I take turns to open. When it is my turn, he helps me with the heavy hinges. I slide off the seat and land on the dirt road, and the smells rush at me—something that will remain in me.

The immense expanse overwhelms me. I am aware of the different air causing an unfathomable emotion in me. It is somehow untouched by humans, like the land lying ahead. And it is filled with ghosts and smells of the untamed. An uneasy madness tugs at me as the wind curls over the land that is turning from solid to sand.

'Come now, Frank, we don't have all day, or night. What are you two doing out there?'

'Come, Nicky, we'd better get in.'

'What were you looking at for so long out there, Nicky?'

'Nothing,' I say, as I would for the rest of my life when I can't explain or (I believe) they don't have the understanding to grasp.

'When are they coming?' my mother asks my father.

'In two days' time; until then at least we'll have peace.' He shakes his head and clicks his tongue to emphasise his displeasure. 'If only she would stop her drinking and leave that useless Jacobus!'

'Just don't let it affect you so.'

'She's my sister, Suzie; of course it affects me. Now the child complicates matters even more. How can that hippie be a father?'

'What's a hippie?'

'A hippie, Frank, is worse than a ducktail. They are disgusting people who listen to crazy music and don't believe in God.' He allows the silence that follows to press home his sentiment. 'Promise me you will never become one, because if you do, I will chase you away and you will never set foot in my house again.'

'Don't say things like that to him; he will believe it.'

'Well, he'd better, because I will.'

'I promise,' says Frankie.

A hare jumps out in front of the car and runs in the light pools that break the shadows of small undulations. Our father laughs and speeds up to chase it, but it darts into the dark ahead of the big-eyed noise. The car drifts slightly over tinned-roof corrugations, and then rights itself. When we go through a dip, the bottom of the car scrapes the gravel and bounces up.

'Three more gates to open, then we're there!'

We rib-run over the cattle grid and reach the place where our father was raised.

The house is set within a big, green lawn dotted with pepper trees. The high roof with the curved covering over the wraparound veranda looks proud and inviting.

There is a formal politeness in the way the two brothers greet each other. Uncle Hendrik and aunt Sannie have a son, Hanno, who also stands on the neat pathway of greeting. He is my age. In him pulses a father-shaped competitiveness, scab deep, barely civil.

It is a place of contrast—the freedom of the spirits borne on the evening air and the mundaneness of my father's family. They seem carefully crocheted into self-righteous squares on which their prejudice rests. There are special voices for God, then in descending steps of deference, for people of the church, authority, old people, friends, children, dogs, and finally the voice they use for the staff.

Long table, respectful children on one side, humble, grateful, then off to bed. We walk down the high-ceilinged passage covered in photographs, to the blank room that Frank and I share. High above the bed a light hangs on a long cord. The frilly, blue lampshade projects in half moons on each wall, with harsh light below the dividing line and mysterious shadows above. We ask my mother to leave the door open. When she leaves, I crawl into bed with Frankie, and we fall asleep hugging each other. Breakfast consists of 'build-you-up-to-play-rugby' helpings that we have to eat in silence. When my uncle asks me a question, I stutter a reply in Afrikaans and my father grimaces.

It is time for a tour of the farm. We reach the barn with the farm vehicles and implements, and the ever-present layer of dust amidst the smell of sheep manure.

Our drive around the farm takes all morning. Frank and I stand on the back of the Ford truck with high railings for transporting sheep. Hanno has a 'you-don't-really-belong-here' attitude and takes up position in the centre against the cab. We reach a whitewashed clay wall and go through a rusty gate leading to the stones that mark the places where our dead forebears lie, contorted as though the hard soil wants to twist them out. My father combs his hair, almost as an act of respect, and returns the comb to his calf-length sock. He points out the different generations to Frank and me, and then we turn to go.

Before the doors of the Ford close, uncle Hendrik says: 'One day we will all lie here.' He starts the engine and drives off. I look at this dismal place, confused and frightened, and turn to Frankie's frowning face for comfort. After lunch we all have to rest. No sound from the children. We wait for the noise to die down, and Frank and I tiptoe through the settled discipline to play with the dogs.

We sit on the red cement veranda squinting into the glare. In the distance a springbok walks by, the heat waves stretching its needle-thin legs into quivering waves of rising air. The corgi that I'm stroking lies panting, its tongue reaching the concrete floor and making wet marks that stay only for a moment before being snatched away by the thirsty air.

In the evening the wind pushes the curtains aside and the spirits look in on us to the beat of the generator. I pull the sheets over my head and hold Frankie tight. Where we touch it is dampwarm and I pray for sleep.

They appear to him broken, dressed in silver, telling him to get up. They carry the boy off through the window; he tries to fight but he is helpless. The chill of the faraway stars panics him as he drifts high above the farm. Below, the old farmhouse is dark and quiet and the land it stands on crumbling. Eyes, behind which a tornado rages, burn darkly and he obeys. The generator is off. Fragile, the sleep of the naive self-righteous . . . he sees them lying, denial fluttering behind their eyelids. The dogs look up and the corgi is calling, but he is too high to hear.

A preacher clothed in piety is talking and has turned his back on a truth of which he has total clarity. Then he takes the hand of a forefather. Both of them are carrying rifles for hunting. It is as though they are pondering a weighty decision and then decide to go ahead. The boy is aware that they have decided against his will. He calls out to them, but no one hears his soundless plea.

Swinging around he sees angels fighting—in the centre he witnesses his own birth in a violent storm . . . recognising them beside his mother, who is screaming in delivery, fighting desperately as they pull him to the square walls until he is dragged within its shadow. When they pass the top of the conifers he kicks and cries, 'No, no!' The one with the gouged features is weighing him down by his feet.

The hard earth opens. Inside the darkness is movement. Now he is begging, 'I cannot go there. NO, PLEASE . . . it's not my grave, It's . . .'

'Nick . . . NICKY . . . wake up!' The words cut through the men standing on the mist. I shake and hold on to my brother, but on the outskirts they are waiting. I know they are there . . .

5

The springbok arches its back and jumps fantastically high, defying gravity. Three times in a row it bounces with majestic grace; head down, horns forward. At the apex of the third leap all its energy suddenly disintegrates. I reel at the sound, cover my ears, close my eyes. Not only against the noise, but also against the destruction I have just witnessed. The shell from uncle Hendrik's .308 rifle clanks onto the metal floor of the truck. I'm still holding my ears when he jumps off the back, gets into the cab and drives off.

I sit on the wheel arch, knowing I never want to hear that sound again. Uncle Hendrik races across the veld to where the animal has fallen. I slip onto the dirt and dry blood on the corrugated floor. Still I don't let go of my ears.

My father is horrified at my performance and orders me to get up, but I stay on the floor, bouncing around with the spent cartridges. By the time we reach the springbok, my father, scarlet with shame, has pulled me up by my elbow. Hanno is laughing at me and calls his father, who looks at me and chuckles.

Through my tears I see the springbok, legs outstretched in a spasm, all its magnificence gone, eyes glaring with dread. It struggles to get up, but the bullet has severed its spine, paralysing the hind legs.

'Here we don't waste bullets,' uncle Hendrik says as he raises his foot above the animal's head and brings his full weight down on its open eye. Then, ceremoniously, he opens his pocketknife and slits its throat. Blood pumps out in thick squirts, and the front legs kick in semicircles on the ground.

My father's elder brother wipes his knife on the animal's soft, white chest. The entrails, released from the belly by Piet's knife, spill out in a steaming heap.

Hanno walks past me and spits, 'Sissy.' Frankie, tight-faced, tells him to shut up. They throw the carcass on the back of the truck and leave the entrails behind.

I beg my father to ask uncle Hendrik to take us home, and Frankie says: 'Dad, please, I don't like this. Please, can we go home?' He looks the other way and doesn't answer us. His embarrassment is palpable; not just one, but both his sons are afraid of one of the most important rituals on this farm.

Uncle Hendrik drives on, slowly, staying down-wind from the other animals. After a while we come across three more springbok, grazing and unaware of us.

'There's one for you, Peet,' uncle Hendrik calls from the front. 'The one on the right, that's your *bok*.'

'It's a ram; the other two are females,' says Hanno, sitting proudly next to his father.

My father takes aim and I start crying. Frank, also almost in tears, begs him not to shoot. Then the shot goes off and the springbok in the centre collapses. Uncle Hendrik makes a suck-clicking noise that signifies disappointment, and my father looks uncomfortable. As the truck starts, the wounded buck jumps up.

'You've wounded her, shoot again.'

'It's a female, Pa,' says Hanno.

'Yes, son, I know.' Our father, visibly flustered, takes aim again.

He uses the cab as a dead rest and fires another shot. The springbok stumbles, starts running and stumbles again. Uncle

Hendrik sets off at a speed while Hanno indicates the direction to follow.

We stop on an embankment. Uncle Hendrik takes out his binoculars and raises his eyebrows to nestle them in his eye sockets. When he removes the binoculars, he blinks to adjust his sight and says, 'Her front leg is badly wounded and she's getting tired. We'll easily catch her now. Do you have a good shot, Peet?'

'Yes, I think so.' I watch as my father takes aim, waiting. The sweat under the rim of his hat runs down his sideburns, trickles down his jaw, and drips on the rifle. He squeezes the trigger. Again the springbok jumps up and stumbles forward, this time with even more difficulty, falling with every step.

It takes another two shots before the animal eventually dies.

When we reach her, I see that the front legs have been shot off above the joint and she has been running on shattered bone. There is soil in the cavities that used to contain marrow.

'*Sy's dragtig, Baas,*' Piet says. She's with young! This time Piet opens the stomach with care and takes out the sack containing the foetus. He slits the membrane and produces a wet little deer. With his weather-beaten hands he removes the phlegm from the animal's mouth and starts blowing gently. The second blow produces a kick and a ragged rhythm of breathing.

'Give it here,' says Hanno and grabs the animal from Piet, climbs on the back of the vehicle and wraps the fragile little creature in a hessian bag from the floor.

Despite our pleas to also hold the animal, Hanno won't let us near it. Before long he loses interest, and when he looks down a while later and sees it is dead, he throws it into the pool of blood between the carcasses of its mother and the ram.

In the afternoon we play at the feet of the women, who are sitting in conversation while the men are cooking meat on the open fire. We drive our toy cars up and down hills we've formed out of gravel.

The three mothers are sitting in a half moon. Aunt Sannie's huge body spills over the sides of her chair, her pink-white legs protruding from under a tight crimplene dress. In between talking she barks orders at the staff. To her right sits our auntie Ester, whom I haven't met before, in a rowdy floral miniskirt. She sips glass after glass of white wine. Her voice becomes sharper, louder and she becomes more careless about keeping her legs crossed. Frank and I build a road to give us the best vantage point.

'What do they call that, hey, Frankie? Is it also called a willy-winkie?' He shrugs and giggles. Auntie Ester is nonchalantly holding her three-month-old daughter on her lap, while her hands are occupied with her cigarette and the wine glass.

Our mother sits to her right, with Bronwyn on a blanket at her feet. I see my mother watching the bouncing child nervously.

Then it's time for a nappy change. Auntie Ester puts the baby down, and with a wine-spilling jerk she drags a pink plastic bag from under her chair. She bends forward, opens the nappy and squints through the smoke of the cigarette in her mouth. Her legs open even wider and the miniskirt moves up, revealing a frilly panty with a dark fuzziness behind it.

There is yellow shit all over the lower part of the baby's stomach and when it's wiped off, I see that where we have a willy-winkie, she has the oddest little aperture. What a shame—she must have got hurt. On either side of the slit are huge, swollen bulges. Maybe she has two bums, I think to myself.

Seeing our attention fixed firmly on the child and our aunt, our mother orders us to go and play elsewhere.

'But she's lying across our road, Mom.'

'Then drive around her, come now, boys.' Auntie Ester's cigarette, more ash than tobacco, is slightly bent, but defiantly holds on to its original shape. Then the ash breaks off and falls on the child's face. My mother picks the child up and takes her into the house.

'Sannie, keep an eye on Bronwyn, won't you. And you two,' she turns to us, 'go and play over there.' She points vaguely to a spot under a tree.

As we gather our toys, auntie Ester loses her balance and collapses in front of us. We hear a slurred mumble as the grown-ups rush to her aid.

I long for Sophie. I now know I will never see her again. I know this from the way she said goodbye.

'Ngizokubona . . . Ngizokubona, Isipho, Isipho, Isipho.'

I start panicking that the ghosts of last night might return. The image of the dying buck is still clear in my mind: entrails spilling out, the soil in the shattered bones, the dead calf.

Certain events are like permanent fixtures in the murkiness of time and experience. I revisit them—no, they come to me. Baggage that can't be shed; only sometimes ignored for self-preservation.

We are often changed by our circumstances. Sometimes they stain our souls indelibly. What we see is just a phantom of the tattoos we carry in our core. And more marks are constantly being added. Only when these marks become dark does the mist fade, punching through the shroud. A glimpse at a person who has been completely stripped could reveal such darkness that we want to shy away, as if moved by our heart's early warning system.

6

It is 1977 and Mr. Klopper's garden has been taken away from him. He has been teaching Agriculture at the school for 23 years and now they've turned his garden into a parade ground—a parade ground to make 'cadets' out of us, to prepare us for the army. The school will play its part in preparing us to defend our country against the not-so-clear or present danger of Communism. A new form of agriculture is being developed—fertilising our brains and sowing the seeds of dread.

Most parents will make their sons obey the 'call-up' instructions, even though they have never fought in any war themselves.

In my matric year I receive my call-up papers. I become a number: 77529220.

7

My mother finds us a home in Welgemoed, a suburb of Cape Town about half an hour's drive from the city centre. It is a new suburb skirted by a few remaining farms. The house is situated on a hill and reached by a steep road. Frankie and I count the grazing cows as my mother's Austin Mini battles up the hill. Our father drives a company car—a Mercedes Benz 230. It has a speedometer that changes colour as the speed increases.

There is a large lawn fronted by a low face-brick wall. The servant's quarters are at the back, as well as a ringworm-infested sandpit full of cat pee.

On Sundays my mother wears a conservative dress and mantilla and goes to the Catholic Church. My father, dressed in a black suit and carrying his hymn book and Bible under the arm, goes to the Dutch Reformed Church. We go with our mother.

Now that we have a larger house we start receiving house guests, and my mother's parents, Gran and Grandpa, are our first visitors. Our father's parents, Oupa and Ouma, also come, but never at the same time as Gran and Grandpa. Gran and Grandpa are warm and friendly and full of fun. Oupa and Ouma are kind, keeping their distance and demanding respect-because-we're-old. Ouma tells us about our Afrikaner heritage and how we took our country from the English, the damned English. With her we have to be restrained and well behaved.

In this antiseptic, secure order of Whites Only the seasons change and we grow older by another year. Of this time I only really remember Frankie. Everything is associated with him.

8

The hours roll on endlessly on the parade ground.

That boy is cute, I wonder if he's gay. Guess I'll never know. The sun is so hot. I wonder if I'll burn a frown that will make me look older. My polish is nearly finished. Has Mom changed? Has everything at home changed? I want to buy a panel van, turn it into a surfer-cabby. Would I be able to afford it on army pay? I'll make a plan; re-design it. Yes, I like that, think it through really well; plan every detail. I'll build it myself, and then fit a fridge, stove, gas and a wood-strip ceiling. I'll plan a trip. Who will I take with me? Maybe that boy, where is he from? We'll do a trip around the country. I must stand next to him in the lunch queue. We'll sleep in the back, just the two of us . . . Don't go there, can't march with a boner. Shit, this is boring. This is so fucking boring. Can't they march? Don't they have any rhythm? Frankie's face . . . Frankie, I miss you, I miss you, my brother. Hope PT is easy. Hate pole PT and buddy PT. I know this afternoon during PT I'll pick him. He seems light, lean and sexy. Think of our first house in Welgemoed. I was so happy at first. Second house in Welgemoed, then Banhoek, Bob Dylan, Joni Mitchell, Black Sabbath, AC/DC, Led Zeppelin. Don't listen to that music, it's evil, devil-music, it's from Satan. Midnight Express, Rocky Horror, Jaws. 'Platooooon, halt two-three . . . bang . . .'

Will I still be able to draw after two years?

'Leeeeeft turn . . .'

Will I be accepted into Art College? I miss Anne. Travel, travel. New York. We are lost. Think of the first house in Welgemoed. I do know what happiness is. I did . . . until that day—when everything changed.

9

I turn five and Frankie will turn seven a little later in the year. It is five days after my birthday.

My mother runs past me screaming, then Gran . . . then someone asks me a question and runs off. Gran carries Bronwyn from the other side of the road, past me, into the house. There is shock and desperation in the old woman's eyes.

Frankie is lying on the side of the road, next to the Ford Cortina. My mother holds her mouth to his, blows into it and presses his chest, over and over. When she blows, she's quiet, but when she comes up, I hear prayers, questions and instructions in an incoherent slur. Each time she pushes down on him, his head rolls to the rhythm flowing through her arms into his tiny frame as she tries to force life back into him.

His head is in a dark pool on the rough, black tar. His hair is wet, and there are small pebbles clinging to the side of his face.

Everything around me is swirling, deformed, and a loud hum twists my perception out of shape. Thoughts and images cram into my head, but they're too big.

Beyond this lies a new pain—a stab that only allows me to stand and look. I am not sure what has happened. I need to think. I must get away from this. What happened? I don't understand.

From a misty abyss comes the image of Frankie running after Bronwyn. Then the mist lifts and I know . . . that's what happened . . . the screeching of tyres and the thunk . . . dull, metal-heavy.

As the events replay in slow frames, a heavy wheel starts turning inside me, unleashing a phenomenal determination: I have to clean the side of his head. I have to change what's happening. I start tearing through the people who have gathered around him. I grab Frankie from my mother's hysteria; call his name . . . As I cup his head in my hands, I feel a macabre displacement, see his changed expression, the dead grimace staring past me.

It takes two adults to pull me away from my brother. I feel the heat from the bystanders, from the tar, from my mother, from the car standing there with demonic indifference. Frankie's leg is twisted under his body, the skin brutally torn. I hit out and scream as they drag me away. If I stay he will be all right . . . I know, I know . . . leave me . . . LEAVE ME!

Every word, every smile, every function . . . stops.

Every story, every game, every sense . . . gone.

Through the afternoon and night I follow the rituals of eating, brushing my teeth, having a bath. I walk into the room with his empty bed. Where is Frankie? Where is he? Where is he now? People hold me and I am given an injection. Screaming, hitting, fighting for air . . . blur . . . fall . . . black.

Never again will I see an empty single bed and not think of Frank. Forever in my soul will be a Frank-shaped vacuum, craving to be filled. Much later I will realise it is both 'best friend'- and brother-shaped.

The nightmares start the night after Frank's death and return every night. There is a cord under incredible tension and I have to keep it from whipping out of control. When I lose control, it becomes knotted and I wake up screaming, wet and petrified, too afraid to close my eyes again.

I start walking in my sleep, spending time with Frankie and telling myself stories at night to fall asleep. I also talk to what people call behind cupped hands 'his imaginary friend.' Who is he? I don't tell. I will never share him again. I will keep him safe. I have a soul mate now, deep inside, that nobody can see, nobody can take away from me, not even time . . .

I should have done something. Did I see the car? Could I have warned Frankie? I should have gone across that road. No, I should have stopped Bronwyn from crossing it in the first place.

10

Each one of the 700 kilometres we travel is like the other. We journey with the hearse following us in grim convoy. We enter a different kind of time—one of long seconds.

We travel to uncle Hendrik's farm, where Frankie will be buried with the other Van der Swarts.

Everything appears to have a sickly, cheap shine—from the glossy little casket to the large hearse. They tell me he is inside this box and it feels so wrong, so unworthy of what it's holding, so far removed from the real Frankie.

Hour after hour I look back at the face of the car behind us, the chrome grill smirking between two cold eye lights. Is he rolling around in there? Is he comfortable? Can he feel? Does he know? Where is he? The tar is like an elastic band stretching between us, never letting go.

This is all there is: Frank and I and the vessels transporting us . . . How can one not want something so much, yet it still happens?

At Laingsburg and at Three Sisters we stop for fuel, and so does the black car. My parents are arguing constantly about the funeral. My father does not want to offend his elder brother, who has arranged for a minister from the Dutch Reformed Church, while my mother, being Catholic, won't hear of it— there has already been a service in the Catholic Church in Bellville. Uncle Hendrik will not allow the funeral to take place without a service and he doesn't want a priest to do it.

Every time they refer to my brother they use the past tense.

When we get to the first farm gate, I get out to open it and close it after the hearse. Dust clings to the black mirror-duco of the car. I hear a hiss of heat through the teeth of the chrome face, then a blowing sound, and then the engine dies. After running without water for many miles, the head gasket has blown.

At the first gate of the many that compartmentalise the road to uncle Hendrik's farm, we move some of the bags to the back seat and put my brother in the boot of our car. The lid won't close, so my father ties it to the bumper. We take the driver, in his weary grey suit that smells of stale cigarette smoke, to the only hotel in Richmond. Then we turn around and drive back to the farm. When we pass the hearse, I notice that it has been sucked closer to the ground, looking melted down and pathetic, close now to its own death.

My father is quiet, my mother is crying, and I go down into the hollow of the seat and turn my face to the backrest to talk to my brother.

There are no hugs between my father and my uncle, just a set way of acting—solemn, no display of emotion. Everybody, even Hanno and the staff, have taken on this 'way' as if from a manual. The warmth of enfold-me, it-will-be-all-right, talk-to-me, that I yearn for and got from Gran, Grandpa and my mother's side of the family at the memorial service in Bellville, is missing here.

All grieving has a structure and it is different for each person. The one I hate is the flimsily constructed sorrow, the temporary, overcrowded sadness with too many words. Here everything is different. I watch them walk and talk, and I don't trust them. They constantly use the Afrikaans words for tragedy, great sadness and sorrow.

I follow them when they remove my brother in his dusty box from the boot and carry him to a cool place. I go unnoticed in the gloom under the mantilla of night sinking over the homestead and outbuildings.

My father and uncle Hendrik put the coffin down in front of a corrugated-iron sliding door. There is a grating sound as the wood connects with the gravel and they fumble with the lock. Inside the cold room a single light bulb casts meat-hook shadows on the wall and lights up the red and white sinew and fat on the carcasses under which they place the casket. The air smells of meat, blood and cold.

I don't cry, nor do I say anything as the sliding door is closed, slicing the view of the casket with the disembowelled animals above it until there is only a shaft of light, a knock and then nothing.

I lie in the bed where Frankie held me when I cried for Sophie. I don't cry; I speak to the hollow emptiness in me, and I learn to understand purgatory—limbo.

The next day the minister comes from town, with an extravagant, patronising sympathy. Everyone is wearing black, and outside the wind is blowing. I meet relatives whom I don't remember and forget again immediately. Nobody talks to me. They just greet me, touch my head, and then they appear to switch on their tears elsewhere.

Five cars drive up to the place where all the dead people lie under the ground. The car doors slam. Women hold on to their skirts and hats, and their white petticoats contrast with the black.

Past the rusty gate is a freshly dug hole. The coloured layers in the walls of the grave reflect the eternity Frankie will be entering. The minister is very serious about this business of putting Frankie into the hole. He reads from the Afrikaans Bible with foreboding, the wind fraying the end of each sentence. He makes me feel that where Frankie is going, he'll be suffering.

The coffin is lowered on ropes. It swings forward and hits the top end of the grave. Some soil is dislodged and falls on the lid, and I imagine Frankie's head hitting against the gravel. My mother and father are beyond caring about the wind or anything else.

From behind the wall I hear voices. The farm workers are singing a hymn for my brother. They are not allowed inside the white people's walls, but their weather-beaten faces are distorted with compassion. They stand in their ragged clothing, under which one can see their emaciated frames. It is they who touch me, for pity is part of their design; suffering and understanding ingrained. It is their anguish I will never forget.

High above us the sky is filled with flaky clouds, like wallpaper on the clear blue of the big, big heaven.

Lunch, tea, and then the drinking. I wander amongst the people. The sounds, the movements, the black clothing all seem to blur into a marsh of indifference. Everything is so completely different now that every molecule of my world has been distorted. How dare anything exist, and not Frankie? How can my life go on when its axis has gone?

As dusk descends, the wind dies down. From where I sit on the back steps of the kitchen, the labourer's cottages beckon me. Their exaggerated shadows from the firelight dance against the walls and their voices are animated.

On my way to the cottages I come across a metal drum lying on its side, and inside I see a corgi with her four puppies. I am still staring at the perfection when Hanno arrives and beats the side of the drum with a stick. Then he strikes again, and this time he hits the mother.

I jump up and grab the stick. Only afterwards do I realise what I've done. He is shocked by my reaction and leaves the stick in my hand, kicks the dog, grabs one of the puppies and walks back to the house. My bravery astonishes me. Halfway to the kitchen Hanno turns back and shouts,

'Get the fuck away from those dogs, they're mine! I will kill them if I want to. And tomorrow I'm shooting that bitch, you sissy, you moffie!'

The labourers only notice me once I am standing amongst them. Their voices die down and they stare at me. They have an understanding of my grief and they don't need to tell me. Their eyes are soft and moist from smoke and alcohol. I sit down on an old tyre, and their conversation resumes. From where I sit, I see the glow of a cold, ancient sun sliding over the vastness of the Karoo. Black paint crawls from the shadows, around the small houses, and stops behind the people at the fire.

I feel the warmth of the circle, different from Sophie's people who seemed to grow from the earth. Sophie's world was mud and grass; this world is tin and poverty. Their sounds are also sharper, whereas the ones at the feet of the dragon are deep, rounder. But the empathy is equally inviting.

They can feel my grief, and to me this is sympathy. Their collective warmth gives me a comfort I have not felt since Sophie. Piet, the one who blew into the mouth of the baby springbok, smiles a toothless grin at me, and the music starts up again.

A big woman with sagging breasts starts to sing. It is more like attrition; weeping, hypnotic cycles. Its strength is not in the lyrics, although they have a raw sincerity, but in the passionate way she expresses them. Her head tilts to one side, eyes closed, her face remarkably dramatic, with round cheekbones like golf balls.

A man gets up, as if in a trance, and dances around the fire with his eyes closed. Puffs of dust fly up as his worn-out shoes drag and beat the ground. His body is skeletal and his arms look remarkably long. His frame is bent over and his arms gyrate as if controlled by a different brain. I have a sense of comfort and honesty, a reality so completely different from the restrained discipline, the formulated emotion that has chilled this day.

By the time they find me it is quarter past twelve. My mother is bordering on hysterics. Uncle Hendrik is angry. He tells me to get home immediately. On the short walk home he is able to talk to me without parents' presence: I am different and badly behaved, an embarrassment to my father; the sooner I change, the better. Now that Frank is gone I'm the only boy. I'm the eldest, I must do what my father tells me, and I must respect my father at all times. I must stay away from the non-whites. He has heard me speak Zulu, which is not good. *We* do not mix with *them*. We are different. If we mix with the staff they will become *white*. We must always show them who is *boss*.

All I want to do is stay with those poor people. Their sorrow is visible; it is raw and honest, whereas in my world it is deep and secretive. I want passion that weeps and holds, not hides and pretends.

When we get to the house I am the centre of different attentions: relief from my mother, disappointment from my father, embarrassment that manifests itself as anger from the rest. I have ended their 'party.'

Uncle Hendrik speaks to my father as if I don't exist. My mother is crying and wants to hug me, but they take her to her room.

'Look what you've done to your mother.' He shakes his head. 'What am I going to do with you?' My father walks me down the long, dark passage, composed but angry-drunk. He holds me by the scruff of my neck, and by the time we reach the room my toes are barely touching the ground.

In the room he removes his belt and orders me to lie over the side of the bed. It's the bed my brother slept in. I am panic-stricken because my mother is not here to protect me. As he strikes the first blow I start to cry. The leather claws around the side of my legs, where it hurts most, like cuts.

Afterwards I curl up on the bed. I can't hear anything around me—the space is full. I have lost my brother and my life.

***

To me there will always be the time before and the time after. A clear line, even though three days pass between Frank's death and the funeral on the farm. The event is so large it takes days to mark. Everything 'before' is drained away like dishwater swirling towards a slurping hole—behind the absolute divide that crystallises over these days.

In the days that follow I rescue one of the puppies and insist on taking it home—this in a house where children don't insist. Dot, my father names her, for the one white dot on the neck of her otherwise brown body. She looks more like a corgi than the others, which are now dead.

11

Bronwyn is the good baby. That's how they refer to her. I have hardly any memory of her before this time. She was invisible to Frank and me. Now she is everywhere.

Affinity is not something that can be created. What was between Frank and me seemed alive. It breathed and grew. It fed us like food; only us. My relationship with Bronwyn, on the other hand, is incomplete, damaged too often. The more my mother encourages camaraderie, the more I recoil. I am even self-conscious when I talk to her.

There is always blame after a death, often invented. It was because of Bronwyn, yes because of her, that Frankie crossed the road. I would have seen the car coming; I should have kept an eye on her; I should have said, 'Don't play here. Mom said we're not allowed to go outside the gate.'

It is easy for my sorrow to turn to anger and then to loathing the one whose fault it was.

12

'This place is so fucking ugly.'

'Yeah.'

'No, I mean it's impregnated with ugliness.' I think I'm very clever using the word, but I've thought about it for a long time, sitting here—long, bored, army-hours against the barracks wall.

'Yes.'

'There is not a single nice thing in sight.'

'Well . . .'

'I'm talking about the place, pervert! It's the surfaces, I think, even the surfaces we're covered in. Actually, that's the intention. I had this art teacher at school who said kitsch is a lack of sincerity.'

'Mm . . .'

'In some ways though these barracks are sincere in their intention. Ugliness does not have to be kitsch, of course, but then the shapes are so unresolved.'

'I can point out plenty of kitsch.'

I laugh. 'Yes, you're right, there's plenty.'

13

'Don't be a sissy, man!'

'I'm not. I just don't want to.'

'You will play rugby! Do you understand me? This is my house, and here you do as I say. Is that clear? And another thing, look at this report! If you are this bad at school you'll end up a tramp on the street.'

'I won't!'

'Yes, you will. And don't think I'll help you. I'll walk right past you. You are good for bloody nothing.'

'I'm good at something.'

'What?'

'I'm good at art!'

'Art! Oh please, Nicholas, grow up. What can you do with art? I'm talking about the real world here! One day you'll have to make money, not play around. I tell you, you are going to suffer. You have no idea of the real world, and don't you ever think I'll help you when you turn out a failure. You'd better start performing at school. At this rate you're going to end up working under blacks, I'm telling you.'

'I want to do the things I like. I hate maths.'

'Nonsense, you're just bloody lazy, that's all. Or are you stupid?'

'No!'

'One thing is certain, from this year on you WILL play rugby. And you'd better be careful—you're turning into a bloody moffie! Do you want that, hey? Hey?'

'No.'

'Bad at school, bad at sport. Why can't you be more like your sister? What are you going to do with your life? Just don't come and cry to me. You're on your own. A tramp on the street! I'll walk right past you . . . Always remember that . . . you hear me?'

And I do.

***

Bronwyn somehow escapes the impact of these events. As for my parents, neither of them openly cries again for Frankie. They're clad in 'the way you behave,' showing the world their strength.

I, in turn, craft a world soaked in him. I set up rituals in his honour; parts of the house, parts of me, reserved only for him. I talk to him and we play together. And I am old enough to know that this will be seen as bizarre.

'Who are you talking to, Nicholas?'

'Nobody.'

'Don't lie to me! I saw your lips move.'

I tell her that I was singing to myself, and she knows I'm lying. She wants to tell me she knows, she wants me to stop, but she doesn't know how. She just wants it to go away.

To me it seems as if my parents don't keep him as close as I do. Frank is carefully wrapped and tied up, like a fragile heirloom from another era, and stored away.

I walk specific paths, open and close doors in a certain way and keep paving stones and routes in his memory, as if the surfaces still carry his touch. I enshrine his shrouded world of undisturbed imaginary relics.

My father, too raw for patience, tries to stop me. But the disfigurement I carry in my heart, that which I haven't let out, and my behaviour as a result of it, deepens the rift between us. Selfrighteousness is the knife he uses to cut this rising dough, but it sticks to the blade that he polishes in church every Sunday, where he believes his outbursts and malicious words are swiftly sterilised.

***

School, Plasticine, powder paint, Mrs. Kreebel, wave patterns, homework, coloured pencils, the smell of wax crayons, lunchbox sandwiches, orange cold drinks in Tupperware bottles, yellow cling peaches, stories, fear of the future, uniforms, older boys, fights, Silverleaf pies with lots of tomato sauce, remember your cap and garters, Matchbox cars, carpets smelling of dust, sit and listen, keep quiet, inoculations, fear, a den in the bushes, rockery with daisies, missing Frankie.

As the years patiently notch up experience, I realise that sport, maths and the sciences are most admired in a system geared for achievers in these disciplines. By some genetic disposition I have neither these abilities nor the desire to develop them. Competence in catching or throwing a ball is held in much higher esteem than the rendering, in words or colour, of a deep emotion, or architecture that sits perfectly in its environment.

By age eight, my third year at school, my younger sister displays remarkable ability in all these categories of this changing world.

Middle-class Welgemoed, and my family in particular, worships at a new cathedral—one of sport. Tennis starts consuming our household.

A coach is appointed to mould the parents' little replicas into winning—a prerequisite for being trendy in this class of South African in the late 1960s. Bellville Tennis Club—catechism for the new religion. At first I also worship there, hating it, but carried by the flood; the only one I know.

Not only the people, but even the leather grips of the Slazenger and Dunlop Maxply rackets have their own pungent identification. The hats, sweatbands and dressing rooms all bear their scent in this island of tar, cement and asbestos. Platoons in perfect formation on a parade ground of competition.

14

They're visiting us for the day at our rented holiday house in Jeffrey's Bay—in-laws of my mother's sister Fran. They're poor, so don't talk about money. They refer to their son, my distant cousin, as Blackie, or Ossie or Oscar.

He has dark skin and hair and a striking presence. I sense in him a gentle strength that I find mysterious and attractive, but because he is related to my cousin Michael I take it for granted that he feels the same about me as Michael does. So I escape on a trip around town, pushing my *draadkar*—my little wire car—with its long steering shaft.

I have constructed a fantasy around saving a man: I am the only one to make it over the final obstacle in time, and in a brave, crowd-pleasing move I rescue him. What he looks like is the best part of the fantasy—I only need to dip my mind into my barrel of handsome boys.

Early evening, deep into their visit, uncle Dirk sends Michael to pour him another brandy and Coke. Then he calls me to the balcony. He has devised a wrestling competition on a dirty mattress lying in the corner. The children have been paired off with those closest to their age, and I see my sister battling it out with the cousin a year older than she is.

The dark corner has an eerie luminosity caused by the light from the adjacent room. A shaft of light falls over the bodies like a chevron.

The boys must take off their shirts. From behind him uncle Dirk puts his arms over Blackie's shoulders and rests his hands on the boy's chest. Michael returns with his father's drink, which he tastes. Then he nods and places it on the balcony wall.

The dust from the mattress makes me sneeze. But there is something more hanging in the air—the fear of shame. Uncle Dirk is swaying, with Blackie still in front of him. His head is turned to the mattress, but his attention is on Blackie. His mouth is in a dog-on-heat smirk. He is somewhere between humiliating me and touching the boy. In the corner of his mouth white spittle stretches and shrinks as he speaks. His right hand plays over the boy's chest, and I see how his thumbnail rubs over Blackie's nipple.

Suddenly I'm angry, confused about my sudden attraction to the boy and jealousy towards my uncle. Uncle Dirk has it all his way. He pretends not to notice the boy squirming under his hand as he stands shouting instructions to the two on the mattress. When he realises that Blackie wants to break free, he puts his head down and rubs his face over the boy's hair.

The round is over. The object of the game is to pin your opponent's shoulders to the mattress. Uncle Dirk lets go of Blackie, and now it's my turn against his son. This is the main event. I find the idea of touching my cousin distasteful.

'Riiiightio, here we have the Flop-Klaas-Kaffirrr . . . annnd Michael!' he shouts into his glass as if it were a microphone. Then, in a softer voice to his son, but still loud enough for me to hear, 'OK, take your time, and I don't care if you hurt the sissy.'

Looking at the man with as much hate in my eyes as I feel in my heart, I know instantly that this is what he wants. He whispers instructions to Michael, holding his arm too tightly, trying to impress on him the importance of this contest. My cousin has fear in his eyes.

Suddenly the world is the size of a double-bed mattress; the fight a religion, invented by this small god of ill intent. His future is under this dim light, fed by alcohol mixed with Coke and tainted by desire. To him his son's opponent is from a different place, an unwilling participant whose future will not be affected by the outcome of this match. No way out, and for

Michael there can be no prospect of losing. I am instructed to remove my shirt and get on the mattress. My first inclination is to simply lose, but the apprehension I feel in Michael is almost amusing, and suddenly the thought of winning excites me.

As we grip each other's bodies, everyone starts cheering for Michael, except Bronwyn and Blackie, who are quiet. Little Dot is confused by it all and she starts yapping.

For several minutes we strain and groan, and then uncle Dirk pulls my feet from under me. Michael plunges down on top of me. Dot jumps on the mattress, barking hysterically, and then I hear a loud yelp of pain. Michael pins my left arm down, moves over me and clasps my other arm. Somehow it doesn't bother me. My concern now is for the safety of my dog.

With unexpected strength I pull Michael upwards. He overbalances and slips off the mattress, still clutching me. In doing so, he pulls me over on top of him. I know immediately that I have him fixed.

'One . . . two . . .' I hear Blackie counting, excitement in his voice. Then Bronwyn joins him, but uncle Dirk stops the counting as the excited audience shout each number, enjoying what they now know is a victory over this adult.

'No, no, it's a disqualification; they're off the mat. Get up, get up.' Irritated with his son, he wrenches me off him. 'Start again and stop cheating, Klaas.' Quite self-possessed and full of confidence I smile at Michael, not with affection or good-will, but with a smirk of knowing the outcome. He is red-faced and flustered.

I win the next round with ease, my opponent being weak with fear and close to tears. When I have him pinned down, his head is over the side of the mattress.

'Come here, before your father says I am cheating again,' I say, pulling him back onto the mattress.

Drawn by the noise and Dot's whimpering, my mother comes to see what is going on and tells us to get cleaned up for dinner. As we walk down the passage to the bathroom, Blackie looks at me and winks.

15

'Hi.'

  'Hi.'

  'I'm Ethan.'

  'Nicholas. I um, I saw you, I mean I remember you . . . the day they cut our hair.'

  'Hardly a haircut!'

  'No shit. How's your back?'

  'OK. Was a little stiff, that's all.'

  'It looked terrible. Shit, those bastards. Fuck, I hate them.'

  'Where are you from?'

  'Stellenbosch. You?'

  'Cape Town. Clifton, actually.'

  'Clifton? That's nice. Do you live near the beach?'

  'Bungalow on Third Beach.'

  'It's terrible here. I feel so trapped. Bungalow, wow what an amazing place to stay.'

  'I can't believe what's happening to us.'

  'Did you ever think it would be this bad?'

  'No way, man, I would have skipped the country.'

  'I had no idea we would be treated like this.'

  'We must get to Oudtshoorn. We must get out of here.'

  'Yes, but they say it's even worse there. Much worse!'

  'At least it's close to Cape Town.'

16

Poofter, queer, moffie, sissy, homo, pansy, fairy, *trassie*—how those words scare me. I'm so terrified of being 'discovered' that I obsess about it. Being a homo gives everybody the licence to persecute one. If I'm found out my life will be ruined. I MUST, AT ALL COST, KEEP THIS A SECRET.

I am gay. Gay—this word and everything it stands for—is what I am at the age of nine, although I have not even heard it yet. I know it, I feel it and, in secret, I start living it.

17

My mother, auntie Sannie, Bronwyn and I, and three servants are in the kitchen. The AGA stove exudes a stuffy heat. The room is dimly lit. The feeling in the rehearsed bustle of cooking is mustard-gloss-paint and depressing. I avoid my father. My underpants are sticking to where his belt cut into my skin. I sit down at the scrubbed table and try to keep the weight off my bottom by resting on my elbows, until that too becomes painful.

Elsewhere in the farmhouse the men are reading, drinking, talking and waiting to be waited on. Everybody is waiting for this time to pass. Fatigue has crept over and into my mother. This new road that has thrust itself on her, seems to possess her. Her one son is gone and the other is 'different.' She feels she must protect me. I see it in her. But she would have preferred it not to be the case. If I could have slotted in, it would have been so much easier. Instead, my grain is anarchistic, and it chafes. She knows this as mothers know their children, but she will not communicate what she realises—not even to herself. Still she supports me on this knife-edge of survival and helps me balance wherever she can.

Until his death, my *wound* always seemed to be hidden by Frankie. And a hidden wound is a healing one, or maybe no wound at all. Now I have to find the strength to deal with it, or the anger to bear it.

From the time that Frankie goes to the angels (after somehow getting out from under all the ground they've thrown on top of him) everything starts going wrong.

18

What is wrong with me? What did I say? Did I carry on too much? Did I try too hard? Was I too girly? What did I do or say that by the time we got to the beach for the cricket match, they already knew they didn't want me in their team?

When the Bellville Tennis Club divided us into two groups, with each captain having an alternate chance to choose a player, why then already did nobody want me in their team?

The heavy, red ball is whacked with a sharp crack in my direction and I know I won't be able to catch it. It flies directly at me. It is undisputedly my responsibility to catch it; clear as a huge, red finger pointing at my inability. It travels in the air for the first half of its journey, and then hits the firm beach, still damp from where the tide has pulled back from this canvas to paint my shame on.

Everybody in the two teams and all the spectators, the entire tennis club, all the people we mix with, all my parents' friends, are looking at me. The ball seems to gain speed as it charges down at me.

On this windy, Sunday-morning, sand-in-the-eyes 'field,' the captain has placed me where he knows the ball is most unlikely to go. Now, in horror and disbelief, I watch it streak towards me on the hard sand of the receding tide, smooth but for a bump created by a shell exactly in the path of the ball, which causes it to change direction ever so slightly and bounce. In the noise of dense disappointment and amused delight from the other team, I think I can hear my mother shout, 'Watch the ball, Nicky!'

Beyond the beach, like a huge horseshoe, the Hottentots Holland Mountains sweep all the way from Gordon's Bay to Helderberg. White Southeaster clouds are being pushed over Sir Lowry's Pass in huge, God-sized handfuls. But my world is the size of one ball.

The ball streaks past me. Angry and ashamed I fly up and run after it. By the time I stop it, the ball has exhausted all its mocking energy. And all the while the two batsmen are running back and forth between the wickets. Those who aren't shouting are counting, and I can feel my parents' shame.

**

There is that fragment of a moment when I know I've pushed him too far, that tiniest of a split second when it's too late. He loses control and I am going to get a hiding. My hands go limp and the spoon drops onto the plate. It overbalances because I haven't placed it deep enough, and it falls, spilling ice cream and chocolate sauce on the tablecloth.

Some part of my brain probably notices this, but it is now occupied with protecting my body. My father flies off his seat and grabs me in a terrible fury.

I have refused to eat my dessert with a spoon and a fork. He said it's good manners and I said it made no sense. He said it's not for me to have an opinion; I have to obey him without question. I picked up the spoon and brought it to my mouth without touching the fork.

Now nothing else, it seems to me, exists in this man I call father, but to hurt me. Gripping a handful of shoulder and shirt and then neck and hair, he drags me to the bathroom, like a dog picked up by the surplus skin on its neck. I am pleading, begging and crying, gripped by fear, not only of the pain, but also of his anger that seems to have no bounds.

It doesn't really relate to the fork and spoon; it is his frustration that drives him.

Like when I wouldn't jump off that rock. All the other boys, the sons of his tennis-playing friends, did. And then, to make matters worse, even my younger sister climbed up and not only did she jump, but she dived into the cold, root-dyed mountain water.

Behind the bathroom door hangs a thick plaited rope and below it the birthday calendar, but whenever I sit on the toilet it is not the calendar I look at. I see only the instrument of punishment that is mainly used on me.

The bathroom smells of Handy Andy and the sick-sweet artificial blossoms of the air-freshener. Were it not for the picture on the can, one would never guess that it's intended to wrap and package the smell of farts into bouquets of spring meadows.

He unhooks the rope. The blows start. It's a whole big thing, the noise of my screaming and the sharp cracks of the rope catching my bare legs. He lashes out at me with large figure of eight swoops, until I am lying in a foetal position with my hands over my ears and face.

My mother is pleading and shouting at him. 'Why don't you just shoot him, Peet, if you want to murder your own child!'

I am hoping the neighbours will hear and come running.

PART THREE

I t is too late to hand out our kit. We are marched to the tents, neatly erected on the side of a hill. There are no beds inside.

Finding a place on the canvas ground sheet, I am so apprehensive that I become consumed by the thought of escaping—all the way home, to understanding parents who are prepared to send me overseas to avoid all this. But like neon writing on a dark wall, I know it won't happen.

And AWOL equals DB.

In a corrugated-iron structure I find the showers and toilets. Sitting on the black plastic seat, I stare at the green partitions on either side, the concrete floor and the crudely constructed door. For a fleeting moment it feels safe to be on my own—secure in this small, hidden space, realising my need for solitude.

Beyond the door I hear the hundreds of strangers I now have to live with, jostling for position, friendship, survival, opinion, showers and toilets. The sounds are somewhere between excitement and foreboding.

At the top of the partition wall I see a series of holes in the shape of a cross. This is a sign, I decide. That I should have chosen this one is a good omen. This space will be my private 'chapel,' *my* toilet. I memorise its position in the row—seventh from the right, my lucky number. Then I summon up the courage to step back into army life.

A whistle sounds and the corporals shout: 'Lights-out in

five minutes. Lights-out, you fucking *rowe*! Lights-out!' With it there is frantic scurrying and nervous chatter.

A single bulb dangles from the centre of the tent, its tepid light sucked from it by the canvas. Then it is switched off.

Dark . . . dark inside and out, dark the future, dark my life.

From under the ground sheet the stones of Middelburg press against my shins as I kneel and pray for deliverance.

During the night I am woken by a thunderstorm. I focus on the grey letters of my digital watch—02:28. Muddy water starts flooding through the tent, and we huddle together on the dry side. Shivering and miserable, we wait for daybreak. I remember the clouds I admired as we rolled into Middelburg. Now even that one thing of beauty has betrayed me, as if nothing has respect for us.

Tired, frightened and wet, I fight hard not to allow panic to whip me out of my precarious control. If that should happen, I know I would not be able to claw my way back.

One week for issuing kit, assessing our physical fitness and health, and then we start basics. If you are classified G1K1, the army regards you as physically and mentally fit. If you have passed matric, you will do the basic training in six weeks instead of three months. Then you are sent to Oudtshoorn Infantry School.

We are repeatedly told that the nine months training at Infantry School, to become junior leaders, is much harder than basics—only a few, they say, ever complete that course.

Swearing and shouting start our day as the lights are all switched on at the same time.

Dripping canvas, unwashed men—sour and pungent—and outside the relentless profanity.

It feels as if yet another door is slammed shut, irrevocably, like a cell door. I am giving up, each step taking me deeper and deeper down.

'Quiet time, quiet time, get in and read your fucking Bibles you . . . you snail-shit, you! Where the fuck is your Bible? What are you? A fucking atheist *poes*, non-believer cunt? Ten minutes and you'd better be on that parade ground, ready. This is a day you'll never forget, so you'd better fucking pray . . .'

I read Psalm 17 from verse 9:

. . . from the wicked who assail me, from my mortal enemies who surround me. They close up their callous hearts, and their mouths speak with arrogance. They have tracked me down; they now surround me, with eyes alert, to throw me to the ground. They are like a lion hungry for prey, like a great lion crouching in cover. Rise up, O Lord, confront them, bring them down; rescue me from the wicked by your sword.

I stop reading and turn to Psalm 23. Yes, I want comfort; I want a table prepared *'in the presence of my enemies.'*

***

'You see,' he says. He is puffed up like a bullfrog, not only in attitude, but his body also seems too big for his small legs. His actions have a cultivated air that is still new and awkward. 'You are all *rowe*. Do you wanna know what a *roof* is? It's a fuck-ing filthy scab on a septic cyst in a dying pig's arse. That's what a *roof* is and that's what you are.' Dispensing his dishwater-wisdom, he says, 'Don't worry, I was one too, hey. But now I'm an *ouman*, I've been here for more than a year . . . but, troops, shit you will shit!'

Nothing they make us do seems possible. Too many people have to shower in too few facilities in too short a time. We wait in lines for food and we have too little time to eat it. We have to clean our fatty 'pig pans'—partitioned stainless-steel plates—in

drums of cold, soapless water with thousands of other troops'
uneaten food floating in it.

Everything is designed to induce panic, and panic causes
insecurity. Insecurity creates in all of us a desperate desire for
survival, and this desire is dangerous and ugly.

In the breakfast queue I look for Gerrie, whom I haven't
seen since we arrived at the camp. In front of me a corporal
seems to self-destruct on discovering that a conscript doesn't
possess the skill to tie his own laces. I wish I could self-destruct,
for how does one relate to, share a room with and fight next to
a man of nineteen who can't fasten his own laces?

The huge mess looks more like a hangar, and behind the
mess is the parade ground. Everything is neat but desperately
ugly. Every shape and colour is purely functional. The buildings seem to stand at attention, permanently disciplined. Tiny
patches of garden look like brooches on fatigue overalls.

***

Each one receives an orange booklet. On the front it has a sun
in the top right corner, with seven rays extending from it. It is
called *Daily Strength*. It comes from the Bible Society of the
Army, Navy and Air Force, to be read during quiet time. Inside
my Gideon's New Testament are lists of passages titled 'Where
to find help.' I look under 'Anxious' and am referred to Psalm 46:

God is for us a refuge and a fortress; found to be a mighty help
in trouble.

Therefore we do not fear though the earth is displaced, though
the mountains reel into the midst of the sea,

Though its waters roar and foam; though the mountains
shake at its swelling . . .

This gives me courage, because my world is displaced, reeling somewhere in space, tumbling towards some baleful abyss.

Then I become still. I make way for Frankie's spirit to visit and console me. He is my angel whose existence I never doubt. I curl up and I pray. With eyes shut tight, I pray from a deep place and I feel God's listening face inside me.

**

We're standing at attention, not allowed to move. My feet feel as if they are not getting enough blood; I cannot feel my little toes. The instructor is shouting, insulting us. Our eyes must not follow him as he moves through the ranks.

'What the fuck are you looking at, troop? I'll suck out your eye and spit it back so deep that you'll look at the world through your arsehole for the rest of your life!' he shouts in Afrikaans.

He stands in front of me, directly in my line of sight. He is telling us how useless we are. He is not much older than I am—last year's intake—but he has the markings of that year. His halitosis comes to me in waves; it smells like shit, as though his vulgarity has an odour. This is the smell of dirty, empty words. The reek is so bad that I have to cast my mind elsewhere. So I study him: His skin is burnt brown-red. In his left nostril is dry snot. It is perched there, like a bird in a nest, looking out, safe in its hairy home above the noise. It nauseates me, but I like seeing him compromised. I picture his fellow instructors laughing at him in the NCO mess at lunchtime, and him knowing that we lowly troops must have seen the muck inside.

2

Most of us arrive with long hair, which in our platoon is shaved off on the third day.

Rumours travel through a base camp within seconds, being systematically warped from mouth to ear, and then they jump base and spread around the country within days. This is remarkable, bearing in mind that there is but one pay phone for thousands of troops, and it is hardly ever in operation.

Through rumour we hear about the brutality of the barber.

In the queue to have our hair shaved, I look at the guy in front of me. I noticed him earlier on, as I always notice the attractive ones.

As we get closer, young men with bleeding heads walk past us. The shapes of their heads are awkward, and their scalps look blue-white—stubble over sensitive, pale skin. The pain that accompanies every haircut kills the humour normally associated with such a transformation.

Closer up we can see into the room. The barber is a civvy who has a contract to shave the new recruits' heads. He is hideously fat, with a potbelly like uncle Dirk, only bigger. He is a mass of blubber contained by expanded skin. His hairy stomach protrudes from his shirt, and sweat pours from his unshaven face.

At nineteen almost everybody still has hope. Later, within a few months, despair will be masked by perseverance—in the fear-fuelled recognition of the truth that lies in the hatred of one human being trained to hunt another.

Each head he shaves he hurts in some way, either kicking the recruit as he leaves the chair or hitting him when he's done. Sometimes he rams the tiny steel teeth into the scalp, hacking out chunks of flesh or nicking ears with the greasy razor.

The boy in front of me is as apprehensive as I am. I wonder what he will look like without hair, for he is handsome, almost pretty. He has long, brown curls with lighter streaks where the sun has bleached them. Suddenly I have an urge to protect this hair; I don't want it to fall on the mountain of hair under the chair.

It's not the first time I've seen Ethan, but this will always stand out as our first meeting. I stand watching him, drawn to him by the way he moves. Then it is his turn.

The barber cuts roughly into the hair, leaving huge, hacked spikes. Then he takes the razor, hanging from a cord, and clears the spikes away. He doesn't tell Ethan that he has finished, just hits him on the ear. The movement carries the weight of the solid razor. It's a knock you feel just by observing it.

'Fuck off,' he says as he strikes, but Ethan doesn't move. Instead he turns around and asks him why he hit him—something not one of the thousands of troops has done. The fat man cannot believe his ears. The skin on his face moves backwards in surprise and drops down in disbelief, and he starts cursing.

Ethan doesn't blink. The contrast between the two men is so sharp that it makes Ethan seem radiant, spiritual, like a monk, with his shaved head and gentle composure. I don't want him to be hurt any more, and in my mind I urge him to go.

When the man stops swearing, Ethan gets up, and as he reaches the door I catch his eye. In that moment I sense the tiniest spark.

Behind him the barber has started to charge like an overfed sow. Grabbing a broom, he shoves it into the small of Ethan's back with such force that it sends him flying forward. His back arches violently, almost curling back over the broom. He loses his footing and falls on the gravel. Then he gets up and silently joins the waiting platoon. At that point I decide: I will know this beautiful boy.

***

In the following days Ethan and I grow steadily closer. I do not hurry the acquaintance—we have plenty of time.

Optimistic thoughts flood into my diary:

I stand on the perimeter of a calm pond, just letting my feet be touched by the stillness, savouring the expectation of submerging into the mystery.

He is so engaging that I don't feel I can absorb much at one time, or I sense I may miss some rare sensations of the experience. I think of him as a rediscovered ancient city, lying with its shrouded civilisations' secrets beneath desert sand. Walking in darkness, running my fingers over the unusual textures, touching walls as slightly as I can, before I look—no sound, no sight, just something lighter than feeling. I want to get to know him slowly, and the army makes this possible, because neither of us is going anywhere . . . for some weeks at least.

I can march or stand at attention for an eternity when he is in front of me. Gazing at his neck and the pattern of his hairline cannot be limited by time. The fine hair curls as if with joy for having been born there. I step out of myself and walk there—brushing just the top of the skin like breath; as in life drawing, where you have to concentrate intently on a line to render it so sensitively that it communicates the full structure of the person you are drawing. Only later do I add smell and touch.

We have tea, and he dunks his rusk five times. Unhurried, he allows the tea to run from between the compacted crumbs, and then brings it to his mouth. There are veins under his brown skin that fork on his forearm where the muscles play as he twists the rusk and puts it in his mouth. A drop stays on the middle of his bottom lip. He lets it linger and sucks it in, his top lip moving over the fullness of the bottom one.

Our surnames, both starting with V, result in us being in the same place during the week of queues. Friendships forge easily under mutual duress, but equanimity assures a more permanent meshing. Foundations of wet concrete do not know the building that will stand on them, or the souls that will occupy it.

Ethan is my first army friend, and for the first week my only friend. Ethan is whom I want; Ethan is the drug to see me through—my medication. We are reshuffled, and by the grace of God we are put in the same tent. For the first time I believe I am going to get through it all.

***

On Sunday we choose the small Catholic Church in Middelburg for compulsory Church Parade. The old Irish priest sweats underneath his heavy cassock and robes. Beside me, high up, the fourteen Stations of the Cross line each wall. I search for the three where Christ falls with the cross. That is where I somehow find a gentle Jesus, as opposed to a God of wrath. The Christ in these low-relief tableaux shows a distorted body in bitter agony. My mind drifts . . .

We stand up to say the creed.

'We believe in one God the Father . . .' I say the words without thinking of the meaning of any of it. The small stained-glass windows seem unusually bright from the African sun blazing through them. I wonder if they were imported from Europe, made for a darker, cloudier climate? Imagine if Ethan and I were in a small chapel somewhere, all alone high up in the Drakensberg. Would that appeal to him? What does he think of God? What are the chances . . . what are my chances with him? Like all the others? Just when I'm completely in love, will he turn out to be straight? Forget that, you can't think about that now; just enjoy the fantasy. I know so little about him. Have I ever seen anybody quite as good-looking? No! We will be friends. I need this friendship. I need this beauty!

'Are you going forward for Communion?'

'Yes, you?'

'Yes.'

'So, you're Catholic? I thought you only came 'cos the Catholic aunties make such nice cakes!'

'Shh,' and he smiles. But I tell myself he has come because I did.

I bless myself and cup one hand under the other, holding them forward as the priest makes his way towards me.

'The Body of Christ.'

'Amen.'

Free on a Sunday is free from training, not free to come and go as you please. We lie on our stomachs on our beds, facing each other and chatting, while others spend hours in queues for one phone call, wash their kit or write letters home.

Just before roll call one of our tent companions, Frikkie, walks in and demands that we clean his boots. We ignore him. Ethan is lying closest to him. Frikkie flings the boots at Ethan. They are tied together and come to rest on either side of his body, with the laces stretched over his naked back. He lifts his body and allows the boots to roll to the floor.

Frikkie walks over and jumps on Ethan, grabs him around the neck and digs his knees into his back. This arouses excited interest from the rest of the guys. I get up protesting, to defend my friend, but it's not necessary. In an instant Ethan has released himself and flung Frikkie off him, over the side of the bed, where he connects with the ground sheet with a thud, Ethan on top of him. Frikkie's face is red with surprise, embarrassment and the discomfort of the fall. Ethan holds him down for a second, asks him if he is all right and quietly tells him to clean his own boots. The whistle for roll call sounds . . . some-how less shrill than before.

'Hell, Ethan, you sure are full of surprises.'

'I did judo; never really used it. But this is one of the last nights we're sleeping in the same tent as those guys. I don't think Frikkie has matric, so he won't be chosen for Infantry School. I reckon he'll be moved out within the next few days.'

We line up for roll call, Ethan next to me. However long it takes tonight for Van der Swart and Vickerman to be called, I don't care. Just standing next to him is enough. Ethan can ask me to leave the army tonight, to risk everything, and I will question nothing; I will obey. In heightened melodrama I fantasise about it.

3

'Don't be a sissy, man.'

'Peet, let him learn in his own time.'

'No, he's going to learn now. I don't have time to teach him in *his* time, *our lordship*. How difficult can it be? Nicholas, do you want me to sell the bicycle, hey?'

'No.'

'I can't hear you. What did you say?'

'For heaven's sake, Peet, the child is four years old.'

'NO!' I beg.

'Well then, come. I'm taking the bicycle to the corner and then you cycle back.'

'No, it's too high!'

'I'll hold you.'

'Promise?'

'Yes, yes, I promise. Come now. Are you ready?'

'Dad, promise you will hold me.'

'Yes, I promise, just pedal.'

'Not so fast . . . you aren't holding!'

'Peet, what are you doing? The child can't ride yet, are you mad? HELP, FRANK, CATCH YOUR BROTHER!'

'MOM, PLEASE, PLEASE CATCH ME!'

At the bottom of the rise in the garden is the sandpit where Frank and I play. We have collected bricks to build with. It is in the direction of these bricks that my momentum takes me. By the time the front wheel snags in the sand I have gathered such speed that I summersault over the handlebars, into the bricks. A moment later Frankie and my mother are there. Everybody is shouting. Frank and I are crying. My face is bleeding and there is a deep gash in my knee.

My mother is furious. Some of the wounds are treated at home, but for the others she has to take me for stitches. My father tells me that when he was my age he was not 'so scared of everything,' and his parents could not even afford to give him a bicycle. If I want to grow up to be a man, I must stop being such a sissy. When we leave for the doctor, we hear the commotion in the house as my father sends Frankie to the bathroom. There he will get a hiding for calling him a bastard when he saw him giving the bicycle a shove instead of holding it.

4

I wake up around two in the morning and feel something is wrong. The sounds crawl into my sleep—muffled giggling on the one side and shock and disgust on the other.

I reach for my torch and shine it in Ethan's direction. There is something dark on his face, and he is trying to get it off. I get out of bed to help, not thinking, simply drawn to him. When I reach him, the odour of excrement jolts me. I take some toilet paper and lift the faeces that have dropped off his face onto the bed.

'Go to the showers, I'll bring towels and soap. Shit, these people are disgusting. You go, I'll be down now.' Then, into the darkness and ignoring an inner warning, I say, 'Whoever did this, you are fucking disgusting.'

There is no light in the ablution block. I pass a row of basins and balance the clothing and towels on one of them. I roll up my towel with the back of the torch in it and jam it between two supports to point where he is showering. He is the only colour in the dark and empty surroundings. Warm skin-colour, as though I am looking at him through tissue paper. I pour shampoo into his cupped hand and take my PT shorts off. When I turn, he is standing with his back to me, lathering his hair. Some of the foam runs down his neck, hesitates on his shoulders, and then continues down his back to between his white buttocks.

Elongated and pale in the light, he looks magnificently fragile. When he turns, I see the dark hair above his penis and the soap running over his chest and down his stomach. Then I turn on the shower next to him and step under the water. I close my eyes and face the spray, hiding my desire under the waterfall.

Over and over we wash what we know we cannot rid ourselves of.

I almost embrace this debasing incident, for the closeness I've been granted with Ethan tonight has a warm beauty and vague sorrow as I hold back its drive. I will resist it, for nothing must jeopardise my friendship with this boy. I cling to it like a mother would if the devil should try to tear her child from her.

Later I would torment myself as I recreate the chimera of this night, eventually warping every glance, every movement of the opportunity so cowardly passed up.

We are re-shuffled for the six-week basic training with the other conscripts deemed physically and mentally fit, for a chance to be chosen for Oudtshoorn Infantry School. We manage against impossible odds to be allocated to the same tent again. These are the buoys that keep me adrift.

The rumours, hearsay and accounts of Infantry School are rife. But nothing draws me to the place other than that *he* may be there.

***

Early on I realise that the only way to survive is not to stand out—not in front, not at the back—but to merge into the middle smudge of brown army rabble. It's not the physical aspect of this situation that is disquieting, but the senseless 'breaking down and rebuilding' that is so devoid of reason.

Bonds start forming within this look-alike cast. I notice that the army has domain over only our flesh, for it is what we carry within that draws us to our own kind, sorting us by language, experience, education and intrigue—the things that make us different, those hidden elements that the eye doesn't see.

After lunch we sit waiting in groups in the sun for the whistle that will summon us to the afternoon's training. Ethan and I and two other English boys slouch against a fence that has bowed in concave submission to years of lazy-on-greasy-lunch troops. Frikkie and a mate are having an argument with Malcolm, one of the English boys.

'I bet you you fucking Englishmen won't make Infantry School,' Frikkie says.

'Fuck you,' says Malcolm, but remains completely calm.

'You English are a bunch of moffies, man. You will not make it in Oudtshoorn; they are wasting the government's money on you okes.'

'Listen, Frikkie, you cunt, you can't even pass a simple army test. What do you know? Tell me, why aren't you going, hey? Are you not physically up to it or are you just uneducated?'

'Fuck education. I know what I must know. You point a rifle at a kaffir terr and shoot. You don't need schooling for that. This is our country. Us Afrikaners will fight until the end, you's just a *soutpiel*, man. They should only allow Afrikaners into Infantry School. They choosing wrong, hey. It's a *blerrie* fuck-up. What you know of war, you traitor English cunt?'

'Wake up, you little closet queen, the South African Defence Force is based on the British system. I bet you didn't know that! Besides, how the fuck will you lead anybody? You can't even read. Most of the people who are chosen are Afrikaans in any case, but you are an insult to them, you thick rock spider.'

'What you call me, hey? Hey?'

'Rock spider. Closet queen. Butt-plug. Nora. And there's more!'

'A what? Queen what? I'll fuck you up, hey!'

Ethan and I turn away, suppressing our laughter. Through one diamond of the mesh fence I frame a picture in the distance, instinctively closing one eye to neaten the composition. I see an instructor who has been drilling a conscript throughout our lunch break. It's called an *opfok*—fucking someone up by drilling him to the point of exhaustion and beyond. At that moment the troop bends over and vomits, but I turn back to the rare bit of entertainment we have been granted, forgetting what could so easily happen to me.

Malcolm sees us enjoying his rally with Frikkie and he carries on. By this time we are so full of suppressed laughter that everything Malcolm or Frikkie says is funny.

'So where are you from?'

'Ellisras.'

'Ellisras . . . wow, that's nice.' There is a hint of a smile when he continues. 'I hear the women there are so tough they snort Drano to clear their sinuses after muff-diving the pigs.'

'Fuck you. Don't you fucking insult our chicks, *ek sê*.'

'No, I hear the women are tough in Ellisras.'

'Ja, better than those Joburg snob bitches.'

'So, if you want to pork your chick in the back of the Valiant bakkie, how do you do it?'

'Don't you know anything, you stupid *Engelsman*?'

'No, tell me, man. You never know. Maybe I'll come and visit you in Ellisras, then I must know how to get a chick.'

'Those birds won't go for an English moffie like you, man.'

'OK, but just tell me what you do, or have you never had a girl?'

'Of course I have! What do you think? Far more than you . . .'

'Well then, tell me! What do you do? Or do you just fuck her in her front bum till her back bum farts so hard you need paramedics to come and rescue you?'

When Malcolm says this the small group around him bursts into laughter, including Frikkie's friend. Frikkie gets up, swears and walks away.

This is how I get to know Malcolm. We never see Frikkie again—he is transferred to resume basics with the other conscripts who will stay behind in Middelburg.

Malcolm, just doing his army training in the Defence Force, by chance ends up in the same platoon as I and our paths cross, never to be uncrossed again. There are three people with whom I form previously uncharted connections here in my living nightmare; three remarkable relationships, so important that they become a part of me, like a vital organ. How ironic that here, where I feel so hopeless, I receive these blessings. But gifts of this magnitude carry a weight—especially the third friendship, the one that awaits me at Infantry School.

'Hi, I'm Malcolm.'

'I've never laughed this much; certainly not in the army.'

And from that day on we are friends.

Malcolm and I are connected by fatigue and army brown aversion for this organisation, and within it we grow effortlessly towards each other, even though we are from vastly different backgrounds. It is much easier than my friendship with Ethan, which is charged and corrupted by my infatuation. Malcolm is light and easy. He teaches me to laugh, and it feels as if we understand each other on all levels. My diary reads:

He is like a hill I walk past and don't notice, its top obscured by clouds. Then one day I am suddenly intrigued and I start climbing. When I get to the mist, I realise it is a fog of prejudice and beyond it is the larger green of a previously unnoticed mountain—I have judged a mountain by its foothill.

There always seems to be a whole lot brimming behind the froth of coping. When he stands, he leans against a pillar or a doorway or a wall, as if he has been stacked there like a rifle, loaded and full of potential.

Yes, it's right for me to compare him to a mountain. He is constant like a mountain.

'Hi, I'm Nicholas.'

'Yes, I know. So you're English? I thought, you know . . . with your surname. I mean, Van der Swart!'

'Yep, mother's English, father Afrikaans, but I was in an English class in a mainly Afrikaans school.'

'What school?'

'Paul Roos Gymnasium.'

'Oh yes, I've heard of it; good school in Stellenbosch.'

'Yes, actually wasn't too bad. And you?'

'I went to Jeppe Boys.'

Malcolm possesses streetwise savvy that runs like a track to his will. If he sets his mind to something, it seems that planets will conspire; constellations obey. And he has decided that we *will* be friends, which carries a measure of security.

He has survived a world I have only heard about, and getting through the army doesn't scare him. I'm attracted to this confidence.

And so I learn a new love; one I have not yet experienced and one I don't understand. It is the love of a friend. As we slip deeper into understanding each other, this love grows like ascending stairs; discovering new treads between the risers.

I think there is a possibility that Malcolm might be gay, and I think he might know that I am. But then I've been wrong so often. It is sufficiently warming for me just to believe that we have this similar secret—a secret boys like us will protect, for our lives depend on it.

The Defence Force distinctly forbids homosexuality, regarding it as an unpardonable offence against God and country, so perverse that it is socially acceptable to mete out punishment to anyone found to be of such orientation. If you are caught, you are sent to the psychiatric ward for shock, hormone, and aversion therapy—you are as good as eliminated. Besides, if he were gay, he too would have lived too long with the fear of the ripples exposure would cause. So we show nothing, not even to each other. I have never met anybody I feel I can trust as I do Malcolm, but it goes against my self-preservation to give anybody such power over my fate.

Malcolm is braver than I am. He tests me with supremely crafted clues, but I would never drop my guard in this purgatory.

5

There is a faint crackle as the needle settles snugly into the tiny groove. Something like static jumps between the speakers. I have listened to this track so often that the distortion has become part of the composition. Due to the off-centre design of the label, the record seems to wobble. I choose my seat and close my eyes to the fantasy I will now put to music.

While I'm waiting for the track to start, I feel the emptiness of the house. In their white clothing, clutching their rackets, they left hurriedly, my mother carrying an ice bucket, sweat-band, jersey and peak. It's like a big blob of noise that has popped out of the house.

First I select 'Bella figlia dell'amore' from *Rigoletto*. When the Duke starts to chat up Maddalena, I am seized by the music and forget to choreograph my fantasy to it. I play the track again, until I have sung it a few times. Then I sit down, close my eyes and allow the music to thread through my daydream. My fantasy will be of a man proclaiming his love, not the revenge of a court jester or Gilda watching her lover seduce another.

I rise dramatically onto an imagined stage in front of a spell-bound audience to act out the drama of the aria. In falsetto I sing the parts of Joan Sutherland and Huguette Tourangeau, not knowing the meaning or the structure of the words I'm pro-nouncing. Then again I do Pavarotti's part, unconcerned about jumping between the two parts, and at the same time I'm directing the London Symphony Orchestra. Needing more space for my theatre, I move the ball-and-claw table out of the way and swoop-dance to the wave of men's voices and the shorter peaking of the women's.

By the fifth replay I start searching through the pile of LP's for *Turandot* and remove it from the sleeve. When I put it on the turntable the needle moves up and down so violently on the deformed record that it looks as if it may become airborne, but 'Nessun dorma' blasts forth at maximum volume.

The most romantic opera and closest to my fantasies of gal-loping over green hills on a white horse is Offenbach's *Tales of*

Hoffmann. Riding bareback, I am holding on to my man with his shirt open, my hands clawing at his bare chest in the evening light.

In the meantime a sow has escaped from her pen, followed by seven hundred others to the green pastures of our front lawn, where they are now exploring their burgeoning new world, digging the air with their round disc-snouts.

My heart sinks, and for a moment I toy with the idea of leaving them there as punishment for my father, but the thought is shortlived. It would take me all afternoon to get my parents' biggest investment back into their pens, so I start the arduous task with Puccini's 'Un bel di vedremo' drifting towards me through the dusty lace curtains of the lounge.

6

It is both an escape and a burden, this relationship with Ethan that I tend to so carefully. I count every word, and each moment is measured, analysed and guarded against over-exposure. I wonder whether this unnatural atmosphere we're in is what keeps us together. If we were in a civilian environment, would we still be so close? How difficult it is to develop a relationship within such complex dynamics. And after all this nurturing it may all be in vain. But my time with Ethan is my cure, the exquisite amidst the dreadful.

The first stage is almost over. I have more than survived; I have fallen in love and made a new friend. Given the choice, I probably would not have had it any other way.

Walking through the rows of neatly spaced tents on my way back from the ablution block, one of my favourite tunes comes drifting towards me. I stop to listen and decide to find the owner of that song. If this is the kind of music he listens to, we will have a lot in common.

The tune is mesmerising. When it ends I meet the owner and we listen to it repeatedly until the batteries of the tape recorder have no power left. We ignore the protests of 'hippie, blaspheming music' from the other tents.

Leaving, I think-hear the words of *Highway 61*:

Oh God said to Abraham, 'Kill me a son,'
Abe says, 'Man you must be puttin' me on,'
God say, 'No.' Abe say, 'What?'

. . .

Well Abe says, 'Where do you want this killin' done?'
God says, 'Out on Highway 61.'

***

Saturday, 2 February, 1980.

When the long, brown hair was shaved off the boy's head, I was watching a monument being defaced in a coup d'etat of a new order. We greeted this new world with a 'number one' hair-cut. The same and yet so different. Now, two days later, blisters cover our inflamed necks where our long hair used to curl down to our shoulders.

The changes thrust on us define the new creatures we become in a world seen from different angles. I have become a planet torn from its orbit, left searching.

The first week of our acquaintance I spend only watching. This boy has a voice as tranquil as a glider in flight, beyond the mess, tests, injections and abuse.

The 'browns pants' we have to tuck into our boots are so unintentionally sexy on him. He is a perfect 32 as he tries on the trousers—a layer of taupe fabric shrink-wrapping my passion.

7

The red ribbon slides between my thumb and index finger like mercury, and I savour the movement. The thin band continues its journey and then gently flies free. The next ribbon beckons, pointing the way to a secret covenant I know I will embrace.

Ethan has told me nothing else but that I should be at this spot, at this time. It is here, behind the tent-town barracks, that I discover the first red ribbon tied to a shrub. For a moment I ponder the magnitude of this tiny symbol. In the tents behind me the other servicemen are resting before tomorrow's early training session. I am probably the only one in the entire company experiencing a sense of euphoria. I turn slightly to the right and see the next ribbon hanging in the still Highveld air.

This is the seventh Sunday in camp, the last one before we leave for Oudtshoorn. I feel a mild sense of accomplishment; partly for getting through this period and partly for the confidence one feels when one is elected to an elite group—even if it entails going to a place one dreads. But for now my world is Ethan, and time is a series of ribbons.

Each one leads me further up the hill. Tonight Mama Africa is again giving so uniquely from her abundant heart. There are no clouds. In the east a moon steals upwards and to the west the setting sun reminds me, for a brief moment, of Storm.

The last ribbon takes me over the hill that now separates us from the army. Ahead of us is a training area that is not used at night and definitely not on a Sunday evening. There is only a slim chance of being caught here, but it is still a possibility too frightful to contemplate.

Ethan is sitting smiling at me. Around him are four candles, and in front of him is food, but at first I only see him. Something reckless wells up inside me, and I feel filled to overflowing.

From a parcel his mother arranged to be sent from Johannesburg, delivered yesterday, he takes imported Camembert,

Brie, Parma ham, bread and pâté—food we only dream about, food not in the vocabulary of most of the troops. For me, just being here, the fact that it is me he has invited to share with, is what centres the night.

'Ethan.'

'Hey, Nick. Let's have some decent food!'

'Ethan, I can't believe this, man!'

'No one saw you, I hope?'

'No, I checked.'

'I hope no one finds the ribbons,' he smiles.

'No chance, they are too far away from the rest and it is already too dark. If you hadn't told me where to start, I would not have found the first one. Ethan, this is very special. Thank you.'

The setting sun on Ethan's face turns his skin a smooth, deep brown. As he breathes in it is as if he inhales the light, which feeds him from within and then shines through his skin and blue eyes.

'We are lucky it is such a stunning sunset, I'll say that for Middelburg.'

'Yes, it is. Ethan, I am speechless.'

He pulls the cork from a bottle of red wine and it sounds like something being freed. The cabernet looks black in the two glasses.

What we are doing is flirting with DB. Alcohol is forbidden for *rofies*, but the ridicule could be even worse. Yet for us this all belongs to another world, outside this ring of candles.

'I asked my mother to put this in. It's a gift for you, but first I want to read you something. This,' tilting a book towards me, 'is the story of a little prince who lived on a small planet, actually on an asteroid . . . uhm . . . asteroid B-612 to be exact.' He shows me an illustration of a timid yellow-haired boy standing on an asteroid. To the left of the little prince some gas escapes from an insignificant protrusion on the tiny planet. Ethan glances up shyly. If I had to give in to my immediate impulse, I would kiss him. 'He would move his chair around the planet to continuously see the sun set. One day he watched forty-four sunsets.' He checks again to gauge my reaction to this information. It pleases him and he smiles.

'Why do you think sunsets are different from sunrises?'

'They are, hey!'

'Nick, do you think they are actually the same, or is it just that we know they are what they are?'

'What do you mean?'

'Well, say I took a picture of a sunrise and then of a sunset, do you think you would know the difference?'

'No, guess not. They would just be pictures of shapes and light. I think we need to experience them to know. I think they feel different.'

'Yes, a sunset actually feels different, doesn't it?'

'You know, I love a sunset, and not just for sentimental reasons.

'I have a theory: In Africa, for me, sunrise and sunset are different not for their appearance, but for the effect they have on me. In the mornings over, say, the Karoo, in the cold, low distance, it stretches far and then rises with promise, looking on a clean and innocent world, but at dusk it sets with forgiveness. It's the grace I find so warm. Sounds loopy, hey?' Immediately I regret what I have said, thinking I sounded pompous and melodramatic.

He looks at me for a long time and I look back, focusing only on his eyes, until a tremor deep within me forces me to look away. I only turn back to him when he says, 'This little guy in the book, I've always liked him and I always think of him when it comes to friendship and sunsets.' This sentence is so beautiful that I smile at him. He looks at me, branding into different parts of me forever something that transcends this plane.

'I want to read you the chapter about friends,' and he reads a short chapter about a fox from Antoine de Saint-Exupéry's *The Little Prince*. I watch him so intently that I have no capacity for observation left to hear the story. I study him with all my senses.

The only part I remember, and only because I ask him to reread it, is, '*It is only with the heart that one can see rightly; what is essential is invisible to the eye.*'

Why, at that moment, do I not touch him, can he not see, can eyes not see, can our hearts not see rightly? This is how profound the barriers are that we carry so heavily around us, the structures of refutation, how complicated our fear; we doubt even the vision of our hearts! Maybe if we knew what was waiting for us we would touch each other gently, but we don't. If only we could know.

I will carry this night with me forever in all its unrealised fulfilment and tortured imperfection. Tonight I let him talk, not only to hear the voice, but for the things that are being said. He speaks of home and of sunsets.

He tells me about the light at the end of day against the Twelve Apostles, the mornings on the white beaches, the sun that spills over Lion's Head and turns the sea into silvery-blue mercury, and the storms that can sweep an entire beach out to sea.

He tells me about it like an invitation to nirvana. His eyes sparkle as though he sees it all in front of him and he wants me to see it with him.

'From Oudtshoorn on a weekend pass you can spend the weekend with me. We will be close enough to go down for a weekend, you know.' But the word Oudtshoorn triggers a tension we don't want here with us tonight.

We stretch the time to just before roll call. Ethan bends down and starts collecting the evidence, then he pauses motionless, as if he is dwelling on a grave thought. The muscles in his legs are visible through his browns, even in this light.

He blows out a candle, then another and another until only

one is still burning. He picks it up, comes to stand in front of me and asks me if I think we will be together in Oudtshoorn.

His face is so close that it feels as if I can see right into him. His expression is one of need—a need for security or something undefined.

'We have to be together, Ethan. We just have to be. I will not make it without you.'

'We will not be alone again, you know . . . before we leave.'

'I know.'

'I hear there will be two trains.' I hear him asking, knowing it cannot be promised. 'Nicholas, promise me we'll be on the same train.'

I promise, and then he looks at me intently. The light from the tiny candle catches his eyebrows, leaving his eyes dark. 'I want to say goodbye here on our hill.' A shudder runs through me, like tiny sparks of electricity racing through every fibre. I hold on to his words. *Our hill*. Did I hear correctly? Did he say that? I keep the words and their sound like a taste. *Our hill*. Then we hear the whistle from behind our hill, where hell still lives and people rush to finish before roll call for the morning inspection that we are so recklessly ignoring.

We look at each other. Then we hug, folding into each other, my face against his neck, so close that I absorb some of him and his smell into me. The body I so yearn to touch, I know so well, I now have against me. The body I would sit and slowly take in for an entire hour every day, not hearing one word of the lecture. Feeling every trace, covering every muscle; touching bone, touching soul. Here it is in my arms. To run my hand down his back would be too much. I put my lips to his neck but I do not kiss, just for some of the taste to linger there or for me to remember that I have *kissed* him. What if I spoil it all by revealing what I am? Can I really spoil this night, this memory? What if he is not like me?

So, in the unwritten contract of correctness and safety, it is a 'bear' hug. Still, after all that has passed, the truth can remain hidden. Or is it just that—a hug between friends at a special time, at the end of a difficult time?

But for me it will be torture again, like it was after we'd showered together, alone in the dark. Questions such as: Who stopped hugging first? Had the whistle blown later, had the hug been earlier, or longer, had I said something, had I said things differently, had I hugged harder, moved my hand down just enough for him to do the same . . . it may have lingered just that moment too long and become an embrace.

But we let go.

8

The shorter the time between the flash of lightning and the sound of the thunder, the closer you are to the actual lightning—so they say.

'One crocodile, two crocodile, three crocodile,' I count.

On this last frantic day we had to be signed out by every department of 4 SA Infantry. It is called *uitklaar*—clearing out—and as with everything in the army, it is done alphabetically. It is a time of queue upon queue and, with a surname starting with V, being at the back of each one.

The V's are still running in the rain, taking abuse from the angry and exhausted storemen, when the A's are already packed and prepared for the journey South. If we don't finish in time, we will simply be left behind.

We run between departments, wait our turn to hand in our kit, and dodge the storm in entrances to hangars.

Looking up, I feel as though I can define the scale of this thunderous send-off, as though I can trace my finger in the sky defining the size of sound. All the while I am wondering what awaits us in the South.

It is dark by the time we are done. We run from the bottom of the camp to our tents on the hill. Tonight we will sleep on our *pisvelle*, our bedding having been handed in. Our packed *balsakke*, looking like the stuffed condoms of some gargantuan prehistoric beast, are on the bed with us, because on the ground there is already a river of water.

I am three metres from the metal mess hall when a bolt of lightning strikes it. This close the thunder is not a rumble but a white, detonating crack. The force strikes us off our feet and we hit the ground, landing in the mud.

By the time we reach our tents, I am soaking wet. For one last time I go to my private 'chapel' to pray. Entering the ablution block, I walk past the row of toilets, count to seven and am relieved to find *my* toilet unoccupied. The bowl is filled to the brim. Someone has even relieved himself on the floor.

This filthy cubicle is my last impression of 4 SAI. As I close the door on this scene, I vow never to return. Nothing will make them send me back here.

On the journey South, we are in exact same coaches, on exactly the same track, and yet everything is totally different.

We are greeted by a group of battle-hardened corporals who were brought to Middelburg to accompany us. They are the best of the infantry best. These men have chosen the army for life.

Ethan, Malcolm and I stay together. As we descend from the Bedford trucks we are formed into platoons on the platform. The cut-off point for the second train is in the row in front of me, and I am separated from them.

From the moment the train leaves the station the torment starts. Two instructors per carriage make us do physical exercises down the narrow passages—goose-walking in a squatting position, push-ups, pull-ups—until we vomit. No sleep. By midnight many of the boys are crying and most of them have decided to request an RTU (return to unit) the minute they reach Oudtshoorn.

But in the meantime we have been proclaimed physically fit, which gives the instructors the right to do virtually anything they want to us.

The train doesn't stop at any station. The journey is swift, and by five in the morning we can see the mist in the shallow valleys and dry riverbeds of the Karoo. By seven, the train pulls into the station—this train of fear and sleeplessness.

The squealing of the brakes is the only sound we hear. Motion has meant delay, but now the images pan by more slowly and linger longer in the frame of each train window. More screeching of brakes, then a jolt . . . quiet for a second . . . and then the shouting.

I have a well-structured vision of myself. Each night before I go to sleep, I refine it, over and over again, through dream and fantasy. Here I develop unhindered, unchallenged, into the person I aspire to be. And over the years this image has started blending with reality.

9

'Never shame me, Nicholas, never shame me.' My father rarely speaks to us, and when he does, he is serious and sombre, with some new form of discipline we should learn.

We eat in quiet submission. I can hear my chewing inside my head, and the meat in my mouth simply won't go down. What does he mean, 'Do not shame me'? Does he know something?

The volume button is missing from the blue portable radio. It looks like a face with only one eye. When it's time for the news we all have to be quiet; but it is not time yet and he has something to say.

My fear is so intense that I can hardly hold my knife and fork. They have been discussing some man at the tennis club who they say is a moffie.

'Never shame me.' Why does he direct this at me?

'There are three things I demand from you children: One, you must make your own money. Look at me when I speak to you, Nicholas. I'm saying this for your benefit. I will not look after you. You can be a tramp on the streets and I will leave you there. Do you understand?'

'Yes, Dad.'

'Secondly, I want you to excel at some sport and at school. If you fail, you can leave this house; you are on your own. Are you listening to me, Nicholas? What is wrong with you, man?'

'Yes, Dad.'

'The third is the most important, and this is for you.' He changes his tone to a sound I have not heard before as he turns to me. 'If I find out that you are a moffie, that is the end.' He waits for the gravity of the words to sink in, looking at me, looking through me. 'That will be the end,' he says in a measured way, stepping slowly from one word to the next.

I am paralysed, because that means it is already the end and there is absolutely nothing I can do about it.

After this talk and others that are also carefully timed, I know that to survive I have to hide the inescapable feelings I carry around inside me. What does he mean by, 'That will be the end'? I dare not ask him. I am walking on a knife-edge and my only defence against catastrophe is my ability to deceive.

Survival. At school I fight for my very survival. Only much later do I realise that threats are only dramatic manifestations of deep fears or desires. But for now there is nobody I can even consider talking to. My security is threatened and I am completely alone. The threats cause anger, and the anger is aimed at me. I detest myself.

I watch my father's thumbs play on the steering wheel, almost touching each other, constantly rubbing over the surface.

'Your mother is going to start farming,' he says, smiling at my mother and checking our response in the rear-view mirror.

'Where?'

'In Stellenbosch.' We digest this. I think it can't be a 'real' farm; a real farm is in the Karoo or here in Namibia, where we are travelling.

'Really? Are we going to farm grapes?'

'No. Pigs.'

'Pigs!'

'I promise you.'

'Really, Mom? Are you really going to farm pigs?'

'What's wrong with pigs?'

'Everything. Why can't we farm something else?'

'Nicholas, we've bought the farm and if you don't like it you can go and live somewhere else.'

'Don't talk nonsense, Peet.' Then to us at the back, 'Nicholas, you are going to high school next year, to Paul Roos.'

'And me?'

'To Rhenish. First to the primary school and then to Rhenish High.'

'But why pigs? It's so embarrassing.'

'It's not the kind of pig farm you're thinking of. All the pigs are in pens that get cleaned every day.'

'Where is the farm?'

'Banhoek.'

'Banhoek?'

'Yes, it's very beautiful, over Helshoogte. Between Jonkershoek and Franschhoek.'

'It's between high mountains.'

Outside, as if to contrast the place they are describing, Namibia's vastness takes its time to slip by. It's as if the world around us died long ago, but has now sprung to life again, rich in colour, becoming in a strange way part of itself—untouched and unexplored.

Banhoek is beautiful, but only in summer. In winter it is much colder and wetter than Welgemoed. Nestled between Buller-skop and the Pieke, the sun has to be high before it peeps over the rounded massif called Bullerskop, and it sets early on the opposite side, robbing the valley of late afternoon warmth.

It is raining; it has been raining all day, as it did yesterday and the day before. Between the showers that come down in sheets on the tin roof, there is the water-torture—the constant tick-ticking as the rain, trapped in gutters filled with pine needles, drips on the dark, wet ground.

It is very cold; the kind of cold when the earth feels refrig-erated. There is snow on the mountains and the wind travels down the valley, collecting the frozen air and pushing it through one like a blade. Grey skies. Depressing. It is dark outside, and I feel like the weather.

10

From the station the *rofie* ride takes us to the parade ground of Infantry School, where a few hundred boys are already wait-ing, brought there from other infantry divisions around the country.

I start searching for two people and become panic-stricken when I can't find them.

The trucks leave and they arrange us into platoons as we wait quietly.

An hour or so later I hear the trucks return from the station in a loud convoy. The first Bedford gears down to turn into the main gate of the camp and passes the duty room, where the boom is already raised.

The trucks stop. I scan every young man barked out from under the Bedford's canvas, dragging his *balsak* behind him.

Then I see Ethan. A shaft of strength is driven right through me, giving me backbone again. I don't take my eyes off him from where he has disembarked to where they assemble. There is tension in his movement.

I am struck by how ragged he looks, how thin and pale. They walk right past us in single file. He sees me and slips in next to me, without looking around, and drops his *balsak*. None of the instructors have seen him do it and we grin triumphantly.

We are called to attention. It is overcast, the clouds trapping the heat and humidity. Drops of sweat collect in my armpits and run down my body. I lift my arm slightly to prevent the moisture from being absorbed by my step-out shirt.

The entire parade ground is quiet and it feels as if the world is holding its breath. The officer in command of Infantry School steps up onto a podium carrying the camp emblem and walks to the microphone. The PA system makes his voice sound metallic, machine-like.

Something is wrong with Ethan. Sweat is pouring from his pale skin, and his eyes are dark and sunken.

'Ethan, what is it? Are you OK?' I whisper at great risk. He smiles, but there is no warmth in it. I want to hold him and love him . . . hold him close and make all this go away. I want to rise above all of what I hear and see, all of what lies ahead and hold Ethan; take him into me. My desire and the contrasting reality are perfectly opposed.

If Ethan starts this day at a disadvantage, he will be among the first to drop out. It could take only one missed meal. I look at his neck below the green beret; his ear with the fine white hair. I follow his jaw line to his chin, the contour of his nose, his eyes—those eyes that have chosen to look at me—his brow. Small drops of sweat cling to the skin where the black band of the beret presses into his scalp.

He is so striking. If beauty is the correct relationship between shapes, where line, texture, colour and space are in perfect harmony, then that is what I am looking at. So close, it's like a jolt when he turns to me. We look at each other. On a parade ground, where everybody is supposed to look at the commanding officer, we are two people staring at each other.

It is a plea that I see, that draws me. His blue eyes are begging. Then they glaze over slightly and dampness collects in the corners; enough for one drop to hover, grow and then fall from his eye. He wipes it away with the back of his hand.

'It will be OK. It will. We're together.' How does one sound convinced? How does one embrace with a whisper? I have to help him, but then we notice the look of an instructor three rows ahead. Ethan bends slightly forward, as if his stomach muscles are shrunk by a cramp.

After the CO's speech, instructors move between the ranks in pairs. One checks the company name (from Alpha to Golf) and the other takes down our names. Ethan is Alpha, I am Golf and we are separated, moved apart, each to be slotted into our rigidly regimented grooves. In a split second of calling a letter in the alphabet, with random fatality, our new destinies are instantly sealed.

'We'll find each other. Think of it this way, at least we are in the same camp!'

'See you, Nick.'

'See you, Ethan. It's going to be OK. Be strong.'

'Golf commmmpany . . . form up, form up, FORM UP!' We move briskly and knit together in a neat rectangle.

'At ease! We are going to march you to your bungalows, and then we are going to divide you into platoons. Do you hear me?'

Silence.

'DO YOU HEAR ME?'

'YES, SERGEANT!' the brand-new Golf Company shouts. He walks to the front of the company and faces us, waits a moment and gives the command.

'COM-PA-NEEEE, commmpaneeee, ATTENNNN-SHUN!' Our step-out shoes strike the dirt unevenly, sounding like machine-gun fire. 'TERRIBLE, NEVER SEEN SUCH A HEAP OF USELESS SHIT. Just you wait. You will see, this will become the best company in Infantry School. You will see, and those of you who can't take it can fuck off to the trains right now! Is there anybody who wants an RTU right now?' He doesn't wait for an answer, because we wouldn't be allowed to leave now in any case. Our days of making any decisions are over. Then he continues, 'COOOOMPANEEE LEEEEFT TURN! Thaaaaat's better. FORWAAAARD MARCH. Hick-ya, hick-ya, hick-ya . . .'

As we march away, I think of Ethan. The yellow dust of the parade ground, tired of being drilled on, tired of rising, but still obedient, hovers around our boots.

An enthusiastic sergeant drives us. He drops the '-ya' at the end of the 'hick-ya' once the rhythm is established. 'Hick . . . hick . . . hick,' on every second beat. It feels pathetic to me, and my obedience to this sound vexes me even more.

As we turn the corner of the parade ground, we come parallel with the groups still left standing. My eyes find Ethan and lock onto him. He is in the last row of his company, looking down. Then I see his *balsak* slip from his hand. He makes no attempt to balance it as it knocks against the man next to him. Then he falls. His body cantilevers over the end of his bag, exaggerating his collapse.

I stop. The person behind me collides with me, and then the next, causing a ripple effect which disintegrates our formation and leaves the front part marching on, unaware of what has happened.

One of the instructors sees the collapse. 'Cooompaannee, HALT, two, three!' but not everyone hears him. The sergeant in charge, proudly parading his troops in front of the entire Infantry School, keeps on hick-, hick-ing until he glances around and sees the elongated formation, some still following him, others having halted, and the rest hovering in between.

His embarrassment at what is happening under his command needs immediate venting. His face is blood-red, the veins in his neck bulging as if they are glued to his skin. The company's sergeant major comes marching towards us. It is clear that the instructors trying to hold us together dread this man.

With everyone keen to shift the blame, I am immediately isolated as the culprit. So many people want to shout at me at the same time, that everything becomes blurred. And all I want is to see if Ethan is all right. I try to keep the group now gathering around him, in sight. Millimetres in front of my face a man is shouting so loudly that his breath, his saliva and his fury hit me full on. 'LOOK AT ME, YOU! Who are you?'

'Van der Swart, *Sammajoor*!'

'Take this one's name. I'll remember you, you piece of shit!'

I try to say something, but he orders me to shut up. The formation is reinstated and all the while I hear the fantastic threats of being driven to an RTU via hell.

Golf Company. My new world. Without Ethan. Malcolm and I land in Golf Company together, and so does Gerrie. Not in the same platoon, but the same company; close enough to see each other, close enough to talk from time to time.

Gerrie, whom I have known for five years, adopts a survival strategy of sucking up to the instructors. Many people do this, as captives often do. So I find that Gerrie and I drift apart. The few moments we have to ourselves during the first months at Infantry School, I spend with Malcolm.

I keep as low a profile as possible, never standing out, never coming first or last, and always keeping out of our trainers' way.

Malcolm and I grow closer, gravitating effortlessly towards each other and establishing an imperishable, uncomplicated and understanding friendship.

But we aren't in the same platoon. If we had been, I might never have befriended Dylan.

***

As we are lugging our heavy *balsakke* into the bungalow, his first words to me are, 'I think we've fallen out of life. No, we've dropped completely out of time.'

He uses the words to test me—a litmus test of the person I might be. Do I comprehend? Do I really grasp? Do I respond? If I don't, I am like all the others, and he will remain where he is—deep inside himself.

He is dark in more than just complexion; silent and hidden. We share a cupboard, and our beds are next to each other. But we sleep on the floor, for the beds are made up with such precision and squared with starch, with our teeth and with irons, that we dare not spoil them.

He doesn't speak often, but when he does, I listen. I am drawn to him, not just because I like him or because I understand him, but because I respect him. I am drawn to his tenderness.

Building a fantasy around him, I imagine that I can see a grown-up Frankie in him. There is no anxiety in our acquaintance, as there often is when one wants a friendship to work. But we are thrown together, and where friendship is normally a choice made by two people to spend time together, here someone else chooses for us.

I am the only one in the platoon he talks to. Only with me does he use words like, 'The problem with these people, Nick, is that they are all deeply sad. They have lived this way for too long; they know nothing else. They don't know how to let happiness in; they have lost the tools to identify it. If you think of it in that way, you could lose your anger towards them.'

Everything we talk about, the way in which he constructs his sentences, even his humour, is different. And these small nuances constantly remind me that he is not like anybody else.

He gives me his favourite book as a gift and uses the word 'betterment.' Then he smiles, for he uses it knowing it is pretentious and knowing that I know it. 'It is the most remarkable book I've ever read and I want to share it with you. *One Hundred Years of Solitude* . . . it's fantastic.'

In the front he writes:

To Nicholas, my friend in dismal places.
May you win the fight against solitude, for I won't.
Love, Dylan

I rarely feel as if I get to his true centre, except perhaps on two occasions, under extraordinary circumstances.

The exposure to such logic, so vividly different from the mindlessness, is like moving beyond a physical level. He never criticises, never resorts to the army bashing we all succumb to, even though he has the most reason to do so.

I describe him in my diary:

Dylan has pitch-black hair; a sallow skin. He is a dark ghost in too sharp focus; remarkably attractive but not affected by it. He does not exude the obvious sex appeal that is flaunted by those wielding the power of such beauty. He would rather you discover the matrix of his hidden self.

Over and above his arresting exterior and unfathomable intellect there is something more: When he listens, he seems to hear more keenly, understanding the history of every sentence as though he can see behind it.

'If we could understand why people do things, absolutely comprehend, then there would never be malice. I guess that would make it easier to forgive, but not necessarily easier to live with.'

Another thing I notice when we meet is a small scab, round and solid, on his hand—on the little triangular web between the thumb and index finger. I notice it subliminally. There is so much to take in during these first days, but I notice it. And later I remember that it was there.

**

Armed with Dylan's unique brand of insight and Malcolm's ease and humour, I discover a way of seeing each day to its end—one day at a time—in Golf Company.

The course is physically exhausting, but I get by and my faith grows. It seems to be all I have, and I walk my days with my Father of the Universe, not with the judgmental God of the *dominee* of the face-brick church in Welgemoed. The God that walks with me is the God of Philippians 4, verse 6:

Do not be anxious about anything, but in everything, by prayer and petition, with thanksgiving, present your requests to God. And the peace of God, which transcends all understanding, will guard your hearts and your minds in Christ Jesus.

Yes, this is what I want: The peace that transcends all understanding . . .

There is an inspection every day, with preposterous rules. One entire set of browns is reserved for the exclusive purpose of being in our cupboards, with so many specifications that one needs a manual for it. We stitch wood behind the facings of the garments within tolerances of a millimetre. We don't sleep on our beds because they have to be made, squared and stitched. Even the fibres on the blankets are brushed into a specific shape. We don't walk on the floors; we shuffle on 'taxis'—rectangular pieces of felt—to eradicate any evidence of our presence.

Then, after sleepless nights and weeks of cleaning, training and exercise, a corporal walks in and dribbles golden syrup over our inspection parcels, breaks the carefully constructed internal spines, rubs dirt on everything, destroys our starched beds and tells us we must have it all ready again for the next morning's inspection. It takes us all night.

This existence erodes the spirit; chips away at one's endurance, and people start requesting RTU's, or in most cases simply give up.

The principle is straightforward: The instructors can do what they want with us. If we feel we can't go on, or will not obey an order, we may request or be forced to take an RTU. Later in the year, only half of the troops are left and the authorities decide to block this way out. They start denying trainees the right to leave. After all, the growing border war needs platoon commanders.

There is no doubt that national servicemen who have had tough times in the eighteen or nineteen years preceding their army training, are somehow able to endure more than the others. More important than just fitness, it is stamina, mind over muscle, that is required. The boys with character persevere.

One afternoon, during a seven-kilometre run—forced to keep the platoon structure, our rifles at 45°, with webbing chafing our backs and our brains frying in the 40°C baking down on our heavy World War II-helmets—one of the guys loses it. He used to be a marathon runner—one of those I saw in the first weeks and thought: Shit, he is so lucky to be so fit; he'll have no problem.

Heatstroke they call it, blaming it on not drinking enough

water. Or is it that the demons inside him just broke free? He bursts out of the platoon formation gasping, pushing the troops in front of him, making gargling, crying noises and sprinting ahead, frothing at the mouth.

As he runs, he waves his arms and drops his rifle—the rifle he was told was more important than his life, should be treated better than a wife and should be worshipped and never, ever dropped. He runs at full speed towards the camp and collides with the security fence. By the time the instructor reaches him, he is biting the barbed wire.

He is immediately taken to the sick bay, where he dies the next day.

On the eight o'clock news the first subject is the announcement of the troops who have 'perished' in skirmishes on the border. Each time I see the black rectangle with the number, name and rank, I think of the families, somehow linked, and how they would deal with this life-altering information.

But it is not only the parents whose sons die who lose their children—their neatly parcelled boys they so eagerly sent to serve. The degree to which they return as whole human beings depends on their individual experiences and their ability to process this serrated incision into their lives.

We are constantly told that 'the army will make a man of you,' but often it just takes you completely. In some instances the men that the families get back are impenetrable sepulchres; caskets they are too afraid to open for fear of seeing the contents.

***

In the background a small portable radio is tuned to 'Forces Favourites.' The volume is turned too high for the small speaker, and the sound it produces is thin and grating as it twists among

us until it is sucked into the wet canvas of the tent. The presen-
ter of the programme is Esmé Euvrard. The song is *Substitute* by
Clout, and it reminds me of high school. The next song is *Ferry
Cross The Mersey* by Gerry & The Pacemakers. I am missing
home and the past and the way things were before, when he
walks in.

He stands in front of me, tells me about the time he went
swimming with dolphins at Noordhoek. There is an urgency in
the way he is talking; he wants me to know who he is . . .

***

Dylan sits opposite me, staring at me intently. He looks focused
and happy. 'I love watching you eat. You attack your food, like
you're really enjoying it.'

'How the fuck can he enjoy this food, Stassen, you arsehole? Do you know what this is?' Basson, who is sitting next to
Dylan, pulls his face in disgust. 'It's called plane crash, man!'
But Basson's reaction has as much effect on my friend's attention as the thousand other boys submerged in the noise of eating on metal tables in this large steel structure.

'En . . .'

'Yes?'

'If you could travel anywhere, where would you like to go?'

'I would like to travel in Africa!'

'Like where?'

'Well, I would like to see the Okavango Delta in Botswana,
and I would like to track the mountain gorilla in the Verunga
mountains. It's . . .'

'Yes, I know, it's between Rwanda and the Congo, or what
is it called now?'

'Zaire.'

'Sounds adventurous!'

'There is no chance though, you know, with a South African passport.'

Basson, intrigued with our conversation says, 'Why the fuck do you want to go there, Van, hey? You fucking crazy *soutpiel* Boer.' Then to the larger group, attracting their attention, 'Do you okes hear, Van der Swart wants to travel to kaffir countries?'

'And you, Dee?'

'Cuba, great music!'

'Fuck, okes, did you hear that? Stassen wants to travel to Cuba. I knew it, you two are fucking communists!'

'And where do you want to travel to, Basson?'

'I want to stay here. I love my country 'cos it's the best and I am loyal to it.'

'How do you know it's the best if you haven't seen the rest?'

'I know what I know. Stassen, do you know that we are fighting Cuban soldiers on the border and you want to go there? Are you fucked in the head?' He leans over to Dylan and jams his own head melodramatically with his index finger, seemingly to drive his point home.

'I don't care for this war, Basson. I don't want to be part of it. Shit, I shouldn't even be here!'

'What do you mean? Hey, you are in this country and you are living off the fat of this fucking land so you must fucking protect it.'

'Only the whites are conscripted.'

'So, you thick Englishman, so?'

'So, Basson . . . so . . . I should not be here!' Now the boys on either side of the table are listening, intrigued. Basson scratches his head.

'So you saying you're a kaffir now?'

'No, I think you would call me a coloured.'

'Fuckin' *hotnot* is what I would call you. AND YOU ARE PROUD OF IT? Are you fucking mad, man?' He almost shouts this out. 'I knew it! I knew it, fuckin' *hotnot*. Did you okes hear?

I tell you . . . fuck me! You should want to hide such disgusting info about yourself and instead you're proud of it. *Kleurling!*'

'Yes, I am.' Dylan is dead calm, as though he is relating something mundane and ordinary, something he might have repeated many times over, when he says, 'Well, I don't know what you want to call me, but my great-great-grandmother— or even further back, I'm not sure—was black or Malay. She was a slave who got her freedom and then married a white man and then all their children just always married white people.

It is dead quiet, as if the entire mess hall is listening, but they are not. 'Shit, and now I'm suffering. Just think, I could be studying or travelling . . . to Cuba . . . instead of sitting here in this hellhole! Wish I could get myself reclassified from white to coloured!'

One guy gets up saying he will not eat at the same table as a coloured.

'Fucking kaffir, I knew it . . . fucking kaffir commie!'

***

'Nick, tell me a story!'

 'Mom,'

 'Yes?'

 'Tell us a story!'

 'No boys, you must sleep now.'

 'Oh come on, Mom, pleeeese.'

 'OK, I'll tell you a story . . . of Jack and Manorie, that's how my story begun. I'll tell you another of Jack and his brother and now my story is done!'

 'Oh, Mom!'

 'No, boys, come, come, sleep now. Look at the time! Let me tuck you in. Sleep tight now . . . I love you!'

'When we used to ask my mother that, she would say, "I'll

tell you a story of Jack and Manorie, that's how my story
begun. I'll tell you another of Jack and his brother and now my
story is done!"'

We're quiet for a while. I turn to him and look into his dark
eyes. They are not just dark; it is as though they are set in the
shade.

'Dee, you are as white as the rest of us, why did you tell the
guys your great-great-grandmother was black? You know it's
just going to cause shit.'

'I just wanted to . . . you know, Nick . . . educate them a little. Basson is so ignorant that I just couldn't help myself. But
you enjoyed it, didn't you?'

'Yes, I did. Nice drama, but we Afrikaners—remember, I'm
a Boer-*soutpiel* mixture—most of us have black or coloured
blood somewhere in our distant past. Very few of us are lily-
white. I wanted to mention that, but what's the point? He
would never believe it. Strange to think that the Afrikaners are
such racists, yet we are all really a mixed race. Fuck, it's bullshit, hey?'

'Yes, it shows you what a church and a government can do.'

'I had that problem when I was in my teens. It nearly drove
me mad. All the questions about other religions, like: How
does one know what the correct religion is? I mean, I was born
into a Christian religion—two actually—but maybe God wants
me to be Muslim or Buddhist, you know. Just maybe He, She,
wants me to serve via a different vehicle? So I asked this
teacher who was like a mentor to me and he said, "Ask God."'

'Wow, I like that. It's beautiful.'

***

I am not entirely sure when or how it starts, but the instructors
develop an aversion to Dylan. I watch helplessly as it seems to

become driven by its own momentum. It is not that he is weak or struggling with the course, which is usually why they start discriminating. With the instructors, it can be caused by the slightest personality clash or provocation. I think it's Dylan's unusualness, his spirituality that they cannot fathom. He does nothing to irritate them, but he looks at them differently when they talk or shout at him. Instead of the humble, terrified look they want, he stares at them fearlessly.

If I lean over slightly, I can see Dylan staring at the corporal in front of him. He is tired. They have made him run across the parade ground carrying a tyre so many times that I don't think he will be able to do it again. His chest is heaving and sweat has stained his shirt a muddy colour in the hollow of his back and in large patches under his arms. His hands, pants and parts of his shirt are black from the tyre.

I want to beg him to be humble and talk to them in the way he knows they want from him, but I know he never will.

'Are you a derrick?' All he needs to say is, 'Yes, Corporal,' but he won't. He says 'NO!' Then the instructor says, 'You fucking derrick *kak* . . .' being the crudest possible abbreviation for a fool. Then the corporal turns and walks away.

He wants to make Dylan run again, but he won't be able to do it, and the corporal knows it. So Dylan stands there, exhausted. He has not taken his eyes off his tormentor. At that moment the lunch whistle blows and I can see the relief on the instructor's face. The situation is defused but not forgotten.

We also have days like these, but for Dylan it happens almost every day.

I can only describe this in the way I see it, which is subjectively. But to my mind Dylan is superior, not only in background and upbringing, but as a person of integrity. And they know it. They don't know what to do with it, so as with most things unfamiliar, they respond aggressively.

They attempt to break or 'crack' him and when they don't succeed, they see it as failure, so they try harder. When Dylan doesn't crack from the physical strains they place on him, I am at first just as baffled as the instructors are, but those with insight would have understood his reasons for persevering.

***

We wait for our first pass like a child awaits Christmas or a birthday. And in the same way it feels like a lifetime.

I get a lift with a guy called Pierre, whose father fetches us because Pierre will be bringing his own car back to Oudt-shoorn after the weekend. The first trip home is not as I created it in well-rehearsed fantasy. Dylan is not with me, yet he is—I carry him unwillingly and uncomfortably within my joy of going home. Dylan is in my head, his haunting face projected onto everything.

We are ready long before we hear, 'Fall in!' This is the parade to see if we are turned out correctly in our step-outs, to show the world how regimented and changed we are. If one thing is wrong, not shiny enough, not straight enough, just not enough, you fail the parade and you don't go home.

When something so valuable, so desired, is in the hands of ruthless people, it is agonisingly fragile.

Up and down the rows the instructors look for reasons to keep us in the camp. Dylan is in the row in front of me. Sergeant Dorman walks his row, slowly, keeping each troop on a knife-edge of insecurity. As he gets to the person to Dylan's right, he flicks gravel onto Dylan's spotless shoes with his boot. Dylan lifts his foot slightly and surreptitiously tries to wipe the shoe on the back of his pants. Of course Dorman sees it.

'What are you doing?' A hateful delight seems to permeate the calm question.

'You kicked some . . .'

'SHUT UP!' Then louder, 'DON'T TALK SHIT TO ME! If you don't want to go home you can fucking stay here. Do you understand, you piece of rat shit?'

'But . . .'

'Don't you say another word, you slimeball. Look at this fucking mess. If you think you're going home like this, forget it, you faggot cunt! You are single-handedly trying to bring down the image of the Defence Force! Is this what you want to show the people back home? You look like a maggot hobo.' He turns and moves on. The rest of the row he handles carelessly and we are discharged, but Dylan has to stay behind.

Dylan was meant to go North, and I am going South. I can't help him. Around me there is a joyous scurry by like-coloured people with like-coloured excitement and they call me to the gate, out for a long weekend, out of the army for the first time. But I can't go.

'Nicholas, you can't help him. You can do nothing for him. We are not waiting. We are going home, buddy. Are you coming? My father won't wait. We're leaving!'

'Let me just speak to the sergeant, Pierre. Please.'

I walk up to him, and as I reach him, I fall into step—one . . . —and come to a loud halt.

'Yes, Van der Swart.' Dylan cannot hear me; nobody can, as I whisper un-army-like, softly, pleading.

'Sergeant, please let him go. Please . . .'

Silence. He turns and looks away while I'm talking. Smoke bleeds from his nostrils and I am amazed at how much there must be inside him. His skin is young yet old; old with large pores, old from within. I can't move until he dismisses me, but he ignores me. It feels like an eternity before he takes another long draw from the cigarette, covering his mouth and chin with his hand—his own personal 'style' of smoking. Behind him, Pierre is trying to catch my eye, miming 'We must go now' in a dramatic way, his eyes wide. Malcolm is waiting to say good-bye; he too is in a hurry.

Sergeant Dorman still does not look at me when he grunts a firm 'No.' He says it so finally, not loudly, just filled with revenge and hate. 'Absolutely not.'

I do an about turn and stamp my foot, then burst into a run. I fetch my bag in our bungalow and there I find Dylan, just sitting, small and sad.

'Dee, I'm so sorry.' He doesn't answer.

Pierre has followed me, urging me on, not wanting to lose these precious moments he sees as freedom. 'Come now, Nick, will you leave him alone now!'

As I leave, I turn around. Dylan is looking at me. 'Have a great time, En. It's OK.' His expression burns into me. There is much more than sadness—a haunting, deep need—and it stays in my head. Or is it my heart . . . or my soul?

As we run to the car, I look for Malcolm. I need his lightness, but I cannot see him. For a brief moment I picture Malcolm getting into a car with other boys for the long journey to the Transvaal, and I pray for his safe return. He told me he would be coming back in his own car.

As we run towards the front gate everything seems quiet, drained of souls; the empty bungalows unmasked and lifeless in their part of this silly endeavour. Dylan is in one of them. I carry that empty hopelessness with me, and something else I do not understand. I will try to fathom it on my way to Cape Town.

'The moment of happiness, that very moment . . . when it's there, you don't really know it; you just live it because this is how things are meant to be. But when it goes . . . when it goes, and life with all that it brings has brought time in between, then you realise that moment was remarkable. They have taken that away, En. That's all. We must have no expectations, then they can't touch us, not even for a moment. They must not be able to touch us.'

***

Dylan and I have made a bivvie—a groundsheet and roof contraption. The platoon has been arranged in groups of two in a circular defence, as if we were on the border. We have to take turns standing guard while our buddy sleeps. This is the first time that we are spending an entire week in the veld.

It is dusk, and we have been given time to clean our kit, which we do lying facing each other on our thin, brown sleeping bags.

His eyes are so dark I cannot discern the pupils. The shape of his eyes, his face and his dark eyebrows are striking.

'What did you look like before the army? Did you have long hair?'

'I'll show you.' He sits up and takes a black wallet out of his rucksack.

'Here's one of me and my family.' He hands me the picture. They are standing in front of a large house. Dylan's hair is long, almost over his eyes, and his body language is inward.

'Let me see the rest,' I say and he smiles to himself, as though in acknowledgement of something he will not share, knowing it is only a wrapped parcel he will show me.

The picture I find most interesting is of him, a man and his mother. Dylan is well dressed and almost exotic looking. I want to tell him that I find him handsome, but don't. Later we talk about the plight of deprived, sick and old people and he says, 'En, there is suffering in this world we know nothing of. There is such unbelievable torment.'

'Like what?'

'Deep stuff.'

'But what do you know about that? You are one of the privileged ones.'

'Yes, I know that's what it looks like. But privilege doesn't guarantee happiness. In itself it can carry its own anguish. Just *looking* at suffering from a position of privilege has its own corruption. No, I'm talking about mental and emotional pain. Healing a mind is much more difficult, because one's inner feelings are so hard to verbalise. It's almost impossible to tell someone. I mean, how can one, if you think about it. You probably think I'm crazy.'

'No, Dylan, I know exactly. I've been there.'

'Really?'

'Yes, and as you said, it's so difficult to verbalise.'

The whistle goes and we have to stop talking.

'My dear En, I am very intrigued. You are a man of mystery. I like that. I want to know about your pain,' he whispers, smiling.

'OK,' I say, grateful for the whistle, 'but not now.'

'Do you still have it?'

'No,' I whisper. 'I'm not *mad* any more.' And at that moment I feel very close to Dylan.

I make sure he can hear the smile in my voice, for I don't want to go into this night thinking back on that time. There is enough here to cope with. Why do those years still terrify me so? It's like constantly being sucked back, but I know that I will never, ever go there again.

'When was this?'

'High school in Banhoek. We'd better keep quiet. I don't want any more shit.'

It is my turn to stand guard. I position myself to look out into the night. Dylan's face is turned towards me and I glance down at him. It has become too dark to see if his eyes are open, but I feel him looking and I feel a smile, a warmth, coming from him as if he has made a decision about me.

Later his breathing becomes deeper and rhythmic. How sweetly the air goes in and out of this complex boy. I move my feet to let the blood circulate. Three and a half hours to go. Far over the valley, a glow unfolds behind the mountains where the moon will soon rise.

11

My first day at Paul Roos Gymnasium. I tell my mother I'm sick from yesterday's tetanus injection after cutting my hand on a bottle. My arm is in a sling. Truth is, I'm sick with fear, sick of trying to fit in, sick of wishing for a gentler, more accepting world.

Bronwyn goes to Rhenish Primary, so she will not be initiated. She is dropped off before me.

The sprawling red-roofed school is built in a semicircle with a dramatic hall in the centre. Three gates are set in the hedge separating the road from the lawns. I walk through the centre gate, overwhelmed by everything around me. Where must I walk? Which gate? What should I say? Will I fit in? Will I ever cope?

At assembly I hear nothing. I study the faces of the teachers on the stage, searching for a friendly one.

'I'm not going back, I will not go back,' I tell my mother after school. 'You and Dad can do what you want; I will not go back. The seniors made this one boy eat his own puke. They beat us up. I hate that school, I hate it!' My words are brushed aside and the next day I go back, taking the bus from Banhoek, over Helshoogte.

It feels as if my entire first year at Paul Roos consists of initiation and a series of hidings from the teachers. There is only one positive note: Mr. Davids, our Biology teacher.

His class is laid out differently. The desks face the centre of the room and everything about the man is refreshingly unusual. Mr. Davids's effect on my life is like an embankment slowly giving in to the flow of a stream. He seems to look at everything in a different way, and I understand it intuitively. It's not only that we discuss different subjects; the attraction lies rather in his unique understanding. It is as if I have had a language coded into me for many years but never used it, and now suddenly I'm having conversations in it.

Only a small group of Paul Roos boys relate to Mr. Davids. During breaks, we congregate in his classroom, irrespective of age or level of education. We are in pursuit of what cannot be seen or worn; we are too caught up in awareness to allow any limitations. The 'others' don't want to rock the boat. Bored and complacent, they sink back into their chairs and think only what has been thought before.

12

There is a slight irregularity to Dylan's breathing; almost like a change to a tighter, double rhythm, and I wonder what he is dreaming. He may not even remember it himself, and I imagine we are poorer for it. I remove my journal from my shirt pocket and use the light of my digital watch to find the place to start the entry, and I write:

They want to be in the drift of continents, seeking movement that is not noticed.

The moon is blazing white and climbs rapidly from behind the distant mountains. Suddenly the valley becomes clear to my adjusted sight and the introduction of light. The night appears bigger with discernable distance. I miss the closed-in intimacy of the black darkness.

The moonlight catches just a part of Dylan's ear and his

cheekbone. He coughs and moves down, sinking into the darkness as if he can feel the moonlight on him.

Go to a story, I tell myself. Why dwell on the bad Banhoek years? It was in Banhoek that I started creating my evening stories into the serial that threaded all the way through high school and arrived here with me, occupying the slot just after lights-out, just before falling asleep.

After Frankie's death I created a world to escape to, but only in high school did it become structured—an alternative existence, a world of my own design, the fibre of which, in the freedom of unobserved thought, took on a new colour as I entered my teens. Ah, the faces of the men I undressed, seeing them so compromised! And the sex . . . the sex with the straight boys!

I learnt from my friends in the valley: the quiet ones and the wild ones. We experimented with sex and alcohol, listening to heavy metal. Everything new or pleasurable was a sin: pop music, fashionable clothing, drinking, sex, movies . . . everything I seemed to like.

I fell in love with a quiet one and in lust with a wild one. At the rock pools fed by clear mountain streams, we masturbated and touched each other.

After the weekends of experimenting under cover of darkness and alcohol, we never spoke about our explorations, but we planned the next trip, knowing what would happen.

For this narrow window of sexual release, I paid very dearly.

Shit, how I hate that word. I remember how I feared being called it, being discovered. And then it happened—moffie . . . moffie . . . you moffie!

13

In high school, with this unwelcome lust whirling inside me, I don't pray for the life my nature asks for. I pray for the life that everybody calls normal and correct. I am disgusted by my own desires, confused and bewildered.

How I pray! Over and over, night after night, the same prayer.

The revulsion I feel for myself, the fear of burning in hell, the fear of being ridiculed, the desire for 'normality' and the sadness of not having anybody to share my uncertainties with—this is what causes the greatest suffering.

I am taught that it is a fight between good and evil, and of course evil is that which I want. I start reading religious books and become obsessed by matters for which there are no clear answers; not only my 'Sodom-and-Gomorrah' homosexuality, but also complex issues of worship.

On a camp with Mr. Davids, I become a 'reborn' Christian, but I can't get rid of the lust I feel for men. And I don't find the answer in the velvet groove of charismatic Christianity either. I don't discuss my problem with anybody, but I soon understand the doctrine, which confuses me even more:

If I am a true Christian, I will be 'cured.' An evil spirit has possessed me, or I am just a slave to the pleasures of the flesh.

Eventually the conflict between my wish for spiritual growth and my physical cravings starts to trigger questions that uncover a myriad of other issues. I find more to worry about, more to question. Eventually I start questioning every question and lose all sense of peace.

I search for my Creator with exaggerated fervour. I read books on religion and spirituality in every spare moment and establish even stronger ties with the one man I trust—a mentor whose patience I test with my delirious perplexities. I don't tell him about the root of my problems, for fear that even he won't understand, so I only pose masked questions to Mr. Davids.

I stop sleeping. In the darkness, I am haunted even more, and by the time morning comes, I am more confused than ever.

136 · ANDRÉ CARL VAN DER MERWE

Eventually my schoolwork starts suffering. My parents have no idea why their son is so introverted and spends all his time behind locked doors.

On two occasions I sink into a delirium and start hallucinating, which makes me terrified to go to sleep. I withdraw totally to this tumultuous inner world, sharing it with nobody, not even with Mr. Davids, who remains my only pillar in life.

Then he is taken away.

14

I take a deep breath, fill my lungs, and when I release the air it sounds like an immense sigh. The soup of self-pity is too thick for me to listen to the voice warning me not to go back to that time.

I watch Dylan for a long time and fight the temptation to touch him. I want to get into a car and escape. I want to get into a well-designed car seat and sit beside a man who loves me. A man who loves me; yes me! Could this be possible? I want to drive off on a road with no link to anything I know.

I sigh again at the realisation of how large my need is for that love; for a life that is not a constant battle.

15

When you think things can't get worse, it might only be the start of the way down. When you truly believe things cannot get worse, you may only be on the cusp of the spiral that is ready to swallow you.

One day a rumour starts circulating at school that Mr. Davids is gay. He is not at school and I can't get to see him at home. The story goes that three boys went to his house and got into a fight with him when he tried to seduce them.

After three days, I see his green Peugeot parked in its usual place. I hear that he has visible scars from the scuffle. When I get to see him, he is wrapped in a camouflage of grim earnestness—a man soaked in disappointment.

A senior student tells me, 'He has been asked to resign and those bastards will go free. I have known Lance, I mean Mr. Davids, for five years and there is absolutely no way that he would have made a move on those boys. Shit, apparently they really hammered him.'

'How did it end?'

'His friend arrived and broke it up.'

'I don't understand how this could have happened. Do you know what happened?'

'They were calling him names, and when he told them to leave, they started beating him up. Neither the school nor the police are taking his side. Can you believe that?'

'But can nobody defend him?'

'His friend was there, you know, François, but no . . . no, they . . . he will not be . . . it won't work.'

'Why?'

'Nicholas, there is so much you don't understand. He . . .' the senior sighs, 'he is in bigger trouble.'

'What do you mean?'

'They are laying a charge against him, and besides . . . well, they're saying that he, François, is the proof that Lance is gay.'

I want to ask, 'Is he?'

I can see the senior is expecting the question, but I can't utter it.

My parents have also heard about the incident.

'He should be fired . . . no, castrated on the spot! The pervert! I have a good mind to phone the principal and make sure he gets sacked.'

'Mom, how can you talk like that? You don't even know the

man. Why do you just accept their version? I can't believe you. He's my friend.'

'Friend? Under NO circumstances!' says my father. 'No son of mine will be friends with a faggot, do you understand? *Do* you understand?'

'I understand, but I know this man and you don't. I *will* be his friend. I can tell you he did not molest those boys.'

'How do you know, Nicholas? You are a child, a naive child, you know nothing about the type of man he is. I don't want to hear another word from you. I'm warning you, Nick, you go near him and they'll call you a faggot too. Is that what you want?'

'I don't care what they call me. And stop saying that he is . . . what you think he *is*. There is no proof.'

'Oh, for heaven's sake, stop it. Nicholas, just do as your father says. Please, this is serious. You don't know what kind of influence he can have on younger boys and what he can do to you. Those types are very devious; they have clever tricks to catch you. These are things you know nothing about. Mr. Davids is evil. He is the worst type of evil, and he will draw you into his web and corrupt you.'

'No!' I cry. 'You don't know what is going on; I know him. Do you think I'm stupid? He will never do anything to hurt anybody. I'm telling you! He is one of the nicest people I have ever met. He treats me like a grown-up.' The moment I say it I know they will read something into it.

'I knew it, I knew it! You see! He has corrupted you already. Now I know! Is he not the one that you went camping with? Peet, this is serious. One wonders how many boys he may have molested on those so-called Christian camps.' Turning to me she continues, 'Nicholas, listen to me . . . tell me honestly . . . did he try anything with you? Please tell us!'

'I will break his neck,' says my father, who never would.

'Listen to me carefully, Mom and Dad. He did not try anything with me or with anybody else, and he never will either. He is not the type of person that would ever harm another being. He is probably the only true Christian I have ev . . .'

'STOP THAT THIS INSTANCE! How dare you include filth like that with god-fearing, churchgoing people, how dare you? THAT IS ENOUGH NOW.'

'I can see I will never get through to you. I'm going to my room.'

A month goes by and nothing really returns to normal. All remains clouded with grey judgment. I wait for it to blow over, but I know it never will. It will just bleed and slowly seep away.

Then the unthinkable happens . . .

When I eventually come out on the other side, systematically shedding the scabs, I realise that all this anguish hinged around my being gay. Being the *unmentionable*, the worst, the utterly sinful, irredeemable, and carrying it all on my own—a secret too large to bear, too devastating to share and too dreadful not to. My mother's Catholic Church, my father's Dutch Reformed Church, all our friends and family, my entire world, it feels to me, regard one thing more heinous than anything else, and that is what I am. Hell is guaranteed; at the end of a living hell that I did not choose.

16

'Dee,' I say quietly. I know it will not wake him. He is still lying facing me, but he has pulled his legs up into his chest. The moon has climbed high enough now to light his face. I lean over him and look closely at his face. He looks intense, even when he's asleep. I touch his shoulder gently. It feels alluring, and I fight the urge to stroke him. I want to stroke his whole

body. 'Dylan . . . hey, Dee, wake up.' More urgently now, for
I'm fighting an urge, fighting myself.

His eyes open, and in a split second he re-enters the world.
'I'm awake.'

'How did you sleep?'

'Well, thanks.'

'Are you going to be OK?'

'Yep. I'm fine, En. Hey, before you sleep, do you want a
couple of jelly babies? I've kept them to keep me company. At
least they're quiet. Do you think I can get one to stand guard
for me?'

'Yes, Dee, just don't use a black one. If they catch you they'll
think it's a terr.'

'Good camo though, for the night. Do you want one?'

'Thanks, no, I'm fine.' He sits up and I take some time to
get comfortable. I use my bush jacket as a pillow. Lying on my
side, I have a feeling of such security, as if he is watching over
only me. He sits above me, the moonlight catching his face
directly from the front, the rest of him in silhouette. Before I
close my eyes, I watch as he flicks his lighter and ignites a Lucky
Strike. He cups the red coal with his hand to avoid being seen,
looks down at me and says, 'Good night, En,' as he blows out
the smoke. There is fondness in the way he says it, almost like
an embrace. I love the way he doesn't use my full name. He
has made the letter his, protecting it like you would something
you own.

17

I wake up with Dot curled up in my arms. I have fantasised
about and needed this first pass so desperately, but now, instead
of giving me peace, the house triggers memories that make me
restless.

Too much time to think, too much of everything—everything I don't want. This first day out of military barracks is not at all as I imagined it would be. How can it be good? At the end of these few days, I know what I'm going back to.

So much has happened to me since I last lay on this bed. I lift the sheet and look down at my body. I am leaner, fitter, harder.

If Mal were here, we would have fun. Next pass I want to spend with him, I decide. Dylan is like a weight I carry that I can't shake and Ethan . . . where is he? The last time I slept in this bed I didn't know any of them.

What was it I saw in Dylan's lowered head, in his dark eyes? What secret lurks there, not revealing itself, just making me aware of its presence?

'You know, you are right, En. I have thought a lot about it.'

'What?'

'We walk on a tightrope, you know, En.' He is quiet between sentences. When he speaks again, his tone is private and deep, as if I'm listening to thought.

'On a thin steel cable, a tightrope that has an end, and we must step off it when we get there. And while we balance and take one step forward at a time, not even that is easy, but we don't look. No, we don't look down. Some of us even flirt with reality, but most of us just plod along blindly and then . . . it ends and we all fall off. We call it death. We all know it's going to happen, and the only way we can carry on walking directly to it is by blotting out the inevitable.'

Then he is quiet for a long time. I don't talk to him because he is staring intently at his bag with the Infantry School crest on it, which we were forced to buy for weekend pass. It is all packed for his first weekend outside the army, which is now denied him. Then he turns to me and says, 'The question is: Why not simply jump off right now?'

Where is Ethan? Something must happen. Anything. The need to see him is so overpowering it becomes an obsession. I decide to find Ethan's house, or at least try.

I walk down the wooden staircase. My mother greets me tentatively. She says nothing, but I can feel her searching glance. She is determined to make this weekend special for me. She makes no fuss, but I am aware of the trouble she has taken preparing every favourite meal, being there for me, but giving me space at the same time. My father greets his son, hoping he has changed for the better.

I ask to borrow my mother's car to go to Clifton to find a friend's parents. I tell my mother briefly about the last time I saw him.

'Why don't you trace him through the army?' my father wants to know. 'Surely that is where you should look? I was hoping you'd wash my car and help your mother on the farm, because I have a tennis match today.'

For a moment I look at my father. How do I explain to him that I need to find this boy because I'm in love with him? How do I explain that the army of the real world would never accommodate my request to search for Ethan?

'And in any case, your mother needs her car.'

'No, Peet, I don't and if I do, I'll use the truck.'

Later she follows me to the car and gives me money for petrol and food.

'It's OK, Mom, I have my army pay.'

'Save it. Here, take this, and don't tell your father. Do you have any idea where this boy's parents live?'

'All I know is that they have a bungalow on Third Beach. Mom, I must do this.' My mother stands next to the car, looks down at me intently, and I know she wants to ask questions but never will. Then I drive off.

During the forty minutes to Cape Town, I fantasise about Ethan being at home and us spending the day (no, the weekend) together. My head is in a reckless cloud—a place I have visited before.

I miss the turnoff, do a U-turn at Camps Bay and drive back to the small sign that reads Third Beach. My heart jumps. On the seat beside me, my black portable tape recorder is playing Rickie Lee Jones's *Night Train*.

For the full length of the song I sit and stare at the plastic dashboard, my mind on the woman about whom the song was written, who lost everything. Well, at least I can't lose what I never had. I cross the road and look down at the steeply arranged, quaint bungalows nestled in the shrubbery above the beach. They are all wooden, low-roofed, humble constructions of similar shape. To get to them I walk down steep pathways consisting mainly of steps.

There are three walkways marked Third Beach, and I decide to start on the left. I have the entire day, so I choose to savour the search. But the first path happens to be the correct one, and at the third door a woman says, 'Oh, yes, the Vickermans, they're just down there,' pointing to a door five metres away, behind an ancient milkwood tree. Everything is calm, green and cool. I press the welcome-worn bell, and the gate opens.

'Good morning, can I help you?'

'Hi, hello, my name is Nicholas.'

The woman's expression changes slightly, as if she is trying to recognise something.

'I'm a friend of Ethan's from the army.' She smiles. 'And your name is Precious.' With this, the black woman starts to laugh joyfully.

'He told you about me, my Ethan? How is he?'

'I don't know, Precious. I haven't seen him in two months.'

'Come inside. I'm sure Mrs Vickerman would like to meet you.'

I enter a small, manicured garden, almost tropical, and then the house. From the lounge, where I wait, I can see the sea over the roof of the house in front. All seems peaceful and comfortable, well lived in and warm. The interior is unaffected, yet sophisticated and inviting. I hear footsteps and see Ethan's mother.

'Good day, Mrs. Vickerman, I'm Nicholas.' Her skin is cared for, her hair well cut but not dyed. Suddenly I am aware of how badly dressed I am in my old jeans and T-shirt, but the woman appears not to notice. I take her hand and squeeze it gently. Her skin is soft.

Still holding my hand, she looks at me directly, focusing deep into both eyes and says, 'Welcome, Nicholas, it's a pleasure to meet you.' Then her hand slips from mine as she moves to a chair and sits down. She doesn't sit on the edge of the chair as if she's about to jump up, but deep and relaxed, making me feel comfortable.

'You're the friend I arranged the food for.' Smiling, she looks at me for what feels like a long time, and her expression becomes a searching look. Then she stops herself, turns and asks Precious to make some tea.

Giving her a brief overview of Middelburg and basics, I leave out anything that might upset her. When I answer her questions, I say that we coped well and helped each other, always using *us* and *we*.

'But, Mrs. Vickerman, I don't know what happened after we got to Infantry School. I haven't heard from Ethan since,' making no attempt to hide my concern.

She tells me that, on the journey to Oudtshoorn, Ethan sustained serious internal injuries when an instructor kicked him while he was doing push-ups.

While she tells me about his burst bladder, the subsequent surgery, its failure, the specialist, and the next operation, her voice is drowned out by a loud humming noise as anger washes over me and I picture the events. I realise that the experience was probably a lot worse than she imagines. People who haven't seen the behaviour of some of the army personnel, have no frame of reference.

I hear a wave breaking in the distance, people shouting on the beach—happy sounds penetrating the thundering passion inside me. At some point I am served tea in a china tea set, but I hardly notice.

'I know Ethan wrote to you. Did you not receive the letter? He did not have your full address, just your rank, number, and the base. He hoped they would forward it to you.'

I have shared more of the army with this woman than with my own folks or friends.

'Where is he now? Is he all right?'

'Ethan is in Pretoria. After the time in the military hospital, they put him on some medics course. I know he is not happy though, but he will have to persevere. It is only two years. I flew up to see him in hospital. He has lost so much weight . . . but he will be fine.' As she says this, she looks past me, focusing on the middle distance where there is probably an image of her son. Then she looks at her watch and says she would have to go, as she is late for an appointment. 'I'll cancel it if you want to talk some more?' she asks.

'No, it's OK, Mrs. Vickerman, thank you so much for your time. I was so worried. Do you have his address for me, please?'

She writes down the words that will put me in contact with Ethan and hands me the card written in beautiful handwriting. It pleases me that something so prized is so well executed.

Then I say, 'Would you mind if I looked at his room? As the words leave my lips, I am sure it is inappropriate, but she appears not to mind.

'You are welcome, my boy. Precious will see you out. I must run.' She puts her cheek against mine and makes a soft kissing sound, does the same on the other side, and leaves.

Precious walks me down the passage to the room.

From the instant I enter, I am immediately surrounded by him.

His bed stretches almost the full length of the wall to my right, with the headboard nestling between the wall and wardrobe in a secure, inviting way. *This is where he lay.*

The phone rings, Precious excuses herself, and I am left alone.

I sit down on his bed and inhale the room: the light, the colour, his surfboard with the stickers of surf brands, the photographs pinned to a crowded notice board.

In one picture Ethan stands on the beach with two boys and three girls, all in bathers, all very tanned, his hair streaked by the salt and the sun. All six of them are pretty. The boy I see there is a different Ethan to the one I know. Ethan comes from a world of light and easy solutions. I don't. Will he move back into this world, replace the loss, and forget?

I open his wardrobe searching for his smell, and then close it. 'I could live there and be half complete,' I whisper to myself, turn and step out into the passage. The minute I leave his room, I miss it. I wave goodbye to Precious, who is still on the phone, and leave.

From the gate, I follow the steps down to the beach, wanting more of him. I walk along to Second and then First Beach, the quietest spot of this different reality. I take off my T-shirt; my body is white, except for my arms and neck, which are a deep brown.

Would I want to be a part of this seemingly carefree, nothing-can-go-wrong world? What a great divide between my world and this one. To my left the waves crash untidily, and to my right there is a good swell and three guys on boogie boards playing like seals.

Before hunger and heat send me back to the car, I think of these words from the book Ethan gave me:

'But now you are going to cry!' said the little prince.
'Yes, that is so,' said the fox.
'Then it has done you no good at all!'
'It has done me good,' said the fox, 'because of the colour of
the wheat fields.'

When I get home, I play Bob Dylan's *Where Are You Tonight?* combing my yearning for Ethan through me. I put the head-phones on and shout the words of longing out loud. My parents are playing tennis, so I lie on my bed and wallow unchecked, rewinding the one track over and over again.

I can't believe it, I can't believe I'm alive,
But without you it just doesn't seem right!
Oh, where are you tonight?

18

Standing on the first floor, I look down towards the back class-rooms. It's about a month and a half since the incident between Mr. Davids and the boys, and nothing has been done to them. The event has been forgotten by most. It is second break on a hot Friday. I have chosen this quiet spot where I can delve un-hindered into the book I'm reading. I lean on the windowsill, cutting off those who pass behind me.

When I get to the end of a chapter, I look at the scene below—too far to intrude into my thoughts. Then I see him.

Mr. Davids is leaving the classroom of Mr. Thorr, the English teacher. The three boys who attacked him are standing on the raised section skirting the back rooms. He walks to the edge of the concrete and jumps down. I see his body stiffen halfway through the movement. When he lands, he turns slightly towards the boys, turns back and resumes his route. I realise that they have said something to him, and from the murmur amongst the rest of the boys, it is clear that it was something one doesn't normally say to a teacher. Then one of them speaks again, louder this time. His voice swirls into the courtyard, amongst the pupils, now captivated, and ricochets against the buildings for all to hear.

'Hey, you faggot, I'm talking to you!' Mr. Davids is halfway across the courtyard. Thorr's door opens and closes again immediately, but he leaves it ajar and stands watching through the slit.

Whispers and giggling spread from the centre like an infection, and in the middle stands Lance Davids. He looks down, as if considering his options, and then he walks on. In that moment that he looks down, I know I have lost the one adult, the one person, who could have been my bridge away from a very dark place.

The boys, who have been shouting, say something again and start running after Mr. Davids. One of them pushes his left shoulder. I run down the stairs, but by the time I get to them, whatever has happened is over.

Lance Davids does not come back to school. Some say he has been expelled, and others say he has chosen to leave. All my attempts to see him are in vain. I leave school early, sneak out during breaks, even skip classes, and ride my bike over Helshoogte to get to see him. But he is either not at home or doesn't answer the door.

My parents find out and I am forbidden to contact him. On the wall outside his house, the word 'Moffie' is spray painted, like a silent scream.

I hear he has moved to Natal, and I never see him again. It is the loneliest time of my life.

***

I kneel, put my elbows on the edge of the bed and bless myself: In the name of the Father, the Son and the Holy Spirit . . .

'Dearest, dearest, Lord . . . please, please, please . . . I beg of you, God, make me straight.' I wait, fighting tears and clamping my hands as I try to impress on God the earnestness of my prayer. 'God, this is not what I want. It is not my choice. I beg you; I beg you, make me straight. I believe that you can, Lord, I believe it. Please, my Holy Father, I pray this in the name of Jesus Christ.'

I think of the words I heard today, words that drove daggers into me: Homosexuals are from Satan. No Christian can be a homosexual. Evil spirits possess them. I shudder and start praying again. It becomes a mournful plea. Concentrate, Nick. Pray, pray! God will hear you. God will answer. He promises it.

Then I hear Lance's words. 'Don't ask for anything directly, always just say, "Not my will, Lord, but thy will be done." Give every situation to God. Don't tell Him what to do. He knows best.' This helps.

I allow the words to settle and I start again, 'Dear Lord, I am a homosexual. I give you this problem to solve for me, and I trust you completely.'

During this year of Lance Davids's humiliation and my inner trauma, I face one more enormous challenge. Why it all happens in one year and what it is meant to teach me, I don't know.

We wait for the summer holidays with our class teacher, Mr. Thorr, for whom I have now developed a deep dislike. He is so petrified of the boys that he actually sucks up to them. He identifies the boys who are a threat to him and befriends them shamelessly.

But my world is different. Around me, the noise doesn't penetrate the cocoon I have built around me and the book I am reading. It is three days before the start of the December holidays. Knowing that our report cards have already been finalised, the boys start nagging and manage to persuade Mr. Thorr to give us the results.

By the time he reaches the V's, two boys have heard that they have failed. The finality of these results, with no chance of reprieve, suddenly grips me. I CANNOT fail! This is not an option. I hear my father's words stretching over the years; painted over time like the line in the centre of a road, from the first day I heard it until now. 'Do not shame me, Nicholas. Do not ever shame me.'

Even my mother contributed to the pressure. 'How would we face your cousins? Nobody ever fails in our family. Failure is for stupid people. It is not an option for a Van der Swart. What would I say to these people? That you are stupid?'

I know my mother does not really mean this. I know she is trying to scare me into passing.

When Thorr gets to my name I know, from the way he moves, that I will be repeating this standard, and the others will go on to finish school a year ahead of me. The reality of this crashes into me with life-changing severity, and when it hits my insides, it explodes. The possibility of failing has always been there throughout my school years. I have struggled to concentrate, always been a dreamer, haunted by worries and fantasies. But this year those were small issues compared to my questioning of religion, eternal life and forbidden lust.

Now I have failed a year. The thought grows, casting a shadow over everything, and suddenly becomes too heavy for its own foundation.

I ask to be excused. I don't wait for permission; I just get up and leave. Every step makes a sound on the same path Mr. Davids walked on his last day at this school. The door to the toilet opens, and then closes with a hollow sound as it bounces back from the frame. Everything carries on as usual, every law of nature, yet in me every law is broken.

I sink down on the closed toilet seat and try to cry, but I can't.

My father calculates how much money I have cost him in this *lost* year; then how much I have cost myself, how much it will be worth as a lost year of earning before retirement.

In bed, sleep escapes me once again. How do I care about earnings at the age of sixty when I don't even know how to get through this night!

To protect myself, I enter my other life. Here I am free. Justice and fairness prevail—at least for me. Bitter revenge visits those who make my life a hell when my eyes are open.

I am fifteen years old.

My mother once said, 'Suicide is a very big sin. It's murder. People who take their own lives go to purgatory. You can't go to heaven if you take a life. That is for God only. It is a cardinal sin.' These words were spoken in my youth, and this is possibly the reason why I could not see past them. Words like that are bigger in your youth and somehow grow with you, more securely implanted.

Everything seems to crack, then crumble from my brain to every facet of my life. I put one foot in front of the other, and long moments turn into days and sleepless nights, which in turn become weeks, months and a year. I can no longer think logically. There is nothing to live for. I am gay, and for me there is no hope or future, not even in eternity—particularly not in eternity.

Everything the institutions tell me I must be, I am completely not. Everything my parents encourage me to be, I am not. I see no hope, I see no joy. I withdraw deeper and deeper into myself.

There is no way to escape other than to remove myself totally. Planning my own death is like being offered the key to a cell that you thought had no door. Knowing that there is a way out is more exciting than anything else.

I had planned an end that would not fail. I shiver when I think back now, for those feelings were so strong that I know without a doubt that I was very close to freeing myself at any cost.

What saved me? Well, it was faith, blind faith in the end that took about two years—a last effort of total trust in a 'Master of the Universe' that I believed cared.

So I came through or, more accurately, turned back from the brink.

19

I can now run the dreaded 2.4 in under nine minutes, with *staaldak, webbing en geweer.*

Ethan is my escape. I submerge myself in my feelings for him and block out the brown world. In the long and boring army hours I have intense conversations with him. I complete him so perfectly in my mind that I know (or think I know) his opinions and thoughts on every subject. So real is the Ethan of my mind, that from time to time the army fades away behind my fantasies. But the army is bulletproof, and soon it gathers around me, regroups and walls me in again. Through it all it is Ethan I ache for—an ache larger than the Defence Force.

Knowing that somewhere out there is someone I love, so purely and simply, is almost enough.

At night I go to the toilet and conquer the copper sulphate they put in our coffee to curb our teenage hormones.

I wake up to him, watch as he goes to the bathroom, returns heavy with sleep, and I know I will feel his hard and swollen morning fullness next to me. I smell him. The smell of his skin is an undiscovered script in a secret tongue for only me to read. It is lovemaking, not sex. Each time in a different place, carefully chosen and finely tuned. The light, the place, and how we come to it, are savoured details in the steps to my climax.

When I've discharged I feel empty. From the warm, light place I am dropped rudely back into the after-climax reality of the glazed facebrick walls of the toilet. While I clean myself and make sure nothing is left on the rim of the toilet or my skin, I pray that no one has heard me or knows what I've done.

'*So, het jy lekker draadgetrek, Van?*' Did you have a nice wank? A familiar question, compiled from the meagre stock of overused phrases.

***

Behind the last row of Golf Company bungalows there are buildings used for storage. One of them houses two rows of Speed Queen coin-operated washing machines—six in total. We all prefer using them instead of the deep concrete basins with the corrugated washboard sides, pockmarked and chipped over the years. But the washing machines no longer work and these rooms are hardly ever visited.

For this reason two boys from Platoon Two choose this place to express their physical affection for each other. It is an affection that has grown over the past few weeks, in this environment of only men, sweat, exercise, PT, communal showers and a system that encourages close relationships between buddies.

A fellow rifleman from their platoon spies on them and calls one of the instructors. The instructor is in the NCO mess drinking, and instead of approaching the two lovers on his own, he is joined by five fellow instructors, each one panting with anticipated retribution.

When the door bursts open, the lovers are kissing. They are still in an embrace when their heads jolt towards the door and their ecstasy is replaced by dread. When they turn to face their superiors, their brown pants are tight with their erections.

The instructors are ready for the attack with towels and pillowcases filled with the working parts of an R1 rifle.

The following day while the boys are recovering in the sickbay, the instructors tell their story to anyone who wants to and doesn't want to hear—a big thing in this small-minded community. Apparently, during the assault, one corporal repeatedly shouted, '*Boks hom, boks hom!*' ('Punch him, punch him!'), and from then on the two are called the Boksom Boys.

The assailants are the heroes and the two young men are further punished by being sent to a psychiatric ward. Their parents cannot help them—they are the property of the State. Going to the press is not an option, as the love between two men is illegal and punishable by law. The parents are told that their sons are mentally unfit and unsuitable for combat or training. This will leak into their communities, where the parents' and the boys' lives will never be the same again.

The army makes it clear that should there be any further such incidents, the boys would not be offered the *humane* option of being *cured, at great expense to the taxpayers,* by Defence Force *professionals*, but there would be a court-martial and they would be found guilty and sent to the detention barracks.

The one boy is from a conservative Afrikaans farming community in the Northern Cape, and the other the son of a minister from a small Free State town. The minister's son stands up for himself, proclaiming his love for the other boy, who in turn says he was seduced and wants to be cured.

In the week before they are sent to the medical facility, while they are on light duty, the troops and instructors seem to have carte blanche to taunt and abuse the two boys. Now there remains no sign of the affection they shared before.

On the Saturday before their departure we are called to the parade ground. The company commander speaks to us about the war, the communist onslaught, the collapse of Christian values and the barbarism of black people. Then he says, 'Will the two pigs come forward.' He says it with a sigh, as though it pains him to even look at them. Someone shouts 'Boksom Boys!' and almost everyone laughs.

The two boys, who are not sitting together, make their way to the front. The minister's son doesn't jump to attention when he reaches the captain, and I fantasise that it is his way of being disrespectful, although that would constitute almost unimaginable bravery.

'This before you,' the commander says, 'this . . . is the lowest form of life you will ever see. Take a good look.' Turning to them he says, 'You are shit, kaffirs, dogs, animals. No, you are not worthy of being called animals; not even animals carry on like you do.'

The minister's son stands upright, his shoulders broad and his head high. Suddenly I am filled with awe for him.

In the evening I see him enter the ablution block and I follow him.

The building is dark and wet. The sharp smell of chemicals and urine hangs in the air. He is in a toilet cubicle and I can hear him urinating. We are alone in the building and I decide to wait for him at the basins, where I turn on the tap and wash my hands.

When he comes out, he surveys the room, hostile towards the world and looking for the route of least possible human contact. But I turn around when he is directly behind me.

'Hi,' I say as gently as I can.

'Hi,' he replies, suspiciously.

'My name is Nicholas.' I hold out my hand.

'Deon.' He shakes my hand but doesn't smile.

'Deon . . .' I want to choose my words wisely, but all I'm able to say is, 'don't let these people get to you, OK?'

'Thanks. I'll try, but at the moment it's difficult.'

'I'm sure,' I suddenly feel tremendous compassion and respect for him. He is tall, with particularly broad shoulders.

'Would you . . . like to chat?' As I say it, I know I'm taking an enormous chance, but at the same time I feel the excitement of taking this risk.

We choose a quiet spot on the lawn in front of the tuck shop. I don't take my eyes off him for a second. Deon tells me that his father's ministry has suffered so much because of the rumours and this incident that he has requested a posting as far away as possible from the town that has now been tainted by this event. His mother has suffered a nervous breakdown and his father and brother told him it would have been easier for them if he had died in combat. There would have been honour in such a death, but now he is dead to them—and has ruined their lives forever. If I'd had the guts, I would have reached out and held him.

Of all of us Dylan is most visibly upset by what has happened on the parade ground.

20

'What! The! Fuck! Is going on here?' Dorman shouts and looks as if he is slowly being filled up with a red liquid.

Someone, somewhere, stitched together two ends of a piece of elastic to make a garter, but didn't do it well enough. The thread unravels, stitch by stitch, until the garter snaps, slips from the leg of Dylan's pants and releases it.

Such a small thing . . . such a big thing.

Dorman is livid. Our platoon has to run back from the rifle range while the other troops ride back in Bedford trucks—group punishment for the loss of Rifleman Stassen's garter.

It has been a day of heat, training and PT. For Dylan it has been far more severe. During our last lecture of the day he was made to run around a tree with his rifle above his head while we had a smoke and water break.

He stands to the left of me, breathing heavily, with his helmet, webbing, browns, boots, and his rifle at 45° over his chest. One leg of his pants hangs over his boot, unlike all the other pants in the platoon, which are turned up and held by elastic garters.

'We are going to fuck you up, Stassen,' someone whispers with thinly disguised hatred. 'You'd better not sleep tonight. When you least expect it we are going to fucking kill you.'

The army's way of disciplining is to punish the group for the misdemeanour of one person—let the group get rid of him if we can't. This reverse psychology is beyond the grasp of most of the troops and turns into the mob justice it was intended to create.

'Platooon leeeeft . . . turn!' We turn left on the balls of our right feet and heels of our left, rifles at 45°, to the count of 'one . . .' The movement to bring the trailing leg up to the left one and stamping it down, is interrupted for two counts: '. . . two, three!' Then with well-rehearsed precision we bang down our right feet to the final count of 'one.'

We start the run back in formation, while someone calls the time. The first Bedford passes us, then the second, until the last one has gone. We are left alone on the mountain, with the sound of our boots, the counting, the dust and the exhaustion. And we will probably not be back in time for supper.

Dylan is running ahead of me. I watch his ill-fitting kit bounce on his back in hypnotic rhythm. The only part of *him* that I can see is between the helmet and his shirt collar. The rest of him could be anybody. Even his tanned arms, bent and straining against the weight of the rifle, look unfamiliar.

If the army says we're no longer individuals, then why do they choose to punish him so severely? They single us out and pick on individuals because they know it doesn't matter how hard they try to break us down and mould us, we are not like them and never will be. Under the browns we are fantastically unique, and they cannot destroy this power.

After running for about two kilometres, some of the boys start straggling and unravelling the formation. But it is the boy in front of me who bears the wrath of Sergeant Dorman's loathing.

It's strange how thoughts can pop into one's head from seemingly nowhere, even if one is exhausted to the point of collapsing. Last night's conversation with Dylan reruns in my mind:

'Tell me a story.'

'I'll tell you a story of Jack . . .'

'Nick!'

'OK . . . uhm.'

'Anything! Just tell me something!'

'My grandparents were children on opposite sides of the Boer War.'

'Wow, and they allowed your parents to get married?'

'Yes, I actually credit my father for that. It was tougher from his side, but he did it.'

'Shows you how quickly things can change. It just takes a few brave individuals.'

'Maybe it can happen between the blacks and the whites?'

'You think?'

'You know there are many really good—no, great—Afrikaners. They're not all like these fuckers. Look at that guy Oscar, for example.'

Dorman halts the platoon, mainly because *he* is tired, even though he doesn't carry any kit or a rifle. He makes Dylan run around a bush some distance away, while we are resting.

When my friend returns, Dorman instructs him to pick up a huge boulder and tells him to run at the back of the formation to prevent injury to the rest of us. He hands me Dylan's rifle to carry.

It is getting dark. We will not eat tonight, which will put us at a disadvantage tomorrow.

Dylan is crying, silently, as he starts lagging behind. Only I see it because I'm running with him. When we reach the camp gate, he has fallen so many times that his pants are soaked with the blood from his shins.

For the last few kilometres we are allowed to help him. Oscar and I drag him, and two others carry his rifle and kit.

We wait for most of the platoon to finish showering. The seven open showers smell of steam, dirty humidity, soap and wet cement.

Our biggest concern is some boys in our platoon who are threatening to harm Dylan. He is under the shower next to me. I have soaped and rinsed, but he is just standing there. My eyes move up his frame to the dark hair leading to his navel on the ashen skin. There is no fat on his body, and every muscle is visible. The water picks its way over the shapes, hitting his shoulders and running down his chest, over his stomach, down to the dark hair where the water collects and runs down his shaft, arching over his uncut penis as though he is peeing.

The expression on his face is distant—not some place away from the pain, but rather some place taken to by the pain. He talks to me, at first without looking, knowing my attention is on him.

'I'm sorry, En. Are you also angry with me?'

'Are you crazy? You have done nothing. Fuck them, Dee. Fuck them. This is just the way things are here, you know that. After a while they will find someone else to pick on. You know how it goes!' As I speak I realise that I am losing him. Strange that I should know this, for there is no change in his expression or the way he stands. I wonder if he might hear me if I speak more calmly, but I am pressing on, desperate to ease his pain: 'Dee . . . Dee, Dylan! Stop worrying! Promise me you will stop worrying.' But I know he isn't listening to me.

'Nick, I don't know how much more I can take; how much more I want to take. It's not just what happened today; it's everything. It's the way those boys were humiliated. You know, the guys who were caught kissing.'

'Yes, I will never forget that.'

'But it's more than that . . . more than just the army . . .'

It is the only time he ever talks about giving up.

'Then ask for an RTU. Who cares? Before you know it, we'll be out of the army.'

'No, you don't understand.'

'What do you mean, Dee? It's not worth it. It's just two years; no, only one and a half left. Dee, think about it: only one and a half . . .'

Why does he not answer me? Is he crying? Too much water . . . I can't see. He just looks down. The water hits the back of his head, flattening the spiky black hair, then streams down his face. His back is slightly bent. Little jerking movements rattle his body as he gasps for air and spits out the water he has sucked into his mouth. He turns the water off and reaches for his towel. He buries his face in the towel and then pulls it down over his drawn features, like a curtain on a new act: composure.

In the dark at the end of the day I uncoil the tension. Knotted by anxiety, I release myself into the warm water of imagined bliss. Before crossing the threshold of mystery, I have a shower with Dylan. It's a different time, later in life, after swimming, his hair long to my imaginings, his body brown, still fragile, his face laughing. And there is that look, the look that I understand, that I know. And want. And need.

21

Uncle Dirk is furious that he's lost the parking space. More so, I think, that it was to a black man whose car he would have liked for himself.

'He may be richer than I am, but he will always be black. Probably stole the bloody car!'

My uncle says something as we drive past him. The black man looks up and walks towards us. He bends menacingly into the open window. He is wearing a heavy silver chain, and as he bends forward it swings like a pendulum, weighted by an elaborate crucifix. There is a thin silver Christ on the cross. The altercation is brief, because it is clear that this man, who is prepared to confront him instead of cowering, is intimidating uncle Dirk.

Today we have to walk a longer distance from the parking to the public swimming pool.

Amongst all the people, the food, the colourful towels and the excited shouting of the children around the pool, I notice a man. He becomes the focal point of my day. He is probably a year or two into adulthood, and he is a perfect specimen. Every part of him is firm, all the shapes flawless, his smooth, tanned skin stretched over muscles of an obviously superior genetic disposition. He is in his prime.

It is alluring to watch a person who is aware of his beauty

and its magnetism. He is wearing an electric-blue Speedo, sexier than had he been naked. He knows the power of sexual desire and handles it with ease.

When he steps onto the diving board I study his exquisite proportions, burning them into my memory for later use in the toilet. The part of him that I look at the longest is the V at the bottom of his long torso, leading into his bathing costume. He doesn't dive in, but jumps up and slips into the water feet first, like going down a kiddie's slide. He makes a very small splash when he breaks the surface and goes all the way to the bottom of the pool, staying there until he needs air. Then he shoots himself out of the water like some exotic aquatic god.

He is my day. I go into the water and watch him swim. I blow out air so that I can sink to the bottom of the pool, which I time carefully as he approaches. Under the water, through my goggles, I see that two tiny silver bubbles have attached themselves to his nipples.

22

'What you doing?' Dylan asks.

'Chilling. Just resting, thinking, daydreaming.'

'What you daydreaming about?'

'Oh, nothing really. What you reading?'

'This . . . shit really, but I don't have anything else. She,' he points to the author on the cover, 'has this patronising way of writing about Africa and the black people, and the attitude of the white characters is nauseating.'

'You mean, some of them are really nice, as long as they don't move in next door.'

'Exactly. The book is actually about the time of the riots. Where were you during that time? I mean, were you affected at all?'

'The valley where we lived had only two roads out, and both ran through black or coloured areas.'

'Radical. All I really saw of the riots was what was on TV. It didn't affect my day-to-day life at all.'

'It was totally different for us. On bad days we had to travel in convoy with Police *garries* to get to school—guys with their rifles sticking through the mesh sides. If we couldn't wait for a convoy, we would use briefcases or our school bags as shields and wind down the windows so the shattered glass from the stones wouldn't get into the car.'

'Not nice. But weren't you scared on the farm? I mean, one is so much more vulnerable on a farm.'

'The valley became organised like for civil war! Radios were issued in case the phone lines got cut; there were coordination points, first-aid classes, and people started carrying guns.'

'Did anything ever happen, I mean on the farms?'

'No, nothing serious . . . I was attacked, well, actually my friend was.'

'Oh yes?'

'One Saturday night this friend and I are riding along a gravel road on our motorbikes and suddenly I hear this dull sound, like aaaugh! And Anton, my friend, slumps forward over the tank of his bike. The bike swerves, but he manages to control it. He can't get any air into his lungs though, so he just starts slowing down. And there are people running after us and shouting.'

'What was it that hit him?'

'A crutch. Can you imagine the blow; the swing and the speed of the bike, how hard it must have connected him? In the chest.'

'Shit.'

'And in front of us more people jump out. It was a proper ambush.'

'No way!'

'And I'm begging Anton, "Go, go, go, go faster!" but he can't. He is just gasping and lying over the tank, and there are people behind us and in front of us. I accelerate and get through, just by luck. But when I look back, Anton's motorbike light moves in an arc to the ground and goes out, and the engine too. Shit, Dee, I was so scared.'

'And?'

'Well, next thing there's this group of people running towards me, with Anton up front. But I reckon they are so drunk they won't be able to run for long. And in any case, they have the bike. So I turn around and Anton hops on, and we clear off.'

'Shit, man!'

'He had two broken ribs and a stab wound, we only discovered later.'

The guy next to Dylan starts playing Carole King's *Home Again* on his tape recorder.

'Mm . . . I love this song. *Sometimes I wonder if I'm ever gonna make it home again, it's so far and so out of sight. I really need someone to talk to, and nobody else knows how to comfort me tonight . . .* Shit, this brings back memories . . .'

We listen to the song for a while. Dylan has stopped singing, his mouth is still moving slightly to the words, but he is thinking of something else and looking very sad.

'Carole King reminds me of boarding school,' I say, trying to draw him from whatever he is thinking.

'You were at boarding school?'

'Thought I'd told you! Loved it. Best year of my life. Everything changed. I sort of pulled myself together, made lots of friends. Booked myself in, just told my folks.'

'They let you?'

'Yep, had no choice. I was earning my own money. What could they say?'

'Wild!'

'You know, if I think of it, that was the day I left home . . . you know, emotionally. I was independent from that day on. No, I was already independent mentally. I think that's actually where independence lies . . . being emotionally independent.'

'How did you make your money?'

'Did a little pig farming of my own. Bought a sow from my folks with sixty bucks I had saved up. She didn't let me down. Always produced a good litter.'

As Carole King starts singing *You've Got a Friend*, Malcolm walks in and asks if I have some shoe polish for him. I spin the combination lock on my *trommel*—my steel trunk—and take out a tin of Kiwi polish.

'Here, Mal, you can have this one, I've got another.' He smiles, takes it, and as he walks off he sings, 'Ain't it good to know, ain't it good to know you've got a friend . . .'

Dylan sighs; I look at him and he says, 'I can't read this. What you thinking about?'

'Actually I was thinking about the year I was trying to pass maths.'

'Yeah?'

'I was forced to take extra maths with this guy, Mr. Leroy. Shit, Dee, I was so bad at it, man, and everybody was making such a big deal about it, you know. My father would say, "You're going to become a tramp on the streets if you don't have maths." And it became like a mountain to me.'

'So how did it go with the extra lessons?'

'Mr. Leroy? Ha, hysterical!'

'Tell me!'

'Mr. Leroy was outwardly friendly, plumpish, short pants and thick, bulging legs, like Little Lotta in Boere shorts. His hair was gone, apart from a U-shape around his head, but he took these impossibly long strands of hair from the one side and combed them over his head to cover the bald part. And he

166 - ANDRÉ CARL VAN DER MERWE

kept it in place with something that hardened the hair, or maybe with sweat, I don't know.'

'Sis no, I can just see it!'

'And under the hair is this head that looks like those travel cushions one uses on a long flight, you know.' Dylan is loving it.

'And?' I keep quiet and think back, trying to picture as much as possible to relate to my friend.

'The table we worked at was between the lounge and the dining room, completely off-centre. I remember how it upset my sense of symmetry. He constantly sucked those hard, round peppermints and they would knock against his false teeth and make a clicking noise. Thing is, Dee, he would move the mint with his tongue from side to side and at the same time dislodge his false teeth and slot them back into position with a sort of a clunk.' We both laugh. 'There was so much going on in that mouth it seemed over-full and busy. There was no space left in it to still teach maths.'

'I love your stories!'

'I tell you, man, it was impossible to concentrate!'

'Who could?'

'But that's not all . . . He would rub my leg as he spoke.'

'No!'

'Yes.'

'What did you do? I hope you just got up and fucked off?'

'No, the thing is he would do it with a kind of affection, not sexu. . . like not meaning anything more by it.'

'Yeah, right! Did you ever tell your mother about it, I mean him touching your leg and all that?'

'No, and you know why? Because I was embarrassed, or I thought she wouldn't believe me.'

I can see the grey sky behind Pappegaaiberg through the small window where I sit struggling with the maths. Before me Mr. Leroy starts writing smaller and smaller in an attempt to save

paper. He scribbles new figures between others, confusing me
even more.

'Then one day—Dee, this is specially for you—he snorts to
clear his nose and after talking through the snot for a while,
you know, with that hollow, wet kind of sound, he spits it out!
Right there!'
    'NO shit, man, no, stop!'
    'Yes, I swear!'
    'Aaugh!'

The Oudtshoorn afternoon is drawing to an end. Our 'off' day
is over. Outside the light has a strange pre-dusk luminosity.
Dylan has told me about his locked-in life, from the school he
attended to the university he has been enrolled in. He tells me
that even his career has been planned for him, and he says he
feels jealous of my life with its freedom of choices.
    We are close and quiet and again we listen to *Home Again*,
uninterrupted.

***

Malcolm, it feels to me, has the ability to get through anything
life puts in his path; not through, but over—comfortably over.
He has an innate awareness and a finely tuned humour. He is
remarkably flexible, yet never loses his identity.
    Malcolm's father never really recovered from his mother's
departure. Mal lived with this heartbroken man for most of his
life and took care of him and Mal's sister. Not financially, but
as I listen to his stories, I realise that he in fact was the stabil-
ity in the house—the strong one.
    It is always easy to be with him, and Mal is tolerant of the
fact that I constantly bring Ethan into our conversations.

Dylan, on the other hand, is dark and inaccessible, but he opens up to me in small, trusting steps, and I have time; I can wait. I will know him forever.

Dylan copes with the training, the pole PT, obstacle courses, and in the buddy PT we are always paired. He carries me, and I carry him. As he runs carrying my weight, equal to his own, it is painful for both of us. When we stand guard, we share the duty, and I am grateful for having him.

'Crack' is a common word in the army. If an instructor doesn't like someone, he tries to 'crack' him. Once cracked, the conscript will request an RTU and leave. Cracking someone with a strong will is an excruciating process to witness. It becomes a contest— one the instructors cannot be seen to lose. It is therefore just a matter of time, but sometimes that time extends too far.

***

'I will die.'

'What?'

'It's just an observation. We're all afraid of it and we all sort of know it, but we don't allow ourselves to *know it*, if you get what I mean.' I don't answer, just keep on looking at him. 'We don't really know that we can die when we *want* to, but we *can*, you know. It's liberating.'

'We don't allow ourselves to *know*, Dee, 'cos we need to survive. We spend our lives fighting the one thing we know for sure will happen! Our whole focus is on survival . . . on just the opposite of dying. What's the point if we expect to die or think about it all the time? It should just hover sort of too far away to think about.'

'No, En, I can . . . I can actually die, and I don't mind it. It *is* conceivable.'

'Don't think about things like that, especially not here. Shit, man, get a grip. Aren't things bad enough? Stop talking like that!'

In front of us are all the parts of our R1 rifles that can be dismantled. The smell of rifle oil hangs in the air. I take a two-by-four, thread it through the copper part of the *deurtrekker*, which we use to clean the barrels, and start feeding it through. I continue until the two-by-four comes out clean.

There is nobody in the bungalow except Dylan and I, but I look up and check again to be sure when he asks, 'Tell me about your toughest time ever.'

'No, not now.'

'En . . . trust me!'

'I don't know if you will understand. It's really difficult. It was a time of madness . . . shit, man.'

'Trust me, En.'

'The thing is, Dee, why I don't think you'll understand is 'cos it involves God.'

'Why do you think I won't understand?'

'I don't know. It could sound crazy to you!' On the gleaming floor in front of me a single ant is searching for a way home, or for food, or whatever. It seems lost in this desert of Cobra polish stretching ahead of it in what must look like a glowing eternity. I know it can't see as far as the edge, or the wall, or the door, for it darts in different directions. Thoughtlessly I try to see if there is a pattern to its search and say, 'OK then.'

'It was just before you went to boarding school, you said.'

'Yes, it was the year before I went to boarding school, but I guess it started way before that.' I tell him everything except the most important thing, the one thing that caused all the fear and paranoia. I tell him the symptoms but not the cause. The rifles stay disassembled in front of us, and all the time Dylan's dark eyes don't leave mine for a second.

I try to tell him about the fear of evil and evil spirits and of sin. I finish by telling him that I know now I had a private kind of nervous breakdown. And then the words start to become thick in my throat.

When I stop talking, I don't regret telling him. He knows this and says nothing, for he knows that I know he understands. After this we are even closer.

'Give me a name,' he says quietly.

'What?'

'Come on, give me a name.'

'I like your name, Dylan.'

'My parents gave it to me, so it's someone else's. I want one from you, En, one to make my own.'

'I already call you Dee. Does anybody else?'

'No, but it stands for Dylan. I want something from you.'

'OK, I'll think of one. Shit knows, we've got nothing else to do.' I tell him I think he is weird, but in truth, I'd like to give him a name.

We are quiet for a while. In my mind I trace our conversation back to his question and ask him, 'Dee, what was yours?'

'My what?'

'Your worst time.'

'It was in New York actually . . . by far.'

'New York? Why there?'

'I often went there on holiday . . .' A whistle sounds, calling us to roll call. In the platoons formation I am not directly next to Dylan.

We shower and then it's lights-out. He never finishes the story.

***

For us, winter starts in a trench—a trench Dylan and I have dug for ourselves, hacked out of rock and shale, where even the soil is as hard as granite. At night we sleep in this trench for the few hours we are allowed between training sessions.

Until now, I have thought I knew what cold is, but what I feel in this trench should then be given another name. We live in this wet trench through a desert night—then another one, then another, until three weeks have passed—in cotton clothing, with no thermal underwear and sleeping bags so thin you can see through them.

At five in the morning I break the ice in my fire bucket. There is a layer of ice on my R1 rifle that sleeps next to me. I shave with the ice water. It is so cold that my skeleton feels a deep and cutting pain, and I vow I will never in my life feel like this again if I can help it.

Our food comes in tins without labels. For three weeks our meals consist of half a tin of beetroot or beans.

By day we leopard crawl over rocks and thorns. Our arms are scarred for life when the wounds on our elbows don't heal for weeks on end. Our clothes are worn through, and then the skin and then the muscle. With our rifles cradled on our forearms we crawl like geckoes, on the sides of our knees and elbows. Flat, like limbless dogs, we drag ourselves day after day on raw sores.

At night, during live ammo training, the ghostly artificial light bathes everything in grey, distorting shapes, warping nature with light-producing mortars.

Alternate lines of men move forward, kneel and fire, while the other troops move between them and repeat the drill. In this way the whole company moves ever forward while thousands and thousands of bullets are being fired.

It is during this kind of training that accidents happen. As the troops move past larger bushes and trees, they lose their formation, while shots are being fired on either side of them.

What are we learning to do? Spending a year to learn to kill. My R1 rifle is designed for the sole purpose of destroying other humans. Our chaplain—the Dutch Reformed *dominee*—reminds us during church parades that we are fighting in the name of Christ. Not a gentle Christ, not a Christ of forgiveness, but a Christ of the assault rifle, a Christ of killing.

77529220BG Rifleman N. van der Swart, blood type O+, training to kill others of his kind, is told about his rifle, 'Memorise the number, this is your new wife, girlfriend, mother. It is your life, for without it you have no life.'

The most significant night in the trench is triggered by rain.

The bleak day gives way to deep-grey clouds that hide the sun and its warmth, drawing the night in prematurely. At five in the afternoon the clouds start relinquishing their contents.

'I don't care if you drown, but if you as much as move from your trench, I will fucking shoot you. Do you understand?' Sergeant Dorman shouts above the rain.

'Yes, Sergeant! But, Sarge.'

'No buts! Are you fucking junior leaders or fucking moffies? This will be a test. We'll see who survives, and if you don't, you are RTU scum! Listen to me carefully: if you crack, you can fuck off. Do you understand, you rotten cunts?' The rain is lashed from side to side by an icy wind, sending it through clothing and any aperture in our flimsy army raincoats.

'Yes, Sarge.'

There is rain in my eyes, water trickling down my neck, under my clothing.

'Yes, WHO?'

'YES, SERGEANT!'

'ARE THERE ANY OF YOU WHO ARE CRACKING?'

'NO, SERGEANT!'

'ARE THERE ANY OF YOU WHO WANT TO GIVE UP, NOW?'

'NO, SERGEANT!'

Through the rain and wind he shouts that the day's training is over and that we can go back to our trench homes.

When Dylan and I get to ours, my bag with all my clothing has fallen over and is lying in a puddle of water. Everything, including my sleeping bag, is drenched.

All attempts to construct a bivvie and a gully to divert the driving rain, fail. In the dying light of day I watch in misery as the torrent outside causes water to gush in, soaking my sleeping bag even further. I try frantically to bail the water with my fire bucket, but it is not big enough. I unclip the dixie—a bigger, square aluminium container we use for food—fold the handles over, and start bailing again.

I am frozen; frozen with the knowledge that I am cracking—cracking like ice.

Dylan gets me through this night by keeping me warm. He tells me to take my wet bush jacket, shirt and vest off and gives me a dry vest for the night. He unzips his bag and tells me to get in next to him. Shaking, I slide into the heat of his stomach as he turns towards me. He puts his arm around me and tucks his legs in behind mine. I shake in large, jerking movements.

I try to talk, but my clenched jaw makes the words shake and rattle, so I stop and I listen. We pull the sleeping bag over our heads. Eventually my body temperature rises and he says I can sleep if I want to, he will watch the time.

If we are caught like this, a far worse hell awaits us, far worse than an RTU or any other shame—DB.

'Don't talk,' he says. 'Don't think about the army, don't think about the cold, think only about what I tell you, OK?'

'OK,' I stammer.

He speaks as if to someone very dear to him, in the way a parent would talk to a deadly sick child, stroking the child's hair and dabbing his forehead. And Dylan's voice is free of its usual tension.

'I'll tell you about love,' he says, and I expect to hear a poem.

'The love I dream about. Just listen and sometime you can tell me if you believe such a love is possible.' At that moment he squeezes me slightly and hesitates. 'I want the person I choose to love one day, and to spend my life with, to know unequivocally that what I give is pure. That person must realise that we are together because I want to be there and not because of a piece of paper or society. I want this person to know that there will only ever be one person for me, forever.'

He keeps quiet and I wait. 'No contracts. The love must live amongst us as a living, tangible thing, even if we are in different countries. I want excellence . . . that unbelievable magic we know is possible . . . that something that comes from here,' his hand moves to my chest and he knocks gently against it like a priest does as part of a ritual in the litany. 'What you get when two people surrender completely to each other. A whole, a completed entity. Think about that. Half of yourself does not cheat or hurt the other half.'

He sighs and I wait.

'I . . .' he waits for a long time and then he says, 'I wonder if it's possible. No, I know it is. What I wonder is if I will be blessed with such a love.'

I understand completely what he says and feel a myriad of questions, almost all of them involving Ethan. He is quiet for a while and I think I should change the subject because I'm afraid he might be talking about me.

'I know,' I say.

'What?'

'I have your name. Remember, my name for you?'

'Yes. I knew you would come up with one. What is it?'

'Well, it's not a regular name. It's more like a description.'

'I prefer that.'

'Dark Flame.' Then I giggle nervously, because suddenly it sounds so pathetic and stupid. 'Sorry, I know it sounds a little melodramatic, but it fits. Guess it would have been better if I could have given it to you in Greek or something. I'm sure it would have sounded more poetic.'

'No, I like it. I like it a lot.' He pulls me towards him as if to say thank you, but the movement is sexual.

Dylan's arm is over my chest; my wrist has fallen into his hand. I hang on to the closeness, the warmth, the giving. I snuggle deeper, pushing into his heat. There is hardness, or is there? Is it his web belt? Can we lie like this and stay like this? We are lying like lovers, and it is too big for me.

Surprisingly I have never fantasised about Dylan, but with this closeness I feel a stirring in me. And so we lie with the enormity of the situation ringing in my ears.

The rain has stopped. Around us the soaked earth gets colder. In front of me I feel the cold trench wall staring at me, and behind me is Dylan's warmth.

'I want to tell you something,' he says and hesitates. There is a tension in him as he says it, the slightest quiver, and he keeps quiet. This is it! He is going to tell me. I don't want to hear it. No, we are too . . . in each other, too close.

If the circumstances had been different, I could have made love to Dylan. A part of me is yearning for it, but my mind wants out. I don't know how to answer any major revelation. Not here, not now. I don't want to talk about it. Talking will put an edge to it. Maybe it's nothing, but I know, I can hear in his tone, he wants to tell me something important.

I do not answer him, and he remains quiet. It feels as if he wants to be encouraged to go on talking, but I wait.

Still he says nothing. Thoughts move into the space and they grow; too many thoughts, quiet for too long.

'What is it?' I eventually ask, and wait, but he doesn't answer.

Does he feel what I'm thinking? Does he know that I don't want complications in this hell, here in the lap of the devil?

Sometimes we live through events that impact on our lives

forever, but while they are taking place we don't realise their significance—pivotal events that end up haunting us.

***

On the last Sunday night in the trenches, the platoon is allowed to make a fire. In the excited warmth of the crowd I hear, 'So I've got her in the Volksie and I'm fucking her silly, her feet against the windscreen, and next thing I know she's kicked the whole windscreen out!'

They all have stories like these, trying to outperform each other, out-penis each other. Hardly listening, I think about the dreams I had last night. I don't know the man in my first dream, but the feeling I have for him is something I recognise and know intimately. The next dream was about my unborn nephews—Bronwyn's children—and I feel a strange affection for her, who will one day carry these souls waiting for bodies.

Then I see him sitting outside the circle, outside the warmth of the fire.

Dylan is holding his cigarette differently. Not delicately with the tips of his index and middle finger, but between his thumb and index finger, sucking hard, flicking the ash and then sucking again. Unaware of my attention.

The following day he has two round sores that look incredibly painful: one on his arm, and one on the side of his hand. It is strange, and I am aware of the fact that I have stumbled upon something secret and intimate. I am not sure that I want to know about it, afraid of what I might find.

It is late the following Sunday afternoon that I ask him why he burns himself.

'It was an accident. No . . . no, it wasn't. I never want to lie to you. That will make me too much like *them.*'

'Well then, why? Shit, it's weird man.'

'Not really. I will tell you—it's no big deal—just not now. Just believe me, when I tell you, you will understand, but there is so much you need to know about me first. Just be patient, will you?'

***

After the weekend Dylan says. 'I know a bit more about the music you like.'

'Hey?'

'Bob Dylan. Not just *Blowin' in the Wind* and *Mr. Tambourine Man*. Really great, En.'

'Did you listen to *It's Alright, Ma (I'm Only Bleedin')*?'

'Yes, you were right. I do like it. It appeals to my sense of . . . how did you put it? Uhm . . . of what lies below.'

'So you've been listening, hey?'

'Yes, all I did this weekend. Do you have *Blood on the Tracks*?'

'Yep. Great, hey?'

'Just couldn't stop. Listened to it over and over. How was your pass?'

'OK, but the strange thing is that as much as I long for them, somehow they always leave me dissatisfied. Yours?'

'Yeah, OK, I guess. My father and I had our usual run-ins. Besides that, as I said, I pretty much listened to Bob Dylan all weekend. Long drive, I was so surprised when Dorman let me go this time. I sort of prepared myself to stay, so the whole weekend was a bonus. Disappointed, why?' he doesn't wait for me to answer. 'Let's go outside, I feel like a fag.' I follow him, and I know there is something bothering him.

As we walk past the TV, which hangs from a bracket in the corner of the room, he hesitates. I follow his gaze to the screen, where long black cars are driving down a wide street in New

York. The camera pulls back and over the city. I recognise the Empire State and Chrysler Buildings. The sound is turned down.

Dylan has stopped and is staring intently at the screen. I look to see what is drawing him. He has an expression as though he is watching injustice to vulnerable people or cruelty to animals, and I recall him saying New York is where he had the worst time of his life. Making a mental note to ask him about it, I turn back to the screen.

'Hey, Van, change the channel to number two, man,' someone says.

Dylan leaves the room. Before following him, I change the channel.

'And turn up the volume. Thanks, man.'

When I get outside, he has chosen a seat on the cement wall between our bungalow and the washing line. His legs are crossed and he is taking a cigarette from a pack of Lucky Strikes. He is bent over, frowning and serious.

'What happened in New York?' I ask.

'Oh, man . . . bad shit!'

'What?'

'I'll tell you some time.'

I can see that I need to be patient. Approaching the subject carefully I ask how often he went to New York.

'A couple of times; got family there. Great art, you'll love it.'

'Lucky you. I'd dig to go, love to study there, seems so full of energy . . . vibrant.'

'Yes, filled with good and bad. Very good and very, very bad. You have no idea.' He taps the back of the cigarette against the pack, making a 'tock, tock' sound, after which he brings it to his mouth.

'Like?'

'Just decadence, brought on by boredom, I reckon. People who have so much are always looking for entertainment, for a thrill, a fix of sorts. I have an uncle there.' He waits a while.

'My father's youngest brother, very good-looking guy. Very, very different from my father; doesn't work, lives in this great apartment, just parties all the time. I've stayed there a few times. Interesting holidays.' He turns to me and looks at me as though he is waiting for an answer to a question I did not hear.

'Interesting in what way?'

I know he is not going to answer my question, for he has been quiet for too long and his expression has shifted.

'Something that has stayed with me is the . . . evolution, I guess; the travel of man's development—a course set by circumstance and the environment.'

His sentences are crammed with the possibility of so many directions that I feel ignorant and uninformed. It irritates me and yet keeps me fascinated.

'Everything is "done": nails, body, hair . . . body hair. If it hasn't been altered, or doesn't cost money, it doesn't seem to have value.'

'You can get damaged people who are not wealthy, Dee, like emotionally or because of circumstance.'

'Yes, but what I'm talking about is different—dark. I must try and explain this properly.' He looks at what he wants to tell me as though he sees it again to record it accurately.

'It was as though she fell harder because she was already so far removed, and the woman helping her was the same, bending down . . . it sort of didn't fit: the stockings on the asphalt, the long, perfect hair constantly in the way, the skirt not designed for the manoeuvre.'

'Deeee . . . you're losing me.'

'When she bent over to give the woman CPR, the bright-red lips and made-up faces were so artificial, I just wanted to say, "Leave her alone, she's been dead for a long time!" It's like she can't be dying; she is not real. And the woman trying to give her CPR was so uncomfortable and awkward, so low to the ground. Like she had stooped to another world.'

'Dylan!'

'Sorry, Just . . . this woman . . . had a heart attack outside Bergdorf Goodman, the side entrance, like between the door-man and her stretch limousine in that small space that ordinary people use . . .'

'And the other woman?'

'She was young. Groomed and perfect. Designer every-thing. Straight black hair, thin, clearly never been so close to a pavement in her life. It was like worlds collided, without expensive Italian leather in between . . . I mean like shoes . . . the dirty pavement and her skin products. Touching, actually touching, weird that the contrast was so significant to me that day . . . but it was.'

'Your uncle, is he one of *them*?'

'Yes. It's just that to me he is synonymous with New York. Hedonistic bastard, just has to have fun all the time, the sick fuck.'

Dylan shakes his head and takes out another cigarette. It is the last one. Before he lights it, he crushes the box, almost like he wants to punish it for being empty.

Then a whistle blows. He looks at the cigarette and says, al-most to himself, 'When you think you've got nothing more to lose, there is always something else.'

'Are you guys coming? It's post parade,' someone shouts as he runs past us.

'Hey, DF, cheer up, man. What's wrong with you?' I say as cheerfully as I can, and I get up. 'Come on, come to post parade and afterwards I want to hear more. Sounds mighty mysterious to me. Come . . . I mean, if you want to.'

'No, nothing for me there, Nick.'

'There might be.'

'Nick . . . En, there are times when things happen, you know, like those two guys who were put on parade in front of the whole company. Things like that—big things.'

'Yes, what about them?' I sit down again.

'Well, I reckon those guys will always be affected by what has happened to them. They will always carry it with them. Things like that can change a whole life. We are just lucky if we're not damaged too much!'

'Dee, listen to me. You must look at the brighter side, man. Shit, you sound scary. Come to post parade. Come on.'

'En, there is nothing I can get there that will change things.'

'How do you know?'

'Let me put it this way, nothing I long for.' A pause, then, 'Nothing that will change anything.'

As I get up to go, I think I hear him say, 'Nothing to save me.' So I say, 'How do you know?'

'I know. I know what I'm yearning for. Go on, En. Go!'

'Fuck, you're a complicated dude. Just come, man.' He gets up and walks with me.

The corporal who hands out the post is in a good mood and has allowed the group to sit on a small stretch of lawn. He sits in front of them on a cement wall, and we stand behind him, waiting for our names to be called. When I turn to talk to him, Dylan is gone. I start looking for Malcolm, find him and sit down next to him.

***

At long last Ethan's letters arrive.

The instructors sniff the letters before they read the surnames of the recipients. Often the senders spray perfume on the pages to their loved ones. The conscript is taunted about it, but somehow the attention just enhances the fantasy of the woman carried in the pages—the stronger the perfume, the prettier the girl. My letters never smell of perfume. Anne's letters are filled with a different scent, more complex, unique—something they can't smell. To me her letters smell of wonder.

'Another one for Van der Swart, you fuck.' The letter is flung at me—its final journey from Ethan to me. I turn it around and beam. Malcolm smiles, because he knows.

Then there is another one; same name but different address. This is the letter he had sent just after our parting. I hold it in my hand. He has touched this very paper, sealed it, and perhaps even licked it?

I sit on my trunk, holding the letters. They feel more valuable than anything man has ever made on earth. Ethan is in hospital. Voortrekkerhoogte. Operation. In great pain. Where am I? Am I coping? Am I in Oudtshoorn? Would I get the letter? He misses me. Mother coming to visit. The person next to him is recovering from a spinal injury sustained on the border. Their Hippo hit a land mine. But the best part: *Love, E.*

The second letter is different. He is on a medics course. Re-classified G2K1. Also Voortrekkerhoogte. So pleased that I have visited his mother. Now knows I'm still surviving Infantry School. Encourages me. So impressed. I must please write. (I have! Three letters! Why hasn't he received them? What if he never gets my letters and stops writing? What if he thinks I don't want to be friends or that I've made new friends? What if he never writes again? I must write tonight, to this address again!)

He seems to like the course. Helping people. Possibly saving a life. Doing something positive in this place. Bored. Frustrated. Missing home. Surfing. When will I be on pass again? Perhaps the same time as him? *He has made a friend.* He has made a friend! But he misses me and signs it again: *Love, E.*

Somewhere in the background I hear a rifle shot. So engrossed am I in this fragile connection with Ethan that it passes by my conscious mind. Only when I hear the screams—no, not screams, more like shouting, raw and anguished—am I shocked back to reality. And I realise that the equilibrium has been disturbed permanently.

Someone is crying, like a child, but the sounds are those of an adult. Someone else is repeating the word 'NO' over and over again. I get up, drawn to the noise.

In the short distance to the ablution block, I begin to realise. The words haven't been formulated, but I know. In my legs I feel the downward pull of a superior gravity, a gravity of another planet, a planet I now occupy, with an awful largeness of load. I don't see Malcolm, who is running straight towards me. Grabbing my shoulders, he says, 'It's Dylan, Nicholas, he's dead! Don't go in there, please, don't go there!'

But I break free and run.

Someone is holding his head, another is vomiting. Lots and lots of noise. People running. More people shouting. One bare bulb lights Dylan's body. There is an expression on my friend's face that burns into me, never to leave me again. It is a horror that can only be achieved when half of one's head is missing. I stand there, breathing and seeing, but I am a crucible about to explode from the thermal shock of molten metal.

There is too much of everything—too much blood, too much of him against the ceiling and the wall, too many people.

Next to him lies his R1 rifle. In the dimly lit room is a smell, partly of the rifle, and another smell for which I have no reference. If I should ever smell it again, I would recognise it instantly, for it too crawls up next to the image that has become imprinted in me forever and now huddles in a dark corner of my head. The concrete floor has cracks in it, and part of Dylan has flowed into them like blood trying to find a vein. This is my last observation before everything in my head switches off.

A doctor at the sickbay gives me an injection when Malcolm takes me there after finding me, shivering, behind the furthest bungalow.

The doctor, an army captain, seems compassionate and kind. I salute him and conform perfectly to my army programming. Within moments the drug's numbing effect takes over and I'm in a dull stupor.

Shock, anger, confusion, hate, emptiness, love and a blunt sense of self-control—this is what I feel. Strangely, the overwhelming emotion I experience immediately after Dylan's death is a sense of survival. If I allow myself to give in to my feelings, everything will spiral out of control. In an environment where there is no mercy or understanding for the expression of love between two men, I need to keep absolute control. So I suppress what is boiling up inside me.

It was entirely my choice, and I hate myself for it. I hate myself for not cracking, for not disintegrating, for not allowing myself to unravel in the face of the army, the other troops and my parents. I despise myself for not breaking down for my friend, as a last token of my love and admiration. Some days later they give the company a talk on the matter of Dylan firing a round through the roof of his mouth. But the talk is about Dylan's weakness, and threats if they should find out that anybody is even contemplating something similar.

'We will not tolerate this kind of weakness here. People like Stassen must go and kill themselves some place else. It's bad for the name of Infantry School.'

At that moment a substantial chunk of respect for mankind is torn out of me, and my soul is scarred. This talk is one of the most difficult things I have ever endured, listening quietly while containing an explosion inside me.

But I do find a tiny degree of pleasure in realising that this event has in fact rattled those higher up in the ranks. And when *they* rattle, everyone below quivers.

The captain keeps quiet and peers at us as if we have thoroughly inconvenienced him. His cheeks, red from burst veins, are puffed out in anger and revulsion.

'We know everything.' Again the pause to make sure every serviceman's attention is on what he is about to tell us. 'It has come to my attention that Stassen had, how shall I put it, a sickness . . . uhm, a perversion, actually.'

I start praying silently, my eyes fixed on the man. *No, no, no, please, dear God, no.*

'Stassen was a *trassie* . . . a homosexual.' It is as if the word leaves his mouth and drives straight into me. 'He was expelled from high school, I am told, for the deviant act of . . . of fiddling with another boy.' Another sigh and mumbling as the captain looks out over his company, allowing his words to sink in. 'You see, it wasn't something the army did. He probably couldn't live with himself any longer, being—how should I say?—sick . . . perverted. According to the experts these people are mentally ill. It's a sickness, and I'm told they hate themselves so much for their evil lusts that they simply can't live with themselves.'

He has everybody's attention, allows them to murmur for a moment, then strains his red face on the sun-beaten neck, twists and waits again. When he resumes, the troops are quiet.

'You know what pisses me off? It's that I must sit with all these homos in my fucking company. What have I done? First those disgusting fuckers, those . . . what d'you call them?'

'Boksom Boys,' the troops chorus.

'Yes, them. First they're caught fucking smooching each other, and now this. Well, I've had enough. I can tell you I don't deserve this. If there are any more moffies here, get the fuck out of my company NOW! That some boys don't know if they're men or women . . . sis . . . sis! And now I sit with the bloody mess. It shouldn't be our job, but what choice do we have? We're given a bunch of sissies and we have to make men out of you before we can hope to beat the shit out of Swapo! What gets me . . . ' he waits for everyone to realise that this is even worse, 'is that we, yes, WE, get the bad name. The papers and the peo-

ple in civvy street think it's OUR fault.' Our officer commanding is so angry he needs time to calm down.

'Yes, it's become so bad that there is a special ward for people like Stassen. Did you know that? Who knows about this
ward?' He looks around. 'Come on, don't you know anything?' A hand goes up. 'Yes, yes, Pretorius.' The boy jumps
up, stands at attention and shouts, 'Ward 22, Captain!'

The captain thanks him in little more than a whisper, and in
a quiet, acid-laden tone he says, 'Ward 22 . . . where all the drug
addicts, madmen and deviants are sent. At great cost to the military. We, WE, have to fix them up. With very little thanks, I
can tell you. To think that you . . .' and he points at us, 'you risk
your lives for people like that, you and I, but that's just how I
am. I've sacrificed my life for this country so that my children
and family, and your families at home, can sleep safe. And that,
yes that, is why I joined the Permanent Force.' Changing his
tone, he shouts, 'It burns my arse that I'm creating a safe country for people like that too.' In an unusually brave move, someone takes advantage of the captain's inclusion of us as the country's saviours and asks what happens in Ward 22.

'I don't know. I haven't been there.' When they see him grin,
everybody laughs, too loudly, for too long. But he does seem to
know. He is the captain and he knows *everything*. 'They treat
them with sophisticated techniques, I am told, and eventually
they give society a perfectly balanced individual who can inte-
grate, get married and have children. What they should fucking do is shoot the fucks! So if there is anybody here who has
even the slightest doubt whether he's a moffie or not, talk to
your corporal and we'll help you. But God help you if later on
this year I find more moffies here. I swear to God I will personally see to it that you're sent to DB if you as much as touch
another man, so help me God. So now is your chance.' He
pulls his nose up by puckering his mouth, and his bushy moustache exaggerates the movement.

'Remember, it's against army rules to take your life. You're not allowed to harm yourself, because you have no right over yourself. Touch army property and I'll see to it that you go to DB. That's a promise on the lives of my children. I swear I'll see you go to DB.'

The army chaplain is a Dutch Reformed minister and he talks to our platoon in one of the instruction rooms. His tone is pseudo kind and he talks about the sin 'this boy' has committed, the pain he has caused his parents and his loved ones, and the cost of this selfish deed to the army.

He looks at me and says that I, as he is told, was the boy's best friend and I should be angry for what he has done to me. I say that I'm not. My anger is so patent that he doesn't address me again. Besides, on my records it states that I'm Catholic, which means that I'm beyond redemption.

Never once do I lose control. I am well trained in such matters—Frankie, failing at school, my religious conflict and my sexual wiring, to name but a few.

Numb perseverance, experience, genetic make-up? I wade through the un-wadable. Unlike in mutual suffering such as my brother's death, I don't have the luxury of being cradled by the sorrow of others, of being inside shared pain.

In the small mirror in the shower complex I look at my own image. Dylan and I showered here . . . just the other day. If I look closely, I can feel him here, in the dark distance of my peripheral vision. He is here in a strange, unfilled way. His words push and strain inside me; all the things he told me, closed, continuous echoes.

I cup my hands under the tap and splash my face. Then I do it again and again, but it doesn't help. I lean on the basin and stare into the small square mirror until it frames my face and I can see nothing else. Just my wet face. Everything else is cut off. But it is not. What I want to remove, I can't. I'm breathing . . . in and out, in and out . . . for how much longer, I wonder?

I look at my eyes as though for the first time. They startle me, for I see inside them something ethereal. Yet all they really are, are round shapes in different browns with small black holes in the centre, from where little flecks dart as if on fire. They are just shapes, that's all, just shapes, but they have the ability to disturb me.

What would they still see? I wonder. Behind my eyes, that's where it all is. In there are the images.

The mirror starts clouding up and I write on it *Dylan, Forever Young.* As I write the words, they evaporate.

Around the building the wind is groaning, cold and agonising. It breathes in and bemoans its fate, incessantly, like a colic child. But this is no sound from a child—it's a beast with an unending ability to express its wretchedness.

***

Malcolm becomes a patient comforter. He stands by me, next to my emptiness . . . no, my fullness, overfull of emptiness.

The comfort of this closeness and understanding is what makes me decide to join Mal on a pass to Johannesburg. It would be easier not to have to face my folks now. Or is the real reason that Johannesburg is so close to Pretoria, so close to Voortrekkerhoogte . . . so close to Ethan?

Instead of giving two more guys a lift to Johannesburg to help pay for the petrol, Malcolm decides that we should travel alone and make it part of our holiday.

He has planned a weekend jam-packed with activities, all

designed to help me forget. If Mal doesn't succeed in healing me, he definitely starts the process with this dizzy weekend, filled with so much excitement that I have no time to dwell on anything else.

We scamper from movies to restaurants, sometimes three in one night for different courses, even on different sides of the city. We play and sing a selection of songs over and over, so loudly that the speakers distort.

He calls me Scank and later puts our songs on a tape that he calls Scank Tape One. Every new day starts with, 'I *must* show you this,' and we burst forth into the next adventure. For this weekend Johannesburg becomes the most exciting city in the world to me.

***

'Nick, are you awake?'

'Yes.'

'Shit, aren't you tired?'

'Exhausted.'

'Well? You must get your beauty sleep, boy, so we can scank it up tomorrow. I've got lots planned!'

'I know. I wish I could.'

'Is it . . .' I don't answer, 'you know . . . Dylan?'

'Yes . . .'

'Try to think about something else.'

'I do, but I haven't been able to sleep since the . . . Sometimes I sleep a little, but it's a restless sleep. I have nightmares and it's like I'm not asleep or awake, you know . . . terrible, half-asleep nightmares.'

'What kind of nightmares?'

'The sight of him lying there, dead. I can't get it out of my mind, Mal. And then all the things he said to me whirl around in my head. It's like I can hear him, I know exactly what he's saying, what he thinks, everything.'

'Maybe you should go for therapy.'

'No, that would be the end of Infantry School, I tell you. They don't want a *malletjie* as a junior leader. Remember, we're supposed to be able to kill. We can't be freaked out by death.'

'Yes, but this is different.'

'I'm not sure they'll see it that way.'

'What is worrying you the most?'

'Well, that I could have prevented it. Shit, Mal, I really think I could have. I really do.'

'Well, you could NOT have, so stop thinking you could. Absolutely, you could not have.'

'I miss him, and you know . . . he was such a gentle guy. I mean, he really was special. And he was intelligent and kind and mature. I just can't . . . I guess I just don't understand it.'

'I never really got a grip on him, to be honest, just couldn't make a connection.'

'Most people couldn't.'

'But you did. You must be grateful for that.' Again we are quiet. I am overcome by the need to tell Malcolm that I think he was in love with me and had I been more sensitive I could have prevented this tragedy. But to do that, I'll have to tell him that I'm gay.

'Malcolm . . .'

'Yes, talk as much as you like, I'm here.'

'What hurts me the most is, I was with him just before . . . you know . . . and he drank some water. I mean, why drink water, what for, if you're going to kill yourself? It just doesn't make any sense, man . . . fuck!'

'Don't think about it. There are things we'll never understand. What did you talk about?'

'Just before?'

'Yes.'

'New York.'

'New YORK? Why?'

'I think it had something to do with people who live a certain kind of life, you know, really spoilt people. He seemed to detest wealthy people. No, not wealthy people, rather people who are ruined by wealth; people who get bored because they have so much. But then, maybe I didn't understand what he was trying to say. I know he was really freaked out by those two guys who were caught kissing!'

'Fuck, that was bad. I wonder how they beat the *blouvitrioel*.'

'Copper sulphate doesn't stop one from falling in love, just from being randy. But maybe they didn't drink tea or coffee. In any case, Dylan was freaked out about that incident. He said stuff like that changes one's life.'

'Nick, you must admit he was a little . . . odd. I mean, one doesn't kill oneself 'cos one doesn't like rich folk!'

'No, Mal, there was other stuff.'

I want to tell him about the cigarette burns, but decide not to.

'Shit, Nick, you've got a strong streak of oddness yourself, you know! Just promise me . . .' he giggles, 'you must know, I'll kill you if you die.' I realise that Malcolm wants to lighten up the conversation, but I'm not ready yet. 'C'mon, Nick, tell me a story.'

'You know, he used to ask me that.'

'What?'

'To tell him a story. But at the moment I only have nightmares to tell.'

'Are your nightmares only about him or about other stuff too?'

'Yes and no. Some are, but mostly they are incidents from my childhood that I seem to relive again. They come up as if they are somehow linked, but they aren't, if that makes any sense. I'm having a recurring dream again. I last had it as a child, after my brother's accident. I swear I haven't had it for years and now I'm having it again, exactly the same! And then

I have these memories that seem so clear, from my youth, like it happened yesterday. I don't know if it's the training, or the lack of sleep, or the thoughts about the border, or what.'

'Like?'

'Like this one thing that happened to me years ago.'

'What? Tell me. It'll be good for you. And at least you won't be thinking about Dylan.'

I lie on my back looking up at the ceiling. Here I am, in a house in Johannesburg with a friend, and my old life knows nothing of me. They never really knew anything about me, did they? Now they don't even know where I am. Maybe it's a good thing, I think, so that if I don't return from the border it will help them that they've let go before.

'Nick?'

'OK. I have an uncle who lives in Namibia. Once upon a time, I had an uncle who lived . . .' I laugh and so does Mal. 'My mother's brother, stunning farm, shit, Mal, wild and unspoiled. Well, one day my uncle and I drive out with this black guy on the back. Mal?'

'Yes, I'm listening.'

'He let me drive; I loved it, this old Landy. You know, the one from the sixties, the one with the lights in the grill, not like the *garries* we use in the army. They have a face, with little cheeks, and he would remove the grill and use it as a braai grid when we did meat over the fire. So clever, those old ones . . . with the dashboard in the middle, all metal, no plastic.'

I lower my voice. Next to me my friend's breathing has become deep and rhythmic.

This room of Malcolm's is so different from Ethan's—like two different worlds. Ethan comes from such wealth and privilege. Clearly Malcolm has had a much harder life. I guess that's why he is so streetwise, so life-wise.

Strange how the army throws us all together, how many different lives become intertwined. Good thing actually, otherwise I would never have met Mal. Under different circumstances, I would probably not have given him the time of day. And now he is the most important person in my life—yes, more important than Ethan.

I wonder what Dylan's house looks like. I'm sure it's really grand. I must go and see his folks, but not now, not this weekend. I need time. Actually, I felt more equal to him than to Ethan, like he judged the world by other standards. I guess I'll never know.

Oh God, take my friend's soul and give him peace and forgive me, forgive me . . .

I must stop thinking of this now. I must sleep, must sleep . . . think of something else.

23

Uncle Ben and I are alone in the Land Rover. It's the same model used in the movie *Born Free*. Bright light is blazing through the dirty windshield and hot air rushing into the cabin through the large openings where the doors used to be. On the back stands a black man with the darkest skin I have ever seen.

Uncle Ben stops and asks me if I want to drive. He knows I would love to. He warns me that it will be difficult driving and if we get stuck it will be a long walk back to the farmhouse.

'It's probably more than a day's walk, and we have very little water. We'll be travelling some distance in a dry riverbed, through thick sand. Do you think you can handle it?' I am blindly confident, not the way I feel when people ask me to play cricket or rugby.

'I'm sure.'

'We'll need the red lever—that's low range—for the next

stretch.' The yellow lever pops out as I move the red lever back. It hooks. I move it forward again and back, and then it slides in.

The concentrated torque causes the vehicle to leap forward.

'You hardly ever need first gear when you're in low range, Nick. Try pulling away in second.' The transfer case gears whine, and the Land Rover is thrown from side to side as it cuts through the deep sand.

'Now build up speed.' There is urgency in uncle Ben's voice. 'We need to get up that embankment. Faster, faster!' Before me an almost vertical riverbank looms, the engine races, and the vehicle starts climbing. Some of the wheels lose traction, then grip again, and we crest the bank.

'Well done, Nick! You're good at this, aren't you!'

We follow a track up the side of a plateau, over large mounds built to cope with the slim possibility of flooding. As we reach the top I look back. Below us the plains stretch as far as the eye can see, and the dry river looks like a darkened line scribbled untidily on the immense expanse.

We drive towards a windmill that has been erected in the middle of nowhere to feed the concrete water trough providing a lifeline for animals of all kinds. Next to the trough is a wire cage. I can smell sheep droppings, and there is a smell of decaying meat in the air.

Uncle Ben walks around to my side, looks down and shakes his head. 'Those bastard baboons,' he says and I walk towards what is left of a lamb. Like a spineless fluffy toy, I think. There is still fur, dirty dull-wool covered skin shrinking around its putrid frame. The animal's head seems hard and old. The eyes have been pecked out and the mouth is open. The expression the lamb now carries is of a forgotten tiny death.

The black man takes a metre long metal rod from the back of the Land Rover and walks over to the cage where a baboon is pacing back and forth in a space probably no more than twice its size. She becomes highly agitated as we approach, exhaustion and thirst forgotten, for she has never been this close to humans. From her back an infant crawls around her for protection—it knows its mother is distraught. When it reaches her chest, her arm moves instinctively to cradle it.

Uncle Ben takes the rod from the black man and carefully chooses a position in the wire mesh of the cage. He rests about ten centimetres of the spear on the bottom V of the mesh and moves the rod so that the point aims directly at the baboon's chest. My uncle and the animal move continuously, as if in sync.

The baboon hesitates for a fateful moment, and the spear drives into her chest. She grips the steel shaft, but the force pushes her against the back of the cage. The metal slides through the fine muscles around the animal's chest, finds a path between two ribs, tears them apart and punctures her left lung. Now she grips the spear with both hands but doesn't have enough leverage to pull it out.

The baby clings frantically to the stricken mother, its eyes wide as they follow the attacker's movements. The third stab penetrates the mother's organs again. The rod is pulled out, coated with mucus and blood. The lung boils through the hole, making gurgling sounds. White, red and pink froth bubbles out over the black hair, and then sucks back. Now the rod gets shoved into her abdomen, lacerating her organs, and eventually the mother's body can take no more shock and she collapses. The baby silently clutches its lifeless mother.

They open the cage and drag the mother out, with the bewildered infant still holding on tightly. The black man tears it off its mother by its back feet, swings it, screeching, through the air and brings it down on the edge of the concrete base. It takes only this one movement to pulverise the little animal's skull.

24

I get up to go to the bathroom and when I get back into bed, I hear a change in Malcolm's breathing. He rolls over.

'Shit, Nick, I'm sorry, I fell asleep.'

'No problem, you sleep. I'm almost asleep too,' I lie. 'Good night.'

'Sorry, man. Good night.'

'Night.'

When we do training with bayonets, stabbing into bags, I know what it will look like when someone tries to pull the rifle out of his punctured abdomen.

'Troops, if the bayonet gets jammed, just fire a shot. It will dislodge your weapon immediately.'

He takes me to dinner at The Bali Hai restaurant in the Landdrost Hotel. We get drunk on white wine and then I say it. 'I'm gay.'

'Really!' Smiling, looking at me closely, he says, 'Wow, I thought so. I mean, I hoped you'd be. So am I!'

'No way! Ssshit, are you really? Oh, thank heavens. How did you know? About me, I mean.'

'I reckon because, well, because I am,' he smiles, suddenly confident. 'And of course it wouldn't take a rocket scientist.' He laughs. 'When one listens to what you talk about . . . no, *who* you talk about all day long! Ethan, Ethan, Ethan.'

Later on, serious for just a moment, he asks, 'Nick, was there anything between you and Dylan?'

'No, no, nothing.' This is not the time, I think. Besides, we're gently drunk, happy, stranded for the moment on this small island of ours before we have to jump into the torrent again. There will be a day when I will share what I believe to be true about the death of my quiet, dark friend. Now is not the time.

Malcolm, who is determined to make everything perfect for me, says, 'Let's try and see Ethan, Nick, c'mon, let's just go!'

'OK, let's!'

'He's little more than an hour away. Tomorrow we'll phone and ask when they're allowed visitors. Ethan, Ethan, Ethan!' he singsongs, laughing.

'Shit, Mal, that would be great. Just imagine if I could see him.'

'I know! And I have another surprise for you tonight!'

'What?'

'I'm taking you to a gay club, Scankie.'

'No way!' But my tone says 'YES way' and I start shaking ever so slightly.

'The Dungeon. It's the oldest gay club in Africa.'

'Gay clubs are illegal, Malcolm! What if we get caught?'

'I say fuck 'em. Tonight we live! Nick, just think about it: when will we have the chance again? Besides, it's Vasbyt next, and then the border. I mean, we're in for hell, man. I need some cherry to think of when I'm on the border. Come on, let's do it for *volk en vaderland*.'

'What? Have sex with a man?'

'Yes. We can't go to the border without spreading a little of our gooorgeousness around . . . for *volk en vaderland*! Tonight they're having Mister and Miss Dungeon.'

I'm trembling, but inside I'm experiencing a wave of exhilaration.

'Hey, listen, are you going to tell him how you feel?'

'No, never. Are you mad?'

'Just tell him! What do you have to lose?'

'What do I have to lose? How about everything.'

'What's the point of being so in love with someone and you can't even . . .?'

'Mal, don't tell me you haven't fallen for a straight guy before.'

He sighs. 'You're right. It's the story of our lives. Fuck, if only we could know; always hoping, thinking they're cute and nice and sensitive, but never having the courage to ask.'

'Especially at school. Shit, if they as much as suspected you were gay, the whole school would persecute you. I mean, you just couldn't take the chance. So I reckon the club is the answer, hey?'

'Yep, Scank-maaaaaaster!'

'Well, although I'm leaving a nineteen-year old closet behind me, I want you to know I still want everything to be right when I eventually get lucky. I'd want the feelings to be mutual. I guess that's why I've never made a move on a straight guy. I mean, not since puberty.'

He laughs. 'Oh yes, do we have a slut in the house then? Ah, a man with a history.'

'Well, I . . . er, we were just experimenting.'

We trade stories about early high school, about the boys we were in love with. Then I become serious for a moment. 'Malcolm, I can't tell you how important it is to me to know there is someone like you. You know, I mean, normal.' We both burst out laughing at the word 'normal.'

'Yes, me too. You secret agent, man, whore you.' Then, laughing loudly he says, 'Agent man-whore!'

'I wish!' He holds out his index finger, I do the same and we lock them together.

'Our handshake, OK?' For a moment we look at each other, the wine, the drunkenness and our fingers locked together, and I feel a new happiness about this friendship—something I have always longed for.

'It's time. Let's go and look for some "mutual feelings" OK? Or do you want to drink some more? Shall we have another bottle?'

'No way, or we'll be the ones who won't remember a thing.'

Mal bribes the waiter to give us a bottle of wine, to open it and replace the cork. He steals two glasses, and we leave with the wine under his jacket.

We finish the bottle in a park. We giggle about everything—stupidly drunk. Through the murkiness of the alcohol I feel a happiness so different from the manic, insecure sexual love I feel for Ethan.

'So, who do you think is the cutest in our company?'

'I don't know, you know I have eyes for only one man. Shit, I can't believe I'm saying these words out loud, it feels so good!'

'The little prince . . . Ethan, Ethan, Ethan. Come now, whoooo . . . iiisss the cutest?' Mal is in no mood for seriousness.

'OK, there's no competition, without a doubt . . .'

'Who, come now, I won't tell Ethan. Who?'

'Oscar.'

'You betcha. Shit, he must be the most stunning boy in Infantry School. Nothing like a cute *boereseun* with a lekker *boerewors*!'

On the way to The Dungeon a memory that was triggered by a word Malcolm had used haunts me. Around me the music plays and the Johannesburg lights block upwards in their concrete stacks. I listen to Malcolm talk but I hear the word punching within me . . . Homo.

Over a weekend in high school, on Arno's farm with a group of friends, reading, listening to music and talking, there is a discussion about an article in a popular Afrikaans magazine—"*Homosexuals: The Shocking Truth.*"

Homosexuality is described as an evil cult, practised behind closed doors. The journalist 'exposes' some people in society posing as 'normal.' Gay men are portrayed as 'despicable and subversive,' perpetrators of the vilest acts.

It is the word 'homo' that for some reason chills me.

There are photographs, grainy long-distance photos, taken

into people's private homes—two men kissing. They appear desperate and sad when they are arrested. It disturbs me deeply, because in a way they have photographed me, arrested me.

There are many references to the Bible and opinions from Dutch Reformed ministers. Sodom and Gomorrah—God's only solution for *them*.

My friends agree with the article and recount, with glee, stories about gay bashing. With sadness I realise I have no friends here, for if they had to know who or *what* I really am, they would despise me.

The building looks a little like a rundown castle. To my surprise most of the men are just regular guys like Mal and I. Some I find really attractive. As we walk towards the building, I repeat to myself, over and over, like footprints into my new life, 'Out and proud, out and proud. I am gay, I am gay,' and for the first time in my life, 'I am OK.'

I feel lighter, intoxicated by the open admission, the madness of words that have now broken free, out in the light, beyond my own bigotry.

'Dolla! Dolla!' A severely wigged, sequin-dressed man swirls around and calls in falsetto to a friend who is some way behind us in the queue, 'Doll-aaaaaaa, did you hear the one about the bi who was looking for a couple?' Hysterical laughter and high-pitched screeching follows while he pivots on his stiletto heels with frightening dexterity.

'It's not always like this. It's just that it's Miss D tonight!'

'I don't mind, I love it. It's wild!'

The show is more entertaining than anything I have ever seen in any theatre: drum rolls, feathers, sequins, the mouldy smell of the smoke generator, the 'old sock' smell of poppers, the overstretched, unbalanced sound, the lights, the overstated, glitzy everything—my first impression of being 'out'!

Mal buys more drinks. The drag artist under the spotlight mimes each syllable of a song with 'her' exaggerated red mouth. The end of each line is like a scene from some tragic Italian opera.

Malcolm beckons me to the loo. I get up and follow him. The toilet fills with pockets of sound as the door is constantly opened and closed, and there is a pervasive smell of urine and sweat. Men make passes at us and we flirt back like teenagers.

'There's someone who fancies you!' Malcolm shouts above the music.

'Where?'

'I'll show you. He's beulah.'

'What?'

'Beulah-beautiful, baby. Just come!'

I laugh excitedly, turn and walk back to the dazzle and the noise. The words swim in the din. *There's someone who fancies you.* A man! And this is fine, and this is normal.

Later, after the show, I dance with Malcolm and then the-manwho-fancies-me asks me to go home with him, but on this night of firsts that will not be one of them.

Ethan . . . tomorrow! I check my watch. No, today, later today I'm going to see Ethan!

Back in bed at Malcolm's house, I pray for my new life, changed around like a windsock by a new prevailing wind, from exactly the opposite direction. And I pray for my meeting the following day.

The landscape of the life I've just left behind starts blurring slightly. From now on I will see everything differently. I will never step back into shame again. I will look at the future from this perspective. And then I sleep.

***

There is a highway between Johannesburg and Pretoria, with urban sprawl on either side. Some day the two cities will become one, connected by office parks, factories and little clusters of nondescript buildings. I find it all so unsightly—untreated sores on the bad skin of a money-hungry city in puberty. On this highway I sit with my heart bouncing around as though it's trapped in a pinball machine.

'Once we know that you can see him, I'm going to leave you two alone, OK?'

'Thanks, Mal.'

Ethan is there and I'm allowed to see him. They send a troop to 'Tell Vickerman there's someone at the duty office to see him.'

Mal shares my excitement, looks at me and says, 'Good luck, Nick. Just enjoy it. But remember,' and he puts on a dramatic, singsong voice, 'there are plenty of fish in the sea!' Then he is gone.

I choose a position from where I can see Ethan walk towards me without him seeing me. Aware of my unsteady heart, wiping my hands on my pants in an attempt to keep them dry, scanning the route and rehearsing my greeting in my mind, I wait.

When I see him approach, my entire body jumps out of focus for a split second. He is wearing browns; his hair is longer, under a new ruby, the medics beret. He stops at the duty counter and asks a question.

Who is this boy? I think to myself in that brief moment before he turns and sees me. Who is this person who commands such supreme dominion over my waking moments? I clear my thoughts, then my throat.

'Ethan!' He looks around. 'Hi,' I say and smile nervously.

'Nicholas! Nick!' He smiles too and I let go of the breath I was holding. He is even more striking than I remember. I'm not

worthy of him, he is too good looking, he will never be interested in me, not even if he is gay, my head races. Breathe, just
breathe slowly. Stand up straight, look sexy, look confident.

'What are you doing here? I mean, how did you get here?'

Is he happy to see me? I search his face, his body language.

'I'm on pass with Mal, you know, Malcolm? Shit, of course
you do. It's our last pass before Vasbyt. We're in the same
company.'

He looks around for Malcolm.

'He dropped me here. He'll be back in an hour.'

'Come, let's sit out here. How are you? Wow, this is so amazing. You are the last person I ever expected!' We walk out and
sit down on the lawn.

'I'm OK. Did you get my letters?'

'Yes, did you get mine?'

'Yep, but only the other day. They took forever to get to me.
Thanks for writing. Shit, the post is slow. It feels like forever
since I last saw you.'

'Yes . . . Nick, are you OK? You look tired, or have you lost
weight or something?'

'I've had a tough time, I must tell you.' I wait a while, look
away and wonder how much I should tell him about Dylan.

'Tell me.'

'Just this whole year, and Infantry School has been seriously
rough. Who would have thought a year ago that our lives
would change so radically?'

'Yeah.'

'How're you finding your course?'

'OK, I guess. It's great that you seem to be doing well. I
mean, we were all so shit scared of Infantry School, but you
seem to be cracking it.'

'You know, Ethan, it's not so much the course—well, maybe
it'll get the better of me yet, because Vasbyt is still ahead, and
the border—but it's something else.'

'What?'

'Something happened that has kind of freaked me out, man.'

'O yeah?'

'My buddy, the guy who slept on the same bunk as I did, well next to me actually—we never sleep on beds there—any case . . .' I notice his surprise and the questioning look; he wants to ask something, but I go on, '. . . he committed suicide.' I put my index finger in front of my mouth and pull an imaginary trigger. I immediately regret having started our time together in such a dramatic way. Trembling slightly, I bring my hand down, my eyes obviously full of pain. He frowns and looks at me searchingly.

'I am so sorry. How close were you?'

'Very. He was my only friend in the platoon. Malcolm is in the same company, but we only really see each other on Sundays.'

'Do you know why he did it?'

'No, well, yes . . . I don't know. They really picked on him, you know.' I keep quiet, convinced that the visit is now moving in the wrong direction. 'I also think he was gay.' The words just plop out. As I say them I can't believe I'm doing it. Am I using Dylan's death to test Ethan's reaction? I look at him.

'Shit, poor guy. I'm sorry, man. We also had a guy, he took pills, and another one died in a car accident coming back from pass. But I didn't really know them. Did you see him?'

'Yes.' I want to cry, but I don't. No weakness in front of Ethan.

'Shit, that's bad. I'm so sorry, Nick. It must have been terrible. Are you all right? Something like this, I mean, it must have knocked you.'

'It's OK. Let's talk about other stuff. How are you, Ethan? You say you like the course?'

'It's all right, but when we finish, they're posting some of us to the border and I think some are staying here for the big parade for the new Head of the Defence Force. General Viljoen is replacing General Malan. They need numbers for the parade. I just hope I don't go to the border. I can tell you Nick, things are looking bad up there. We see the guys here at 1 Military Hospital, and we hear the stories.' He keeps quiet, then he smiles and says, 'Do you remember Middelburg? It feels so far away . . . so long ago, I should say.'

'Yes, I do. I'll never forget that sunset, that Sunday before we left that shit place.' He smiles, looks past me into the distance. Is he thinking of that evening on the hill or of something else? 'Ethan, what happened to you on the train?'

Before answering, he smiles, but it's more like a grimace.

'When we left Middelburg I ended up in a coach where the sergeant in charge was the biggest cunt ever, an Infantry School sergeant.'

'Dorman?'

'Yes, I think so. In fact, I'm pretty sure. How would you guess that?'

'I don't know, it's like that man . . . our paths were made to cross, or crash. Shit, he's such a bastard. Can you believe it? He's my platoon sergeant. He's the guy who hated my friend Dylan so fiercely, and I swear it is he who pushed him over the edge. You know, the last straw. Fuck, I can't believe it . . . the same guy!'

'Well, he gave us an *opfok* all night long, while he was getting pissed. Early in the morning he made me do push-ups. Eventually I just couldn't do a single one more. I knew if I went down I wouldn't come up, so I just kept the prone position and he kicked me. From underneath on my lower tummy!'

'Fucking bastard!' I say, knowing I'm talking too loudly and reacting too strongly. 'The bastard! Oh, Ethan, I hate that fucking bastard.' But I've seen much, much worse; it's just because it was Ethan. 'So what happened?'

'He ruptured my bladder. Shit, Nick, I've never felt anything like it. I think getting in and out of the Bedford afterwards was what really did it for me. I passed out on the parade ground.'

'Yes, I know, I saw it, but they wouldn't let me go to you. I stopped the whole Golf Company. They almost put me on RTU that first day.' He smiles, maybe at the thought of me stopping the whole company for him.

'Well, they took me to hospital, operated, then to 1 Mil, because I wasn't getting better. Turned out the op in Oudtshoorn was a stuff-up, so they operated again. My folks came up and organised a specialist.' He waits a while and changes the subject. 'What did you think of my mom?'

'Great, she was really nice to me. Shit, I love where you live.'

'And you met Precious. Fuck, I miss home. I've only been there once since the op; my folks flew me down.'

'Precious loves you, hey. How is your stomach now?'

'I have a scar,' he gets up, grips his shirt and pulls it from his pants. Just seeing the small sliver of his tummy is hugely erotic. The scar is below his navel on the neat little path of hair linking his bellybutton with his pubic hair. I have been there a thousand times in fantasy, and to the mystery below that— almost too enormous to contemplate now. His stomach has beautiful definition, and he is slightly tanned. Then he lets go of the shirt, loosens his web belt and the two top buttons of his pants, and tucks his shirt in. I see his underpants, the fine hair running through the scar; then I look away.

'I missed you.' As I say it, I regret it. I always say stuff like that out loud, without thinking. Shit, how many times have I told myself, 'Jeez, you're pathetic'?

He says nothing. Why the hell not? He seems so far, so distant. Oh shit, it's over! He stays quiet for a long time. So do I. But eventually he says, 'Yes, me too.'

Is he saying it because I've left him no choice, or does he mean it? I know nothing any more. Vasbyt starts as soon as we get back. Dylan is dead, I still have more than a year and a half of this, my pass is almost over! Then there is the border and those bastard instructors, especially Dorman.

I have a brief realisation of how, in this short time, my emotions reach extremes, even changing in the space of one sentence, and I despair.

'How are the guys you're with?'

'They're OK, I guess.'

'What about the friend you said you've made?' Ignoring my own warnings against later misery.

'I don't see that much of him.'

'Why not?'

'I reckon we're just too different.'

I bet he fell in love with you, I think. You're straight, I knew it! But then he says, 'He's not like you.'

I want to scoop him up, all of him, his whole past and future, and hold him, enfold him, drink him into me, to stay inside me forever.

'In what way?' I'm more confident now and smiling. Those words are enough to hold me up like crutches under a limp Dali balloon.

'You know, I wish you were here,' he smiles. 'So tell me about Vasbyt.'

'I'm kind of nervous about it. The ones who make it, go to the border and then, well, I reckon it costs so much to train us that at that stage an RTU will be too bad an investment.'

'Shit, the border . . . if I'm not chosen for the parade I'll be going there pretty soon too.'

'Be careful up there, Ethan.'

'We'll be in a hospital. It's you guys who have to be careful. You'll be on patrol.'

'Yes, I know. I can't even think about having to shoot people, or being shot at!'

Our time runs out unnoticed, as I am too scared to look at

my watch. Then I see Malcolm parking his car, getting out and walking towards us. He reaches us and smiles, but suddenly everything feels awkward. Mal looks at me for clues and cracks a joke. Ethan says he is only allowed an hour and should go. We say we must go too, and Mal says goodbye. I want to hug Ethan, but I shake his hand.

I watch him walk away. He is looking down, and again I notice how perfect his body looks in clothes. He stops, turns to wave and then moves out of sight. Gone.

I don't remember how many times I re-run every single word he said, reliving it, questioning and chastising myself for a wrong tone or interpretation, wishing I had said more, or less, or something different. I carry it with me during Vasbyt and then the border; but then, it often carries me.

***

On the way back we listen to Joan Armatrading singing *Willow*.
'Mal, I want to tell you something.'
'Tell me.'
'I want to tell you, I have this need to say it out loud, to relate something that straight people can do all the time, but I've never been able to do.'
'What?'
'I want to tell you about my love for Ethan.'
Malcolm takes his eyes off the road for a moment, smiles at me and says, 'It will be my pleasure.'
'It's . . . like . . . well . . . just to hear him say my name. I crave it, I yearn for it, you know. In a different way—like with love, like I've never experienced. I long for him to say my name in that way, to look at me . . . just he and I, and he says it softly. It would be the most beautiful thing ever.
'And then there's this desire I have to say *his* name as a

lover, you know . . . Ethan. I want it so much that it hurts . . . to hold him and hold him and hold him . . . to look at him all night while he's sleeping.' I smile, and to break the seriousness, which I know Malcolm doesn't like for too long, I say melo-dramatically, 'Ethan, Ethan, Ethan.'

***

On the trip back to Oudtshoorn, we are quiet for long periods, unlike the over-excitement of the trip up. I think about the recklessness of telling Malcolm that I'm gay, I think of Ethan and too often about Vasbyt and the border.

The Karoo night around us feels starless and dark. Ahead of us lies the long straight road lit by our headlights. The white lines suck towards us rhythmically, and I picture us slurping them up, filling the car as part of the weight of distance.

'I knew someone who was in Ward 22, you know,' Malcolm suddenly says into the darkness.

'Really, is it as bad as they say?'

'Worse . . . much, much worse. This guy, well, he was . . . is, totally fucked up now.'

'What did they do to him?'

'Everything. Hormone therapy, shock therapy, aversion therapy. You know, the sad thing is, he was a great guy, good-looking, fun, masculine, fit, sporty . . .'

'So how did he end up there?'

'Because he was going to study drama! Can you believe it?'

'No way!'

'Yep.'

'They put him in this platoon, the reject platoon, as they called it, with all the druggies, gay guys and fuckups, and he just rebelled, so they punished him. I believe all the gay boys they catch out,' he turns to me and the lights of an oncoming car reveal a cold smile on the side of his face, 'end up there too. First the psychiatric ward, then DB.'

'Shit. How did you know him?'

'He was three years ahead of me at school.'

'Was he gay?'

'He was. I didn't know it at the time, of course. Never slept with him or anything like that, but shit, I would have loved to.'

'And?'

'No. He's still gay, but he's so fucked up, man.'

'Like how?'

'Well, the hormone therapy changed him. He says he has hardly any libido, but he definitely still prefers men. The shock-aversion-therapy was a bad joke; apparently really painful, but with no results . . . real crap sort of Nazi experiments. He'd act like he didn't like the pictures they showed him and afterwards he'd wank soon as he got the chance. But I think it was DB that finally fucked him up. He didn't want to talk about it, you know; constantly beaten up, slept on a concrete floor, no blanket . . . tortured all the time. Must break one, I guess.'

We are quiet with our own thoughts again, and after a while I say, 'Mal, did you ever think it would be this shit?'

'No, and it's going to get worse. Vasbyt and the border . . .' As we go underneath the bridge that carries the railway line north to Potfontein, Poupan, Kimberley and Johannesburg, Malcolm says, 'Hey, Nick, we're close to Hanover and there's a hotel that does the best ever *boerekos*. I'll stick you a dinner.'

'We won't make it back to Oudtshoorn on time, Mal. There's no way we'll get there by midnight if we do that.'

'Fuck them, I'll tell the duty officer we had car trouble.'

A truck passes us, and the Golf shudders from the displaced air. If it had hit us, we would be dead now, I think.

'OK, that will be great. I'll drive after dinner.'

25

Tomorrow we start Vasbyt, an excruciating five-day route march with full kit and minimal rations.

In the small hours of the night I dream the same dream that came to me night after night following Frankie's death. I see my brother lying with the dark pool of blood under his head. But then it becomes Dylan's head—my friend who I feel I betrayed in the trench. DF, my dark ghost in sharp focus.

I can tell you, I write in my diary, as if to some alter ego, *I've figured something out about fear. Fear has different patterns. It takes on different shapes under different circumstances. It's like the way that every room has a different feeling, only with fear you experience it much more acutely—at the tip of every nerve; from the outside in. This is how it is with fear. If you've been exposed to dreadful situations, you realise that they are all different, like a living evil, with a personality and a specific intent. My feeling about Vasbyt, for example, or knowing there are people who want to kill me, is totally different from the feeling I had with the Bellville Tennis Club, where everybody was watching and I couldn't catch the cricket ball.*

'Hey, Scankie, do you think he's gay?'

'I don't know. He's really different from the rest.'

'No shit, different looking too, different class. Fuck, he's hot. Nice name as well: Oscar.'

'You just like everything about him. You're the scankie one. Stop thinking about him and pack your kit.'

'No, I need something to take my mind off all this. Man, imagine lying naked next to that guy, all sweaty after a long sex session!'

'Like you stand a chance! Do we really have to pack all of this? Step-outs too?'

'Yep.'

'I can't fit it in!'

'Roll it real tight and just squash every layer.'

'It's so heavy, I don't know if I'll be able to even pick it up!'

I finish packing, put my pack on, and the only way I can get up is to go on my hands and knees and then stand up.

***

Way, way above, yet dramatically close, Lion's Head towers. With its body stretched behind, the lion lies vigilant, protecting the life nestled close to its belly above the ocean of the Cape of Storms. Clifton at the end of day—the warm light of the setting sun reflecting orange against the blue rock faces of Lion's Head and the magnificent Twelve Apostles with their feet in the water.

But the true magic lies in the early mornings on the four white, sandy, rocky, bungalow-encased beaches of Clifton. When the sun rises over the distant mountains, the sea absorbs its light. Bands of colour form in the sky above the mercury horizon, turning into turquoise, then crimson and fading into silver.

Through the haze of sun-saturated, wind-still, cold-sea days one can see ships journeying around the foot of the Dark Continent. Far on the horizon they float by, not silhouettes, but soft air, a tone darker, like smoke blown along by a gentle breath.

It is here that I picture Ethan and myself most often. Clifton and an Ethan of my own design is what I think of lying in bed, waiting for the day that will bring the start of Vasbyt.

***

When the body has given up, but the mind ignores the pleading and drives the body through the pain and the protests . . . that is Vasbyt.

Vasbyt starts on a Sunday afternoon, after being frisked, completely nude, even up our arses. We are not allowed any cigarettes or extra food, only the sparse provisions they give us.

On our backs we carry our *grootsak*—literally, big bag— filled with our kit, and below it our webbing. To the front straps we attach the heavy army radio with its face-whacking aerial, which we take turns to carry. Our epaulettes are modified to carry the weight of our rifles; the buttons are stitched with nylon gut to prevent them from sliding off our shoulders.

Altogether we carry more than our body weight. This we will be hauling over very difficult terrain for many, many kilometres.

We walk from Sunday evening to Tuesday morning—approximately 33 hours—and this counts as our 'first day.' This day is a thorn driven into my memory and stuck there, never to fester out. Most of the route is over mountains, between Oudtshoorn and Calitzdorp. There are crevices so wide that each and every one of us falls, and the weight we carry causes some to break their coccyx, others to sprain or break ankles. Alouette helicopters casevac the injured.

Almost every man in the platoon is driven to tears, but not me.

Our food again consists of half a 'mystery-can.' The only thing that is not a mystery is what we find inside—something simply and utterly awful.

Water, cool drinks and food are thrown down in front of us, and we are not allowed to touch it. The instructors know that Vasbyt is their last and easiest opportunity to break us. If we haven't 'cracked' before, this is the time that we probably will—these five days.

One foot in front of the other. Keep your mind off the pain. I do this by thinking of Dylan. I carry him with me. I fantasise about him. In his absence I can love him freely, not sexually, but with a love of regret. And its noise is louder than my body's pleas.

If I had angels, they've deserted me. They are far away, absent, unconsoling in these days, or are they with every foot dragged in front of the other, helping just enough? But if they are helping, then why so little? No, they've betrayed me, for I don't get what I so desperately need: superhuman strength and to be carried—carried away.

On the third night we are high up in the Swartberg mountains, where the temperature drops dramatically.

To get into your sleeping bag, you have to worm in without bending your legs. If you bend them, multiple cramps seize you in painful spasm.

Tonight a powerful PA system plays recordings of horribly disturbing sounds—babies screaming, a sick, continuous shrieking, sounds of animals howling, dying; but merciful exhaustion prevents me from having any reaction to them.

At around two in the morning, I am kicked in the stomach. It is an instructor who demands that we get up and line up. In front of us are two massive silver containers, one with hot soup and one with coffee. We stand, stiff with cold and exhaustion, holding our fire buckets in anticipation.

I am aching all over. It is raw where the straps have cut into my shoulders, and my swollen feet are throbbing in my boots where blisters have burst and are rubbing against my socks. We dare not take off our boots; if we do, we will never get them on again.

I obsess about the liquid; there is nothing I crave more. Steam gushes from the mouths of the huge containers, turning yellow in the gaslight and contrasting sharply with the desert night beyond.

When everybody is lined up, Sergeant Dorman starts a speech. I watch the dark clouds that seem to have gathered to look at the madness going on down below. Like a group of people staring at a road kill, they crouch low, pulling the bleak moon down with them. I pray that they will go and weep about us somewhere else, for if we had to be drenched again, we'll surely not make it. And I focus on the hot soup.

Vaguely aware of Dorman speaking, I hear how he works himself up. Then he kicks over the containers. Within seconds the steam with all its promise of warmth has dissipated over the freezing ground.

Only an hour to sleep—if we are lucky—then the day starts.

Light only starts breaking faintly through the clouds much later. We are in a line again, and again we're being shouted at. For a start to the morning, we are given human excrement to pass hand to hand, all the way through the company. Nothing smells as awful as human shit. We have to squeeze it with both hands before passing it on. With no soap and very little water, we have nothing to remove the smell, even if we could, but we are not allowed to clean our hands, so everything we touch is contaminated. I rub my hands in the sand, which helps to a certain extent, but we'll be walking with the smell for two more days.

From time to time I see Malcolm when our platoons pass each other. We're not allowed to speak, but we have a sign. We hold our fingers out, as for our unique handshake, and over the distance they interlock and we share our secret.

On the fourth night, high up in the mountains, we are even betrayed by the weather. It starts to rain. I believe I cannot go on. I try to stop the water running through the long grass in an attempt to keep my pack dry, for if it becomes waterlogged, it will be so much heavier to carry. The voice inside me, encouraging me to carry on, has become small and weak. My need to give up has almost become an obsession. I am wet, cold—no, not cold, bone-freezing, ice cold—stiff, hungry, sore and desperate. The half of the company that has given up is kept apart, but close enough for us to see that they have warm food and tents to sleep in.

On the last day, those of us still holding on are merely plodding; dragging ourselves forward. Attached to every footprint you can see the drag marks, if you have the energy to look down.

We are in a small group and Sergeant Dorman starts to speak about Dylan. He theorises about the reasons for Dylan ending his life. Because these instructors have such authority over us, they are treated with reverence, and in their ignorance and arrogance, this power soon spirals out of control.

'Stassen was a moffie, a weak moffie, a fucking fudge-packer. If he stood in front of me, I would tramp his balls off.' He brings the heel of his right foot down violently and grinds it into the dirt. 'The world doesn't need shit like that!' The words hack into me, each blow fuelling a hate in me, so pure and so strong that in that moment I understand clearly how it is possible to take a life. I feel like beating him so thoroughly that what drives such words is completely destroyed.

'He wasted our food and air. Do you know how much it cost the army to train him, hey? Now it's all wasted. They should sue his parents for damage to state property, but his parents are probably just as weak and pathetic. Fuck, I hate those spoilt *poeses*. They should just have shot the *doos* on the first day.'

Wanting to get out of earshot, I fall back, but he sees me.

'Hey, Van der Swart, get back here! Are you giving up, you little cunt?'

'No, Sergeant, I will never give up,' I hiss dramatically, showing him how badly he is affecting me. As I increase my pace to catch up, I decide to channel this anger to drive me to complete Vasbyt . . . for Dylan . . . today.

'Van der Swart, you were his little arse-fucker, weren't you? Did you two have a lovers' quarrel? Yes, that's probably why he couldn't take the punch, hey? Hey! I'm talking to you. Answer me, you little shit.' I don't answer.

'So it was you!' He draws out the *you*, making it slither like a worm from his mouth. 'You murdered that little fuck!' His head is nodding affirmation, as if choreographed for effect.

How much can one take? Much, much more than one would ever believe, and still I don't react at all. Because I know that the best way by far to honour my friend, is to beat this man and get through this hell.

My brain blanks out. Black blurs of fury shut my mind down, like a short circuit. Only one tiny clip of logic holds me back, for I know that the man *wants* me to attack him.

He can see that he is getting to me. The energy I am using to fight my emotions comes from a place unknown to me. Dorman waves down a *garry*, which I didn't even hear approach. 'Get in, you fuck!'

'No.'

'Get in or I'll fucking break you. I swear you'll wish you were never born. Van der Swart, GET IN!' But I know, for as long as I carry on, I'm winning.

'No.'

'No, who, you shit-licking fuck?'

'No, Sergeant.' I say firmly.

We are standing still. Everybody has stopped, looking at us, but mainly using this time to rest.

His face contorts, sick with frustration and loathing. In my eyes he sees only revulsion and abhorrence; that much I know.

'Your friend,' he says and I look straight into his eyes, his mouth deformed as he spit-whispers, 'was a fucking fag, fairy, moffie, queer *poes*! And I hate his type.' He knows that there are some troops in the group who enjoy this kind of talk. 'He deserved to die. If he hadn't, I would have killed him myself.'

Against every bit of better judgment, my resistance crumbles, my hate overflows and I whisper, 'You did.' As the words leave me, I know I have crossed a boundary.

'What did you say? WHAT THE FUCK DID YOU SAY?'

Then softly, 'You have started something here that you will live to regret. You have fucked with me and I guarantee you, you will be pleading for mercy. I will see you beg!' But now it is about me and no longer about Dylan, and I have regained control.

Realising that I have not answered him, knowing he will need a witness, he demands again that I repeat what I'd said. Centimetres from my face he screams, 'What the fuck did you say? You answer me now, or as God is my witness I will fucking kill you. I swear I will fucking kill you, troop . . . if it's the last thing I do!' At that moment a Bedford truck stops next to us and a sergeant on the back asks if anybody wants to get on, wants to give up. Now the audience is too large. The moment is broken, and he waves them on. Then he whispers to me, 'I will get you, mark my words, not now, but one day. We still have the border ahead and you, Van der Swart, will not see the end of this year. If you had any sense, you'd give up now . . . give up now, take RTU and get away from me; save yourself.'

He takes me by my backpack, whips me around and uses the momentum to run me off the track, into a tree. I fall. Dorman spits on me, kicks me and walks on.

Someone tries to help me up. I look up, straight at Oscar's dark eyebrows. He pulls at my webbing and I roll over to my knees, from where I somehow lever myself up.

Dorman makes us run the last few kilometres. It is more like shuffling, but it gets us back to base.

When your rifle dangling from your shoulder hits you on the side of your leg and the muzzle hits your face like a bruise being beaten for days on end, when your shoulders are cut by the weight on your back, when your feet are raw and blistered and every part of your body is pleading for you to stop, when your skin is boiling with sores . . . it eats into you like acid.

But the body doesn't really remember the suffering. We know it was awful, horrific, but the way we felt in that moment is not remembered—all the minuscule stimuli, the smells and sounds are imbedded like garlic cloves stuck into a leg of lamb. Everything retains the flavour, but we never actually taste the garlic again, and this is good.

They don't send us home until most of the outward damage has healed. For some weeks we can't wear shoes. The black-blue bruise where Dorman kicked me takes almost two weeks to heal. Our feet start festering. But it is a relatively easy time, because we have made it and we know we'll be going home.

Inside me I have started a war; or is it a war that was started in me?

PART FOUR

1

T hings change more in the way one perceives them than in themselves. This I realise more acutely when I come out of the closet.

***

'It's all *your* bloody fault that I'm sitting here.'

'Shoo-er it is.' Malcolm bounces the words like a ping-pong ball.

'All this Infantry School shit . . . it's all because of you.' I might as well be hugging him, for the amount of blame in my voice.

'Would you rather be with what's his name, the head-shitter?'

I laugh. 'Frikkie. I wonder what's happened to him. Shucks, no way, Mal. I wonder where he is? Just imagine . . .'

'No,' he says melodramatically, 'no gratitude, no, no, no gratitude!' and he feigns hurt for a lack of appreciation. 'You go to head-shitter, your neeeeew best friend.' He digs his fingers into my side below the ribs. My body doubles up with pleasure, and we start wrestling. I am aware that we are too close, too deep inside each other's space for the army, but I don't care.

Then he rolls right over me and lies still next to me. High above me is a cloud that looks like a rabbit, and I think that clouds often do . . . rabbits and dragons, shapes with liberal boundaries, one gentle, and one mystical.

With a small shock I realise that I am happy, happy in that moment.

'It's amazing . . .'

'What?'

'Mal, it's amazing, you know. We're sort of coping, aren't we? I mean, we're still here, and so many have dropped out.'

We sit up on the lawn across the way from the wash troughs and both notice Oscar at the same time. He is doing his washing, shirt off, muscles flexing as he twists a browns shirt, and I know we are both thinking what a magnificent creature he is.

***

After the RTU's of the boys who did not make Vasbyt, the shrinking company is reshuffled at random for the departure to the border.

I am allocated to Platoon Two. Mercifully, Malcolm is too. We have a new lieutenant, corporal and platoon sergeant. We are free of Dorman!

Just before everything is finalised, I see Sergeant Dorman talking to my new platoon sergeant. Then he walks over to me, pulls me out of the ranks and places me in his new platoon, Platoon One.

The three platoons that now form what is left of Golf Company are in relaxed formation as the corporals walk down the lines, taking down names. Somehow Malcolm manages to change places with someone in Platoon One without being detected. This seals his fate, for Dorman's hatred of me will surely spill over to him as well.

Gerrie is also in Platoon One, in our bungalow, and I notice how much he has changed since we stepped over from our previous world to this one. His choice of survival has been to attach himself to the instructors, even at the cost of being ridiculed by the rest of us. In my war with Dorman, Gerrie is not on my side.

There is one more important person in Platoon One: Oscar.

A man with a similar disdain for others as Dorman leads the platoon. His name is Maurice Engel. 'Engel' is the Afrikaans for 'angel,' but this man is a fiend. If one cannot understand why Dorman carries such a deep hate of life and people, with Engel it's clear. Not even his fellow officers like him. In the world beyond these petty rules strung on rank, he is nothing. Engel is simply one of those unfortunate people who will never be popular.

Because he has a primary school teaching diploma in wood-work, he holds the rank of lieutenant. He did not complete the same training that we, or for that matter, Dorman did; yet he has the power to make our lives miserable, and from the out-set it is clear that this is his main aim.

Dominating everything now is the border, dangling in front of us like a hangman's noose. Until now we have faced only the immediate obstacles, one after the other, with the border lying somewhere behind them. But now it is with us.

We are issued with dog tags and instructed to hand in our last will and testament. Each man's blood type is determined and indicated next to the buckle of his web belt.

During this period of preparation (mastering rifle grenades, hand grenades, Claymore mines and shooting at the Swartberg or camp shooting range) something happens that seems insig-nificant at the time. But perhaps nothing is ever really insignif-icant.

Gerrie decides to befriend Malcolm, and with the same zeal that he attached himself to Arno and me at school, and later to his superiors here, he pursues this friendship. And then it abruptly ends. After our last weekend pass, Gerrie is chosen as the lieutenant's right-hand man, which means he even sleeps in the same tent as the instructors when we are out in the veld. Gerrie is thus pretty much guaranteed rank at the end of our course, and protection on the border. His position of intimacy with Dorman and Engel does not bode well for us, and on the day of the inspection by the commanding officer of the entire base this is confirmed.

Before an inspection we stand at ease on our taxis until just before the command to brace. Then we step off them and hide them under our un-slept-in, sharp-angled beds.

Mal is at the door and sees Gerrie standing on his taxi.

'Gerrie, you've got my taxi,' he says, clearly alarmed.

'No ways, Bateman, it's mine.'

I shout from the other side of the room, 'Gerrie, give him his taxi!'

'Fuck you, Van.'

'Gerrie, for fuck sake, there's no time for this bullshit!'

'It's mine, Nicholas, and I said fuck you!'

'Listen, Gerrie, we can sort it out later, just give it to him so that he can get to his bed!'

'If Bateman is so *slapgat* to lose his taxi, that's his problem.'

'It is his, you fuck! I can prove it. It comes from the same piece of felt as mine. Look at the green stripe.' Through the window I see the inspection group approaching.

'Fuck you, Nick, you're always defending Bateman.'

'Give him his taxi NOW, Gerrie! You're going to get us all into shit!'

'Bateman is going to get us into shit, not me.' There is determination in his voice. I see he will not relinquish anything, so I step off mine and throw it towards the door. It veers off to the right. Oscar is nearest to it and he shuffles forward, picks it up and flings it to Malcolm.

Malcolm starts his journey between the beds, past the entire platoon already standing at attention, each in his own way silently imploring some higher force for a successful inspection. If prayer could fill space, his passage down the middle of all the beds would be thick with pleading for a favourable reception by the CO. But Mal doesn't make it in time.

The light that shines on the gleaming floor through the open door is darkened by the figure of a man. It is Dorman.

The inspection group passes the last windows, and like a strip of film slipping off its sprockets, everything starts to move too rapidly. Dorman stands in the door. If we fail, it will reflect badly on him.

The CO pushes past him as he calls us to attention. Behind him are the company commander and the platoon commander, Lieutenant Engel. Everybody is standing at attention, but Malcolm is still halfway to his bed.

The CO walks directly to Malcolm and starts finding fault with everything in his inspection. He doesn't address Malcolm, who is too far beneath him. Instead he insults our company commander in front of the whole platoon. This is not good for us. A flame-thrower has ignited under the captain's skin, snaking like a high-pressure hose out of control and turning him red from within.

Very early the next day we are woken by corporals, lieutenants and sergeants. They are all shouting at the same time, shoving us around and kicking the metal cupboards and the beds.

Soon we are running to the parade ground on the outskirts of the camp, on our way to Swartberg. We are going to have a company *opfok*, in *staaldak, webbing en geweer*.

The sky is overcast. This is good, it will be cooler, I think to myself as we pass the tuck shop. I am already feeling tired. Strange how fear saps one's energy. When we arrive, there is an ambulance and a water truck.

***

My folks wait for me at the Klapmuts off-ramp, the closest point to Banhoek on the N1. From a distance I see the Chevy's rear lights. Then I see the two heads, small on thinner necks in this light, as we pull up behind my parents' car.

My father gets out to talk to my travelling companions, who can't wait to get away. The back door of the Chevy hesitates over the two knuckles of its predetermined positions as I slam the door shut. Inside the car I step back into a small world linked by cables of memory in this space infused with the smell of cleaning products, vinyl and my parents.

My father asks a few questions, but I say very little. It's all polite and very superficial. My mother watches my expression in the light of the traffic sweeping past us, blasting our small space with a sudden flash of brightness. She wants to know how I am, how I really am, without asking me outright. She has a positive response to everything I say, as she mostly does. It is familiar, but at the same time it frustrates me, for I nurse a need for a deeper empathy.

It is the first time since Dylan's death and after the open, if slightly tipsy, expression of my gayness, that I see my folks. I feel strong knowing I have grown beyond their prejudice—one step forward, many steps sideways.

Light catches the side of my father's face, like spray paint catching a raised surface. I see his goatee in silhouette and the lighter hair under his bottom lip bobbing up and down like a switch going on and off, on and off.

Did his sperm make me? Am I linked to this man who is so detached from me? I want him to know as little as possible about me—even the things that might please him, like the fact that I outlasted the toughest.

I sit back in the seat and start fantasising about making love to Ethan, stroking my hard-on through my step-out pants, dirty and sweaty—lust-revenge lovemaking. I picture my father walking in on us and me not cowering, being proud, waiting for him to see the smirk on my face before I turn back to my love. In the dark of the back seat, I enjoy my spiteful fantasy, even though I know that life hardly ever follows desire, for in constructed perfection we leave out the bits that reality will not.

He sent a closeted child to the army and got a homosexual man back. I will choose the time to tell him carefully, for the best effect. He may have made me feel worthless, but I don't need his approval any more. From now on I will have to look back to see the damage he has done.

Dot comes running out from the kitchen, frantic with joy. Pudding, the bullmastiff, has only two settings between sleeping: eating or greeting.

'Shame, she's getting old now. She really misses you.' My mother smiles down at her. 'Nick, will you feed them for me, please?'

The farm smells wet and cold. No, it reeks of gloom. Sheets of winter rain start to fall from the black night, close and enfolding. On the roof the sound is ominous, and I can almost feel the dampness bleed into the walls.

I hesitate at the threshold of my room. Ahead of me the space is stale with remembrance, with emptiness and waiting. It is as though the empty room is not ready for the change.

So often I have masturbated on this bed, fought my desires, and now the room is the same but I am so different! I will never cower again, never again allow the self-loathing that comes from being caged and tortured by duplicity. If they don't want to hear, I won't tell them, but I will not change or lie to them. Fuck anybody who doesn't accept me.

This weekend before leaving for the border, I reveal so little of myself that I might as well not be there. And soon I am sitting waiting for my lift back to camp.

Pierre is late. My mother and I wait under a bridge on the

N1 in the Datsun. From time to time Mom turns the ignition two positions to the right. Red lights glow on the dashboard, and the windscreen wipers complete two swoops. The whirring sound of the little motor and the shuddering of the rubber over the glass grate at my nerves.

This time I'm going back to war—to two wars in fact: one against Swapo and another against Dorman. I will fight and possibly die for an institution that makes laws against me and my kind.

***

'Do you guys want to stop for food?' Pierre asks. None of us is hungry, but I know that I must keep my energy up. We will get to Oudtshoorn very late, maybe only at one in the morning.

'Yes, OK. Where do you want to stop?"

'Maybe at Worcester.'

'Shit, we have so far to go still. Maybe Robertson or Ashton. At least it will feel as if we've covered some distance. Or even Barrydale. There's a garage . . .'

'No way, that food is shit. Let's just stop, Vannie. We must just be very quick. I have to fill up before eight in any case.'

If we get there at one, that means I'll probably get to sleep by two, no, one thirty . . . one thirty, two thirty, three thirty and a half . . . shit, that's only two and a half hours sleep.

I think of all the boys who might have died travelling to and from pass. If I die tonight, it must just be quick. I shudder when I picture the car crumpled up and mangled, full of tar and blood—our blood on hard tar—and the flashing lights of police cars and an ambulance. But then it will be all over . . . all gone. Whatever comes must be better than this. Is this how Dylan felt? I picture my bed waiting at Infantry School and the rest of the company arriving, the base, the smells and the depression. Think of Jeffrey's; think of anything but Infantry School, I implore myself.

'There, that place makes *lekker* chips. Stop there, Pierre, stop!' Jan says from the back of the car.

'OK, OK. *Fok, hou jou in.* I'll drop you guys off and I'll fill the car up at that Shell station. Hey, Jan, you haven't paid me yet. Have you got bucks on you?' Then to me, 'Vannie, do me a favour, man, get me some chips and smokes.'

'Sure, what do you smoke again, those French ciggies?'

'Yep, Gitanes. But I don't think they'll have them. Then try for Gauloise.'

'And if they don't have them?'

'Then just get Stuyvesant . . . the regular ones, I don't want those light sissy fags.'

The car smells of vinegar. I like this part of the drive, from Ashton to Montague, weaving between the rocks and the cliffs with the fantastic formations. It's too dark to see them now, but it's enough for me to know that they are there and we're passing close to them.

In the distance I see the faint light of a farmhouse. I imagine being there, a man undressing in front of me, slowly and deliberately. I watch his every move, every item of clothing leaving his brown body . . . there in that house, all on our own, in a world that has no army. He has brought me here. A large fire lights the room, forming patterns on the raised stones of the walls. There is a wrought-iron bed in the room, and above us rough, gnarled poles hold the thatch. We are sitting facing each other, our legs around each other's bodies, warm and naked. We feed each other. I don't think so much about the sex as I do about the closeness, the light on his skin; that soft, flickering light that makes skin glow.

Our closeness surpasses sex—it is an unfathomable affection, a tender worship of two lovers. Who is this man I have created? His body is perfect—for what I am discovering, must be well packaged. Ah, his face, so strikingly attractive. And he is the other half of my soul, because he has grown up with me, into me. It is when he listens that I am most intrigued, because he understands everything; even the things for which I have no words.

All the way to Barrydale I rerun the fantasy. I run my nose up his neck and I inhale him. We fit into each other when we sleep, entwined. Now, the image of the first man, the one who eradicated all hope of change in me, burns through my fantasy. When I saw him all those years ago, I knew, yes, I knew beyond a shadow of a doubt, that I would only ever want to be with a man.

Some people's imprint stays on the map of one's life forever, having nudged it into a new direction—something one has longed for without even realising it. I wonder if Storm ever knew it.

2

We approach Jeffrey's Bay—wild, warm and windswept. The house we have rented seems relaxed about our invasion. Bronwyn and I run down the passage with Dot following, barking, slip-sliding, her nails scratching on the floor as she tries to keep up with us.

Behind the kitchen is the toilet, made out of corrugated iron on a wooden frame. Looking down into the pit at the right time of day, the light shines through a hole in the roof, illuminating the brown shit, yellow toilet paper and flies.

Jeffrey's Bay in 1970 is a small village. We shop at Ungerer's for groceries, and Coetzee's for fish and *slap* chips. The tanned surfers who stop there in their beat-up VW kombis captivate me.

Even on holiday, my father is always neatly dressed, with his hair impeccably in place, his comb always ready in his sock. His tight, checked shorts are ironed, and he never takes his shirt off, except on the beach.

The 'hippies' wear no shoes, no socks to house a comb. Their baggy shorts hang low on their hips. Around their necks are beads, and their hair is long and wild.

They irritate, even anger, my father. 'I'm telling you, those hippies are all queer and they don't believe in God. They're like bloody girls with that long hair. They disgust me. They look like hobos. *Agge nee, sies, man.* Their poor parents. They probably don't even know where their children are! Just promise me you won't turn out like that. If you do, I'll *bliksem* you. Are you listening to me, Nicholas?'

'Yes, Dad,' I say, and then, 'But, Dad, I like their long hair.'

'You'd better believe me, if you decide to grow your hair like that one day, you can find yourself another place to live!'

'How do you know they don't believe in God, Dad?'

'Well, have you seen them in church?'

'No, Dad, but would they be allowed in?'

'Not looking like that, they won't! But if they cut their hair and dress properly, well, maybe then they would.'

To me they look relaxed and happy, and at this tender age I decide to like everything my father dislikes.

I surf the foam on my lilo. Then I lie and tan and watch for beautiful men with brown bodies.

A 'bunch of hippies' are camping in the dunes close to our house, much to my father's aggravation. To me their kombi is like a lively puppy inviting a new friendship. The only inconvenience to my parents is that we have to pass them on our way to and from the beach.

On my way home from my shell-collecting spot, I cut across the beach to the dunes, past the 'hippies.' The sun makes its way through the branches of the candlewood and the dog-smelling milkwood. Where it touches white sand, the contrast is harsh against the shade of the old shrubs. The pathway winds ahead, each plant's smell hanging, waiting to be disturbed as it opens in front of me and closes behind. But today the walk has a new dimension for me. Not only is the car there, but its owners are there, reading in the shade.

The man is lying on his stomach. As he turns around, he reveals his naked torso. His hard shape picks at the nerve between my legs, at the base of my penis. I experience this so strongly that it feels as if I'm carrying a sign reading: Look, look at Nicholas, he has sexual feelings for this man!

The man is the most beautiful being I have ever seen. He seems to glow, radiating sex. His girlfriend is thin, with long, curly hair. In the light and on the white sand they belong as though by invitation. The shade is a complex mixture of flecks on their tanned skins. Then he rolls over again and carries on reading. I find myself irresistibly drawn into their space.

After lunch I wait for my parents to take their afternoon nap, and I climb through my window, lifting Dot out, with a wide-eyed Bronwyn watching us. Charged with excitement, I melodramatically swear her to secrecy and walk down to the hippies.

'Hi.' Not 'hello,' but 'hi'—so sexy I can hardly contain myself.

'Hi,' I follow suit.

'What's your name?'

'Nicholas. What's yours?'

'Storm.'

'Storm? That's a funny name.'

'And this is my girlfriend, Tracy.'

I stand staring and smiling, but soon I relax and, with uncommon bravery, I ask to see the inside of the kombi camper.

Afterwards, we settle into conversation. He answers all my questions patiently, while Tracy makes freehand drawings of him and me. I tell them about Frankie, school and Welgemoed.

Storm has light brown hair below the layered, weather-bleached curls that spill over his face and down his back. Around his neck is a leather thong threaded through three shells. From his bellybutton, fine hair runs down his flat stomach and disappears into his baggy shorts.

Tracy's hair is a similar colour. She is wearing a sarong around her tiny waist, with a bikini top over small, firm breasts. After handing me the drawings, she makes tea that smells of flowers.

'Don't drink that, Nicholas! Get home this very second!' My mother marches up to me and grips my arm so hard that my tea splashes onto the sand. 'Are you totally mad? Didn't you hear one word of what I said about these people? Get home immediately.'

Storm looks at her respectfully, and when she has finished, he says, 'We mean no harm to your boy. I can understand that you're concerned for his safety, but he's quite safe here.'

This reaction seems to surprise my mother too, and, as we leave, Storm speaks again, this time to me. 'You're always welcome, Nicholas.' Excitement swirls inside me. I beg my mother to let me stay. She stops, turns, and looks at them briefly, but says, 'No, we're going to have dinner now.'

Walking home, I tell her about them: the car, the sketches, and the kindness. I know I need to finish telling her before my father can hear.

Just before we get home, she stops, looks at me for what feels like a long time, and then says, gently and lovingly, 'I guess it would do no harm, but don't tell your father, Nicholas. For God's sake, don't let him know. And if they do anything strange, promise me you will tell me, OK?'

Later, in bed, I close my eyes and concentrate on the image of his hair, his chest, his torso. I stroke my body, running my left hand over my chest and tummy, and slipping my right hand under the elastic of my pyjama pants to feel the erection pulling there.

About a week into our friendship, Storm teaches me to surf—
further down from the main beach where my parents swim and
at a time when the wind has chased most of the swimmers
home. His way of teaching is different from what I'm used to,
where there are threats, deadlines and frustration. He teaches
calmly, enjoying it, and laughing often. I ride countless small
waves on his board, at first lying down. He holds me, and I
revel in it all—my skin touching his, the salt, the noise and his
patience. The board is long, carries my light frame easily, and
before long I stand for short stretches.

Afterwards we sit on a dune overlooking the ocean. There
is no hurry; this seems to be part of the lesson. Then he puts
his arm around my shoulder and says, 'To surf, all you need to
know is this: you must be one with the ocean, the waves, the
energy, your board and your body. You must feel it . . . like
with everything. Like everything, Nicholas. You must trust me
on this. It's important to feel this connection and then to grow
into it . . . the whole universe. It's like that with everything . . .
feel the energy . . . be in it.'

When he asks me if I understand, I say yes, but in truth, all
I really know is that in me is the *feeling* of what he says, even
if I don't understand exactly what it means.

The next day he takes me down to the water's edge. 'Nicholas,
I want you to look . . . but to feel, rather than just staring at it.
Experience it, sense and taste it. When you walk on any surface,
be aware of how it feels under your feet. Feel it all. The wind
. . . air has emotion, you know . . . taste and smell it. Use all the
senses God has given you. You will find that things don't just
have colour and form; there's much more to them.'

'Yes, OK.' Thinking about what my father had said about
hippies, I ask him, 'Do you believe in God?'

'Yes, I do, but I worship God as a power, a little differently
to the way I imagine you know. You see,' he waves his hand,
sweeping it over the ocean and beach, 'this is my church.'

I smile to indicate that I understand, and I think of our friendly old priest in the Bellville Catholic Church and wonder if he would approve.

'If you look at these waves, but you look at them upside down, they will look different.' Laughing, we bend over and look at the reflected light through our legs. Everything suddenly does seem different, more vibrant, from this unrehearsed angle. I hear everything and promise to discipline myself to 'feel' everything. I don't understand all of it, but I carry his words with me, for the textures and emotions to reveal themselves over the years to come.

I am now soundly in love with Storm. I take the step across that line beyond which I have never allowed my mind to go. Until now I have lived in denial of my true genetic engraving. It will be a long time before I fully embrace it, but I no longer deny it.

3

The hum of the engine remains constant all the way from Calitzdorp to Oudtshoorn. Hard as I try to sleep, anxiety has taken hold of me. I know this last part of the journey so well.

Over the next rise we'll see the lights, then pass the place where they searched us for food before Vasbyt, the road that leads to the mountains, the hill they made us run up during lectures. Then Pierre will slow down, take a left past the college, maybe stay in third gear, and turn left again into the main entrance to have our passbooks signed. We will walk up to our barracks and he will take his car to the civvy car park, where it will stay when we leave all this behind.

***

It is four days before we have to board the freight plane to the border. There is a slight relaxation in the tightly woven rank structure of the camp, like a carpet taken off the loom, to hang on its own. Malcolm and I are in the barracks, going through old copies of *Scope* and rating the male models in the cigarette ads out of ten. We have three categories: my taste, his taste and a combined list. We debate, and often argue playfully when there is a man we both find attractive.

Anyone wanting to know what we're talking about would have to listen very intently for quite some time. And that is what Gerrie does.

When he eventually breaks his cover, he calls us queers and immediately leaves to tell some of the guys in the platoon whom he still regards as his friends. Over the next few days some of them start calling us moffies, but it never goes beyond that. We ignore it, as one does with news of little interest.

Dorman is the only person in authority who encourages the name calling, which, in my case, he has been doing since Dylan's death.

***

The target we aim at is a picture of a 'terrorist' storming towards us. The centre circle is around his heart. We run to the shooting range at Swartberg or shoot at the range behind the camp.

I am a good shot and soon get a *skietbalkie*—a little emblem of an R1 rifle—that I have to put on my step-out jacket and wear with pride. I lose mine, or it is stolen, and I never replace it.

From the shooting range, one can see down the valley all the way to the airport, from where the Hercules freight planes, called Flossies, will take us to the border. Tummy-planes, airoplanes . . . that's how she used to say it . . . that's what Bronwyn called them many, many years ago. Now I'll be going in one of those tummies.

Of all the memories I unwittingly gather during this time, it is the second last day before our departure that stands out.

Malcolm and I are blamed for something the platoon has done, and Dorman decides that the whole group will be punished. This, in army mentality, will cause the other troops to resent us and make our lives even more difficult.

'There is a certain element in this platoon that must be eradicated,' he says. Everyone knows to whom he is referring. 'Some people here need to be sorted out. Because of this element and the *slapgat* attitude of certain individuals, you are all going to carry your *trommels* from one shed to the other. And if you think they're going to be empty, you're mistaken. They're full of fucking ammo.'

The other troops' animosity towards us is tangible and further fuelled by Dorman and Gerrie. What worries me most is that these are the people who will be on the border with us, in a war, and we will be relying on them for protection.

The metal trunks are impossibly heavy. After moving the first one, I feel like crying. The handles are thin steel bars that cut into one's hands. When you put the *trommel* down, your fingers remain clenched and numb.

Exhaustion and hate are reaching boiling point around us. 'Fucking faggots! I swear you're all going to hell! Just being near you makes me sick.'

I don't react, for deep down I believe it is only their pain talking. What does upset me though, is the fact that Oscar is also there, because to me he is better than all of them, and I want his respect. He listens, but says nothing.

We are given a short break. Most of the platoon collapse against the incline of a concrete embankment. Malcolm and

I, with one or two others, sit on the level, facing the embankment.

Gerrie is the leader of the group that has been calling us names, and now they start discussing the degrees of sin. Johan, whom we call Vrugtevlermuis (the Afrikaans for fruit bat), says that sleeping with a black is tantamount to bestiality because blacks are not human. Gerrie says that, according to his *dominee*, homosexuality is the worst of all sins, much worse even than murder. Nowhere in the Bible did God ever punish as harshly as he did the cities of Sodom and Gomorrah, and that was because of their homosexuality. He also argues that being gay is a sin of choice, a premeditated decision, whereas murder is often a result of passion, war or an accident.

Against my better judgment I say, 'You're talking shit. Show me where in the Bible you read this. The way I understand it, sin is sin and we are all born into it. If you read the Ten Commandments, it doesn't say that some fall in the category of unforgivable! Surely Christ died for everyone, for the absolution of all sins.'

'*Ag fok*, Van, man, I can't remember the exact verses. I'm not a fucking computer. It doesn't really matter, because my *dominee* says that Jesus died for sin, but not for that sin; that's a different kind of sin. I promise you, Van, you better be warned, mixing with Bateman . . . sleeping with dogs, you know, you end up with fleas.'

'Fuck you, Gerrie,' Malcolm says. 'We all break rules of the Old Testament all the time. There are even things in the New Testament that would be considered un-Christian today.'

Gerrie is outraged. 'What did you say? How dare you blaspheme like that? This whole country is built on Christianity. Are you saying the Bible is wrong?'

'He's saying there are things in the Bible that are ludicrous,' I lend my support to Malcolm.

'Like what?'

By now the entire platoon is watching, waiting for me to defend the indefensible, waiting to crucify me. If ever there were a moment that I've been grateful for my torturous years of spiritual searching, it is now, because I do in fact have some ammunition—passages I have memorised for exactly this kind of situation. I am also acutely aware of Oscar's attention.

'Well, for one, the Bible supports slavery. Check Titus 2:9, where Paul tells the people that slaves must be submissive to their masters and give them satisfaction in every respect.'

For a second there is dead silence. All eyes are on me, and I know nobody is arguing because they don't have the knowledge to do so.

'Bullshit,' says Gerrie, but I ignore him and take advantage of the rest of the men's attention.

'And what about 1 Corinthians 14:34, where it says that women should be silent in church, that they must be in submission, because it is disgraceful for a woman to speak in church? You know how patronising the Bible is about women. They are not even allowed to ask a question. They must ask their husbands at home!'

'I don't believe it!'

'Read it,' I say, and then, to drive home my point but probably undoing the good I've done, 'or can God or the writers of the Bible change their minds any way they like?'

'Who do you think you are, Van? Smarter than a *dominee*, hey? No wonder you're defending moffies. Fucking *gatgabbas*, that's what you are!'

As if from nowhere, interrupting Gerrie's diatribe on deadly sin, Oscar pipes up, '*Ag kak, man.*' Just like that, and Gerrie shuts up.

Oscar gets up, walks over to me, bends down and kisses me full on the lips. He looks at the group, then up at the sky, stretches his arms out as if being crucified, palms up, and says, 'Strike me down, God, for I have kissed a man. Kill me now, or for heaven's sake, *donner* these people, or give them some hint of truth or a brain, because I can't take this shit any longer.' He drops his arms and looks at the group. 'Fucking hell, stop talking this *kak*, man.'

With all eyes still on him, he slowly turns to me and says, 'Fuck them, Nick, just fuck-em all.'

At this instant I am filled with adoration, love, hero-worship, all mixed up into one emotion. And it stays with me—a support system cherished by my subconscious.

***

The Hercules C130 is under constant threat of attack from the ground, and for this reason the pilot spirals down over Ondangwa while two Alouette gunship helicopters search the ground for terrorists who may have Sam Seven heat-seeking missiles trained on us. The Flossie needs to land quickly. It's during the final approach, just above stalling speed that we are in the greatest danger of being shot down. From inside the aircraft we can see nothing. We just sit in the sling seats, our backs against the fuselage.

'It's odd to think that some of us won't be going back, hey, Van.'

'Malcolm, don't talk like that. You and I are going back, and that's it. Besides, I'm not used to you being so negative.'

'OK, but maybe some of these other fuckers won't.'

'I don't want to think about it.'

'Did you, like, say goodbye differently . . . I mean, to your folks . . . sort of *this could be the last time*?'

'Stop it! No, not to them. But I did spend the last Saturday with my friend Anne. You know, the one who always writes the long letters. I told you about her. We went to art classes together.'

'Oh yes, the one who sent you the letter with the butterfly wing in it.'

'Yes, we went to the Botanical Gardens in Stellenbosch and decided that we would visit a certain tree when I get back and have a picnic there. Silly, I suppose.'

The pilot lands and taxis. When we stop, the roar of the engines is replaced by a whining sound. Then the rear door opens and the border air rushes in—dusty, hot and dry . . . in mid-winter.

The camp in Oshivelo is like all other camps, the same depressing feeling, except that the buildings are mainly tents—fatigue green army tents on red sand.

It is here, with the great expanse around us and the closeness between us, that Malcolm and I really get to know each other; bit by bit, like turning a precious stone over and over and studying its every facet. When you can tell someone absolutely anything, it's like therapy. For the first time I totally share those parts of my life that I have kept secret for so long. I invite him into my now empty 'closet'—going back and peeking at the cramped interior that I had occupied for so long, never thinking I would be able to leave it.

Oshivelo is a training base for the war we will step into in just a few weeks' time. We are taught to put in drips, which we must practise on ourselves and our friends, digging for veins with butterfly needles.

Our toilets are long drops, with seats we call go-carts—row upon row of them, all under one roof. We pee into plastic funnels, called *pislelies* (piss lilies), dotted around the camp, and we shower in trailers, queuing naked outside in our platoon groups.

'Hey, Van der Swart, why are you here? You just want to see dick, hey! Bateman, you homo, don't perv here or get a hard-on, oke!'

'Not for your small pin-prick dick, you *tornaaier.*'

We cut down trees to build a structure to hang our kit on. We have inspections, stand on parade and have longer quiet times. We train day and night in what they call 'modern-day guerrilla warfare,' using vehicles protected against land mines, V-formation patrols, roadblocks and ambushes.

Almost every night before lights-out, except Sunday nights, we are given propaganda briefings, clipped onto us like weights. I am instinctively sceptical of everything they tell us, but when something is unavoidable, it is better not to dissect it.

One troop is chosen from each platoon to sit in on the briefing by the company commander. In our platoon it's Gerrie. He takes notes, which he then has to convey to us.

He walks into the tent flushed with his own importance. He says he isn't allowed to tell us everything he has heard—only a *select group* is allowed that. It's clear that he has swallowed their propaganda in huge gulps.

He tells us about the spoor that has been spotted close to the camp and the large numbers of terrs that have crossed the border in the past few days. 'This is highly confidential,' he says and waits before delivering the next bit of information. 'Not the newspapers or the people in the States know this; you have to keep it absolutely secret. Do you understand?'

I am beside myself with irritation. He uses the language of the border: terrs, States, gooks, PB's, kuka shops and clicks. I can't keep quiet any longer and let out a loud sigh—so charged with irritation, it might as well have been a sentence.

'What's wrong with you, Van? If you don't take this seriously . . .'

'Oh, Gerrie, for fuck sake. It's propaganda, man, and what's this States shit, we're not in America or Vietnam. Don't get so fucking carried away by the drama. They want to scare us and get us all worked up. You know how the army is. Let's keep some balance here. Besides, who the fuck can we tell? We can't phone home, our letters are censored, so what's your story, man?'

Malcolm follows, 'Fok, Gerrie, don't *ruk* the *hol* outta the *hoender*,' and someone else says, '*Hy ruk sommer die hele fokken hoender van die stellasie af, ou!*' Everyone laughs, except Gerrie. He moves awkwardly on the chair, crossing and uncrossing his legs.

'You can believe what you want, Van. If you have a problem with the information, tell the captain.'

When he leaves, he looks at me with undisguised hatred.

The next day I am summoned to the tent that Lieutenant Engel, Sergeant Dorman, Corporal Smith and Gerrie share. Corporal Smith marches me in. The manoeuvre is awkward: the doorway is lower than my head and I walk crouched, but at the same time try to be as upright as possible. It feels ridiculous, and I wonder if they also see the humour, but as I enter the tent, I feel their self-importance and know that they do not see the absurdity of this sideshow. The tent is too small to allow for the halt, which is a three-step manoeuvre, and I collide with the centre pole and then Lieutenant Engel's bed.

But they are the ones with the power, and that is what they use in this kangaroo court. My 'sentence' is sandbag PT with full kit in deep sand. During the sentencing, it is my anger that gives me the strength to face the fear—courage I know will be tested during the night that lies ahead.

The tent appears to breathe around me as I process the sentence.

Gerrie sits on his fold-up bed. This strikes me, because the rest of us sleep on the sand. He is cleaning his boots soundlessly, but his whole body is leaning towards what is taking place in this tent he has made his Judas home.

Dorman sits crouched over, legs crossed, his elbows resting on his knees. His right hand cups his chin while his fingers are

246 · ANDRÉ CARL VAN DER MERWE

stroking his nicotine-stained moustache. He says nothing but his eyes scar the space between us.

On his own bed sits Lieutenant Engel, bent forward, his legs open and firmly planted, his short torso awkward, too dumpy for the legs clawing over the side, like a vulture with exaggerated talons.

But it is next to me in the corner, the silent boot-cleaner that I feel most. Our history fills the space between us like smoke.

Corporal Smith, standing at attention next to me, marches me out, calls me to a halt and dismisses me. Before we separate, he looks at me for a brief moment, says nothing and turns. 'So much over so little' is what I like to believe I read in that expression, or 'Fuck Gerrie, the little squealer.'

It's the waiting I hate. The terror that prevents me from eating or drinking anything sits inside my stomach like a hard rubber ball. Some of the troops revel in reminding me how often people die from an *opfok*.

'Hey, Van, you're going to *kak* this afternoon. You got gyppo guts? Suffer, baby, suffer.'

I have a full day of training, then PT, after which I have to meet Dorman at the sandy road, dressed in my browns and boots, with rifle, webbing and *grootsak*.

I adjust and readjust my laces and the straps of my bag. I worry about the lack of fuel in my empty constitution. Malcolm mixes some Game and pours it into my water bottles. With all my kit on, I am very hot. Just the walk to the road is exhausting.

Dorman shouts at me to run. When I do, the weight displaces itself through my frame, and my feet sink deep into the sand. He shouts a constant flow of insults, and I hear Dylan's name too, but today I can't allow aggression into the space where I carry love. I have to use my all to get through the next few hours.

Nobody is allowed to watch, but they all do. A medic is

placed on stand-by. I am allowed one bottle filled with tepid, plastic tasting water. Dorman pours out the Game Mal has mixed.

First I have to run to a *pislelie* and back. I know I must pace myself to last long enough for Dorman to feel that he has executed the sentence and that I have suffered enough.

Up and down I run, up and down . . . then push-ups, dips, more exercises and more running through the sand with my rifle and sandbags, not thinking of what I'm doing, only running the prerehearsed fantasies of revenge through my mind.

He lies under a bridge on a piece of disintegrating foam rubber, in vomit, faeces and urine. He has descended to this point on a stepladder of loss, and I have relished the collapse of each rung beneath him, the final tread having been the artificial support of the dark soul of drugs.

My visions are now just snippets of disjointed images. The pain of mind and body is too loud and consuming to allow me to be creative as I run back and forth over the same route.

'If I fucking . . . for one fucking moment, see that you don't give everything, Van der Swart, you will be on the first RTU when we get back, I swear it. But before we get back you first have to survive the border with me. I'm going to rip your balls off, you cunt-faced fuck.'

A dirty needle forces into a wasted arm full of welts and puss. He is searching among collapsed veins to inject the poison. Sickblue, under a transparent skin and seething with filth. Begging with craving . . . like my body is now begging for relief.

My rifle keeps on hitting my face where it swings clumsily on my shoulder. It's impossible to push the strap higher up, because both arms are carrying sandbags. Then it falls from my shoulder, into the fold of my elbow, and hits my knees, swinging and snagging between my legs.

My lungs rasp, chafing as I suck in bits of air, and I taste blood. There is a noise in my head that drones at a monotonous pitch. Time has taken on a different dimension. Long, long seconds are delayed through sandpaper lungs, and then the next one strains into place.

My dragging foot falters. I try to move it, but it doesn't obey. Dorman is shouting millimetres away from my face, spit flying at me. I don't flinch. He hits me and I fall.

I get up, but my kit rides up over my head and overbalances me. I leave the sandbag at my feet. Dorman kicks my leg, it buckles, and I fall again. He is shouting, completely out of control, but the sound is blocked outside the coating of my exhaustion and the noise in my mind. I manage to get up on my haunches and pick the sandbag up. The rifle pivots and hits my face, but I'm on my feet and manage another run past the *pislelies*.

Dorman walks next to me, shouting, 'Beg me to stop, beg me.' Then, whispering, 'I've got all night. Beg me, you *poes*!'

Two laps later, I fall again, and this time I know I will not get up. He knows it too. He puts his boot on my head and drives my face into the sand.

Then he stands back and kicks me in the stomach. There is a sharp pain, my stomach contracts, and I start vomiting. Bile burns my throat and into the back of my nose, and I gasp for air. Pain fights for recognition, but I can only compute some of it. I try to spit, but I can't release the shiny gum from my lips. The vomit pools on the sand, too thick to drain away, frothing along the edges. I spit and spit, then vomit again.

I move into a kneeling position, with the kit on my back hanging to one side. As Dorman knocks me on the shoulder with the inside of his hand, the weight of the ill-fitting pack shifts forward and rides over my head again, but I manage to get up and stay on my feet. I am aware of the medic trying to give me water. Driven now by a kind of madness, I shuffle forward. Nothing works—my vision is obscured by sweat, sand and tears from the vomiting; my face is caked with puke and sand. Everything starts swimming before my eyes. I hear voices, but I can't move. There is water running over my face, but I can't react.

I spend the night in sickbay.

Dot is at the side of my bed in Jeffrey's Bay. I motion to her and she jumps up and crawls in under the sheets. It's our secret; she knows we are sharing disobedience. In her coat is captured the smell of the sea with the collected dog smell. When she gets too hot, she moves out from under the sheet.

I feel a deep ache of longing cutting through the headache and the throbbing in my bruised knee. I miss her so much—her simple, unconditional love. I think of how she waits for me when I'm swimming, and her relief when she sees me in the shallow water while she was still searching for me beyond the waves. The simple, uncomplicated honesty of it all . . . *that* is so much more important than *this* . . .

***

I lift up the canvas sheet that is hung at the door to stop the flies from getting into the toilet tent, and find the place empty, except for Gerrie sitting on a toilet in the corner. He is the last person I wanted to see here, but there is no way out now.

At first, we don't talk, but the space becomes loud with what we're not saying. I run through sentences in my mind, and by the time I start speaking, it is as if I am some way into a conversation already.

'What has happened to you, Gerrie? You're not the same person I knew in high school. Shit, man, you were my friend, remember?'

'One has to do what one has to do to survive.'

'But betray your friends?'

'You were asking for it, Nick, and besides, you stopped being my friend when you got so friendly with that Malcolm moffie.'

'Fuck you, Gerrie. Malcolm is an amazing guy. I'm lucky to be his friend. You've betrayed me, and you will always carry that with you.'

'This is the army and I'm going to survive at any cost, that you must know. In civvy street all this will be forgotten, but here it's the survival of the fittest.'

'That's where you're wrong. This is who you really are, here and in civvy street.'

He bends forward on the plastic go-cart. 'I don't care a shit what you think,' he sneers and clicks his fingers when he hisses the word 'shit.'

At this, a fly takes the opportunity to disappear into the hole behind him. I pray that it will stay inside and not come and sit on me after being on Gerrie's arse.

'You think you can walk away from this, but it will always stay with you, Gerrie, always. That's the type of person you are, and you know it. You know it, and you will never get away from it.'

My words have struck a chord. He leans forward again, this time to take some toilet paper, and pushes his hand between his legs to wipe himself. He drops the paper into the hole without checking to see if he needs another wipe, gets up and pulls up his pants. As he gets up, I notice his cock—small and shaped like a little missile, with a long, taut foreskin sitting in a bush of dark hair. The ugliness of it gives me a delicious sense of victory.

At the tent flap he turns around and says, 'It was me. I'm

the one who split on you. And I'm glad I did it. I have more power than you think. Engel likes me. You will never be an officer, Van, I'll see to it. NEVER. You will be a corporal at the end of this course; that is if you survive! I will see to it that you're placed at the border for your next year, doing patrols and fucking getting killed. You mark my words, you fucking faggot.'

Then he is gone.

Fear and anger creep up inside me. He could really bad-mouth me sufficiently with Engel and Dorman and succeed in all his threats.

***

After the weeks of training at Oshivelo, we leave in open Magirus trucks, sitting on our kit. The first stop is Ondangwa. Here we sleep propped up against our kit in a demarcated area, before we are transported North in landmine-protected vehicles. Now we are soldiers; soldiers in the operational area.

In a twist of fate, of all the Infantry School companies, Golf Company is deployed with Koevoet.

Koevoet means crowbar. There are few South Africans who haven't heard of Koevoet and its activities on the border. It is known as the most ruthless killing machine in the world.

'They have by far the most successful kill rate,' our captain says with a grimace. 'They are a division of the South African Police and seem to have developed the most successful anti-insurgent tactics. Most of the members are Ovambos. We are going to work with them, to study their strategy. They have just started this technique of hunting terrs . . .'

We leave at first light. As we get into the Buffels, I feel as if I'm carrying some slender remnant of the dream I had the night before. All day I feel this presence; like dust I can't shake off.

A Buffel is a smallish landmine-protected vehicle that sits high on its Mercedes Unimog chassis. It feels as if it wants to pounce—far more agile than the heavy Hippo. The driver sits in an armoured capsule next to the exposed engine. Behind him, two rows of troops sit back to back. In front of each one, a half circle is cut into the armoured sides for our rifles to rest in. During a contact or an ambush the sides can be let down, allowing the occupants to get off quickly.

We sit strapped into firmly moulded seats. If the vehicle detonates a land mine, this is what gives us our only chance of survival. We are told that the terrorists have started stacking multiple land mines on top of each other. When triggered, the explosion is fierce enough to somersault the vehicle and rip its chassis to threads.

In our row, Malcolm is first, then I, and to my right Oscar sits reading during most of the day's journey. When we stop, he draws or writes.

I rub my index finger on the side of my nose to make it oily and draw an 'E' on the matt paint of the armoured wall in front of me. Malcolm sees it, whispers, 'Ethan, Ethan, Ethan,' and I smile. He does the same, but draws an 'O'.

Above the steel side of the vehicle the immediate foreground blurs past—from time to time small settlements of huts can be seen, with bored people in makeshift doorways. A little girl, watching other children playing soccer, leans on a home-made crutch on the side where her leg was ripped off by a land mine. They don't even glance up as our convoy passes.

Other pockets of existence float past, each little kraal pitted by war, with emaciated cattle scattered around the huts behind which the bush moves forebodingly past—further, slower, darker.

4

I celebrate my tenth birthday on the last day of our annual holiday in Jeffrey's Bay. It is a beautifully warm evening, and after dinner my mother suggests we take a walk on the beach. On the cool sand, under a clear summer sky, she points out the Southern Cross to us—the two markers and how to determine south.

It all feels big and calm at the same time. I am happy. Light-specked vastness above, and from the sea the white water of each disintegrating wave pushes cooler air in front of it, carrying the salt and the sound of the crashing waves. At the calm end of its journey a black sheet is spread for reflecting the stars, washing over our feet, before being called back to the deep.

Standing guard on the border, I will remember this night many a time, longing for my mother. I will watch for six hours as the Southern Cross moves like a watch around the celestial south.

At the end of the beach, where the fishing boats are launched, we turn back. The lights of the town are left behind as we approach the spot where we usually walk home through the dunes.

We are leaving tomorrow and we follow the familiar path for the last time. Between the milkwood trees we can see light from Storm and Tracy's kombi.

Their cosiness, enhanced by the firelight and the soothing sound of Tracy's guitar, attracts me, as always. When we get to the closest point of passing, I stop and ask my folks to wait for me. I walk over to them and Storm jumps up when he sees me. Tracy carries on playing, smiling up at me.

'I've come to say goodbye. We're leaving tomorrow,' I say. Tracy stops playing, calls me closer, hugs and kisses me and says softly, 'You will be loved by many; carry that love in your heart, Nicholas.'

I can't think of anything appropriate to say. Storm takes my hand and leads me back to my family. Halfway there he lets go of my hand and rests his hand on my shoulder. When we reach them, he greets them politely.

He tells my parents that we have shared the waves together and that I have the ability to really see things sensitively. Again I don't quite understand what he means and neither, I think, do they, but I am proud of his praise.

He wishes them a safe journey, goes down on his haunches and hugs me. With his hands on my shoulders he says, 'Stay free, Nicholas . . . never stop searching.' He looks at me, our faces the same height, but with the light of the fire behind him, I can't see him clearly, only feel his presence. He smiles, gets up, turns and walks back to the fire. I burn the image of his silhouette into this parting, thankful for the dark, because I'm sure the glow I feel must be visible.

I never see Storm again.

5

'My mother left us when we were very young.'

'Mal?' His bush hat is rolled up under his epaulette. The wind catches his hair, which jerks in sudden movement. He looks far ahead into the bush, not focussing. 'I know I told you she had died, but she met someone else and left. She's dead to me, so I guess I didn't lie to you. I've never told anybody the truth; no friend, I mean. But I can't keep secrets from you.' I see the chain holding his dog tags below the top two buttons, which are undone, his skin sunburnt and young, his mouth firm.

'In a way my father died the day she left; just opted out of life, started drinking. He was always too gentle . . . I hated her.'

'Hell, that must have been shitty.'

'It had its good side too. We had total freedom. We raised

ourselves, actually. My father didn't even know whether we were at school or not. Don't think he even knew which high school we went to. But he always gave us what he could.'

'And your sister, Mal?'

'My sister and I hardly see each other. She's married to a chauvinist fuck-face and all she thinks about is him and the children. He hates me, calls me a moffie, so I don't see her. Not that I want to in any case. They're reborn hypocrites; think I'm evil.' Then he is quiet.

'Were you two close?'

'Yes, very. We did everything together. I used to think that is why I'm G-A-Y.' He spells the word soundlessly, glancing around to make sure that no one else sees it.

'I also only had a sister after my brother died, but I know that's not why I'm gay. I was born this way, no doubt. We were so different. She always split on me. It was like having three parents. Did you have many friends at school?'

'Yep, but never really close ones. I was always hiding who I really was from them, so there was always a kind of barrier. Terrified of being identified, being called a moffie, you know.'

The drone of the engine and the buffeting of the hot air blend with our voices, with what we are sharing.

'You are my best friend, Nick. I want you to know this. We must look out for each other.'

'I will be there for you, Mal, I promise.'

'Best friend.' We do our two-finger greeting. To my right Oscar sees it, but says nothing and carries on reading amidst the shaking.

Looking into the shrub, it seems ominous, dark with mystery, and dense. Strange to think that killing takes place in there . . . all this is so bizarre. In bush like this I will walk, with my rifle, with full magazines and a live round in the chamber.

'So, Nick . . .'

'Yes?'

'How did you deal with your G-ness? I mean you are a believer and all, aren't you?'

'Well, I had this mentor . . .'

'Yeah, the guy who was accused of being G?' We now no longer use the word 'gay'—it's G, with H for homosexual and M for moffie.

'Yes, and he taught me to just have blind faith, against all odds, blind faith. So, over time I have developed this totally honest relationship with God. I reckon that is the most positive thing that ever came out of my "affliction." I decided that if God knows everything, well then He must know I didn't choose the way I am, or He must change me if it's so terrible. I just told God everything: my fantasies, infatuations, everything.'

'Even your fantasies?'

'Yep, every single thing. I trusted God completely with everything. And over time I just thought, bugger what the church people say, God is quite cool with it, and He understands.'

'Well, you should have got some help, 'cos you sure as hell don't seem well to me!' he laughs.

'Yeah, and you? You would need an army of psychologists, Blondie.'

We stop for 'lunch' or smoke break or piss break, whatever we need to do.

Mal and I sit in the shade of the Buffel, against a tyre, sharing our rat packs.

First, we lay out the contents to see what this unlucky dip holds: biscuits (which we call dog biscuits), instant porridge, coffee, tea and sugar. For the main meal, we have three small tins (mince and noodles; steak, onion and potato 'salad'; and a compressed meat spread) plus an energy 'milk shake,' and an energy orange drink we mix with lukewarm water from the water car that is towed by a Buffel. For dessert, there are sweets and the only worthwhile thing in the whole pack: condensed milk. Our cutlery is our *piksteel* or *fokken* knife and spoon, as it's called.

Not far from us, Corporal Smith joins a group of men, and we overhear their conversation.

'So, when an instructor gives troops a hard time, I believe they put a shined-up bullet on his pillow, which means he's a marked man.'

'Yep, if we don't like you, we can kill you here.'

'You can shoot one of your own buddies if you have some beef with him, like if he stole your chick or something, and you'll never get into trouble. "Killed in action," is what they'll say.'

'Ja, why do you think there are so many casualties up here. Guys get shot by their own *tjommies, ek sê.*'

'No shit,' someone says, and I hear Dorman say, 'But remember, it also works the other way round.'

'What do you mean, Sarge?'

'Well, if I get fed up with one of you little cunts, I can take you out.' Then he turns around and looks at me. I hold his stare until he turns back to the group.

'I think you should talk to the captain, Nick. Dorman has it in for you big time.'

'He's just trying to scare me.'

'No, Nick! You don't mess around with shit like that . . . fuck it, man.'

'What can I tell the captain that won't make me look like a fool?'

'Well, if you don't do something, I will.'

'OK.'

'I'm so *gatvol* of this Buffel. How much longer before we get there?'

'No one knows.'

'Tell me a story, will you?'

'OK, I'll tell you something I thought of when we were talking about our sisters.'

'Is it a true story?'

'Yes, now listen. I have this uncle—my mother's brother. Uncle Ben lives in the southern part of Namibia, on a beautiful farm. Well, I like it, it's real desert. He had a problem with baboons, so he speared them to death by hand.'

'Bullshit. I thought it was a true story.'

'No, it is. He trapped them in cages first, but that's not my story. He had captured this cheetah on the farm and kept it in a cage behind the shed where he fixed the trucks, and there were some pigsties and storerooms and trash. Anyway, this cheetah fascinated me. I tell you, Mal, this animal was so unbelievably beautiful, you know, up close. I couldn't bear to see it in a cage. So I decided to free it.'

'What? You crazy fuck!'

'Well, I reckoned if I attached a long cord to the latch I could wangle it loose from a distance. In fact, I could do it from a window in the shed. But I didn't think the plan through properly, because when I pulled the latch, I thought I'd be able to pull the gate as well. But there wasn't enough leverage. So the latch opened but the gate wouldn't budge. Eventually I plucked up the courage to go outside, and just as I get to the cage, the cheetah flies at the fence. Shit, my heart stopped. So I thought bugger this, I'm not dying for this cause. But the cheetah flies at me again and this time it hits the unlocked gate, and it opens. And I'm standing this far away from it.' I point out a distance quite a bit shorter than it really was, of course.

'So?'

'The cheetah slowly pushes past, scampers out and runs off in the opposite direction. I nearly shat myself. A few minutes later, I hear this *moer* of a commotion behind the house, dogs yelping and screams and shouts—huge drama. I managed to get back to the room unnoticed, but just as I slip into bed, Bronwyn asks, "What have you done now, Nicholas?" Not "Where have you been?" but "What have you done?"'

'Go on!'

'I gave her some bullshit story and swore her to secrecy. But shit, Mal, I was shitting myself. The next day I find out that the cheetah has mauled uncle Ben's staffie. Man, he loved that dog like a child. But the best was that he thought it was some guy who worked for him who was pissed off and wanted revenge, so I was off the hook. What does the Bron bitch do? She goes and tells my folks.'

'You must have been in deep, deep sheila!'

'My father beat the crap out of me. Eventually my mother came into the bathroom and begged my father. "Why don't you just shoot him if you want to kill him," she said.' Malcolm finds this highly amusing.

By this time, the sun has moved behind the trees, changing to a deep red. Suddenly I'm overwhelmed with a desire to hold on to it. Up to now it has always been 'before.' But tomorrow it's the real thing. If only I could hold on to this day. But through this bush of death, the sun just carries on sinking and the convoy seems to gain urgency as darkness starts to fall around us. Or is it simply the uncertainty that dusk brings? Why we go on travelling at night and when we will arrive at our destination, is not for us to know. Not that I think anybody really cares in this state of fatigue and with the noise of the demons in our heads.

Just after eleven, we stop at a base, where we are instructed in muted tones to line up. We march into an area surrounded by high 'walls' made out of sand. There is no light. In the walls are guard bunkers, and I also notice a lookout and water tower silhouetted against the inky-blue sky. This is where we will spend the night, amidst the smell of unwashed men and diesel—diesel from a spill, which penetrates every fibre of my kit and will forever remind me of my time with Koevoet.

Where the base now stands was probably once a prosperous

cattle farm. Parts of the buildings are blown away, and others damaged by shrapnel. What is left of the buildings is for the officers and a sickbay; out of bounds for us.

There is a baobab tree with a trunk that splits into two close to the ground. I find it the most beautiful of plants. The Bushmen believe it has mystical powers and medicinal properties, but this poor tree has chosen such a bad place to grow. Now, hundreds of years into its life, man has decided to have a war here, and it will bear huge scars of this short time in history. Three quarters of the way up the tree, the two thick trunks have been cut off to be used as a base for a lookout post and to house a machine gun.

At times discipline can furnish one with a sense of security, especially when it feels as if the world around you has gone mad. But in Koevoet there is no such sense. There seems to be no discipline, and the men are completely wild. They have established their own methods and seem to be accountable to nobody. When we ride in the vehicles, we have ways of climbing on and strapping ourselves in that are rehearsed so many times that we can do it in our sleep. Not Koevoet. They ride on the sides or on the roofs, anyway they care to. Our vehicles are all exactly the same, always parked as if in a platoon, ready for parade. Their vehicles are left haphazardly wherever they have stopped. The cars are dirty, painted and personalised, with parts missing and crude modifications, like machine guns fastened to the tops of the Hippo APC's.

Their personal appearance entails whatever makes them feel comfortable—long hair, torn clothing and a scruffy craziness.

Towards the evening we are told to go and look at the 'kill' of the day in a roofless, battered building. There isn't always a kill, but today there are five.

***

The Hippo comes to a screeching halt in a cloud of dust. Shouting soldiers waving their rifles hang over the top rim of the vehicle, and along the sides are hanging what look like half-filled sacks, but they are in fact bodies dangling awkwardly, doubled over. Then the bodies get thrown from the vehicle like trophies, as uncle Hendrik's workers used to do with the springbok after a hunt.

Parts of the bodies are missing where machine guns have eaten away at them like chainsaws through soft timber. One terrorist's head is completely crushed, with varying shades of yellow pulp squeezed out where bone has torn the skin. A twisted jaw pushes teeth through the one cheek. His face is held together only by skin, covered in dirt from being dragged through the sand.

How resilient God has made human skin. But where is He now? I wonder. Why is He looking the other way?

Here I see a new kind of death. Not a family shattered by the loss of a loved one, not the pain and guilt of a suicide, but a death flirted with, scoffed at, celebrated. I am not observing something from some other civilisation, but one I am trapped in. My subconscious sprays it into me—this colour of brutality.

It is critical that I guard against this with all my might, because I'm dealing with a force that is staring at me. And I'm staring back, knowing I've been changed by it, and I sense it smiling. I feel my brain shaking me, telling me to take note.

The corruption is swift as I notice how many of the boys start joining in the perverse rejoicing. There is a quiver in their laugh, which is like a taut cable binding the hate inside them.

Two of the victims lying at our feet are teenagers. We have heard stories about the terrible conditions in which they live in

Angola. I've dismissed it as propaganda, but here are the examples—wasted bodies, dressed in rags.

***

It is our third day at the Koevoet base, and our platoon leaves early for the first patrol. It would have been tedious if it hadn't been that we were hunting people and they were hunting us. Even so, during the long hours on patrol the initial fear of finding a terrorist behind every bush starts eroding.

At midday we dismount and start walking. The vehicles wait for us as we make our way through the thicker vegetation. There is a Koevoet tracker in front and we follow in a V-formation. We are following a spoor none of us can see. The tracker, we are told, can tell everything about the person he is following, what he is carrying, as well as his physical stature and condition.

At first, as with everything in the army, I question this, but in the weeks that follow I am astonished at the abilities of these trackers. Not only are they good at tracking a person walking, but they can also track people who are equally skilled, for the insurgents are just as accomplished in anti-tracking tactics. For example, they put the treads of their shoes on backwards, or keep to hard ground, or walk in shonas (pans often filled with water in the wet season).

Koevoet tracks with vehicles in small manoeuvrable groups and hunt until they kill, going for a week at a time into the bush, searching for spoor, which is pursued even if it takes them deep into Angola. Our platoon is used mainly as decoys or stopper groups for Koevoet's manoeuvres. We lie in ambush as part of their strategy, or form part of a group that chases the enemy into Koevoet's hands; but we seem to me to be of little help.

On our way back to base, at nineteen hours twenty, our convoy is stopped. We hear the corporal repeat the instruction into the radio handset—stay in this position to defend a line; Koevoet is chasing terrs towards us. But even before the order is given, we hear gunfire in the bush north-northwest of us, and almost simultaneously, the crackling static of the radio, 'Contact! Contact! Wait out!'

It takes a split second for reality to hit and drive us through the drills. Corporal Smith shouts, 'Circular defence! Circular defence!' This means we have to dismount by opening the sides of the Buffel. The person sitting opposite the handle must open it. Malcolm's handle won't budge. The corporal goes on shouting, 'Circular defence! Circular defence! WHAT THE FUCK IS GOING ON THERE? GET OUT! GET OUT!' Behind us, the other half of the section is already on the ground, but we're still inside. It feels comical—almost as if we have decided not to play along—sitting in a neat row, while around us everybody is frantically scurrying and leopard crawling for cover.

Someone starts swearing at Malcolm, and then the corporal shouts, 'Go over the side, go over the side!' He sounds hysterical. It is too high to jump, but most of us do, because climbing down the side, with our backs to the enemy, would make us even more vulnerable. We hit the ground, with rifle, webbing and full magazines, take up our positions and lie in wait.

In my mind, I see black men running towards me, and I struggle with the concept of taking aim at them. I am lying on my stomach with my R1 rifle in front of me. Remember now, *Nick . . . two shots, poppop, poppop.* For the fourth time my thumb slides over the safety catch, making sure it is disarmed.

I start analysing my position. Is it good enough? I leopard crawl towards a tree stump in front of me and take aim. Plotting a V in front of me, I determine my parameters and watch for movement within them. Again I hear the pop-pop sound and the reverberation of machine guns in the distance. The sounds are further away, which is heartening.

We wait. There is no more rifle fire, but I can hear the labouring of engines. Then behind us, Corporal Smith and Dorman shout, 'Get on, get on! Fucking run and get on, GET ON!' We scramble up the side, pushing one another for position. Before we are seated, the motor is running and the Buffel lurches forward.

Between talking on the radio and the overwrought sounds of the engine, Corporal Smith spits at Malcolm that he has put the whole section in danger and that he will go on orders.

'This fucking thing.'

'What happened?'

'I don't know, Nick, I guess I pushed it down too far.'

Some of the troops shout that he is a derrick—an airhead—but others are more threatening, accusing him of wanting to get them killed.

The Buffel in front of us veers off to the right and drives straight at a small group of huts surrounded by a fence of rough branches. Our driver follows suit, and the troops start cheering. All I can think of is that there might be people behind the fence.

The vehicle bursts through the branches. It hits a large clay pot used for making beer, and it explodes on impact. But the destruction is futile, for the insurgents have fled, and they will keep on running all night.

There is much excitement in the vehicle. The soldiers vow to cut off the terrorists' ears and balls and dry them for jewellery, as they have seen Koevoet do. The boy next to Oscar has a grenade over the end of his rifle barrel, and he is playing with the nippleshaped trigger on the one end of the device. It looks like an art deco spacecraft, with an arrow that can be set to LIVE or SAFE. If the arrow is on LIVE, the knob is depressed and the rifle is fired, the grenade will explode.

'Are you crazy?' I lean over Oscar. 'If that thing goes off, the shrapnel will ricochet inside this vehicle and we'll be in fucking shreds!' He looks at me, smiles and holds his thumb over the nipple, fondling it and then pressing it down. When it can't go any further, he pushes harder, releases it slightly and then presses it down again.

'Bang, bang, bang,' he says. 'Hey, Van,' I try not to react, as he no doubt wants me to. 'Hey, Van!' I glance over and watch him. He is twisting the head of the grenade from *Safe* to *Live*. He does this slowly, looking at me with a half smile. After arming the grenade again, he starts fondling the trigger with his thumb. In my head I rerun the words I've so often heard on the news: *'An entire section was killed in an accident when a grenade exploded inside an antilandmine vehicle. The names of the deceased will be released as soon as the next of kin . . .'*

'Fuck, are you crazy? I didn't come to the border to be killed in a grenade accident!' I turn to Oscar, 'Tell him to stop, man, help me here.' I am aware that my reaction is exactly what he wants, but I can't ignore what's happening. Before Oscar can react, he depresses the nipple again. The grenade doesn't go off. Oscar rips the thing from the barrel of his rifle and disarms it.

On the next patrol we follow spoor with a vehicle following us, carrying our kit and towing a water trailer. Into the first day they radio us to say the water is contaminated. We carry on, not even allowed to drink water from our water bottles. The trailer's water is poisoned. Even though we use purification tablets, it's not safe. When we get tired, we lie down in a shady spot, with two men on guard, waiting for water.

My every thought revolves around water. I tell myself stories, but they twist towards water like an addict's urge, frightening in magnitude and persistence. I have no control over it. Every moment drags by like thick glue. After two days, they bring us water.

I try not to let my mind wander, watch for the odd shape,

something shiny, something other than the natural line of a bush or tree. I think of Ethan, of home, but also of Dylan and Frankie, Dorman and Gerrie; incomplete thoughts, unresolved emotions.

There is a different kind of boredom on patrol—it's tedium on the move. I look down at my feet and observe the rhythm: one boot showing, then the other; right, then left, then right, then left. The sun bakes down on my shoulders, on my brown shirt, smelling now of old, sour sweat. Is someone following my spoor? Why don't I care? It feels good not to care. We are repeatedly warned against POM-Z booby traps with green tripwire. If you trigger one, your feet and legs are turned to pulp. As the hours drag by, my vigilance wavers. The thought of dying also feels painless in this heat-induced trance. Like a camel, I rock on my feet, my rifle and the medical bag constantly in the way.

My head snaps back as a hard thump drives into my right shoulder. I stumble but don't fall. Then the pain moves down my arm. With the pain comes the jingle of the buckles of Dorman's rifle strap, the now familiar sound, when he hits me with his rifle butt. I lift my head and align my rifle with my chest. Dorman says nothing and walks back to his position in the formation. The pain allows me to nurse my loathing.

In the early evening we establish a temporary base, referred to as a TB. From where we lie in our sleeping bags, I see a black *korhaan* climb into the sky, its call like an underpowered diesel engine. It climbs at an impossible angle, then appears to run out of power and plummet. Malcolm has also noticed it.

'Is it going to crash?'

'No, that's how it flies. It opens its wings just before it gets to the ground, but you don't see it land because of the long grass, so it looks like it's crashed.'

'Crazy, hey?'

At the base we do not interact with Koevoet. They don't talk to us; we are low-fat milk and they are jet-fuel.

***

Malcolm and I are sitting outside the base, on the concrete strip against the wall of a shed that contains spares for the Hippos and Buffels. The bush is beautiful, but from where we sit, we see only parts of cars, a gravel road, a water tower and a kuka shop, with the trees way beyond. It is our time off, and we're talking about the music we like.

'What's the first LP you ever bought?' Malcolm wants to know. 'Can you remember?'

'Neil Diamond, *Hot August Night.* I loved it. But you know, Mal, just because it was pop music, I thought it was evil. I tried not to like it. That's how fucked up I was.'

'Evil? Neil Diamond!'

I start singing, 'And the time will be our time, and the grass won't pay no mind . . .' Then, louder, 'Child, touch my soul with your cries, and the music will know what we've found, I'll hear a hundred goodbyes, but today I will hear only one sound . . .' Now my voice is booming, 'For the moment we're living is NOW, NOW, NOW! . . . and . . . now . . . I can't remember the words . . .'

We both laugh, but suddenly we become pensive and peaceful, with an unspoken understanding swaying between us.

'Imagine, Mal, if I could be lying next to Ethan, kissing him, feeling his hair, feeling him, just being there with him, you know. It's almost unthinkable . . . especially here. Do you think it will ever happen?'

'You and Ethan?'

'No, just experiencing that feeling with someone you love.'

'For sure it'll happen, otherwise what's the point of living?'

A Hippo comes travelling towards us on the road we use for patrols. Dust billows from under the large tyres. Tied to the front grill is something dark. Malcolm and I carry on talking, but then we see that the dark shape is a man and he is alive.

'It's an anti-landmine tactic, but it will only work if he planted the mine himself.'

The man tied to the bumper dangles from the ropes in agony. I'm sure they wouldn't even hear or see him if he had to shout or wave at them over the bonnet.

A little later an Alouette lands in a halo of dust. Koevoet uses helicopters in what they call a killing partnership. Koevoet is still young, taking shape and finding its feet. But in a short period of time they have become so strong that they set the record for the most kills per unit and developed hitherto unused tactics for guerrilla warfare.

For all my aversion to the war, there are still certain aspects I find interesting—the sound of a turbine when a chopper starts up, for example; the pilot running through the checks; the huge machine lifting off, with all the noise and upset to every-thing around it.

One day, during our time off, Mal and I hear excited talk-ing from behind a building and I get up to see if our position has been discovered. I see a pilot and six men walking towards an Alouette. The pilot climbs into the machine, and behind him two Ovambo Koevoet soldiers are dragging a black man who is tied up. I notice that it is the same man who was tied to the front of the Hippo. There is an older Ovambo walking close to the prisoner, talking to him.

Malcolm and I find a position behind an old Hippo engine block and sit down to listen to the muffled sounds coming from the group. The black man is begging, his speech fast, and his eyes darting from the older Ovambo to the two officers who are obviously the decision makers.

The pilot has headphones on and is concentrating on the controls between the seats and in front of him, flicking switches and looking at dials. Then he turns and looks at the officers.

The most senior of the group signals to the pilot, twisting his hand above his head as if he too has become a helicopter. The pilot applies himself to the controls, and slowly the top rotor starts moving. At the same time the tail rotor starts flipping over and over until the stripes on the blades blur into circles painted on air.

The captive's voice rises with the sounds of the Alouette's motor until it becomes a howling whine. One man signals to the two Ovambo's, who start dragging their captive to the open door of the chopper. One of them takes a bag out of his pocket and tries to pull it over the man's head. He buckles in protest. The downward force of the helicopter blades rips at their clothing. One of the men, dressed in browns, runs towards them, bends below the blades, pulls the hood violently over the prisoner's head and ties a rope around his neck. He and the older Ovambo load the hooded man in the chopper and strap him in.

I will always remember that face just before the bag covered it: puffed up, the black and white contrast of the terrified eyes, teeth clenched, neck pulled into his shoulders, howling and writhing to get away.

The pitch of the blades changes, and a mini dust storm develops as the chopper lifts off. It climbs a short way, and the pilot tilts the nose down while it moves upwards and forward. Then the pilot flies around the base, pulls the craft into a hover, stabilises it and moves slowly down towards the place where he took off. The Alouette floats just above the ground for what feels like a long time. Something appears from the side and falls to the ground. In its short fall we see that it is the insurgent. It is neither hard nor far but it is bound in terror. There is a dreadful tension in his body as he lies shaking on the ground. The chopper moves a short distance away and lands.

Everybody but the pilot, who does not shut down the motor, gathers around the insurgent. They are bent over him, the one Ovambo listening with his ear close to the man's mouth. He straightens up, cups his hand and talks into the senior officer's ear.

The chopper leaves, and the men start dragging the prisoner back to wherever he is kept. Soil is glued to his frayed clothing where sweat and urine have soaked it. But the real damage is not to his frame; he is shredded from within.

'We can never talk about this, Nick.' Mal is waxen, goose bumps on his arms.

'No, we have to get out of here. If they know we've seen this, we'll be in deep shit.'

I fondle the wire-bound diary in my top pocket. I want to record what I have seen, but decide against it. Removing the little book, I look at it as if for the first time, even though it is so full of my thoughts and feelings.

There are poems I wrote about the war, my infatuation with Ethan—referred to as 'E' and never as *he*. There are two good gesture drawings and many small sketches for sculptures, which I decide look way too much like Henry Moore's.

Most of the writings in the book are prayers, and surprisingly many of them are prayers of thanks. I analyse concepts; interpret my experiences. There is much about joy and love, and even more about death, woven between plump Picasso-esque drawings with turbulent expressions and figures of skeletal children.

6

'Good night, Mom.'

'Good night, you two. Did you wash behind your ears?'

'Yes, Mom. You always ask us that.'

'I know, and your necks?'

'Yes, Mom, you always ask us that too.'

'You should see what your collars look like. Don't worry, boys, I believe you. Come here . . . mm, you smell so nice.' She has both of us in her arms, me on the right and Frankie on the left.

'Say good night then, and run along. I'll come and tuck you in later.' We kiss her—left cheek, right cheek and then on the lips. When she lets go, I can feel her need to hold on.

'Good night, Dad,' we chorus.

'I'll tuck you in tonight,' he says, and we leave the room, which is warm with the glow of the paraffin heater. Mom calls after us, 'Remember your prayers, boys! Sleep tight, don't let the bed bugs bite.'

Our father follows and tucks us in.

'Tight, Dad, please, tight.'

'No, Nicholas, not too tight. Then you can't kneel to say your prayers,' Frankie says.

'Tonight you can just lie on your backs and say your prayers. It's OK, God will understand. Good night, boys.'

'Good night, Dad,' we say in unison.

'How much do you love me, hey?' he asks.

'We love you as much as all the ships.'

'And trains . . . and planes,' Frankie adds.

'And cars . . .' Then we start naming them—Pontiac, Chev, Ford, Valiant, Volkswagen, Mercedes, Land Rover, Mini, Austin, Citroen, Renault . . . Uhm . . . Aston Martin, Ferrari, Jag . . .

'OK, boys, that's enough. Sleep tight now.'

7

'The coffee's ready. Where's your fire bucket?'

'Here, thanks.' I unclip the handle and swing it around,

then secure it with its slide to make sure it will not slip out and tip the coffee over me.

'What's the time?'

'One-ish.'

'Shit, three more hours to go.' In the bunker the smell of the coffee mingles with the dust from the sandbag walls. In some places the hessian is torn and sand has leaked out. Ahead, over my R1, is the shoulder-high slit we look through. Hour after hour I watch as the Southern Cross does an almost 180° turn on its invisible axis. Over and over I mark south and recalculate the position. It's very reliable, and each time I remember Jeffrey's and saying goodbye to Storm. He would not approve of me being on the border.

Through this little window of war I feel the power of the stars. Their eternity makes this conflict that is so large in my life seem tiny.

To the right of us, in no man's land, is the shower trailer, and on the other side of the landmine area stands a house. Must have been the foreman's cottage before the war, I think. The house is dark, and I imagine that it would have been a good cover if I were planning an attack on our base. I should keep my eye on the building. But it makes me uneasy. To the right of the structure, much further behind it, is a palm tree, which is my marker for south. I close one eye and line it up with the sights of my rifle. How far in that direction is home? I wonder.

The coffee tastes better than anything I have ever tasted in the army.

'Hey, Mal, this is awesome. What did you do? I mean, how did you make this?'

'I made it with long-life milk, no water.' He is proud and happy that I like it. 'And lots of coffee.'

'Shit, it's nice. But where did you get all the milk?' That is the question he has been waiting for.

'I stole it.'

'WHAT? Are you mad? What else did you steal?'

'Oh, you're going to love me!'

'I already do, that's why I want you to be careful. I'll crack if you end up in DB.'

'Biscuits, and not dog biscuits either.' He produces a packet of Romany Creams.

'Jeez! We'd better push the wrapper in between the sand bags, or burn it.'

'Yes, Dorman doesn't need much of an excuse to get rid of us.'

'Have you ever hated anybody so much?'

'Yes, my sister's husband.'

'Oh, the macho dude.'

'Yes. And I put pool chlorine in his hair-growing lotion.'

'What!'

'I stayed with them for a while. He was such a *doos*, such an absolute fool, I can't tell you. Telling me I'm a sissy and that kind of shit. But he had this receding hairline and he religiously rubbed in this hair-grow stuff. My sister also had to rub it in from time to time.'

'And?'

'Well, I just sort of doctored it a little. He got such a rash he stopped using it. Even my sister's hands would burn. And now he's completely bald.'

'Wish you could do that to Dorman.'

'You know what was the most fucked up thing of all? I lusted after him!'

'Man, you're a mess.'

'Let me tell you something else.'

'NOW what have you done?'

'I sheila'ed in Dorman's bush hat.'

'No!'

'And pissed on his clothing before I hung it up to dry.'

'Fuck, you like living dangerously. He's going to know it's you!'

'And you? Who do you hate that much?'

'Mm.' I look out and for a fleeting moment I imagine seeing shadows crossing no man's land. A shudder scuttles up my back.

'There are so many *dooses*, but I reckon the closest I ever came to hating was this one uncle . . . *oom* Dirk.'

'What did he do?'

'He was just always really mean to me. He had huge, pap tits that hung down, with big, hairy nipples. I'd make up these fantasies and have my revenge on him. Boy, did he suffer.'

'Hell hath no fury like a moffie scorned.'

'Look, LOOK! Did you see that?' I urge as a shooting star streaks across the night sky. 'You know, a meteorite actually hit the earth here in Namibia some time ago. At Hoba, near Grootfontein. We did this trip to uncle Ben's and then to Etosha.'

'Nick, do you know what you're going to do? I mean, after the army?'

'Sure. I'm going to study art. And you?'

'Marketing, I guess. I want to do something that I can use in other countries as well.'

'Why, you're not going to leave, are you? Shit, am I going to have to travel to New Zealand or somewhere to visit you?'

'No, Canada! Vancouver. I hear it's great.'

'No way! Do you have any idea how hideous the weather is there? You just stay here. Shit, where will I find another best friend?'

'Well, you never know. Things aren't looking good here, man. I mean, we all know it has to change, and I don't see how it can without major shit. These Boers will never give up without a fight.'

'I really love this country, I mean South Africa. I can tell you, I've been overseas, and I don't want to live anywhere else.'

'The blacks hate us, man, and I don't blame them. Look what we've done to them.'

'The only hope is for the Boers to give up apartheid and pray that the blacks forgive us.'

'Yeah right, dream on! By the way, do you know what they call the guys you like over there?'

'No . . . gorgeous?'

'No, twinkies.'

I know Malcolm would rather talk about men than politics, but I'm thinking about the future, which is now, after the army, real grown-up stuff.

'But I also can't go with the commies, you know, Mal.'

'Yes, well, if the commies take over, we won't even be allowed to decide what work we want to do. They'll decide for us! What happens if the commies tell me to be a gynie?' He pronounces it *gaaaynee* and we both laugh.

'We need a miracle, a fucking miracle, with no precedent in this world; something so outrageously against human nature, something that has never been seen before . . .' I say this quietly to myself, as though thinking it aloud. For some time I look out over my rifle at the great Namibian night.

Behind me Mal has fallen asleep on the ground, leaning against the sandbag wall. The future seems darker than the night ahead. How will we resolve it? I feel heavy, tired, and I check my watch: almost three—one more hour.

'Mal . . . Malcolm.'

'Hm?'

'You asleep? Chat to me, man, I'm falling asleep too.'

'OK,' he yawns. 'Who's doing the last shift?'

'Oscar and Pieterse.'

'Hey, Nick, I'm going to wake them, OK?'

'Sure, why?'

'Maybe . . . Mmaayybee Oscar has a *pishoring*, and I can have a cheap thrill.'

'Pervert!'

'I have to go and sheila.'

'OK, you go for a shit and let the twinkie defend the base all on his own.'

'You're no twinkie, sweetness, look at these muscles.' He grabs my biceps and squeezes them.

'Go shit, just don't fall in the long drop, and I hope Oscar has a hard-on just for you.'

Just imagine how this base will erupt if they had to hear shots. Please God, let us not be attacked on my watch, please. But what if I save the day and become a hero? I might even get a medal for bravery. I wonder if it merits bravery? No, I'd rather there be no action.

8

'Bronwyn is a good girl, you know, Peet,' uncle Dirk says with deliberation. 'She's going to make some man a good wife; such a well-adjusted child.' My father returns the compliment, pausing between sentences, which seems to add sincerity to what he says.

Then uncle Dirk says something that will stay with me for the rest of my life. 'Such a pity Niklaas is such a flop.'

With a ringing of amplified emotion in my brain, I look at my father. *I'm sitting right here next to you. How can you let him talk about me like this?* I ask wordlessly.

My father avoids my stare and busies himself with stoking the fire. The wood releases sparks that rise in a twirl and light my father's face, revealing a frown; but there is no protest.

Flop, structureless, nothing forgiving about it. Flop, flop, flop, soft and spineless like jelly, tormenting me, over and over, each time hating him more, and my father for not defending me. I can't tell my mother, I'm too embarrassed. I start obsessing that there is something really wrong with me.

The Afrikaans pronunciation of my name—Niklaas—is intentional, to stress his dislike of me. He emphasises the last part—Klaas—which is what Afrikaners call a slave. Then he drops the first syllable and calls me Klaas.

9

'We have a gift for you, Nicholas,' Storm says with a smile. He places a loosely folded paisley bandanna in my hand. Wrapped inside are three shells threaded on a thong. It is like the one he wears, and there is something almost sexual about the gift. He hangs it around my neck and adjusts the length for the shells to lie in the indentation of my breastbone.

When I walk back to the house, I take my shirt off to feel the movement of the shells against my skin. I bend over to the side to see if they can touch my nipples. When they do, I feel a hardening, a tingle in my pants, and my nipples become erect with excitement.

I know this gift is going to cause a reaction. Uncle Dirk's Zephyr is parked outside. They are all in the lounge having tea when I walk in, dressed only in my red swimming trunks, with the shells lying on my tanned skin. They are in dark suits, dressed for church, filled with restraint.

At the window the thin curtain billows, then the moving air can no longer hold it, and it falls back—for a few moments the only thing moving in the room.

In uncle Dirk's mouth is a biscuit, and he stops halfway stuffing another in. It just waits on his lips to be worked in.

They stare at me. My mother's face drains, and suddenly I feel as if I've betrayed her, driven by my need to show how different I am. In my father's face is the shame I see so often.

278 · ANDRÉ CARL VAN DER MERWE

Then the room fills with cousin Michael's shrill, 'Look, Pa, Nicholas is a moffie, a hippie, just like you said!' There is another squeal of glee from Michael. My father gets up and moves towards me.

'Take that thing off, you bloody little girl, you disgust me!' My mother jumps up and moves towards me. My father reaches me first, grabs the necklace, but it holds and my neck gets jerked down. One of the shells breaks in his hand. Then he takes the thong on either side of my neck and rips it apart.

Clearly on his way to get rid of the necklace, my father starts heading for the back door. I have sunk to the floor and grabbed his leg. He walks with me like a weighted shoe, my mother in tow, begging. The Hoffman men jostle for position to watch the spectacle.

Nothing can stop my father from opening the corrugated door of the outside toilet and dropping my beautiful gift into the stinking, dark mess.

In the evening I watch the sun set over the distant hills. The haziness allows me to look directly at the sun. Far on the horizon the deep red disk hovers above a hill in perfect complementary contrast. Then it distorts to an oval slipping into a void. Eventually only a sliver hangs over the horizon, not letting go of this day, as I never will.

10

I only hear him once he's in the bunker; the sandbags block sound as well as bullets.

'Hey, Oscar, you still have fifteen minutes to sleep.'

'Hey, Vannie. Howzit, my man? No, it's cool, I was awake anyways.'

'*Lekker*, howsa sleep?'

'*Kief.*'

'Where's Mal?'

'Trying to wake Pieterse. Here they come now. You guys can go, you have *min tyd* before roll call and first light. *Lekker slaap, ouens*, good night.'

Pieterse is less willing to start his guard duty earlier. He has been bitching with Mal for waking him. When we leave the little tunnel of the bunker, Pieterse says, 'Enjoy your wank, Bateman!'

Malcolm stops, turns around and with a glint in his eye, he says, 'Fuck you, Pieterse, *druk jou vinger in jou hol en kielie jou kak, man.*'

***

With my head on the ground, I lie looking at the Milky Way, obscured on one side by the embankment that encircles the camp. I turn to Malcolm lying next to me and pull my knees up into a foetal position. There is a smell of stale diesel on my kit and webbing, and I try to block it from my senses . . . make it like when we used to play house; when we used to make a tent contraption out of an eiderdown at the old house in Welgemoed. I remember the feeling of cosiness, the security, Gran, Mom and Frankie.

I think of my mother with an ache of longing. Strangely, I don't get the same feeling about Frankie. I wish he were here, to share all of this with me, but I don't miss him or long for him like I do for my mom. Maybe this is what they mean when they say time heals. But at the same time it gives me a dull sense of betrayal. I wonder if all the troops are as mixed up as I am and go through the same kind of emotions.

All through the night I am haunted by fears and questions, memories and doubts. Will I still be able to do my art? What will people think of these elongated faces I'm drawing? What if the army gets hold of my diaries? DB for sure. Maybe I should destroy them . . . but what about all the stuff I've written and drawn? I can't just destroy it all. Gerrie and Dorman are the ones who shouldn't see them.

Malcolm . . . will our friendship last? Not after the army, never. But I can't tell him that. We'll probably drift apart. I mean, with him in Johannesburg and me in Cape Town, how will we see each other? It's a different world after the army.

When I eventually fall asleep, I have my recurring dream about flying—drifting effortlessly over vast stretches of the Free State, floating faster, with the exquisite scenery lit by the warm light of the sun as it completes its daily journey.

I wake up, and the contrast of the hard surface and the lightness of where I have just been is overwhelming. Then I turn around and dream of Oscar.

When I walk to the toilets the next morning the dream is close and inside—there is a fragile casing that just coats the soft centre that will be my nourishment for today.

***

We go on another random patrol. When we return, we hear that Platoon Three was involved in a contact. They are elated and wear the event like rank. I am pleased that I wasn't one of them, but most of the troops wish they could have had a part in it.

During the night there is an explosion outside the bunker walls. As usual we are told nothing, but then mortars start flying over the embankment from our side and explode in the no man's land that surrounds the base. For about half an hour we hear the metallic sound of mortar sliding down the tube, the explosion as it fires and rockets over the wall and falls with an earth-shattering thud on the other side.

Three more days before we leave for South Africa.

***

Today was meant to be an easy day for us, preparing to leave Koevoet and start the journey home. After breakfast our platoon gathers for the morning briefing, which is of little consequence, as we are leaving within a day. Dorman asks for two volunteers to accompany a Buffel to make a 'delivery up north.' He usually nominates Mal and me, but today we are out of his line of sight, sitting beside a diesel tank. All eyes try to avert his as he scans the faces, and then I see Gerrie leaning over and whispering something to him. Dorman's face lights up and he shouts, 'Bateman, Van der Swart! Where the fuck are those two *naaie*?'

We are told to accompany a Buffel to deliver a gift to a chief in a village 'just around the corner.'

'You'll be back for morning tea. You two must just help unload the stuff.'

We ask someone to watch our kit, then take our rifles, webbing, ammo, bush hats and water bottles, and walk over to the vehicle.

On a trailer attached to the Buffel is a forty-four gallon drum, tied to the one side, weighting it unevenly. We clamber up the metal steps and wait. Four Ovambo Koevoet members climb on after us, and a fifth one approaches the vehicle with a radio, rifle and attitude—clearly the leader of the pack.

For a moment I wonder why it should take seven people plus a driver to deliver this drum, but in the Defence Force you don't question a command. 'It is not for you to question who or why, but to do and die!'

The leader climbs on the first step, whistles, and the driver pulls away. Then he casually completes the climb and swings over the side, unslings a radio, which he balances on a seat, and places his rifle in the rubber-based rack. There is a constant crackling and clicking sound from his radio. The flat metal aerial rattles like a metal tape measure, slightly concave. To shorten its length it has been bent over and tied. Unlike our other patrols and excursions on the border, where we were hardly ever informed of anything, the leader talks freely. He doesn't buckle his harness, and after a few kilometres we all undo our safety belts and hold on to the roll bar in the centre, the warm wind tugging at our clothing and short hair.

He tells us he was trained by Cubans in Angola, to fight for Swapo, but didn't like the way they treated him, so he changed sides. He is young, with open features. He wears a balaclava rolled up into a hat. His shirt is army issue, but there is a rectangle less faded than the rest, where the nametag has been removed. His rifle is a battered looking AK-47 that looks as if it has a long history. I look at it and wonder how many lives it has taken—from some Russian or Chinese firearm factory to Swapo, and now used against its creators and first owners.

On his chin are unshaven black curls. They appear to be screwed in at random. He looks like a boy, but his eyes seem older. He is wearing shorts, and the skin on his blue-black legs is so dry that it has a scale-like quality.

He tells us the fuel we are carrying is for a sympathetic local chief.

I decide to enjoy the ride. The hot, dry air buffeting me, and the freedom of driving through this wild country, remind me of uncle Hendrik's farm.

I tilt my head down, facing my hair to the road, the follicles tingling as my hair moves from left to right, combing the sensation over my scalp.

'What's your name?' I ask the leader, knowing that he knows I'm not entitled to ask him his name. But on the border, in ops, they often don't wear rank, because it draws the first fire. He tells me his surname, which I try to pronounce, but then he smiles and gives me his English name: Ben.

'I'm Nicholas, and this is my friend, Malcolm.' We shake hands.

'Friend?' Mal feigns annoyance.

'I mean best friend.'

Ben moves away, and Malcolm and I start talking about what we want to do on our first pass after border duty. We decide that I will go to Johannesburg with him again—not home to Banhoek. I feel the tingle of reckless independence. I will see Ethan and tell him how I feel about him. That's what I'll do!

The freedom of invented possibility excites us and we start singing songs we hardly know, creating our own lyrics, humming where we fall short. Ben looks at us quizzically, smiles and looks away.

The Buffel slows down and we turn into a narrower, less used road. Ben indicates to the straps dangling from our seats, and we buckle up. There is clear apprehension on his face and an almost imperceptible move towards his AK-47, now balancing in the gun port.

'What happens if we suddenly hit a contact?' I ask Ben, who says that there has never been contact here, but there is the possibility of land mines in the road.

How rapidly things change. Just a moment ago we were having a good time, and now we are reminded of the real possibility of being maimed. It feels as if we were given a gift, which we had to rewrap and return.

'Mal, teach me the words.'

'Which words?'

'The gay ones.'

'OK.'

'Where do they come from?'

'I don't know. I think from the airlines. Right, you know dora . . .'

'Yes, drink, drunk, booze, wine.'

'And nora . . . nora no brain . . .'

'Yes, *dof*, stupid.'

'And HILda,' he says, stressing the hil-part.

'Hideous, ugly old hilda, right?'

'Yes, like hilda army, hilda Dorman and . . .'

'Hillll-da Gerrie!' The longer the 'L' is held, the uglier the person is!

'And grizelda . . .'

'What? Grizelda?'

'Yes,' he laughs, 'Gri-zellllda is even UGLIER!'

'Ah! Gri-zellllda Gerrie!'

'Beulah is beautiful, like me!' he says, smiling. 'Beulah blond!'

He thinks for a while. 'Oh yes, priscilla is the police . . . and iris is irritating, like if you iris someone, like Dorman irises us.'

'How do you remember them all?'

'Vera is vomit, cilla you know . . .'

'Yes, cilla cigarette!'

'Clora is coloured. Bella is bash . . . see, I'd like to bella-bash that iris grizelda Gerrie till he veras all over the *fokken* hilda Dorman!' We laugh.

We reach what seems to be a small town. There are a few build-ings, which are used as kuka shops, and a post office. There is a booth that once housed a phone. People are sitting around as if that is all they have ever done.

On either side of the buildings there are kraals—bundles of existence, with huts seemingly growing out of the soil, their rough branch-pole fences holding parcels of lives. The square flat-walled structures appear to have been placed uncomfort-ably on top of the landscape.

The driver slows down, pulls to the side of the road and goes down a small embankment. I glance back to see the lopsided trailer strain against the pull of added gravity. Then we stop.

There is constant talking on the radio next to Ben—a broth of hissing and fuzzy chatting. The men get off the vehicle and talk to the gathering villagers, while the driver, Mal and I stay behind. The scene is extraordinarily calm in the overwhelming hush of the shut down engine. The little community seems weighted by a sheepskin of heat draped over it. I feel the urge to paint or sketch the scene.

Mal unbuttons his shirt and sinks down in his seat, legs apart. His dog tags are gleaming between his pecs, on a chain that, with its hundreds of ball links, looks like it should hold a bath plug. The two tags are stuck together with Prestik to prevent them from jingling. His abdomen reveals three rows of bumps where no fat, only skin, covers his stomach. My friend looks unexpectedly sexy.

The driver gets out of the Buffel, squints at us, and then walks across the road and past the shop. To the right of the structure he picks a spot. He glances around, moves his arms to the front of his pants and widens his stance to have a pee. Everything is quiet, except for the high-pitched choir of the insects—the Africa sound of heat and waiting.

'Zulu Delta, Zulu Delta, this is Zulu Alpha, come in, over.' Why do I hear this clearly when all the other talking on the radio was just a hiss? Then again, 'Give us your position, over.'

'Shut that thing up, please, Nick. You're closer to it. It's interfering with my well-being,' says Mal, smiling and squinting against the sun.

I lean over the seat and turn the volume down slightly. I couldn't possibly reply to the radio call, because even though we're using an army Buffel, this is strictly a Koevoet operation—Ops K, as it is called.

'I'm not turning it off. They'll know it was us.'

The driver is walking from the opposite side of the road,

286 · ANDRÉ CARL VAN DER MERWE

chewing a twig, which he rolls around to the side of his mouth. He stops in the middle of the road, places his hands behind his neck, looks down at something, then up, and moves from side to side as though he is looking down the road and stretching at the same time. He drops his arms and continues crossing the road. With every step there is a crunch under his boots. His stride seems choreographed to the whirring insects. In slow, slow steps his boots displace the grit on the road in pleasing, crackling sounds that change as he walks off the road and stands in the shade of the silent Buffel—except for the radio that is babbling quietly to itself. Then he flies up the side, grabs the radio, turns up the volume and shouts, 'Are you two fucking deaf?'

He presses the button on the handle. 'This is Zulu Delta, go ahead, over.' Now every word from the apparatus is clear— they have been looking for us for some time.

'Stand by, over.' He drags the radio over the side and runs to where Ben has disappeared into a hut.

When they return there is a new urgency. The driver reverses the trailer to level ground and instructs us to unhitch it.

'Aren't we supposed to unload the fuel?' I ask, wanting to buy time, hoping that somehow everything will return to normal.

'No, no, just leave the trailer here.'

'What's going on?'

'We've been called to help in a contact.'

'Why us?'

'We are the closest. It's just a few clicks north of here. Get in, quickly!' We scramble onto the vehicle. The driver keeps the revs high, waits for the instruction and releases the clutch. The vehicle leaps forward on its long coil springs. Ben talks on the radio, leaning over the driver, shouting directions. Then he sits down and listens . . . and talks as if he can see the people in front of him. I look at Mal for comfort, but he is angry.

'That fucking Gerrie, it's his fault that we're getting into a contact the day before we leave. I'm going to *moer* that fucker.'

'No, Mal, you know it's my fault. It's me Dorman is after. Since Dylan died . . . and Vasbyt, you know . . . and you heard what he said to me the other day. That guy hates me, man.'

We head north on a dirt track. The Buffel sways, rips branches from the bushes, which scratch the side of the metal like nails being dragged over a blackboard. The motor loses momentum as the driver tries to engage low range in the thick sand, and the gears grate. I feel something crawling on my arm. It's a massive spider with a yellow body. I lift my arm and shoot it over the edge with the index finger of my right hand.

The driver brakes violently as we arrive at the entrance to a kraal. There is an evil presence all round. From inside a roof-less room we hear scream-wailing, like a mechanical sound switched on with the press of a button. Then the woman gasps for air with a raw sob that cuts right through us.

Ben speaks to his troops, who jump off and start looking for the spoor of the terrorists and Zulu Bravo's vehicle.

'OH MY FUCK, NICHOLAS, LOOK AT THAT! AAAUGH! OH, GOD, NO!' Mal turns his head away, his eyes closed.

'What, Mal, what?'

'There . . .' He doesn't look around; points backhanded in a general direction. A vein has popped up on his neck, like implanted blue rope. He rushes to the back of the Buffel, bent over by contractions.

'Above the entrance!' Then he vomits. My eyes dart around the huts. Then, on a tree, just metres away from us, I see the head of a man impaled on a stick.

A vice clamps the concept within me, prevents me from thinking rationally, shutting down my ability to assimilate the picture. The head is full of sand, as if it has rolled around in dirt. Soil has dried on the severed neck muscles, pieces of bone, sinew and veins. It is impaled through one eye, and the other eye has been ripped out. The lids are hollow and dark, crusty with dried blood. Strings of nerves hang from them.

I take a step back, my calf snags on a seat and I sit down with a thud. But I jump up immediately and move over to Malcolm. I put my arm around his shoulders. A silver cord of saliva is dangling from his mouth.

'Spit, Mal, spit.'

'Nick, I don't want to be here. I can't . . .'

'Are you OK?'

'Yes.' He puts his head down on his folded arms.

There are only the sounds from the wailing woman, the chirping of a few tiny chicks and the constant jabbering of the radio. The leader has spoken to the driver, the trackers are pointing sticks at the ground, speculating, and waiting for us to follow.

As we leave, the woman runs after us, past the head of her husband. It looks as if she wants to rip the pain from her chest, her shredded clothes flying around her like ribbons. There is desperation in her pleading, and all I can think is to pray that I may never ever see or feel this again.

As we round the fence, I see her looking up at the head. I don't see one of the soldiers lifting his rifle, pulling it into his shoulder and squeezing the trigger. It is only when the bullets tear into her and she falls, face down, that I register the lethal explosion in the chamber next to me.

I claw for self-control.

The Hippo's track is clear. The trackers jump on and ride on the sides for a while, until the branches bully them inside. Adrenaline makes Ben forthcoming.

'The terrs were here just before Zulu Bravo got here. We were tipped off by people who had fled to a nearby village. That woman's husband . . . they tortured him.'

'Why?'

'They thought he was an informer. They raped her, got drunk, slept out here, played soccer with his head.'

'Fuck no! How many?'

'Ten or twelve.'

'TEN OR TWELVE! Shit!' I turn to Mal to see if he has heard, then decide to keep it to myself.

'We can see ten, but with heavy anti-tracking there could be more.'

'How close are the others?' The radio interrupts us. Ben gets up and shouts instructions to the driver, who increases speed. We churn through the sand, swaying violently on the channels cut by the wider track of the Hippo. A flare climbs up above the trees, slows down and falls. It seems very close to us.

'The other group is stuck; they need our vehicle.'

'Can this day get any worse?' I say to myself, or perhaps to God. I go through different scenarios, but they all look bleak. I want us not to find the terrs, but as if he has heard my thoughts, Ben says, 'They're heavily armed, so they won't get far.'

We travel like this for about ten minutes. To my left a black man ducks the branches, cradling his rifle in his lap with his right hand, the other used for balance. On the opposite side another man sits twirling a piece of red fabric between his fingers. His nails are cigarette-stained. Suddenly the men on the back of the vehicle start cheering.

I follow their gaze to a body on the ground. Then I see another one. It has been flung back and lies suspended, crucified, in the fork of a tree. Blood has pooled under the tree and is still shining wet on his soaked shirt, flies all over it.

'They got three here,' Ben says, 'and wounded two. That's when they got stuck.'

I cannot stop feeling the presence of the guest that has now possessed the people on this vehicle. I am terrified by the complete absence of goodness and their almost tangible desire to destroy.

Being so far removed from anything good and kind makes me yearn for my mother. I see her face in front of me; I hear her favourite phrases, like 'dash-it-all' and 'lovey-ta.' Suddenly I feel remorse for all the things I've done wrong. I'll go home after the border to see her. I won't tell Mal now. I'll wait until we're safe. Oh God, will we ever be safe again? Will we make it through this?

We get to the stricken Hippo. Some of the men climb onto our vehicle, others start passing the radio and ammo up the side—grenades, a Russian RPG-7 rocket launcher, rifles, magazines, bullets for the Bren and webbing. As they scramble aboard we hear the repetitive pops of an automatic rifle. It sounds far away. Via radio, we hear that the group in the other Hippo has found and killed one terr and is closing in on the others.

Four men and two of our companions stay behind with the damaged Hippo. They are instructed to keep looking for the spoor of the other five insurgents.

'Ons gaan gou daai ander terr vrekskiet en as ons terugkom, wil ek weet waar die ander loop. Vandag gaan daai fokken gooks hulle gatte sien.'

One of the men who has joined us, looks at Mal and me and says, 'Today you'll see how it's done, your mates in browns know fuck all.' Another shouts something and points to a smoke grenade somewhere in the distance.

When we reach the other group they are standing casually next to their Hippo, with another ragged corpse between them. The trackers are dripping with perspiration, their black faces shining with a mixture of pride, exhaustion and excitement. They have waited for us to change trackers, and they know their prey stands no chance—one wounded man against fresh trackers, two vehicles and all of us.

The chase resumes. It becomes a 'running spoor'—clear, red markings, the blood and prints of the wounded man leading us to his death. It's ironic to think that the very liquid he needs for life now points like an arrow to his ruin—as though it has changed sides.

'Why must we join them and stand by and watch? Surely one vehicle is enough?' I ask, not wanting to witness the killing, but at the same time knowing that the alternative would be to start tracking the other, larger group of insurgents.

'Man, it's better to be two, *ek sê*, when we cross the Yati, but those terrs are not going far. We gonna get those okes, you'll see, or at least a couple of them. Depends if they split up . . .'

'But what about the guys at the broken Hippo? What if they are attacked?'

'No fucking way. Those terrs know they'll only pick up *kak* there. We are too many and they have cover. No, they're *kak* scared, they're running, but those cunts are *moeg*, hey. I tell you, they're finished!'

A soldier picks up the slaughtered terrorist's rifle, checks the rounds in the curved magazine and then exchanges his own rifle for it.

With remarkable energy the trackers chase the spoor in the heat. They run with the two vehicles flanking them. The wounded terrorist is not far ahead.

We reach a pan, the Hippo to our right slows down, and the leader indicates that we should hold our fire. A quarter distance into the pan we see the wounded man. His step has changed to a mere shuffle, but he still seems driven, by fear or something else. In his right hand his AK47 twists slightly as he tries to lift it, but he doesn't have the strength. The weapon's muzzle digs into the ground and rotates lazily as he squeezes the trigger. The impact shudders through the right side of his body; it takes a split second for the sound of the two shots to reach us.

292 · ANDRÉ CARL VAN DER MERWE

Then the rifle drops from his hand; he stumbles, but stays on his feet. The bush khaki colour of the back of his pants has become saturated with a shiny maroon-red, which now streaks down the black of his legs.

Faltering, he looks up at the sky, his head loose on his neck, almost like a drunk, but this is a man dying. Everybody is watching, the engines still idling and the bush sounds uninterrupted. Then a calmness drifts through the man. He caves in as though he's dissolving, and falls onto his face, probably dead before he touches the ground.

'They're so full of drugs they run until they don't have any blood left in them.'

The other vehicle drives up to the body. They casually pick up his rifle, remove the magazine and pass it through the back doors of the Hippo.

Mal leans over to me and says, 'Fuck, Nick, I hope we can go home now. This is hilda sheila, man.'

The car commander standing behind us hears him, but Malcolm doesn't realise this and carries on, 'It's past lunchtime. I'm sick of all this death and shit.' The big Afrikaner grabs him from behind, twists his shirt in his fist and pulls him violently back over the seat. 'Go back, you little sissy. Get out; find your own way home. If you wanna go . . . go! Fuck off, moffie . . . GO!' He releases his grip when the radio calls, and Mal slides back over the seat, red-faced, gulping for air. The car commander takes the handset, listens and says, 'Right, we're coming . . . over and out.' He smiles, but it carries no warmth; it is an expression of a different kind of pleasure. He turns to Malcolm and hisses, 'You aren't going home until we've killed some more terrs. You two are sleeping in the bush tonight, you fucking little turds.'

We reach the Yati, turn left and make rapid progress over what feels like a highway, travelling east on the wide, cleared strip between Namibia and Angola. We travel in silence, each with our own thoughts and fears, until the radio tears us back to the present.

'ON THE RIGHT!' I look up. 'RIGHT, RIGHT, in the trees!' The body of the Buffel reels over to the left as the driver turns.

'How are you doing?' I ask Malcolm.

'OK and you? Are you all right? I saw you bending over just now. Were you praying?'

'Sort of.'

'I'm not scared any more, you know.'

'Strange thing, I don't think I am either. Just kind of tired of all this . . . just so thrown by all those people dying.'

Mal looks at me, turns to make sure he won't be heard again, and says, 'We're going to be fine, Nicky. This is not for us. Let them shoot each other.'

'I've been worried the whole time that I got you into this shit just because of Gerrie and Dorman.'

'Forget it, do you think I'd want to be in the base now, without you and missing all this sheila?'

'Yes!'

'No, no. I'd much rather be out here shaking my teeth loose, hungry, killing terrs, being shot at . . .' he smiles at me. I hold my finger out below the seats for our handshake.

We stop on a slight rise. A grenade billows yellow smoke just above the trees to our left, and we burst into the bush again, crashing over trees and shrubs.

***

We reach the trackers. Downwind I can still see traces of the smoke grenade hanging like synthetic mist amongst the bushes—a veil in artificial colour. I wonder if the plastic air affects the insects and birds.

The trackers are beaming. They have done well, and their superiors are pleased. We are winning in this game. Nobody wants to rest; they all want to be part of the chase. There is something childlike, primitive, about the hunt. Grown-ups' hide-and-seek. If you get caught you die.

'Mal, Dylan once said to me that he . . . that he was ready to die.'

'What?'

'Ja . . . but you know, I'm not. I can't see myself . . . I mean . . . this being my end.'

'Don't think about stuff like that, dammit, you're just making it worse!'

'Dearest Lord God, please, please don't let me die!' I pray.

But then I remember what Mr. Davids taught me. Starting again, I pray, 'Lord, here is this terrible situation. People who are alive right now are going to be dead. I can feel it; it's all around me—it could even be me. If it's your will today that I die, please let it be quick and painless and, dearest Lord, forgive me, forgive me, forgive me for all my sins. May your will be done today. I give you this situation. I trust my life unto thee. I pray this in Jesus' name . . . amen.'

All the while I keep my eyes on the metal barrier in front of me, riveted, to seal off the world of death around me.

The spoor changes direction, from east to northeast to north. They are heading for the border. I constantly check that my rifle's safety catch is off and I hold it ready, not in the gun port, but against my chest and slightly up . . . *my* rifle. Instinctively I say the number, casting an allegiance with the awful device.

Suddenly we are at the Yati again, and then we cross into Angola. The insurgents now know we are close. They don't even attempt any anti-tracking. They have thrown away everything they were carrying, except their rifles, and are running for their lives.

Mal and I are told to shoot only if we are sure it's not a tracker, but best to hold fire. They don't trust us, but we don't care.

Firing breaks out to our left. I hear the radio, 'CONTACT, CONTACT!' And again, *'KONTAK, KONTAK!'* Then we are on top of them, the bush erupts in a mad spectacle of cordite, smoke, dust, tracers and a confusion of noises and men shouting.

I register small fragments of sounds and scraps of movement and colour. Staccato detonations of mechanical engineering. Little springs pushing each bullet up in the magazine as the spent hot cartridge ejects from the chamber. Blazing hot slugs travel through the air at exquisite intervals, hit with equal uniformity, and drive with tissue-shredding force into trees, people or just the soil. All of this becomes indistinct, manic, with tortured screams of ricocheting white-hot death.

When there is automatic-rifle fire from a shrub to our right, we drive straight into the line of fire. I pull my R1 into my shoulder, squeezing off two shots at a time, as we were taught. I fire at a point just below the volley's origin.

This is it, this is it—this is when I kill or die! When the machine gun stops firing from the top of the Hippo, I realise that everybody else has stopped too.

I start shaking. The thought of a bullet travelling towards me from the shrub is suddenly paramount. I know it is not aimed at me personally; it's what I represent. The man is shooting at a government I never even voted for. I know this, but I don't think about it. I am entirely fixed on one goal, and that is to shoot at anything that is a terrorist. Suddenly I understand how people who enjoy this feeling can become addicted to it.

When we stop and the soldiers get off the vehicles, I feel only relief. As if the threat to my existence comes only from that one place, I walk with my rifle at my shoulder, aiming my right eye through the sights, my left eye open to detect any other movement. But it is unnecessary, for the man whose remains lie almost cut in half, will never be a threat to anyone again. It is clear that it was the machine gun that got him. I did not kill him.

In total there are nine terrorists dead—it has been a good day for *our side*.

***

'Listen to that sound . . .' I exaggerate an expression of expectation, holding my hand close to my ear.

'What sound?'

'That, that, listen . . .'

'What is it? Do you mean that?'

'Yes, it's a nightjar.'

'A what?'

'It's a bird, a fierynecked nightjar. I love that call.' Mal listens intently. I look at him, he looks back and smiles.

'There, there . . . listen, you can hear it again. Do you know what it is saying?' I don't wait for an answer but lay the words over the haunting, plaintive sound of the bird's call, 'Good Lord, deliver us. Good Lord, deliver us.'

I become aware of movement towards us. As the shape moves into the light of the fire, I see a person approaching. Above and around him the sinister hard shapes of the vehicles reflect the flickering light.

'*Het julle manne iets geëet?*'

'*Ja, dankie, die een man het vir ons 'n* rat pack *gegee.*' Malcolm answers in Afrikaans with a heavy accent.

The car commander changes to English and there is a definite mildness in his voice.

'Do you want more food?'

I say, 'No thanks,' but Mal says, 'Yes, please, I'd like some more condensed milk.' The car commander turns around and calls to one of his staff to bring more rat packs.

'When are we going home?' Mal asks, now clearly relaxed, 'It's just that we are meant to go back to the States tomorrow.'

'Ja, they radioed for you two. Your platoon is fetching you tomorrow and bringing parts for this fucking thing,' indicating to the broken-down Hippo. 'O ja, and coming to fetch the dead terrs before they stink out the place. Nothing stinks like terr, especially a dead one.'

As the car commander turns to leave, he says, 'You must be careful. Don't sleep under the Hippo. If we are attacked with mortars, the shrapnel ricochets down from the V-angle and will kill you. Rather sleep over there.' He points to a tree.

We make a bed on a groundsheet and blanket given to us. We pick the tree next to the broken Hippo for cover and listen to the sounds of the bush. I feel the urge to hug Malcolm, sleep in the love I feel for him, hold him, and sense his warmth . . . my best friend.

This incredible day starts drifting out of me, out of my muscles. Tomorrow my body will be strong again, with no scars, but my mind will carry them all.

'Nick . . . Nick, are you still awake?'

'Yes, kind of.'

'What are you thinking about?'

'Just this day. So much has happened.'

'You must let it go. Don't think about it too much. Things like these can make one go *bossies*—totally cuckoo.'

'Yes, I know. What are you thinking about?'

'Nothing.'

'Bullshit, you're thinking about Oscar.'

'Mm.'

I must pray, I must thank God for protecting us today, I remind myself, turning to lie on my back. I see the stars above me, turn my palms upwards in meditation and say thank you;

softly and sincerely. I don't want to ask for anything, I only want to express gratitude.

***

Before we leave the next morning, I walk past the Buffel Malcolm and I were in yesterday. I see the neat little scars on the armoured side where AK-47 bullets, fired on automatic, travelled towards us. I climb the large tyre to the rung of the side step, holding on to the dew-wet metal edge of the bulletproof side. From this point I can see where I sat yesterday. I follow the trajectory of the spaced abrasions. There is a lesion just below the ridge. I see that the next bullet would have travelled over the edge directly to my exposed head during the contact. Did he miss, or was he killed just before he fired? I touch the last mark as though I am somehow linked to it. Holding on for a while, I stroke the inside of the lesion; then decide not to look at the marks again.

The early morning bush, so rich with life, so clean and good, contrasts sharply with our journey from where we camped to where our platoon is going to meet us. We are carrying the bodies of the nine men killed, polluting the air with noise and fumes, and damaging everything in our path.

Mal and I try not to look at the blank gazes, bodies with chunks missing, empty rib cages, bags of lifeless meat. The dark skins now have the dull colour of death—muscles lie formless, yet stiff, as if they never really functioned.

I try to feel some kind of hate for these people who tried so hard to kill us; but there is none. All I know is that I'm alive and they are dead.

It is still early morning when we arrive at the four vehicles with our platoon encircling them. The previous day has covered us like a membrane—invisible, but there forever.

'I don't think they'll believe that we slept out here last night without standing guard,' Mal says quietly.

Lieutenant Engel and Corporal Smith want to know everything about our 'major contact.' Dorman asks no questions, but listens to our answers. When we scale the side of the Buffel to take up our designated seats, we are bombarded with questions from the rest of the troops.

I clip and tighten the straps of the seat, but already I have to fight the desire to travel like the Koevoet men—standing instead of being strapped in. Oscar takes his position next to me.

'Vannie, it's good to see you, man. I'm so glad you're safe!' On my other side Malcolm nudges me.

'Thanks, thanks a stack, Oscar,' fighting Malcolm's prods.

Malcolm and I both dodge as many questions as possible, and eventually they stop.

Below us the Koevoet driver who dropped us at the meeting point, talks to Lieutenant Engel and the driver who will lead our convoy, recommending a shorter route back to base.

They decide to take it.

Malcolm sits next to me as he has done every day on vehicle patrol; no need for us to talk any more. Time and compatibility have wrapped around us, and within this union we start the first of many legs back to South Africa.

When the driver changes gears, all ten of the occupants facing the sides rock as one—forward then back, like bottles in a crate. Then we move sharply forward as the driver slams on the brakes the moment the vehicle ahead of us detonates a land mine.

We were drilled to loosen our belts, release the catches on the sides, get off and form a circular defence as soon as the vehicle comes to a halt, because a triggered land mine is often followed by an ambush. The training has the intended effect— we all obey mechanically. Malcolm still carries the memory of the stuck handle and immediately starts attacking the lever.

Our driver, focusing on the Buffel ahead, that is now on its side, with dust and smoke billowing from it, lets our vehicle roll slightly forward instead of stopping dead. In this short distance our right front tyre triggers a fuse that, in turn, triggers another mine.

The only release for the device's energy is upwards, towards the tyre that activated it. The force then travels to the wheel, suspension and body of the Buffel in a wave of terrible power. This invention is designed to cause maximum damage, which it does, particularly to the troops who are busy climbing out.

There is blood somewhere. Sun in my eyes. I try my best to see. Am I sitting? I'm not upright. Bright, bright light. I can't see. No, no. I'm lying, but where? I can hear nothing on the outside, but inside everything is loud. I'm lying on the moulded seats. Yes, that's where I am! Thick, sticky. Something is running into my eyes. I want to wipe it. I can't. My arm is stuck. There is someone with me. Or is there? More people. I close my eyes. I open my eyes when I hear sounds far, far away. Hollow, heavy sounds that clog together and move in and out, in and out. The noise that I can't see is there. No, it's here. Yes, I hear it. More. There are large spaces in between these small bits of recognition. Comfortless, harsh, jarring. I'm lifted. My hand is free. Obscure, hazy sounds from the people. Hollow, wobbling sound. Questions and more questions. I just want to wipe my eyes. If only I could wipe my eyes, I will hear. More comfortable now. Flat. Moving. Blur. Different sounds now. Silver buckle. What is that noise? It's hot. More noise. Mechanical. Smell. Jet-fuel. Where is the buckle? Fumes, petrol. So tight around my head and ears. Under my chin. Tight, tight! Tube. A drip!

On my forehead I feel something crumbly. I rub it and it comes off. I can see a little better, less discomfort in my eyes. I'm sitting. Blood and people everywhere. Outside is far. I look at the metal loop.

Just relax. The side is open, and far below I see the earth streaking past. I can see the other side too. From time to time there are people moving in front of me from the darkness. When they do, their faces distort and I can't hear what they're saying. One looks at me. Talking. Looking and talking. But I can't really hear him. I don't understand. He touches my leg and then my hands, but mostly he looks into my eyes. Then he leaves me and melts into the dark shapes silhouetted by the bright light—a steady, fluid light with shapes.

The Puma helicopter lands at Oshakati. I can see now, and I know what I'm seeing, but in a confused and fuzzy way. I can identify simple things if I'm asked to, but I don't ask myself to give anything a name.

We are lifted into army-brown ambulances. On the inside, it is white and there is a light, opaque whitish, with a shiny silver fitting attaching it to the roof. It is a short trip from the Puma to a prefab hospital, where I lie and wait.

A doctor removes a bandage from my head and a medic cleans the blood on my face. He gives me an injection, shaves my head and stitches a cut. They ask me questions, which I answer lazily. The medic who is seconded to Koevoet says, 'Two Buffels hit land mines—yours and the one ahead of you. Most of the casualties came from yours. It hit while you guys were getting off. The driver says he must have rolled forward.'

'Where is my friend?' I ask.

'Who? The one who was looking after you?'

'Malcolm!'

'I don't know your friend. But it's probably the guy who took care of you. He's fine.'

'Malcolm, his name is Malcolm.'

'I don't know who Malcolm is. Don't worry, just rest,' and he leaves. Above me is a metal roof. I notice the way it is constructed. It has hooks that pull the sheets of metal to the angle-iron rafters. It feels like a cheap barn, harsh and unforgiving—

302 · ANDRÉ CARL VAN DER MERWE

no place to heal. Above me is wire stretched across the room, resembling a washing line. Drips dangle untidily from it.

There is still this buzzing in my ears, like bees trapped in a tin—a persistent whirring, unwavering, with electronic steadfastness.

A scream weaves through a cleft in the humming, entering through my right ear and flooding my cognisance with sound, driven by the way a brain interprets information as life-threatening—from fright to pain, and interlaced with it the smell of hospital. Only then it reveals itself: Something has happened . . .

As the thread of events unravels, I am gripped by concern over Malcolm's absence and I call out, but nobody responds. I become aware of a heavy pain in my head and a burning ache on the surface. My back hurts when I try to move. I am carried on a stretcher down a narrow corridor to a room.

The medic who stitched my head comes in. 'Listen, troop, I don't know who Malcolm is, OK!'

'How many people got hurt?'

'Five of the ten on the back, mostly compressed fractures. One guy's hand is fucked.'

'Are they all alive?'

'No . . . one guy bit the dust.'

'No, SHIT, who died, man? Find out! Fuck, NO! Please! Please just ask . . .'

'OK, OK! Calm down, china. What's his name?'

'Malcolm!

'No arsehole, his *surname*. What do you think this is, a holiday farm?'

'His surname is Bateman . . . please, Bateman, remember, Bateman!'

'OK, I'll check, I'll check. Fuck!'

'He's my buddy. His name is Bateman,' I say again.

He returns almost immediately. 'Your friend is the one with the fucked-up hand.'

'Shit, how bad is it?'

'I don't know. He'll probably need an op. States *toe* with him, china.'

'Where?'

'1 Mil.'

'Dammit,' but I am relieved that Malcolm is alive. 'Besides his hand, is he OK? Can I see him? Where is he? Is his hand going to be all right? Can I go and see him?'

'Listen here, troop, just don't come in your panties! You're not getting out of that fucking bed, and I don't know how bad his hand is. I'm not a specialist, OK? But it's bad . . . OK, china?'

'Shit!'

'You okes are all going back to the States once you've stabilised; all except the oke who's fucked, that corporal whoever.'

'No way . . . is he dead . . . shit, really? And the sergeant?' I ask.

'Ah, him? He was in the front car, a little shaken, like the others, but no bad hits, just some backs, as usual.' Must write this down, I think, and then, with sudden alarm, I swing my feet from the bed.

'Where the fuck are you going, troop? *Is jy fokken doof, ou?*'

'Listen, there is something I must get.'

'What?'

'It's in my shirt.' Sliding forward I move to transfer the weight of my body to my legs, and my head spins.

'Lie down!' the medic says, almost panicked. 'What is it with you, *ou*? Seems like that mine fucked up your brain, or are you deaf? OK, OK! What is it? I'll get it!' When I move forward, he jumps up and pushes me over onto my back. 'Wait here. I will get your shirt. What's your name? Mm . . . Van der Swart,' he says, not waiting for an answer as he reads my dog tags.

He hands me the garment and I fumble through it to the top pocket for my diary. The top half of my shirt is covered in blood, which is now dark-dirty and almost dry. When I retrieve my book, the red wetness has stained the cover and seeped onto the rim of the top few pages.

Through the pain and the drugs I am at Malcolm's side all the way South. From the makeshift hospital in Oshakati we are taken to Ondangwa in a Unimog ambulance. From there, we fly in a Dakota to Grootfontein, where we board a Flossie back to South Africa. After landing at Waterkloof Air Base we drive through an unaware South Africa to 1 Military Hospital at Voortrekkerhoogte, near Pretoria.

It is like moving between two seasons in the space of a day, or two generations, or mindsets—from a deserted rubbish dump to clean porcelain on an opulent dining table.

I am sent for observation for the knock on my head, but it is clear to me that apart from the concussion, my injuries are minor.

I sit next to his white metal bed, under which a grey, army-clean floor mirrors the dragging of time in darkened half-reflection. The white blanket that covers the white sheets is pulled tightly over the frame, and under it his body appears slight.

Surrounding us are damaged young people, lying in similar beds, their lives crippled to different degrees. Most of them believe they will heal, and most will—on the outside. But I focus only on my friend.

Malcolm moves between two planes—a drugged stupor and angry pain. When he is lucid, frightened and suffering, we talk, but when his lids lie half-mast over his eyes, I pray and beg, like a chant, that he will not lose his hand.

Mal's father and sister arrive. Leaving them alone with him, I look back for some outward sign of the blood that links them, but again I don't see any.

After his visit I walk with Mal's father to his car. He says that the doctors have told him Malcolm may lose his hand. He lights a cigarette, sighs, and says he feels the doctors know what they're doing and he will support their decision. What else can he do?

I picture Malcolm with a stump at the end of his arm.

'No!' I interrupt him, almost too loudly.

'It's out of our hands, my boy,' he says gently.

Does he really believe that they are competent enough? Or is it that his fight is depleted? He cares for his son, I can see that, but life, and everything it has done to him, has yanked all energy from him. Now this older man appears to have no drive left to fight, or the power to *will* something so strongly that you somehow make it happen.

'We must go,' says the sister.

'Mister Bateman,' I urge, 'Malcolm has his life ahead of him. He can't lose his hand,' but I realise that my desperation means nothing and I have no power over these events.

'Nicholas,' he says softly, a little smoke escaping with my name, 'they're going to operate and see if they can repair the damage. Only then will they make the decision whether to amputate or not.' It infuriates me that this exhausted man is the only one with some say, and that he has made the decision not to interfere.

'Besides,' he says as I look at his dull eyes with baggy layers of skin under them, 'I have no say, you know. He belongs to the army. So do you. It's out of my hands.'

I walk to the doctor's rooms to find out who will be performing the surgery. All I want is for him to try harder. If there is the slightest chance to save the hand, he must. This is what I have to impress on the man.

I am surprised when the doctor, a commandant, is willing to see me. He is irritated by my arrogance, but he listens. I'm standing at attention in front of him, searching for any mercy he might have, any care and compassion that he is not showing me, but that might just be beneath the surface.

He rides back on his chair, his hands behind his head. It

looks as if he is enjoying the power he wields in this situation. 'Wait, Rifleman Van der Swart,' he says as I do an about turn, stamp my foot as part of the manoeuvre, and proceed to the door. 'Let me explain. We will not simply amputate, except if the wound is threatening the rest of his body or his arm. The first operation will be to start the restorative process. You must realise your friend may require a number of operations. First we are going to clean it up and have a look-see. Amputation is the last resort.'

'Thank you, Commandant, thank you,' I say softly, with as much humility as I can muster.

Walking down the passage, I think of how often we encounter people who have life-changing power over us and the only weapon we have is to plead for mercy. People we may never see again. And I wait.

They chase me away from where I'm sitting in the hospital passage, close to the operating theatre door. I pretend to move away, but I don't.

It feels far longer than just 48 hours since the Buffel triggered the land mine. In this short time, I have watched something settle over Malcolm, like a creeper that has netted around him. And this is what I fear most: losing him, losing the Malcolm I know.

Eventually they call a sister with rank—a staff sergeant—to get me to leave. 'Wait outside, Rifleman, and that's an order. If I see you sitting here again I'm sending you back to the lines. This is bloody nonsense. Is there no *donnerse* discipline in this place?'

I wait directly in front of the entrance to the theatre block, where I know I will be noticed. I don't hear the cars, the people or the birds. My attention is focussed on the doors that will bring news, and on God for intervention.

'Nicholas! Nicholas . . . is it really you?

'Ethan!' Everything in me becomes unsteady. I feel hot and cold, blood gushing in my ears, his name exploding around me.

'Nicholas, what are you doing here? What happened to your head? How are you?'

'I'm fine, but they're operating on Mal's hand.'

'But your head . . .'

'I'm fine, I'm fine, Ethan. We were in . . . Ethan, I can't believe it's you, right here!'

'Nick, what happened?'

'A whole lot of stuff. In all this confusion I forgot that you were at this base, or rather that you were still here. I've been in a kind of a *dwaal* since this . . . this head thing and all.'

'Nick, tell me, how bad is your head?'

'No, not bad at all. I think my rifle must have connected me here.' I stroke the bandage at the spot where they stitched the cut. 'I was out like a light and a bit confused, but I'm fine now; no headaches or anything like that. The staff here have been pretty understanding. They've allowed me to sort of stay with Mal.'

'How long have you been here?'

'Since yesterday.'

'Where's Malcolm?'

'In the theatre. They're operating on his hand. Our Buffel triggered a land mine. I had a little concussion, but Mal's hand was crushed.'

'Fuck, how bad is it? I mean, what do they say?'

'Not much to me. You know what they're like. What I *do* know, is that this first op is to clean up the hand and start the reconstruction—the reconnection of tendons and resetting the bones—or, what I don't even want to think about, amputation.'

I say his name, 'Ethan,' and again, 'Ethan . . .' The person I've carried inside me is now crouching down in front of me, looking at me, reading in my eyes what I can't say, and staring back with confusion.

'In a way it was my fault, Ethan, mine . . .'

'But you said it was a land mine.'

'Yes, but he wouldn't have been on that patrol if it hadn't been for me. We were there because Dorman sent us to deliver fuel.'

'What?'

'It all started with Dylan. I actually think he killed himself because of . . . shit, I'm not making any sense, am I?'

'Wait, let's take it one step at a time. You're obviously going to be here for at least a few days. You'll have time to tell me everything.' I know that Ethan has noticed how close I am to tears. He gets up and says he wants to check on Malcolm.

When he returns, I have regained my composure.

In the short period that Ethan was away, something inside me had sunk into place, almost like a dog curling up on its favourite blanket—a mixture of thoughts for which there suddenly appears to be a home.

Without thinking it through, I say, 'Ethan, I need to see Dylan's parents.'

'OK, I'll take you. Do you know where they live?'

'No.'

'I'll speak to the Welfare Officer. He's quite cool. I'm sure he'll help us. Nick, I'm so sorry, but I have to go now. What ward are you in?'

Before he leaves, he squeezes my knee and we look into each other's eyes. It has happened to me only a few times in my life that a look has travelled right through me.

***

I sit smiling next to Malcolm while he sleeps off the last of the anaesthetic, his hand still intact. When he has shed the last of the drugs, I tell him about Ethan and my plan to visit Dylan's parents.

'So, how does he look?'

'Amazing . . . you'll see for yourself, Blondie. He'll be visiting you a lot. Listen, I don't know how much longer they're going to let me stay here.'

'No way, man!'

'Well, at least Ethan will be here. Don't you steal him now!'

'I'm not into twinkies, you know that. Only real men for me, thanks.'

I sigh, and after a pause I say, 'I need to tell you something, Mal. When we were doing section leadership, Dylan and I slept next to each other one night.'

'You little tramp! In the trench? Fuuuuck me! Why didn't you tell me?' Malcolm is hugely excited by this information. It does more for relieving his pain than the pills do.

'I don't know actually. I guess the whole Dylan thing is just something I wish I could escape, but I realise I'm going to have to work through it.'

'Go on.'

I tell him about the night in the trench, the freezing cold, how Dylan dried me, gave me his shirt, and held me from behind when we lay together.

'So, did you guys, you know, have a poke-in-the-whiskers?' he asks, laughing.

'No, we did not. Shit, you know, that's all you think about. We just lay really close; his arm around me. He may even have saved my life that night . . . makes me feel even worse. You remember how closed Dylan was? One never really knew what he was thinking, but that night . . . I think he wanted to tell me that he was gay.'

'And did he?'

'No, but I felt it. You know what it's like when you just know what someone is going to say, but you don't want to hear it.'

Suddenly Malcolm is serious. 'Nick, there's something I need to tell you . . . seeing that this is truth hour and all.'

'Yes?'

'It's not just you that Gerrie has it in for. I've been wanting to tell you this for so long, but I didn't know how to. We have a history.'

'NO! No way! Don't talk shit here, Mal!'

'Well, the weekend before the border I was at the club on the Saturday night, and I'm like really camping this hunk. Remember, I told you? I was going to tell him it was his duty to be nice to me, because I was going to risk my life to protect him and all that. I wonder if it would have worked.'

'Yes, I'm sure it would have, but tell me about Gerrie, man. Besides, you said you didn't go home with the hunk.'

'True, but I never told you why. That little *poes* Gerrie suddenly appears—in the D!—and he won't leave me alone.'

'Gerrie! In a gay club! Are you serious?'

'Yes. At . . . the . . . Dungeon.' He pauses between each word for effect. 'And he won't leave me alone and says that he has no place to stay and please can he come home with me. So I said yes. I mean, he was one's *makker* and all, you know, you do that for your buddies.'

'So why is he so nasty to us?'

'Guess because he knows I know his secret. He made me promise that I wouldn't tell you, but I reckon you should know.'

'But I still don't understand, Mal. Surely he knew you had some serious ammo against him. I mean, remember, we even had that argument about homosexuality and all.'

'And Oscar kissed you!'

'So *that's* why Gerrie did it, to discredit the two of us in case you ever said anything. The little bastard!'

'But wait, I'm not finished.' Malcolm moves up against his pillows. 'So we get home and, as you know, I only have the single bed, so I make him a bed on the floor and we say good night and so on and then . . . .. Ooooh, I'm so tired.'

'Stop that! AND?'

'Well,' laughing, he tries to yawn but goes on, 'a little later I feel him getting into bed with me. And of course I tell him I'm not interested and that I don't feel comfortable, but you know, a man is not a stone, and I had a lot to drink and all, but I still say no.'

'Thank goodness.'

'But then he says I must just lie back, I needn't do anything. So I reckon cool, I'll get a *lekker* blow or a hand job, what the fuck. But then, instead of him giving me a blowjob or some-thing, he starts licking me, all over, until he gets to my feet, and then he jerks himself off and leaves me. Doesn't say a word, cleans himself and gets back into his bed.'

'What?'

'The next day he's like ice towards me, makes me swear on my mother—he obviously doesn't know her—says he must go, and never talks to me again.'

'Wow! Now it all makes sense. That's why he went on and on about us being gay and trying to get the whole platoon to call us moffies. Shit, what a warped cunt. Tell me, when he was licking you,' we suddenly find it funny and burst out laughing, 'did you, like, touch him and stuff?'

'You know, Nick, that's the thing; I didn't. It was as if he wanted the humiliation more than the sex. It wasn't sexual for me at all, and when he came, I was just too happy it was over. It was so mechanical, and he was embarrassed, not like wow, full-on climax, you know.'

'It's actually quite sad, isn't it?'

'Yes. But I just wanted you to know so that you'd stop feel-ing so guilty about my hand . . . OK?' For a while we're quiet.

'Thanks, Mal, but from now on no more secrets, right?'

'Right.' Then he smiles. 'I shouldn't have told you; could have milked you. Come now, Nick, it's your fault, now I need to be relieved,' pointing down at his groin.

'Mal, does it make sense to you, this Gerrie thing?'

'You know, I have no problem with it. I reckon each to his own, as long as nobody gets hurt.'

'Yep, guess there are some strange sexual habits out there.'

'Perversions.'

'Maybe we shouldn't call them perversions. As you said, each to his own. Fuck, if a guy wants humiliation, or bondage, who cares? Provided it's not abusive, or with underage kids or animals. It's their choice.'

'Yep, but in our case we've been persecuted simply because of the way we were born, man.'

'And it's going to be like this forever if we don't do something about it. If you think about it, we're the most victimised minority, and yet we're not a threat to anybody. But people are so thick, most of the discrimination is because most straights don't even know the difference between a homosexual and a paedophile.'

'Do you remember those two Boksom Boys?'

'Of course!'

'Do you know what the worst thing was for me? Not the fact that they were so badly beaten up. But when they walked into the mess and the whole place went silent and they stood there and someone started chanting "moffie, moffie, moffie" and everybody joined in.'

'Yes, I remember.'

'Nick, I swear, I don't know if I'll survive that. I'm proud of being gay, but there's no way that anybody in the army must catch us out, you know. It's just too dangerous.'

'No. You know, to me the saddest thing is that they split up. I mean that the one oke betrayed the other one. But I tell you . . . that guy, he stood proud. He lost his friends and his family, but he told me that night they would not get him to be dishonest; that's all he has. I've always felt so guilty for not being able to help him in some way.'

'Shit, Nick, what could you do? Hell, man, thank heavens

you didn't try, otherwise you would be in Ward 22 with them, being fucked up for life.'

'I still felt like a traitor. Isn't it pathetic that we've become so used to living in secrecy and hiding our feelings that it's become second nature? We just accept the way we're treated. Shit, we don't even know what it must feel like to have an open, caring relationship with a partner. It's like these older guys who live their whole life together as "friends" and never come out, not even to their closest family. You know, we're actually as badly persecuted as the blacks in this country. Even more so. At least it's not illegal to be black!'

'Did you ever wish you were straight?'

'Of course I did. Prayed for it.'

'Do you think it will ever change? I mean, will we ever be treated like "normal" people?'

'No, not in this country, not with this government. And the general public will also have to change their attitude.'

'Nick, when we get out of this shithole, we're going to have a good time, man, I guarantee you. The first thing is, we're saving up and going to America: New York and San Francisco!'

'Yes, and have all the sex we've missed out on.' I look at my friend and I know somewhere deep inside there will be good times ahead for us—very good times. And in that moment the fears that I have had of the two of us drifting apart after the army, is gone. I recognise the cables that have bound us, and suddenly know that we will be friends forever.

11

The Welfare Officer contacts Dylan's parents, who say they will see me, and they send a driver in a black Daimler Double Six to collect me.

The house that Dylan left for the army is set in green abun-

314 · ANDRÉ CARL VAN DER MERWE

dance. It exudes a comforting feeling of tradition, of perpetu-
ity, of a strong foundation. Uniformed servants are manicuring
the garden as we drive up to a pillared veranda.

Inside there is the stillness of antiques and heavy drapes,
mingled with the light of marble and crystal. I am led to an
enormous patio at the back of the house, with sloping gardens
leading to a large pool, beyond which are more lawns, a tennis court, stables and a forest. The furniture on the terrace is
covered in a pink-and-white striped fabric. The woman sitting
under an umbrella gets up as I approach. She is tall and elegant,
but she seems to have a tenuous composure. Her black hair is
so perfectly in place it makes me think of black candyfloss. Her
mouth is drawn in a blemish-free face, the skin on her forehead
and around her eyes tight.

'Welcome, Mr. Van der Swart, can I offer you something
to drink?' At her side, a servant steps forward, awaiting her
instruction.

'Please call me Nicholas,' I say.

'Very well, Nicholas it shall be. Something to drink?' she
asks again as she sits down.

'I'll have a Coke, please,' I say as the chair that has been
pulled out for me is placed gently against the back of my legs.

'I am told you knew my late son.' When she says 'son' her
mouth quivers, her voice slightly high and gaunt.

'Yes, Mrs. Stassen, we shared a bunk bed and a cupboard.
I was his closest friend.'

'Dylan never had many friends. Introverted boy, my Dylan.'
Her words are pensive, and I struggle to think of something
to say.

'He was very quiet, but we were good friends. In fact, just
before . . .' I stop. What am I saying? Nicholas, pull yourself
together. I look at her and say, 'We were very close,' and then
I wonder if she might misinterpret *very close*.

'Dylan should never have gone to the army. Lord knows,

with all John-Andrew's connections we could have got him off, or sent him out of the country. None of our friends' children ever went to that beastly place.'

I hear my father's words: 'Yes, these rich people just live off the fat of the land and are not even prepared to send their sons to the army!'

She keeps quiet, but I see her thinking, wanting to say more. Or perhaps it's the vodka delaying her speech. 'What a waste . . . oh Lord, what a waste. What have we done?'

'Mrs. Stassen, I'm so sorry. I just want to say I really, really am.' She doesn't listen. I want to reach out and take her quivering, manicured hand laden with rings—just to touch her, to steady her. But I don't.

'My beautiful, beautiful, gentle boy.' I look at her eyes. She is weeping more than just tears. She is broken inside, under the veneer of expensive skin products.

She opens the catch of an ornate little pillbox and takes out a capsule, which she swallows virtually unnoticed. A man, clearly Mr. Stassen, approaches from the opposite side of the terrace and sits down at a table that is set for lunch.

The butler invites us to join Mr. Stassen at his table, which stands beside dramatically high arched windows and doors with stone surrounds. A male servant assists Mrs. Stassen to the table. She starts introducing me, but her husband interrupts her.

'Yes, Margaret, I know who the young man is.'

'Good day, sir, I'm Nicholas,' I say, extending my hand. After a cursory handshake I take the seat indicated to me while he picks up the white cordless phone brought to him on a tray.

Before me on the glass table is the finery of Dylan's life that I never knew. He could have held this silver knife and fork in his hands and sat in this chair, I think as Dylan's father talks on the phone. Between sentences he indicates that I should start on the hors d'oeuvre placed before me. How difficult the change to the crudeness of the army must have been for Dylan.

Mrs. Stassen, in the grip of her tablet, hardly speaks, and when she does, she is ignored.

Mr. Stassen puts the phone down, turns his attention to me and starts asking me about the army. He is particularly interested in what is happening on the border. I gloss over Koevoet, the contacts and the little I know of the war, but tell him in detail about Malcolm and his injury. The friendship between Malcolm, Dylan and me is an easier place to visit than Koevoet.

As I sit making small talk in a setting that seems to have no bearing on the friend I have lost, I am suddenly filled with regret for encouraging this meeting and I have to fight the urge to leave.

Why am I here, and what can I tell them about their son, apart from the fact that we were friends? Am I here only because they felt it would be inappropriate to refuse me? Were we good enough friends for me to have crossed this divide? I can't tell them about my love for their son. How does one explain such a love, discovered deep within, months later, in a war? And how is it that I can love two people? Do I only love him now because he is forever out of reach? How much did he love me? Did he, after all, really love me?

As we eat, Mrs. Stassen sinks deeper into the exit of drugs and alcohol. She sips her chardonnay without appearing to allow the liquid over her lips, but the wine steward continually fills her glass until Mr. Stassen indicates to him to stop. She uses the leftover vodka, which she has not allowed them to remove, to swallow another pill.

'You,' she suddenly says, pointing at her husband. 'You,' she says again. I glance at him and see him stiffen. He has an expression of anger and apprehensive expectation, but he remains composed. 'You,' she says for a third time, 'you killed Dylan. You just won't admit it, but you did! Go on, tell the boy!' He doesn't reply, but simply indicates to the staff to help her inside.

As they transfer her to a wheelchair, she tries to fight them off with arms that have forgotten how. Her refinement and poise prevent her from raising her voice and using force to resist. She sinks into their charge as she has probably done all her life; trapped by privilege.

'I'm losing her. You cannot believe what a regal woman Dylan's mother was, but the drugs have taken her.' Something tells me that before this tragedy he would never have shared something so personal with a stranger.

'Surely there is help, treatment? It's only been a few months,' I say and immediately wish I hadn't. But I am so nervous that I need to talk, so I talk before thinking.

'Nicholas,' he says, ignoring my question. 'I've read all Dylan's letters again. He often spoke of you.' Suddenly I find it difficult to hold my knife and fork, so I balance them on the side of the plate and look up.

'I think he was very fond of you. You were a good friend.' My mouth and throat are like sandpaper. He looks at me, into me, as if he has already been inside and is just re-checking something.

'Not good enough, I'm afraid. I feel I should have tried to prevent what happened.'

'The thing is, Dylan was always a sensitive child. I thought the army would make a man out of him. How wrong I was.'

'He *was* a man, Mr. Stassen. Really. He coped with all the PT, the training, in fact, better than most, despite . . .'

'Despite what?'

'Well, despite the fact that our sergeant seemed to pick on him, which is what they do; it's just the way the army works. But I don't think that's why Dylan, you know, ended it all.' There is silence and I wonder if I have opened something that should have remained closed. What happens if this man with all his power starts an enquiry and I am asked to testify?

'What did this sergeant do?'

'He just sort of picked on Dylan. The thing is . . . they . . . it happens to all of us at some point. I guess they want to see how much we can take. Dylan could take it. Believe me, he was really tough. The thing with Infantry School is that we are there voluntarily, provided we are physically and mentally fit. So the instructors are pretty much allowed to do anything they want with us. We can refuse, but that would mean leaving the course. If it all got too much, Dylan could have left, got an RTU, but he had this tremendous tenacity. Mr. Stassen, please know that your son was a man . . . the finest there is!' I want to say, 'Whatever *a man* may mean,' but I decide against it.

'Thank you,' he says. The jumbled sentences twirl around my head. Did I say something I shouldn't have?

'What is an RTU?'

'Return to unit. The unit we were first posted to. But Dylan chose to stay, and I can tell you he was one of the toughest people I know . . . knew. It was not the training, Mr. Stassen, I'm sure of it.'

He looks past me, pensive for the first time. Just as I expect him to ask me what I think the cause of Dylan's suicide was, he says, 'No, it wasn't the training . . .' A long silence follows, and I wonder why this man is implying that he knows why Dylan ended his life. Then he asks me.

'Nicholas,' he says, looking straight at me, 'why do *you* think my son killed himself?'

'I don't know.' How do I do this? 'I think it was everything—just life generally. Dylan never really opened up. We shared many things but he never told me his deepest feelings.'

'It doesn't really matter any more, does it? Some things cannot be undone. Now it's just a matter of learning to live with it. I just hope my wife pulls through.' He sighs and looks up at what must be her bedroom window.

'Mr. Stassen . . .' We are already out of our seats when I say this. It is clear that the time set aside for me is over, but I sink back into my chair and he follows suit. 'Mr. Stassen, I think maybe I could have avoided what happened.'

'Why do you think this?'

I talk despite the screaming in my head telling me to stop, bracing against the decision that I would NOT tell him I think his son was gay, or in love with me. The words flow out as if I have no control over them; words I decided must absolutely remain unsaid.

'If I had listened more intently, if I had allowed him to speak, maybe he would have told me, or maybe he even did. But I wasn't sensitive enough to realise that he wanted to tell me. I think . . . one night he wanted to tell me something, and I wasn't a good listener. I think it was difficult for him to even start telling me, but I just didn't want to hear.

'Don't go on. It's not your fault, that I'm sure of.'

Now that I've started, I want to go on, but he has stalled my momentum. I feel a sense of collapse. He reaches forward and puts his hand on my shoulder.

'Never blame yourself, and don't talk about it. It is not your fault that my son took his life.' By now we both have tears in our eyes.

'Come with me, my boy.'

We get up and he leads the way down a wide passage. On the one side glassed arches look out over the estate, and on the other side paintings and antiques are arranged on a wall that leads up to a vaulted ceiling.

To me this splendour becomes a new epitaph to Dylan, that mystical phantom. I decide to lay him down in these environs from now on, rather than in the harsh Defence Force. Now that he has gone, he can rest here . . . in my mind.

Mr. Stassen has stopped and appears to be wrestling with some private thoughts, and I leave him to it. We are in a huge space with a massive staircase curving upwards between carved wooden balustrades.

I can see Dylan moving down these steps, skipping down the last one and swinging on the end of the balustrade to turn left and walk down the passage.

'I've decided to show you something,' Mr. Stassen says.

I follow him to his office. He removes a key from his oak desk, opens a cupboard and starts turning the knob of a safe. The door is released with a thunk. He reaches for a letter in the safe with the familiarity of someone putting his hand on his own heart.

'This . . . I intercepted it. He had posted it just before he took his life. I must insist, for the survival of my wife and family, that you never talk about its contents. I know now that you need to read it.' He passes a blue envelope to me.

My dearest, dearest Mother and Father

I know I am about to cause you great pain, but what I am about to do, cannot be avoided. I cannot go on. I REALLY CAN-NOT. I have debated this decision for many years. There is something about me that I am unable to change; something that will cause you great pain and shame.

I am a homosexual; I am gay. I know this is not tolerated. I know that you see it as a weakness, as despicable. I know how you feel about the shame this would bring on the family, but believe me, I CANNOT CHANGE. It is for this reason that I have decided to end it all.

I am not miserable because of the army; it is in fact here that I have had a glimpse of the happiness I will never have. Mom and Dad, I have fallen in love, and it is a love I know I can never have. I have avoided this in the past, but now it has consumed me. I simply cannot live like this, you must under-stand, because I know and you know I will never be allowed to live with a man.

I am sure the man I love is also gay. To know that it is right

there and to know that it can never be, is more than I can bear.
It is all I think of, constantly, and I feel as if I am going mad.
I am so very, very sorry for the heartache I will be causing
you. I want you to know that I understand and do not blame
you for anything. The world we live in is to blame, not you.
I beg of you, know that I am not doing this to punish you;
I am doing this to free myself, to free you . . .
Your loving son,
Dylan Edward

Something inside me has broken. Tears wash over my face, my shoulders shake and I have neither the strength nor the wish to control it.

I cry for the irretrievable waste, for the loss of Dylan's life, the complexity of it, for the fact that I didn't love him when he was with me, for the suffering, for not trying to prevent it, for not being sensitive enough, for Ethan being there at a time when there was a Dylan. I cry for Mal who might lose his hand, for the bodies that lay on the floor of the Buffel, for the woman who was raped and then murdered, for her husband who was decapitated in front of her, for everybody and everything sad. Had I known, had I known . . . I would have, yes, I would have stopped it, because I could have made a difference.

And I cry for my non-existent relationship with my father . . . and for holding on.

I sit bent over, my head on my arms. He comes to comfort me, puts his arm around me, and I can feel him sobbing too. Eventually he says, 'You are that boy, I mean man, he was talking about. My son was in love with you, wasn't he?'

I nod. 'Yes, it was me. He never told me, but it was me. You see, Mr. Stassen, I could have prevented it. How can you ever forgive me?'

'No, Nicholas, it's not your fault. I think it's clear from this,' and he shakes the blue pages gently. 'We are the ones . . . no,

I . . . I'm the one who failed my son.' The last words come out in gulps of emotion. He says 'no, no' over and over, and then he repeats Dylan's name and cries. Eventually he says, 'Thank you for the letter you sent; it meant a lot to me. I should have contacted you.'

'You did write.'

'Yes, I did, but I should have done more. Thank you for coming. Do you know we used part of the poem you had sent as an epitaph on his stone? You were so important to my son, and we made no effort. I'm so sorry, Nicholas, I failed you too.'

'No, Mr. Stassen, I understand. Really, I do. My father and I . . . it's never worked out between us. He knows nothing about me, and he doesn't want to either. I understand how difficult it is for a father.'

'Perhaps you should tell him, talk to him?'

'Yes, I will, but he won't understand. I know that.'

'You know,' he says, 'Dylan was right. I wouldn't have accepted it. But only now, after this loss, do I realise how wrong I would have been.' Again, he is quiet for a long time. Then he says, 'He will be like the words you wrote in your letter: forever young.'

I notice a photograph in a walnut frame. Dylan and an attractive man stand on either side of an impeccably groomed woman. Dylan has that intense expression that I know so well. When Mr. Stassen sees me looking at it he says, 'Dylan with his grandmother, and that's my younger brother, good-for-nothing; lived with my mother in New York. She spoilt him terribly, that's why he ended up the way he did. I wanted to be sure Dylan didn't end up like him, so I was always very strict with him; perhaps too strict.'

We are both still looking at the picture when he says, 'Dylan was with her when she died, just outside Bergdorf Goodman . . . massive heart attack.'

I gasp, but decide not to say anything about our last conversation, hoping he reads the gasp as one of sorrow.

'Is there anything I can do for you? Anything?'

Without having to do much thinking, I say, 'Yes, there is something. Would you be able to get good medical care for our friend Malcolm? I really don't want him to lose his hand.'

'Consider it done, Nicholas. If it is medically possible for his hand to be saved, you can rest assured it will be, whatever it takes.' He asks for Malcolm's full names. I give him his number, rank and name, fleetingly thinking how conditioned I've become—giving Malcolm's number before his name.

When we eventually get to the car, he says he would like me to stay in contact and hands me an envelope. 'This is for you. I should have seen to it that you got this, but I just . . .' his voice trails off, but he knows that I understand.

'If you ever need me, Nicholas, I will be here.' I thank him and extend my hand, fighting an urge to hug him. When he takes my hand, he places his left hand over our grip.

The driver, who has been standing attentively beside the open door of the car, closes it after I slide from the grip of his employer. I wind my window down. Dylan's father leans on the door, pressing down on it with a weight I can feel as if it is me he is leaning on.

'I would have been proud to have you as . . . as . . . my son's friend. How I wish things could have been different.'

I whisper, 'Thank you.' He taps the door gently, and the driver pulls off.

***

How hopeless is hopeless? Where does one stand in oneself when one takes everything, every single thing, one's very breath, one's thoughts, one's history? Forever . . . What is forever when a life is ended? Is forever not just the length of a lifetime? How are time and distance and living measured where he is? Where is he? Surely I was there when the decision was made? Somewhere close. Surely he carried it around with him? Yet I never noticed. What did he think just before he squeezed the trigger? Did he hurry into the act? How large is the argument? Is there an argument? Is there a part that disagrees, makes a case for life?

12

An hour after lights-out I crawl out of bed to the toilets, choosing a cubicle below one of the two exposed bulbs. I carefully open the letter Mr. Stassen has given me. Inside I find a page from a standard issue army notebook and a bunch of small pages pinned together. On the single sheet Dylan wrote:

Empty is not when there is no longer anything inside—but when a container can never hold anything ever again.

Lonely is not when there is nobody; lonely is when there IS and you walk away.

Desperate is when they rip your soul from within you, dangle it in front of you and then dry it and cage it.

Pain is not something you feel, something you can package and identify; pain is when anything . . . anything else is better, including the complete unknown.

On the other papers he wrote:

Fate stares at me disdainfully, as though we have just come upon each other. In her stare I can see there has been preparation.

She beckons and I follow to a cliff. 'Look,' says Fate, 'look down there, all the way to the end; there peace is waiting.'

Before me my life lies clear, well lit in perfect sight, no distant perspective, even though it is far and long—it's all clear, I stare into its black, icy face.

Deepgrooved valleys like tracks
Deepgrooved valleys like a maze
Deepgrooved valleys like a jail

There are other, untidier writings with corrections crossed out, and in some places he wrote three words before finally choosing one. I don't understand every sentence, but it is clearly desperate.

Does the moon miss man? Why does it look at us all the time? Proclaiming our pain. What a hassle this coloured castle! Don't bother to have a party.

She takes another gin
The tin still has a din but hollower than before
Every negative space in my forest is a masterpiece and my fullness is depicted by taste

The following day I am issued a travel pass and a ticket back to Oudtshoorn, for 'light duty' until the stitches are removed. On the same day, Malcolm is transferred to a private hospital.

That night I board a train.

***

'Hey you, Scank-muffin.'

'I must say goodbye now.'

'No way, really?'

'Yes, they're sending me back.' In the background, The Sutherland Brothers are singing *Arms of Mary*.

'No, Nick, think of something. Complain about headaches or something!'

'Well, I sort of did, but they say if I had concussion they would have known. The doctor had me sussed. In any case, he said I could phone anytime to find out how you are. How's your hand?'

'Shitty. I'm so pissed off about this. Why did this have to happen to me? Shit.'

'They're going to sort you out.'

'Yes, I know. Thanks for organising it. I still can't believe everything you told me about Dylan. Shame, man.'

'He must really have been hurting, Mal. It must have been terrible. I just don't know why I didn't see it. His dad asked me not to tell anybody, but I reckon, well, Dylan was one of us, and we're family.'

'Yes, *boet*, or should I say sis?' He laughs and says, 'Funny, you'd think he had everything to live for, and actually he had nothing. Look at my folks, my background . . .'

'I reckon in a way your background gave you the strength to cope. I mean, your dad isn't going to put any pressure on you. That's a huge gift, you know. You're blessed with a different kind of wealth.'

Just before I leave they play *Substitute* by Clout.

'Shit, Mal, this song reminds me so much of Paul Roos. I can't believe it, but it was just last year that I was still at school. It feels like another lifetime.'

'Not even a year, Nick . . . not even a year.'

'Hey, Nick, I love you, my best friend.'

'And I love you, Blondie.'

Walking away, I know he is watching me. At the door I turn, smile and wave.

Ethan drives me to the station in the MG he was given when his mother got a new Range Rover.

'Before we leave I must quickly drop this off at Ward 22.'

'Ward 22! That's where they send the gay guys, isn't it?'

'Not only the gay ones, all the people the army thinks are "subversive" or different.'

'Shit, I didn't know it was right here.'

'Yes, 1 Mil.'

'Wow. Can I come in with you?'

'OK. But I must warn you, Nick, it's not pretty. Those guys are buggered up, man.'

'I've heard stories.'

'Nothing you've heard comes close, believe me.'

At an office we are told to go to a room at the end of a series of wards. The sealed file that Ethan has been instructed to deliver, has to be handed to a certain staff sergeant and nobody else.

There are about six beds in each ward, most of them empty. Where there are patients, they seem to be very ill—curled up and staring blankly at nothing. The entire area feels covered in a layer of despondency. Suddenly I am overcome with fear that they could decide I'm sick too, because to them I am.

'Ethan, I think I'm going to wait outside.'

Walking back, I feel vulnerable and try to look as un-mad as possible. As I step outside, I see Deon sitting with a group of patients in a demarcated area.

I greet him, but he looks at me like a dog that wants to please its master, struggling to understand what is required of him. He is clearly drugged and searching for a memory, tilting his head slightly and narrowing his eyes.

My first instinct is to remind him who I am, which I do. Eventually he seems to start remembering. Should I remind him of the *bokshom* boys, or that evening before he was taken away? Or would that do more harm than good? His speech is slow and lethargic. I get the impression that he knows what he is saying, but finds it difficult to formulate the words. But it is clear that he trusts me and knows that I am from the 'outside.'

'They're shocking me,' he says idly.

'Why?' I ask.

'Because I'm gay.' There is a long silence in which he looks at me with sad, milky eyes. I know he wants to say more, because he moves his head and throat in a way that suggests he is trying to almost regurgitate words. I want to put my arms around him and tell him it's going to be all right. While I wait for him to get the next sentence out, I notice how thin and wasted he looks. When the mind is damaged, the entire body becomes infected.

'It's OK,' I eventually say. 'It really is. Just take your time.'

'They are . . . they . . . they do bad things to us.' There is no correlation between the words he is saying and his body language.

'Like what?'

'Can you tell my parents that I'm here?'

'Don't they know?'

'No, none of these people, none of their parents know where they are.'

'How do I get hold of them?'

'I can't give you the number now. If they see me . . . I can't take the chance.'

'I have a way,' I say, knowing that Ethan will help.

'How?'

'I have a friend; he works at 1 Mil.'

'Please, please, I must get out of here. I'll die. I know I will. People disappear here.' He glances at the medics sitting in the corner, who also serve as guards. Instinctively I move closer to the door to get out of their field of vision.

'What are they doing, Deon?'

'If they catch me trying to get out, they'll send me to Klippies.'

'What is Klippies?'

'It's a sanatorium.'

'Why would they send you there? It doesn't make sense.' I see that the thought of that place makes him withdraw, so I change the subject and ask how long he has been here.

'I don't know,' he says unhurriedly, appearing even more distant.

'Since Infantry School?'

'Yes.' He tries to pull himself together, looks at me almost calmly and says, 'People disappear here . . . completely. The next morning their beds are rolled up and they're gone.'

'Surely they are just taken to another hospital, or maybe they're just sent ho . . .'

'No, no, they are gone forever,' he interrupts me. 'It's the really sick ones, the ones that . . . that . . . are weird. When they go mad from the stuff that these people do to them.'

'What kind of stuff?'

He starts talking, but then he bends forward and shakes his head saying, 'No, no, NO!' over and over. He shivers, and suddenly he starts sweating. I steady him and help him to sit down. He hangs on to me, but I try to keep my distance, for it feels as if he won't let go if I allow him a hold.

'Deon,' I urge him, 'you must be careful. If we attract attention, they'll send me away.' But I am more nervous that they might keep me 'in.'

He starts talking again, this time deliberately, lucidly and eerily calmly. I get the feeling that he is talking without picturing the things he is saying; just knowing he has to get them out.

'They put us in a mortuary with body parts. It's like a cool room: dark, very, very dark. One at a time. Everywhere you look there are just bodies or pieces of dead people.' His voice has become loud and he is sobbing.

'Deon, shh. Not so loud. Take your time.'

'They turn off the lights and they leave us there, alone, for a long time.' For the first time he seems to be beating the drugs that are chaining him. It attracts attention from a patient near us, who starts making howling noises. He comes towards us, and as he focuses on us, he starts wailing. Deon tries to shoo him away, but the situation quickly unravels. Another patient gets involved, starts talking gibberish and then starts barking like a dog. Deon grabs hold of me and starts crying.

Two guards rush towards us and start pulling Deon off me. They grab his arms and twist them behind his back. The other two patients are pushed so roughly that they fall on the asphalt. Deon is cowering and wailing. One guard twists his arm further and pushes it forcefully behind his neck. Deon buckles over, crying and begging. Within seconds they have him up the steps and away. I am told to wait outside the complex, but before I reach the door, Ethan is at my side.

'Sorry it took so long.' Then, looking at me, he says, 'What's wrong, Nick, what happened?'

'I'll tell you in the car.' Which I do.

'Nick, I have a friend who worked in Ward 22. We must never talk about this. Please promise me you won't repeat this to anyone.'

'I promise.'

'My friend who worked there asked for a transfer, which didn't come easy. If it weren't for his parents' contacts, he would never have got out. They make those medics and guards do dreadful things to the patients so that they are kind of part of it. He made me promise never to tell anybody. He told me they put the guys in the mortuary for two days and two nights, with body parts all over the place—people who died on the border, pieces lying open on trays, everywhere, man.'

'I was hoping it was the drugs talking.'

'There's a boxer, and they have this boxing ring, and all the officers sit around watching this guy fuck up the patients. They put gloves on the guys and then he carries on until he has knocked them unconscious. This champion boxer . . . against patients on Stelazine.'

'What's Stelazine?'

'It's a tranquilliser, sort of makes you not care, but only some patients are on it.'

'Shit, Ethan, I've heard of the hormone treatment and the shock treatment, but this is torture, man.'

'And there's nothing we can do about it. Property of the state, remember!'

'But you will try and find out where Deon's parents are, won't you?'

'Of course.'

Ethan puts the roof of the car down and we drive in silence, enjoying the feeling of freedom. Sitting next to him, I resolve to get on that train tonight knowing I have achieved something, feeling that we have progressed in some way, no matter how small.

As we approach The Fountains, I tell him about the little steam train that used to run there and how it was the highlight of our visits to Pretoria as kids. To further dispel the misery of what I have just witnessed, I force myself to think pleasant thoughts: kissing Ethan, holding him. Wouldn't that just make everything worthwhile?

Then something inside me falls into place. 'Ethan, you know, I survived the border and it was the most profound experience, but I will not allow it to scar me. I'm going to take all the positive out of it and learn from it. I will not let the shit get to me.'

He smiles, looks at me for a moment and says, 'And at the end of next year we're finished with the army, except for camps.'

'Forget camps, Ethan, I will never do them. You can count on that. I've seen enough. There will be a way out, and I'll find it. I will never do a camp. And I won't allow any of this to get to me. If I do, they've won. Our happiness does not depend on what life deals us, it's how we deal with it!' This makes me think of Dylan. 'You know, because Dylan came from such a privileged background he actually suffered a lot more. His whole life was plotted for him and he just had to fit in: school, university, what to wear, how to act. He once told me that he didn't have a choice of what to study. It was decided for him—a business degree—and he HAD to excel.'

'What did he want to study?'

'I think literature. He wanted to write, be creative. More than anything else, he wanted freedom. Malcolm, on the other hand, had no pressure like that. Do you know, even at primary school he took two buses to school on his own, bought a newspaper and read it. Best of all, his father didn't even know where his school was!'

'We have family friends whose father has this massive company, really wealthy—been our neighbours in Clifton for years—and all the children, three boys and a girl, are made to work for the company. No choices, no compromise, you work or you're disinherited.'

'Pretty much Dylan's situation.'

'Did it help to speak to his parents?' he asks, looking at me and gearing down.

'Yes, but it has sort of changed my memory of him, if that makes sense. It has helped to give me closure, to realise that maybe I couldn't have prevented his death. But I will never know for sure. Some part of me will always feel that I could have done something.' Deciding to change the subject, I say, 'I'm going to miss you, Ethan. When's your next pass?'

'It's actually this weekend.'

'Wow, lucky you! What are your plans?'

'I don't know, my folks will fly me down to Cape Town, I guess. Listen, when we finish the army at the end of next year, let's take a holiday together, say up the Wild Coast for a couple of weeks. What do you think? Can you surf?'

'Not too well. Shit, that would be great, man. I can't wait! That's a deal, OK?'

I feel a pang of pleasure and pain in my heart. Eternal, I say to myself trying to describe the feeling, this thing that has grown in me that hurts but at the same time has become my most important need. Eternal . . . to last forever.

***

'There are only three things that will last forever,' I can hear Mr. Davids so clearly. 'Faith, hope and love. One day you will understand hope. It can't be taught. It is something you will understand; it will come to you.'

Love was easy, wished for, given and received, causing different reactions. Faith has been a journey for me. At first, I just leaned on it, then clung to it, and then it supported me.

Hope only made itself known to me in my nineteenth year. The army, Middelburg, basics, Infantry School, Vasbyt, the border and Koevoet taught me hope. I now realise it is not just some desire beckoning on the horizon. It is the trust in a future, lying there like a safe harbour.

Travelling with Ethan gives me hope, a colour to drench my time in, a brighter pigment. I want him to talk, because then I can look at him, study him. I want to burn his image into me so that I can take him with me, in my Wild Coast fantasy, all the way to Oudtshoorn.

After saying goodbye on the soot-stained platform, I turn to get into the second-class carriage. He calls my name. When he says it, we step towards each other and he hugs me and says he will see me as soon as he can. He whispers it into my ear, too precious for others to hear.

I find my compartment, press the silver bar at the top of the window with the springbok head etched into it, and release the catch. The glass drops down and I lean out for the last few words.

He promises to spend as much time with Malcolm as possible, and the train starts moving. Only when the rhythm is well established and I can no longer see Ethan, do I draw back into the compartment and the real world.

13

'My name is Pranks.'

'Hey there, Pranks, I'm Nicholas. How are you?'

'Shit, thank you.'

On the high-backed seat sits a woman who came in while my interest was still focussed on Ethan.

'Is that your boyfriend?' she asks, drawing on a cigarette. She is dressed like the cigarette: all in white, with gold shoes and a gold chain around the waist. Without waiting for an answer she goes on, 'Don't worry, your secret's safe with me. I won't go to the police or tell your friends in the army. One of my best friends is, you know, like *that*.' Between every phrase, she draws in more smoke. The cigarette lingers on her lips, and then her tongue pushes the butt out.

I try to cling to Ethan's smell, and all I can think of is how the smoke from this woman's lungs is displacing it.

'Come on, what's your name? If we're going to share the compartment . . .'

'I told you. Nicholas.'

'Well, hello, Nicholas.'

'Why did you ask me that?' I stutter.

'What? Oh that. Just the way you said goodbye, you don't look like *trassies*, but two beautiful boys like you, what a waste. Shit, you guys are going to break some hearts. Would you like a drink? How about some Tassies? Tassies for the *trassies*!' and she bursts into spluttering laughter.

From her white handbag with a gold plastic flamingo on the flap, she takes a half-jack of brandy. 'Or some Klippies an' Coke? When you see the trolley, be a dolly and get us a few Cokes.'

'No thanks, I won't have a drink.'

'Oh, come on, don't be a moffie.' She is halfway through the word when she laughs a smoker's chortle, thick with phlegm, ending in a cough.

'OK, maybe later, after supper.' I feel like crying, for Ethan, for his sound, his walk, his smell. I need something to relieve me of this heartache. I want to run or somehow just escape, but the compartment closes the smell of the woman's perfume and smoke in around me.

'When you introduced yourself . . . Pranks, is it?'

'Yes.'

'Well, Pranks, you said you felt like shit. Why did you say that?'

'I am shit.' She is clearly pleased I've asked. 'My family has discarded me; husband found a younger *bokkie*, traded me in, and the children have sided with him. He has the money. Money, that's what it's all about. Don't you agree?'

'No, not really.'

'You will see, you will see. Money, that's what it's all about.' She sings the last words. She looks at her dim reflection in the glass where the night is perforated by lights changing the glass pane into a mirror. 'Discarded, thrown away like trash, like shit; that's me. And now I'm going to live with my sister in Bloem-fontein.'

I make my bed on the top bunk, safe from her spilling brandy or falling on me. Lying on my stomach and raised on my elbows, I write about Ethan:

This is love that should be renamed, the type that can make you mad. The type you can never live without, once you are addicted to it. This world will coexist next to such love—it's bigger than the planet where it was born.

When I close my eyes, I see blood seeping in between the frames of the destroyed people of Ward 22, the killing and the lost lives. And then the shouting starts. When this happens, I don't sleep.

I get up and go to the toilet at the end of the carriage, splash my face with water and talk to myself quietly, my face close to the speckled mirror. I put my shoulder against the side of the cubicle to balance myself, lift the lid and take my penis out. Standing at an angle, I aim at the stainless-steel toilet. The pee twists from between the two small lips.

Running my hands against the sides of the passage, I walk back to my compartment, steadying myself in anticipation of the irregular movement of the train.

From the other end of the passage, a man is heading towards me. I recognise him immediately as the medic who stitched my head on the border. When we come face to face, I say, 'Hi, do you remember me?'

'No, china. Hey, yes . . . maybe, hey! But I'm *lekker op 'n stasie.* Pissed as a parrot, china. Who are you again?'

'You stitched my head on the border. What are you doing here?'

'Goin' home, my mate, for *lang pas.* Now I remember. You're the oke with the head, and the friend with the hand. I still came up with the doc from the base. Ja, ja, I remember. So how's your wound, *ek sê*?'

'Pretty good!'

'Fucking good stitches,' he says looking at my head. 'So, where you goin'?'

'Back to Infantry School.'

'I'm getting off in Bloemies early, so I reckon rather like *dop* all night!'

'Well, I'm going to try and get some sleep. Enjoy your long pass.' He shakes my hand and we push past each other.

'Hey!' he shouts after me. I turn around. 'I remember, at the bang site I didn't really have to look after you. There was this guy from your platoon, fuck, he was amazing, took care of you like you were like this.' He crosses his middle and index fingers to indicate closeness. 'I just left you with him.'

'Really, who was he?'

'Fucked if I know. But the amazing thing was, this oke was so together, not rattled at all. *Fokken* strong china, that *ou*. Solid, hey, solid!'

'What did he look like? Can you remember?'

'Ja, good-looking. The kind of *poes* that gets all the chicks at the disco. Black hair. Shit, china, you don't know him? He walked all the way with your stretcher to the Puma. Big help, that oke, big help.'

'Thanks,' I say, and just as I wonder if he has heard me, he raises his hand, index finger and pinkie extended—the safe-my-mate sign—and stumbles on without turning back.

Oscar is the object of my thoughts before I fall asleep.

Somewhere during the night Pranks starts talking and tries to engage me in conversation. Everything about her depresses me. She becomes so drunk that she no longer cares if I listen— probably used to being ignored. The only words I remember her saying before falling asleep again are, 'It's when you don't matter to anybody, when nobody cares, when you have no meaning, *that's* loneliness.'

Early the next morning she gets off at Bloemfontein without saying goodbye. Her blond beehive is pathetically skew. Searching the platform to see if there is someone to meet her, I see her looking at her own image in a shop front, trying to adjust her hair. Next to her is a suitcase of tartan fabric that seems barely up to the task of holding her few possessions. There is a thud, then another one, and we start moving.

As the sober Karoo morning slips past, I think of uncle Hendrik, auntie Sannie and Hanno, and the times we spent with them. But mostly I think of the weekend of the funeral.

14

There is an incredulous silence in the 'sacred' dining room where I'm standing, demanding that the dog be taken to a vet. An alien could just as well have entered the room and asked for sex with auntie Sannie.

They are stunned. Hanno is enjoying this—my behaviour vindicates him.

'Nicholas, get out,' my father hisses. I don't move. 'GET OUT NOW, THIS MINUTE! We're eating. Get that dog out of this house. Did you not hear what uncle Hendrik said? No dogs in the house. What in heaven's name is wrong with you?'

Still I don't move, which is unheard of. In this house things operate within the parameters of the rules laid down by the men, generation after generation. But there is weakness in their disbelief, feebleness in their overreaction. How can something so small cause them such angst? This gives me the courage to speak, and I direct it at the only person who seems sane to me.

'Mom, please, the dog and the puppy are suffering.'

My mother surprises me by turning to uncle Hendrik. 'Hendrik, will you please do something about those animals?' Now everybody starts talking at the same time, in disbelief, wondering why everything seems to be spiralling even further out of control. There's a dog in the house, even worse, in the dining room. Where is the discipline? How dare these people break the rules like this? What's with this child and this Catholic woman?

'For the love of God, please,' my mother asks again.

Eventually uncle Hendrik seems to regain his composure. 'Will you please see to it that I'm not disturbed at MY table, by YOUR child, while I'm eating? Then, and only then, will I consider looking at the bloody dog. Does your child have no manners? Who is in control, you or him?'

'GO NOW! Get out this minute! Do you want another

hiding? Embarrassing me like this,' my father shouts, red in the face. His words are desperate and angry, but there is also an air of pleading. He is in a corner, and I realise that I too have power.

'Please, my boy, wait outside,' my mother asks, beyond caring about their rules. She just wants this to be over.

15

The train stops at Colesberg. There I have to wait for the rest of the day and night for the next train to Port Elizabeth. I spend the time in a rowdy two-star hotel, hiding in my room one floor above the bar. From PE I change for the last time at Klipplaat, to an ordinary passenger train to Oudtshoorn.

Next to the brownish grey station building there is a tickey-box. The black rubber earpiece smells of dirty hair, but it is my only way of connecting to 1 Mil, to Ethan and news of Malcolm.

The unhelpful voice tells me he doesn't know where Ethan is. After asking him to connect me to anybody who can give me news about Malcolm, he keeps me holding on for so long that I run out of coins.

With a heavy heart, I wait on the slatted bench for the duty driver to pick me up. I move my bum over the slats, bending forward to find a moderately comfortable position.

Unbuttoning the flap of my shirt pocket, I take out my little book. Thinking of Pranks makes me write:

She possesses something sad, a cold wisdom when completely stripped down. I wonder if there is some freedom in that.

By the time the army minibus arrives, I am exhausted, and the driver's news that the entire Infantry School is on pass doesn't help my mood. I missed the pass by one day—the first pass since border duty.

The driver's chatter is negative and empty. Delighting in my misfortune, he says, 'You are *shnaaied, broer . . . naaied* in the eye, my mate!' And again, 'You're fucked, bro, all the way back from the border and fucked out of a pass. Now that's a bummer.'

'It's Friday. The army will give me a train pass.'

'No way, you're out of luck, man. There's nobody to issue it. Besides, I know the schedule, and there are no trains to get you to Cape Town in time. You'd better hike.' I know he is right. It will take longer than the pass to complete a return trip. If I had to start hiking tomorrow, I'll have two days on the road and two days there, if I'm lucky with lifts. I decide to rest first and to make up my mind tomorrow.

The clothes I have worn for three days, stick to me like grease. Looking around the streets of Oudtshoorn, I get that strange feeling of having been away for a long, long time, yet it feels as if I'd left only yesterday. We enter the camp gates, and everything I look at has an uncomfortable memory.

It is strangely humid for late winter; strange . . . maybe it's spring? Or early summer . . . what's the date?

I'm waiting to report to the lieutenant on duty, but he is shouting at a troop who has driven into his car with an army Land Rover. Every expletive, every possible form of verbal degradation, is used to belittle the young man in front of all those present in the duty room. He was one of the first troops to drop out of the course. Suddenly the lieutenant turns to me, points and says to the troop, 'You see this man? He is the elite. You don't deserve to tie his shoelaces, you fucking failure. He has done the whole course; not a wimp, piece of shit loser, like you. Look at him and give him fifty.'

The young man turns to me and stamps his foot. His face is red and sweaty, there are tears in his eyes, but not enough for him not to recognise me—and a wave of shame passes across

Hanno's sorrowful face. Instead of enjoying the moment, as he is doing fifty push-ups at my feet, all I think of is how strange it is that we haven't bumped into each other before.

Later I feel a sense of triumph. My cousin Hanno, against whom I always seemed to fall short, could not make it here, yet I did. I have all but completed this course, an even greater achievement considering my nature. And suddenly I am filled with pride. For the very first time I feel that I will succeed, that nothing, not even Dorman, will stand in my way.

The old face-brick barracks of Golf Company stand deserted. I take four steps into the room where I spent my first months in Infantry School. The bunk beds are as they were, the mattresses rolled up as if dried out without human contact. I look at the bunk Dylan and I shared, our grey metal cupboards and the polished floor.

This is where my *trommel* stood. Right here I sat praying during our ten-minute quiet times, morning and evening, where I pleaded with God to save me from this. Here I scrambled for the working parts of my rifle and struggled with the combination lock, losing vital seconds during drills. Over there is where I slept, and that is where Dylan slept . . .

The atmosphere holds more than just my memories. The angst is still here, clinging to the walls, waiting in this deserted space to seep into you when you enter.

The ablution block next door looks dark and wicked, but somehow smaller than I recall. Then I go back to the bungalow of Platoon One, from where I left to go to the border.

The kit of those who were wounded was put on their beds. I sort through it and pack everything back into the cupboard with the clanging doors. I notice that much of my gear has been stolen. I put Malcolm's kit in my cupboard as well, lock the stainless-steel handle, and gather my toiletries and clean clothing to go to the shower complex.

In the distance I hear thunder; some of the crowns of the clouds are shining brilliantly against the dark sky. There is the promise of rain—Little Karoo shrubs releasing their scent to the wind running ahead on the breath of the storm.

I choose the shower *we* used, drape my towel over the basin *we* shared, recalling a strong Dylan and trying to still the turmoil inside me. The shaft of light from the high windows sparkles in the cold drops deflected by my chest. I stand there with an in-explicably mixed feeling of joy and sadness, an expectation of some undisclosed promise.

As I walk to the *Kamp Kafee* across the road from the duty office I hear the words, 'Hey, you!' floating towards me. 'Hey, you,' the duty driver who collected me from the station shouts again, 'there is someone for you at the front gate. Shit, I didn't know where to find you. I was just going to forget it; never thought I'd find you.'

'Who is it?'

'Fucked if I know. Go down there. I'm off duty now.'

On the way to the front gate, the rain starts coming down. There is a whipcrack and white light and then a sharp boom that rumbles off between the valleys.

When I get to the duty room I am drenched, water streaking from my hair and running into my shirt.

The person leaning on the duty counter looks around as I enter the room.

'Ethan!' I blow the water from my lips, blink, and wipe my eyes to see if it's really true.

'Hi, Nicholas,' he says softly. 'I've come for you.' The duty room and the people in it have ceased to exist.

Tears are streaming down my face, but the water of the storm outside hides them.

'Come with me.' He turns and I follow. Outside, it's raining harder and we run to his car, laughing out loud as we close the doors.

'What are you doing here?'

'I've come for you!' he says again. The rain coats the windows of his MG, and the drops fall loudly on the canvas roof. With his arm over my backrest, he turns to me. He moves closer, smiling, his skin wet, like mine, rain on his eyelashes; and then he kisses me.

The earth revolves around moments like these: feeling the firmness of his lips, taking in his smell and his taste, my hand on his neck—that neck I've watched and studied for so many hours. He pushes his beret off his head, his tongue licks the water and the tears from my face, and then he finds my mouth again.

I hug him, hold on to him, not like I did before, but with all the need for him released—released on a lover, *my* lover.

'I've booked us into a guesthouse . . . very romantic, actually.' He laughs and starts the car. 'I was hoping just to see you for a bit, to tell you . . . Then I got here and heard that the whole camp was on pass, and I thought I'd driven all this way for nothing. And then the driver said you were here!'

'This is so, so good Ethan. Your timing is perfect. Just drive, nobody in my company even knows I'm here. I have the whole weekend—four days. I can fetch some clothing tomorrow.' He smiles, rubs his leg, revelling in the mischief as he says, 'You won't need any. By the way, we must phone Malcolm when we get to the guesthouse. He must be climbing the walls by now.'

'Now I understand. He told you!'

'Yep. Why did we wait so long, Nick? We've wasted all this time.'

'I've loved you since the day that bastard cut your hair and hit you. Do you know that? Do you know how many times I've wanted to tell you that?'

'Me too, shit, me too. And there's good news, Nick. Malcolm's hand is going to be fine. It seems the army doctors did a good job—full use, they reckon. Looks a little scary, pins and metal goodies and all, but he's going to be fine.'

***

Early Monday morning I watch Ethan's MG leave through the Infantry School gates, and I feel invincible. I seem to have all the answers, having been divinely anointed, touched by the finger of God and having had a glimpse of eternity. I feel the simple wisdom of utter happiness, when all else seems inconsequential. At the same time, there is the dramatic pain of parting, still camouflaged by the bliss of the weekend; a pain I dwell on, take in in large swigs, using it to remind me of our time together.

This is different from the pain of our previous separations which were without hope. This is an exquisite pain made unbearable by the promise of return.

Past the main parade ground where they divided us into companies all those months ago, climbing the embankment to the tuck shop, I realise that I have no ammunition against this feeling. Even if he should be lying in my arms, get up in the middle of the night for a wee, I would immediately feel empty, craving him until he folds into me, knowing exactly how far to pull up his legs for mine to fit in behind them; every single body part like a void waiting to be filled—arm over chest, hand in hand, cheek against shoulder, penis against bum.

It is for this that we were born. So when it arrives, we know it, we recognise it as our ultimate destination.

***

When rank is handed out, it is no surprise to me that I become a corporal and not a one-pip lieutenant—Engel, Dorman and Gerrie's last show of power. How much of it is Gerrie's doing, I don't know. However, making me an NCO is not enough revenge for them. They also manage to place my name on a list that I only find out about when base allocations for our second year are done.

Some weeks before the passing-out parade, we are allocated to bases around the country, or sent for active border duty. The method of allocation is nothing short of barbaric. We take position on the grandstand, and on the cricket field in front of us is a number of tents, each representing a base. There are only a few places one would want to go to. The rest are bases on the border one wants to avoid at all cost. A person with an intercom shouts out the name of a base, and we have to sprint to that tent and stand in line. Only a few candidates are chosen, and the rest have to return to the grandstand. The officer enrolling the members at the 'new' base doesn't indicate how many men he requires, which leaves one waiting in a line where you might not be placed, thus giving up the chance of getting into a second or third choice of base.

This must be how the gladiators felt—walking out into a ring, fighting their own for a chance of survival, depending solely on physical ability to outrun and outshoulder the others.

After my third try, I manage to get to the front of a queue for a training base. I am one person away from the front when I hear my name being called over the intercom, with other names I don't recognise.

Being singled out for anything in the army spells danger. My brain races through questions and possibilities. Should I not just get my name enrolled here before I respond? Then my name is called again, with number and rank. The person in front of me has completed his enrolment and the officer calls, 'Next!' Before me are two roads, completely different in direction, but I have no choice because the person shouting over the intercom is now instructing people to look for me.

At the podium, an irate staff sergeant informs us that we are the only group not allowed to 'choose' our base. We are allocated to one which, of course, nobody wants to go to, as it is infamous for its high contact rate. The answer we are given when we ask why we have been singled out is, *'Fok, ek weet nie, maar julle moes kak drooggemaak het! Julle op hierdie lys is diep in die oog genaai!'* ('Fucked if I know, but you guys must have fucked up badly! The ones on this list are really fucked in the eye.')

The tent we have to go to is on the furthest corner of the cricket field. I am brimming with panic and hatred, but even more with humiliation, as I walk behind the staff sergeant with this bewildered group, trying to figure out some kind of solution and praying furiously.

We are halfway across the field, and I am lagging behind by about two metres, when I notice our company commander some distance away. Without a second thought, I turn and walk towards this man who has been my leader for a whole year, but to whom I have never spoken.

From the way I halt, stamp my right boot down and salute him, the man must detect my desperation. As I speak, I cannot believe that I'm addressing an army officer in such a way. I don't say I 'cannot,' or 'please, could I not,' I simply say 'I will not' go to the border. He looks at the symbol on my arm—the black and green triangle with the semicircle like a parachute above it—and sees I'm from his company, Golf Company.

He looks at me and then past me, and all I can think about is the way he spoke about Dylan and the two boys who were caught kissing in the laundry room. He doesn't look at me again, not even when he says, 'Follow me.'

It is his job today to sign people up for a base called the *Danie Theron Krygskool,* and I am duly enrolled.

***

The passing-out parade, which my parents attend, is over the weekend of 13 and 14 December, the parade on the Saturday morning and Church parade on the Sunday. On Saturday evening there is a military tattoo in which each company takes part.

Golf Company gets to do the best part of the program. We are to enact a contact situation on the border, where a section of the SADF completely annihilates a group of terrorists, with only one wounded soldier on our side, who is then speedily case-vacked. The contact is complete, with blanks, smoke grenades and helicopter. I am the medic who administers a drip, and the person helping me harness the 'patient' to the helicopter winch is Oscar.

I feel an obscure sense of pride, mainly for having succeeded in completing a year so totally against everything I stand for. But the satisfaction makes me feel as if I'm betraying myself—allowing this system I hate to make me a part of it.

I am also confused about being pleased that my father is given the opportunity to be proud of me—that I'm excelling at something he believes in after all the shame I caused him by failing at school, cricket, rugby and everything that is important to him. But strange as it is, despite our destructive relationship, I still harbour a subconscious desire to gain his respect.

There is obviously no way for him to know exactly how huge this achievement really is, or how difficult the year has been; least of all my 'coming out,' Dylan's death and falling in love with Ethan. But it is enough for him to know that I am now part of a small elite, of which all the parents and visitors are constantly reminded during this weekend.

After the tattoo, we clean the black-is-beautiful from our faces, shower, change into step-outs and are allowed to spend the evening out. My passbook is signed, I get into the Chev Constantia and go to a restaurant with my parents. The collective excitement of the camp and being part of the 'stage production' is carried into the car, and not even the news that some distant family members are joining us for dinner can spoil my mood.

'Nick,' my mother says, 'don't you remember them? You met them in Jeffrey's once.'

'No, Mom. When?'

'You were in standard three.'

'Mom, really, I was ten. How are we related?'

'Uncle Dirk and aunt Fran.'

'Just not them!'

'No, uncle Dirk's brother, Jan.'

'They call him Jannie,' my father corrects my mother.

'No, it doesn't ring a bell,' I say, sounding disappointed at the prospect of spending an evening with uncle Dirty Dirk's family.

'I'm sorry, darling,' my mom says, 'but we had no option. Their son is also here and they don't have very much, so we offered to take them out. Just make the most of it, OK?'

'Is he in Infantry School?'

'Yes. I can't remember his name, but they call him Blackie.'

'No, I don't know him. I don't really know the people from the other companies. We hardly ever mix.'

Parking outside the restaurant, my father says, 'Are we late? They're here already.'

'No, we're not,' says my mom.

'How do you know they're here?' I ask.

'Because that's their truck,' my father says, pointing to a black breakdown truck with the words *Jannie and Son* dramatically sign-written on the door. Below it, in a straight line, are the words: *Best prices, speedy & honest.*

I am appalled, picturing a drunken version of uncle Dirk being rowdy in the restaurant, in the presence of other members of my platoon or company.

'Where do they live?'

'Somewhere in the Transvaal.'

'And they travelled all the way in this!'

'Yes, uncle Jannie said the car was not reliable, or something like that.'

'Nick, it's the right thing to do, OK? Be nice to them.'

'Of course,' I say, mildly irritated.

The establishment is in a beautifully renovated old house that once belonged to a wealthy ostrich farmer.

'Yes,' says the maitre d', 'Van der Swart! The rest of your party is already here. Please follow me.'

I stand back, like a well-mannered boy, to let my parents seat themselves, and only then do I see Oscar sitting at our table. My immediate reaction is one of embarrassment that he might see my distant relatives, but when my folks greet the two people sitting with him, I realise that Oscar is their son. He gets up to introduce himself to my folks. Then he shakes my hand, smiling. 'Howzit, Vannie.'

It takes me a glass and a half of wine before I am relaxed enough to respond to Oscar's attempts at small talk. My father directs most of his questions at Oscar, as if I have never had anything to do with the Defence Force. Oscar answers politely, until he too has emptied a glass of wine, when he says, 'Uncle Peet, do you know that of all the troops in Golf Company it is actually Nicholas and a friend who have had the most combat experience?'

'What?'

'Yes, he and a friend were the only ones to actually go on patrol with Koevoet and have a major contact!'

'I don't believe it!'

Everyone is quiet. My father looks away from Oscar, appears to think for a while, and then starts talking to uncle Jannie.

I am flushed with wine and Oscar's support. Our parents start conversing in twos—the women with each other and the men too. Oscar smiles, notices that I see the smile and says, 'Let's go for a jol tonight, you and I.' Then he turns to his father and says, *'Pa, ek wil vanaand die trok gebruik, OK?'* ('I want to borrow the truck tonight.')

The adults decide to travel back together so that the youngsters can go and 'chase some chicks,' and without waiting for dessert we leave.

After trying the bars and finding them too crowded, we decide to go to the Holiday Inn. We order a bottle of wine in the lounge, where it is quiet enough to chat. We talk mostly about the past year, and particularly about the border. I am keen to talk about the time he kissed me, about helping me after the land mine explosion, and the last day of Vasbyt, when he picked me up. As Oscar pours us a second glass of wine I say, 'Listen, I just want to say thanks for the times you've helped me.'

He smiles and says, 'It's nothing, Vannie, nothing.'

I look at the condensation on the silver ice bucket, run my finger over it, look up at him and say, 'I know it was you who helped me after the land mine.'

'Oh, man, forget it!'

'And I won't forget Vasbyt either!'

'Oh, that.' He is slightly embarrassed, but I look straight at him and manage to say what has been uppermost on my mind. 'And what about the day you kissed me!'

He bursts into nervous laughter.

'I just had to thank you, man. I tell you, it meant so much to me. It was so fucking brave of you. It like blew me away.'

He looks down smiling, then the smile fades, and with an intense look he says, 'It had to be done.'

This gives me the courage to go on. 'Oscar, there is something I want to tell you.'

'Vannie, you don't have to. It's cool with me, whatever it is.'

'No, I want to.' I wait a while. The silence between us is not awkward; it is a moment we both need to prepare ourselves for a revelation. 'I . . . I'm gay. I just wanted you to know that.'

In a split second, I become completely sober. I sink back, as if I have used up all my energy, and sigh, 'I hope you understand.'

'That's OK.' He leans over, straining to get closer to me, and says, 'It really is OK, I promise you.'

'Shit, I'm relieved. I don't know why, but I needed to tell you.'

'I'm glad you did. Just to put you at ease, I want to tell you about this guy I knew. Probably the most important person in my life. He sort of helped me see life differently. You see, where I grew up it was a bit rough. Well, this guy was my Art teacher and became a close friend. He is gay, and I tell you he was, and I guess still is, like a guru to me; definitely the most amazing person I have ever met. He told me early on that he was gay, and I spent a lot of time with him. Sometimes it would even be just the two of us in a tent, because we did many hiking trails together. Think about it, me a schoolboy and he a gay man, on a five-day hike, and I tell you I never ever felt the slightest bit threatened.'

'Wow, I knew a guy like that too, sort of my mentor as well.'

'Van, there's something I must tell you too.' Seeing my expectant look, he says, 'No, no, I'm not gay. It's something else. Do you remember that we spent a day together many years ago?'

'My mom told me you visited my uncle when we were in Jeffrey's. But I don't remember meeting you.'

'Well, we were staying in the caravan park that year. And that uncle . . . well, he's not a nice man.'

'I hated him.'

'Do you remember that wrestling match?'

'Yes, of course! No way, NO WAY . . . You're *that* Blackie! Blackie, no way, man, no way!'

'That's me.'

'Wow, man, I can't believe it. Shit, and we were together in the army this whole year and never . . . What a coincidence. I also bumped into a cousin of mine here.'

'It's actually not such a coincidence, Vannie. I mean, most of the guys who matriculated the same time as we did are in the army now. Do you remember how you beat Michael that night?'

'Yes, but it was a fluke, I think.'

'It wasn't. I remember it like it was yesterday!'

'Oscar, I hated that man. I could go to hell for the thoughts I've had about him.'

'He tried to feel me up, and my sister too, the sick cunt.'

'What? In Jeffrey's?'

'No, we went down to Margate on a family holiday with them. He was a pain, trying to touch me and shit, but I wriggled away each time. I never really felt threatened because I knew he stood no chance. But then one afternoon, while everybody was resting, I went to the loo and passed my sister's room. I heard her sort of talking, but more like moaning. I could hear she was distressed, so I opened the door and, shit, there he was, his hand down her . . . front.'

'Fuck!'

'I lost it, Vannie, totally. There was a lamp next to the bed. I grabbed it and started hitting him. And then,' Oscar smiles and sniggers softly, 'the shade went flying and how exactly it happened I don't know, but it was one of those lights with the switch under the bulb, you know. So the switch went on and the next time I hit him the bulb broke and I shocked him!' We both burst out laughing. 'So he tried to get off the bed and block the strikes, yelling at me to calm down, but I just went on hitting and hitting, using the broken bulb like a cattle prodder!'

'And the rest of the people in the house?'

'Aunt Fran was first on the scene. She knew immediately what was going on, so she got me to stop and sent him out of the room. The next minute my mother is there asking what's going on, and poor aunt Fran says there was a little accident with the lamp. But the way she looked at me, almost pleadingly, I knew that she knew.

'Later I felt bad that I hadn't done something about it. Someone like that is sick and needs help, man. What if there were other kids, or even his own? But you know what it's like with family and shit. Plus, I was only about ten or eleven, so what would I have been able to do?'

*

Before we go back to the base, Oscar gives me a gift—something that means more to me than material things ever could. We drive out of town and turn off the tar onto a gravel road. He drives on for about two kilometres, stops on a small rising and says, 'Let's get out.'

The Milky Way is so powerful above me that it feels as if I'm looking up at one enormous, solid, heavenly body, and the vast energy of our entire galaxy comes flooding towards me.

'Listen to this, Vannie,' he says and puts on a tape in the truck. And there, on the edge of the great expanse of the Karoo, with the smells of the veld where I had slept and trained for nine months, under the stars that I watched for countless hours on guard duty, we listen to *Beim Schlafengehen*, one of Richard Strauss's four last songs.

The music swirls around me, then cuts into me and seems to link me to the cosmos—to the greatness of friendship, my admiration for Oscar and the love I have for Ethan. The Karoo air, with just a hint of dust and the scent of the bushes carried within its cleanness, gives me a feeling of unshakable power.

On our way back to camp, we drive through Oudtshoorn. The town is emptying out after its brief siege of army personnel, junior leaders and their families. Taking a shortcut past a late-night bar, the truck's lights fall straight on Dorman, walking down the street. He is drunk. Oscar slows down and follows him. I ask why, but when he doesn't answer, I don't ask again. Dorman's Datsun bakkie is parked in a side street, next to a pine tree. He fumbles for his keys, finds the right one for the door and gets in.

Then he looks down, trying to find the ignition. This man that has caused me such endless hardship looks small in his drunken state. He doesn't look up at the lights blazing on him and flashframing his image into me as Oscar completes the turn and lines up directly in front of his bakkie. He eases up against the Datsun's bumper. Dorman's head immediately snaps up and he tries to block the light from his eyes. Oscar gently pushes the vehicle back until it is sandwiched between the tree and us. There is the sound of metal buckling, glass breaking, and the revving of our vehicle's engine, but it is so gentle it's almost muffled.

Then Oscar gets out, walks over to Dorman, and I follow.

'Come here, Vannie,' he says quietly as he stands looking down at Dorman, who is sitting in the car without a sign of the malevolence for which we have known him all year. In fact, he starts talking, and it sounds pretty much like pleading. Then he stops, and both he and I look at Oscar, who is undoubtedly the one in charge of this situation.

'You have done wrong,' Oscar eventually says in a steady voice, still not looking away from the drunken, trembling man in front of him. It is as if God himself has spoken on Judgment Day and there is no reprieve for Dorman.

'I want you to know this, Dorman; I want you to realise that you have done terrible things this year. What you have done will never go away!'

I hear Dorman swear on the name of God, I hear him refer to Oscar's rank, which is now higher than his, and I hear him make promises, but none of it has any truth or carries any weight. Then Oscar and I turn around, get back into the truck and drive off.

PART FIVE

After the older man has run his hand over the boy's chest, stroked the smooth, young skin of his torso and seen the hard shape grow in his Speedo, he slowly eases it out. The young penis is so hard that it looks like skin over bone. It is clear that the boy is blistering with lust. When the man touches his scrotum, there is a jolt of pleasure in the younger body.

They are lying at a pool on beds designed for tanning. It is a hot night. Both of them have drops of water on their skins, in which the silver-blue light is now trapped. The water in the pool is still moving from when the two bodies were in it; from the chasing, touching and finding. The only light that is on, is inside the water, and it is now herding sharp sparks of silver light against the deserted pool house.

As the older man moves closer, the boy rolls over on his back, opens his legs and spreads them. They are exquisitely defined and youthful, almost tender under the stroke of the older man's hand moving over taut, elongated muscles.

Soon the boy ejaculates. He is still on his back, resting his head on the arm of the man lying on his side next to him. His penis stays hard. In this light, his pubic hair is black against his white skin, and a line of fine hair runs up to his navel.

When the alcohol has worn off and they had sex one more time, the older man starts telling the boy why he shouldn't tell anybody about what has happened. The boy doesn't tell him, but there is a good reason why he won't tell anybody: he is in love and wants to spend the rest of his life here, with this man, whom he would never ever want to hurt or jeopardise. In fact, he will do anything for this man.

But soon the one who has lived longer, who should be the more mature, begins to realise his hold and starts abusing this love. He has had so many men fall in love with him that he reads the signs easily. And after a conquest, he gets bored and looks for other stimulation. But the young man with the long, black hair is so infatuated that he will do anything, which is when things start going wrong.

By the time the weekend is over and they are driving back to the city, he has shared the boy with a friend while he watched. Without consent, he also filmed the boy being fucked. But it is his obsession to hurt the boy that scars this beautiful man-child for the rest of his short life. He doesn't understand why his uncle would want to burn him with a cigarette while he is entering him, but it helps that he is either high or drunk when it happens.

When he turns to go to the first-class lounge at JF Kennedy Airport, after checking in his bags to South Africa, his uncle reminds him of the Super 8 film he has taken and will keep as an insurance policy. He also reminds him to keep his back and buttocks covered until the scabs have healed.

EPILOGUE

It took me twenty years to pluck up the courage to look at my diaries and start reconstructing the events of that year. In all this time, Ethan's visit was the one thing that stood out—everything else remained buried until I started the process of writing this story.

Life simply seemed to carry on, even when it felt as if the planet should stop and take a breath to reassess what had happened. Everything just goes on with the momentum that life gives it. I guess a story never really ends. It certainly doesn't remain in the 'ever after,' but it does stay with us 'forever after' in that it has changed us, made us grow, or scarred us.

My second year in the army turned out to be surprisingly comfortable. I was based at Danie Theron Combat School with Malcolm, and after receiving rank I worked in the media centre as a graphic artist. I was close enough to Pretoria for weekly visits to and from Ethan, and the year passed on the wings of first love.

After the army I enrolled at art school and Ethan at UCT. We rented a small bachelor flat and shared a year of uncomplicated bliss. But in that year, while we had everything our hearts could desire, we were introduced to something more dangerous than prejudice—the darkness of substance abuse. That, however, is a story for a next time.

My friendship with Malcolm has stood the test of time and distance—a distance that has since grown to the western shores of Canada.

There are nights when I wake up from dreaming about the army—about conversations, acquaintances and emotions that emerge from somewhere deep in my unconscious. They awake in me a sense of longing that lingers for that whole day and leaves me slightly confused. How it is possible to have hated a time so much and then to discover that somewhere inside, one is yearning for certain aspects of it?

My only explanation is that when one has an experience that is so traumatic, it knits itself into your very fibre while you are raw and ripped open. Then, when there is a really good moment, it can be so incredibly fine that it surpasses all other, because of the acute contrast.

GLOSSARY

Balsak	Large canvas bag used to carry kit (literally: ball bag)
Bivvie	Temporary shelter
Blerrie	Bloody
Bliksem	Used as a noun: scoundrel; used as a verb: to beat up (literally: lightning)
Blouvitrioel	Copper sulphate; mixed into beverages to reduce libido
Bok	Antelope; goat
Boer	Afrikaner (literally: farmer)
Boerseun	Young Afrikaner male (literally: farm boy)
Boerewors	Traditional South African sausage
Braai	Barbecue
Broer	Brother
Buffel	Buffalo; also name of anti-landmine vehicle
DB	Detention Barracks
Deurtrekker	Plastic coated cable to clean barrel of rifle
Dof	Stupid
Dominee	Pastor
Donner	To fight; hit
Doos	Derogatory word for female genitalia
Flossie	Hercules freight plane
Fok	Fuck
Fokof	Fuck off
Gatgabba	Derogatory term for homosexual
Geweer	Rifle
Gharries	Army Land Rover
Grootsak	Army rucksack for carrying kit on route marches
Hippo	Anti-landmine vehicle
Hotnot	Derogatory term for person of colour

JLs	Junior leaders
Kak	Shit
Kerk parade	Church parade
Kief	Nice
Kleurling	Person of colour
Koevoet	Name of police division on border (Literally: crow-bar)
Krygskool	Combat School
Kuka shop	General dealer for local population on the border
Malletjie	Crazy person (Literally: little mad one)
Min dae/min tyd	Literally: few days/little time (referring to time left before being discharged from army duty)
Moer	To hit or hurt
Moffie	Gay; homosexual
Naai	Fuck
Nafi	Lazy (Acronym for: No Ambition, Fuck-all Interest)
Oom	Uncle; also term of respect for an older man
Opfok	To give a hard time
Ouens	Guys
PB (Plaaslike Bevolking)	Local population
Pikstel	Knife, fork and spoon set
Pislelie	Plastic funnel used as urinal (Literally: piss lily)
Pishoring	Erection (Literally: piss horn)
Poes	Derogatory word for female genitalia
Shona	Water pan in border area (only appears during rainy season)
Skietbalkie	Badge received for exceptional marksmanship
Slapgat	Lazy
Soutpiel	Derogatory name for English South African (Literally: salty penis)
Staaldak	Steel helmet (Literally: steel roof)
Stasie	Station
Terr	Slang for terrorist
Trassie	Derogatory term for a homosexual
Troep	Troop; infantry soldier
Trommel	Large metal trunk
Uitklaar	Clear out (term used for leaving the army)
Volksie	Volkswagen Beetle

ACKNOWLEDGEMENTS

A s a gay man with deep spiritual desires, my only way of
processing the confusion I felt about my sexuality was
to write about it. The church regarded me as sinful, the
government told me my sexuality was unlawful and the rest of
society considered it offensive.

Although based largely on those writings, I have to stress
that this novel is essentially a work of fiction and although the
story follows the course of my life, the relatives of the main
characters are all fictional.

In 2001, I lost pretty much everything I had built up in my
life. Had it not been for the friends who stood by me, I don't
know how I would have got through that time. Starting a new
life at the age of forty was probably one of the most daunting
challenges I have ever faced. It was then that I discovered the
real meaning of loyalty.

I am eternally indebted to Nico Bacon, Neil Carse, Manuel
Tarre and Raymond Langston, who extended a helping hand,
without anyone knowing about it, in that bleak time.

My deepest appreciation and thanks go to Sam van Wyk—
the first person to read the manuscript of this book—for the
many hours he spent encouraging and indulging a very insecure
writer; to Richard Butt for introducing me to my publishers; to
Dennis Banks and his staff at DesignZero3 for the cover design;
to Bernard Johnson, Jan van Tonder, Grant Bacon, Nonene
Mthini, Gordon Jones, Brett Gage, Wayne Dunn, Graham
Chivers and Olga Godinho for their constant love and support,

and to Helga Steyn of Penstock Publishing, for her tremendous insight, help and understanding of what was a very raw manuscript when she first opened it as a courtesy to Richard, and thus started our long and interesting journey together.

I must also thank my three mentors from school: my English teacher, David Taylor, who started me off on keeping a journal; the late Annie du Toit, our school librarian, who was my friend and spiritual guide, and Pieter Bredenkamp, my art teacher, who laid the most solid foundation for my creative career, which has now extended into writing.

I am most grateful to the late Michael Collins for his valuable advice; to Lin Castle for her enormously positive response to the manuscript, which came at a very crucial time.

I have been greatly blessed with a mother who has loved me unconditionally and has always been there for me. There is such tremendous power in her quiet strength and wisdom. To her, my deep love and thanks.

During the final year of editing this book, a man came up to me at gym one morning and introduced himself as Shiloh. He told me he had heard that I was writing a book about the hardships of being gay in the National Defence Force. Then he said, 'I was in Ward 22.' Shiloh is not gay, but was sent to Ward 22 because his spiritual beliefs did not conform to conventional Christianity. He told me that over 80% of the 'patients' in Ward 22 were in fact there because of their sexual orientation. He has substantiated all my references to Ward 22. For his willingness to be interviewed and to spend hours recalling a time in his life that must have been more torturous than most of us would ever know, I owe Shiloh my deepest gratitude.

André Carl van der Merwe

Cape Town, 2006

CPSIA information can be obtained
at www.ICGtesting.com
Printed in the USA
JSHW031140151122
33234JS00002B/95

9 781609 450502